OFFSET

CHILDREN OF THE GULF

WRITTEN BY DELVIN HOWELL

ILLUSTRATED BY HANS STEINBACH

BEYOND PUBLISHING CARIBBEAN

OFFSET: CHILDREN OF THE GULF

Cover art & Illustrations by Hans Steinbach
Book Design by Thomas Anderson, Tristan Roach

Published by
Beyond Books
A Division of Beyond Publishing Caribbean
40A Friendly Hall
St. Michael
Barbados, West Indies
BB25064

offsetseries.com

Barbados National Library

ISBN 978-976-95902-7-4

Printed in the United States of America

THE GROUP THAT SURVIVED

Collins felt a chill as he approached the bus stop. It wasn't cold. The sun had authority amidst the blue skies, scorching everything (living or otherwise) beneath. The breeze blew across the coastline, riding the crashing waves and bringing salt to the air. The tourists loved it. They loved the colorful beach cottages—the peaches, the limes, the pineapples. They loved the pearl white shores. They loved the sparkling aquamarine sea. They loved it all. *It was just like the brochures!* But Collins couldn't care less.

He didn't look it, greeting every passerby with a friendly nod, which they returned in kind. They didn't notice the apprehension in his eyes, or the quiver in his gait. And though Collins hid this fear, he couldn't help it; after all, he knew too much.

The bus stop was a skinny wooden pole about eight feet tall, painted in segments of black and white, with a flat, red-and-white circle on top which had the words TO TOWN printed in the center. An insignificant object, which enabled one to catch any public service vehicle running along the route. But Collins experienced a different form of transport last year, where the sign zipped him from one location to the next in one breath.

Collins had no idea how, and frankly at the time he didn't

care. Many bizarre incidents happened that night: a living forest, a group of man-sized monkeys, a giant rampaging behemoth made of wood, so in the midst of everything else a magical bus stop didn't seem so weird. Without it, Collins would've died for certain so he didn't raise any questions at the time.

Still, the staccato in his chest could not be ignored as he sauntered towards the black-and-white pole.

A minivan sped up the street with the heavy bass set beating from the distance. The word BRIDGETOWN was on a little sign up front.

"Hmm … I hope it got seats."

It was empty. Collins slipped through the narrow aisle of the van, noting the vandalized seats full of graffiti and gouges and opting for the back. Eyes followed him along the way, appraised him.

As a pretty boy, Collins was accustomed to prolonged looks from strangers. His athletic physique (hidden today by a black graphic Tee, some three-quarter Cargo pants and a pair of slippers) often made the girls spare a glance. Local or no. Thin chocolate dreadlocks stretched down the back of his neck, all tied in one with a neat rubber band. That's probably it; for better or worse, his dreadlocks always placed him in a stereotype he didn't necessarily belong.

YOU DON'T HAVE BE DREAD TO BE RASTA.

Morgan Heritage played as Collins took his seat; the reliable hum of the engine urging the bus towards its destination. On occasion, the other passengers would glare but he ignored them, instead bracing for the rough corner turns that made him slide in his seat.

"Man… It sucks I ain got de car today." Collins sighed, but then a stray thought entered his mind. *You, I should check and see how Nadia doing.*

Rummaging down his pants pocket, Collins felt the cutlass sheath hidden along his leg. Now that would really make them stare!

He caressed the smooth hilt for a moment, then fondled his phone and scrolled through his contacts, stopping at Kyle Harding's name. Kyle Harding, the man responsible for his anxiety. For it wasn't until he met Kyle Harding that Collins discovered the monsters that lurked within this island.

It had been months since they last spoke, and that conversation was short and lackluster (well, more so than usual). Knowing Kyle, he wouldn't have anything more to say than last time, so with that in mind, Collins skipped the number and continued to his girlfriend.

A cute, exhausted voice came through the receiver. "Yes, Damian."

"Hey, Nadia. Just giving you a shout." Collins said tentatively. Even though she was his lover, Nadia still detested ill-timed calls (like when she was in bed or behind the wheel).

"How de exam was?"

"It was okay. Just that I ran out of time before I could finish all de questions."

"That is you all de time," Collins let out a chuckle which was just above the booming music.

"You mussy want to write out the whole book, nuh?"

"I study the whole thing so I could as well write it out, too," Nadia replied with a sweet slur and sucking teeth. "Stupse!"

"Heh! So that's an A, then?" Collins asked. By now heads were turned towards him, their expressions coated with dis-approving frowns.

"...I ain sure about that."

"Yeah, right! Don't be shame. I know how hard you was studying...."

A group of teenagers ambled through the door, all five decked-out in hoodies, T-shirts, scarves and caps that blocked out their eyes. The other passengers didn't pay them any attention, but Collins did, watching intently as they took their seats.

"Hello? Damian, you there?"

"Huh? Oh, sorry about that...." Collins said, noting the overly large headphones over their ears.

"Wha happen? You seem distracted."

"Nah, it's nothing. Just had to get some bus fare for de con-ductor." It wasn't a complete lie. A man clad in a yellow jersey came over with arm outstretched to collect three copper coins.

"Oh, okay. Well. As I was saying, the exam was manageable

but—"

Collins didn't hear another word Nadia said. His ears deafened by every fidget the teenagers made. The way one reached into his pockets to pull out two bills. The way another bobbed his head to a beat, which didn't seem to match the mellow one playing in the van. Two more were chatting amongst themselves, while the fifth kept his gaze outside of the window. Each act seemed so normal, so why was it that Collins couldn't look away?

"Uh-huh… Uh-huh… Yeah…"

The fifth teenager turned in his direction.

"Damian? You ain listening to me!"

"S-Sure I am, babes…." Collins felt a nasty, murderous spirit spilling beneath the teenager's cap. It was only for a split second, but there was no mistake.

It was a year since his last real battle. A year since Bewitched Gully. Collins had prepared all this time for the enemy to resurface, but he didn't expect them to be normal kids. They weren't strange enough. Even so, Collins kept his fingers on the hilt of a concealed blade, anxious to draw it should the need arise.

"No, you're not!" Nadia continued. "If you listening, tell me wha I say just now?"

"Uh…" Collins sighed. Now was not the time for this nonsense.

The other passengers dwindled with every stop. Two had just exited the vehicle, and from the way the final few groped their bags they were sure to be disembarking soon.

Through the window, the round tips of red buildings protruded high above blurring trees; an antique cannon appearing just beyond the stretching field. They were at St. Ann's Fort, Garrison Savannah. A beep pierced the music as one commuter disembarked. Only Collins, the teens, and the minivan workers remained.

"Look, Nadia… I gine gotta call you back, 'kay, babes?"

"Huh? Damia—"

Collins tucked the phone into his pants while pretending to ignore the teens' movements. Everything slowed with each breath as the passenger stepped onto the sidewalk. It was amazing he never noticed him before; a decrepit old man, hobbling away from the vehicle with washed-out dress clothes and a battered hoe wrapped in a crocus bag. At the back of his mind Collins wondered why people kept staring at him, when *that* character occupied the bus, too. But there were more important matters to think about, as the group shuffled in their seats.

He had to be delicate; any sudden movement might spark a preemptive strike. Aside from the fact he was outnumbered five to one, Collins noticed they were average in size and didn't pack much bulk. This could mean they were agile, but he couldn't be sure till they made a move. They didn't have weapons either. *Maybe I'm just imagining things…*

Collins tightened his grip around the cutlass when a sudden burst came from the adolescents. Two of them darted over three seats towards Collins, plunging one arm at his chest to catch him off-guard. Pity the Rasta wasn't.

Clang!

The chime of fist upon metal rang through the minivan, shattering the music and forcing the driver to turn away from the windshield.

"What de rass wunna feel you doing?!" He barked, but the six in the backseat didn't respond. He focused on Collins who had his cutlass drawn, with blade intercepting the blow and a keen smile on his lips.

"…Guess you guys ain wasting no time, nuh?"

Two of them exchanged glances before resuming their assault. More punches were hurled at Collins's head but they only landed on dreadlocks. The remaining passengers were on their feet now, struggling against better judgment to peep at the battle unfolding before their frightened eyes.

Bam! Collins planted two slippers into his assailants' chests, and sent them flying to meet their other three comrades. "Come on." He jeered, trying to bridle his nerves.

DANCE WILL NEVER DIE.

Elephant Man serenaded the five teenagers who maneuvered across the cramped vehicle. Hurdling over seats with a gazelle's grace, they advanced on the waiting Rasta with an organized onslaught. The closest one had arched his right leg above Collins and brought it down hard like an axe. But the cutlass was there; surely the enemy would lose his foot should he follow through. That was what Collins thought, until he saw the flash of steel glint from the teen's sneaker. *Shing!* Sparks flew from the clash of two blades: the one belonging to Collins and the one on the foe's heel.

…*That's different.* He regarded it for a second before two more blades were curving towards him. *Shit!*

Collins needed more space. He stumbled over the seats, grating his knee on metallic rails as he passed. From behind, Collins heard the sounds of iron and leather being gouged by the flailing slashes of hidden blades. Beyond him, the spectators had finally gotten the sense to leave the area, scuttling with frantic steps out the van door. This was just as well, since it gave Collins more room to play with. Upon reaching the middle aisle, he parried a strike directed at his neck with the hilt of his cutlass.

Fast! Collins thought while returning a flurry of sword strikes to keep them at bay. *But I've faced faster opponents!*

Compared to certain specters and man-sized monkeys, these teens were standing still, but they had dexterity to compensate. In a narrow vehicle, which couldn't be more than ten paces long, they skipped away from that cutlass, effortlessly using the surroundings to their advantage.

Collins kicked and slashed at the opponents, but every attempt missed completely. On one effort, his cutlass stabbed into leather after being evaded. That mistake cost him a gash on the shoulder. Collins was shocked; he didn't expect to shed blood from such minor foes. Marveling at the scarlet splotches floating next to his cheeks, he thought: *I gotta get more room, boy. Otherwise I gine be in some serious trouble!*

The Rasta caught his balance while surveying the stationary vehicle. There was only one exit point (aside from many open windows), and that was the front door which everyone came through. Fortunately, he was the one closest to it, though the enemy was determined to lock him down with three pairs of sneakers blurring at him. There was no escape.

The driver was horrified at the damage inflicted on his precious ride. "A-aye! Try and get off my rangate bus, man!"

"Gladly!" Collins answered with a wild slap of his cutlass,

which sent the enemy stumbling backwards to avoid it. The opening lasted seconds as two other teens bolted towards him. Though by the time they reached Collins, he dove onto the sidewalk, scratching his elbows and knees in the process.

Salvation had presented itself. He was free to move around and reevaluate the battle. That is, until the sound of crashing glass caught his attention. *Shit…*

The group had broken through the windows of the van, shards adorning their airborne bodies with utmost splendor. Collins rolled away to avoid the landing, and found himself near the Garrison Savannah racetrack. It was a vast field filled with many shades of green, from chartreuse to olive. Stretching several furlongs, the pasture was divided by numerous white barricades which formed tracks within the circle. People were often seen running the same route built for horses to keep in shape, but today only battle was displayed.

Parrying the sharpened blows aimed at his shin, Collins finally understood their fighting style. Not only did they have blades hidden on their heels, but the enemy also wielded them dangerously.

Beyond them, Elephant Man's track was pounding and with each beat the teens seemed to weave with it. Thrusting his sword forward, they dipped away from the edge with a sort of cadential flair. Collins had a bad feeling. He'd seen this sort of movement before, where the enemy had shifted its body according to a rhythm that made it difficult to hit. Music was playing back then, too; and with each change in tempo the enemy's actions seemed to change as well.

It's just like they're dancing. Just like the Shaggy Bears!

Except there was no flute song to control their movements. In fact, the teens aligned their motions with the music instead of acting like marionettes. They weren't as acrobatic either, so Collins kept them at bay with ease.

Clashing his cutlass against another pair of sneakers, he felt a wave of relief. *These guys are only human!* With renewed fervor Collins pushed against the group; his blade matching the ten against him. Still he failed to cut them down, brushing mere apparel instead of flesh whiles the teens weaved through each swipe.

Damn! They really are dancing! Two of them were break-dancers, spinning on their backs while swaying their legs with lethal flares: fluid and deadly. The others were closer to home, with their dancing styles mimicking several Passa Passa moves.

The one nearest Collins was dipping his upper body from left to right, dodging the agitated cutlass completely. While the remaining two slid across the ground, right foot bent to provide support, and left foot extended with sweeping motions. If Collins didn't back-flip in time, the attack would've severed his ankles.

"Stupse!" Collins sucked his teeth and resumed his stance. "Wunna men ain easy at all...."

The minivan parked in the distance, and spectators for the skirmish had more than doubled; including the driver and conductor who minded their vehicle, and the queue of backed-up vehicles curious to know what blocked traffic. To call it a spectacle would be an understatement.

*I got to end this quick...*Collins ran through the next strategies in his mind. But before he could act on them, a voice called from behind.

"Um... Hello there, young boy." The courteous drawl came from the old man who disembarked from the van before.

Part he come from now? Collins inspected the old man, whose clothes looked tattered now that he was close. *Was he here all along?*

"Could you spare dis old soul five dollars, please?" the old man asked.

"Get outta here, Pops. It's dangerous sticking around."

"Please. I just want a piece of chicken from de shop down de road. Uh hungry."

"Wait, Pops, you deaf? It ain safe here. Besides, you ain catch de bus just now?" The latter point caught the old man off-guard as he scrambled for an explanation.

"Well I... Uh, you see, I figure I was gine get something when I get home. But the sun so hot and my belly just start rumbling...."

Collins sighed. He didn't have time for this, not with the

enemy lurking nearby. At any moment they could pounce and tear this old man apart, Collins couldn't allow that to happen. But the old man saw his fidgets as a sign of weakness; now was the time to strike.

"Please, youngsta...." His eyes tearful and mouth pouted like a starved-out puppy.

"All right. All right..." Collins fished five dollars from his pocket and glanced at the teens. *They're gonna move soon. Mek haste and leff, Pops.*

But the old man didn't leave. With many bows he continued, "Thank you, young boy. Now if I could just get a lil dollar for extra bus fare..."

"Huh? You fuh real?!" The blade on one sneaker glinted menacingly in the sunlight, the others braced for a sudden bolt. *Shit!*

Then, in a coordinated dash, the five took stride towards Collins and the old man. "Get—"

Brax!

The closest one was sent reeling into the air with blood pouring from a shattered nose. But Collins didn't even move. His stance was still intact.

"Aye! Can't you see I doing business here?" Collins looked down at the old man, who now had a disturbed look on his sallow face. In his grip was that rusting hoe from earlier, which dripped scarlet at the square blade's tip.

"What the—" The teens shared Collins's sentiments as they backed away. This old man was strong.

"Young people these days just don't know about patience. Only force people to raise dem blood pressure...." He waved the garden tool like a knight waved a lance. The remaining four glanced at each other, and then after silent accord, they darted forward in a counter attack.

"Look out, Pops!" Was what Collins sought to exclaim, but there was no time for that, those four hoodlums had already ambushed the old man in a simultaneous assault. A refrain of metal upon flesh echoed throughout the savannah, and after seconds, they were punctuated by thuds. The spectators couldn't follow what happened, but Collins did. "H-Holy shit!"

At his feet the enemy lay: lifeless and utterly defeated. Various wounds were on their bodies; one was bleeding from the head, another from the torso, another had a dislocated knee and the fourth a shattered collarbone. The old man wiped his hoe in the dirt, and then turned towards the bemused Rasta. *I...I barely saw him!*

Then the old man resumed his hustle, painting his face with courtesy. "Now, sonny boy. As I was asking yuh earlier ... about de extra for bus fare?"

Collins stared, forcing the old man to clear his throat.

"Oh yeah, right... Here you go."

"Ah! Bless you, sonny. Hear?" The old man beamed, pocketed the two green bills, hoisted the hoe over his shoulder and left the Rasta to gawk in his wake.

Police officers arrived at the scene, their gaze singling out Collins as part of the disturbance. "Right dey, Offisuh! Dem is the people that wrecked my blasted van!"

Crap... Scampering across the savannah, he regarded the vanquished foes. *What the hell gine on? Who were those guys? And who was that old man...?*

These questions rang above frenetic cries as Collins made his escape. No doubt, Bimshire was about to get lively again.

On the other side of the island, away from the violent scuffle on the south coast, a young man ambled idly along a lonely hillside. At the right of him, vehicles of all sorts passed by, their drivers taking mere moments to eye the boy as he walked. He was, by all accounts, an average pedestrian except for the piece of sugarcane holstered on his shoulder.

Kyle Harding noticed the stares. He even nodded at the few who sped past with unrefined interest. This was standard fare for the past eleven years, so Kyle didn't mind the attention. What bothered him more were the hot beams of sunlight beating against his body. Few clouds were in the sky, leaving the golden ball overhead free to shine on everything below. Still, as hot as it was, Kyle didn't complain. He rarely carped about discomfort, so at most he fished a handkerchief from his pocket and mopped the glistening sweat off his brow.

"Just another normal day." he muttered, while regarding the white building far behind. Kyle left the University not too long after finishing his final exam before summer vacation. Some of the cars speeding past him were packed with other students eager to indulge in their newfound freedom. But Kyle didn't have this luxury. He never did.

Kyle had too much on his plate; even now, he was on his way to a part-time job to pay the mounting bills at home. This had been the norm ever since his mother died, leaving him to mind the family affairs in her absence. But as stressful as this was, bills alone didn't sully Kyle's vacation.

He hopped over a steel barricade, which kept passersby from the steep incline next to the sidewalk. Most people wouldn't even consider this a short cut, but Kyle did, so he ventured down the rocky path, much to their curious looks. This area was also part of the University's expansive property, though most of it was left idle. The only exceptions were a newly constructed, cream-colored building with burgundy trimmings and a sign marked UNIVERSITY OF THE WEST INDIES – ARCHIVES DIVISION, and standing in contrast a couple meters away, was a rundown wooden structure with the same words hanging askew over the front entrance. Kyle thought it abandoned since most of the cars were parked next to the newer edifice, and there was a yarn of lianas and vines across the older building's walls.

He passed the compound and ventured through a little woodland track leading towards the main road. Just like the hillside earlier, cars were hurrying by with oblivious fervor. Of course, the passengers were too far away to see his cane, but Kyle regarded their fret as they honked and steered on the crowded street.

How could they be so carefree? Kyle sighed, giving his forehead another wipe. A sudden frustration flowed through his body, followed closely by fatigue—but not of the physical kind.

Weathered, green benches were scattered along the area. Someone thought it was a good idea to put them out in nature, where they were subject to the elements; nevertheless, Kyle sat on the nearest one to catch his breath. For a moment the exhaustion disappeared but not the aggravation; in fact, it only grew the longer he stared at the busy road. "…Don't they know what's out there?"

Kyle posed the question to the sugarcane on his lap, taking a few breaths to recall every event they experienced together. From the time it left his mother's dying grip that cane had always been surrounded by unnatural phenomenon. Thunderous rumbling on the rooftops of his house, flashing lights that poured through his bedroom window while he cowered in fear—all of this mere minutes after holding that cane. Then many years later, after a term of peace and security, Kyle heard that patter again; only this time eerie flute music accompanied it, along with the gaze of unseen eyes.

Then the observer revealed himself— or itself—for the being wasn't human. Those glowing eyes still haunted Kyle's core. That sand, flowing steadily from the wound on its torso, still imprinted in Kyle's mind. "…Things like *that*…"

He inhaled deeper and recalled even more treacherous opponents: a serial killer with an abnormal right arm who reaped people's hearts, a towering wooden behemoth that carved fissures into the ground. If it weren't for his cane, and some help from Collins, he would've surely died by now. And one could only have so many second chances.

"Damn!" He shuffled on the bench, scraping his jeans across the dry wood. Magic existed. And not only did it exist in Bimshire, but it was a product of an underground industry known as the *Dark Arcs*. A business; where miracles happen in exchange for a fee. And the clients better pay, lest they suffer the consequences.

Of course, none of this concerned Kyle, until he heard the term *Inheritor* and what it represents.

That sugarcane is like an invoice to us. Surely you know it's not normal, right?

It was a product of the Dark Arcs, conjured by his mother

before she died. However, as it was still unpaid for, Kyle became burdened with a vicious debt; one that invited the supernatural and treacherous to his wake.

"Why am I thinking 'bout useless things?" He shook his head. "And I supposed to be at work, too…."

Tucking the sugarcane across his back, Kyle resumed his stroll towards the main road. It was on his fifth step that he came to a halt; when the thin, black-and-white frame of the bus stop popped into view. Bus stops were the first magical artifacts that he'd ever encountered. Its flat red-and-white circle-top would flicker each time he approached, sprouting goosebumps on his skin.

Kyle gazed at it for a while, his sneakers firmly rooted into the ground and unable to move. He didn't know why. He broke his gape and began scoping around the surrounding trees. Verdant canopies glared back at him from their timber thrones, and the faint chirps of blackbirds filled the park. But there was something lurking behind this lush ambiance. Something sinister. Lethal.

It was as clear as the sun, though the moment he stepped forward the sensation dulled. *I know you're here, you bastards…* Kyle squeezed his sugarcane, careful not to alert his hidden foes.

Who will it be this time? A Shaggy Bear? A Mocajambe? Kyle listened for the flute music—thankfully, there was none.

The answer would come in the form of atmospheric change; where the air was pierced by malice and murder. It surged towards Kyle at a pace that made the very leaves rattle. *Fwip!* That sound—the only sign of the projectile—which Kyle twitched his head to avoid.

"…The hell?" He was afraid, but his excitement drowned out the fear. Though it was only whistles, the enemy had finally returned.

Crap! Three lines were torn in the air as Kyle skipped along the park for cover. It made no sense hiding behind trees, as one dart ripped through the foliage like mere sheets of paper. Force aside, the projectiles moved at blinding speeds which made it difficult for Kyle to evade.

But he did, just barely. Ignoring the gashes across his bag and shirt, Kyle maintained his mobility. He combed the canopies for his attackers. *...By the angle, there should be at least three of them in all.*

However, the two darts gliding towards him proved that he was incorrect. Choking his breath Kyle dove underneath them, yet three more were fired from the same positions as before, forcing him to scramble forward.

Fwip! Fwip! Fwip!

Tiny explosions brushed his heel but he was unscathed, sliding away to safety. *Tch! Close. Too close.*

The sugarcane was still wrapped in its cloth, dormant until its wielder deemed necessary. Kyle skipped along in zigzags to avoid the next series of attacks; with any luck his enemies wouldn't have enough time to take aim. However, there was one flaw with this plan; it counted on knowing the exact number of opponents, and since that wasn't the case, it was inevitable that another dart would come flying at him.

"Shit!" There was no time to dodge. Within seconds Kyle shed the crocus cloth, drew forth the sugarcane, and placed it in between the oncoming missile and his face.

Clang!

The dart's tip bent from the impact, and its body twirled away from Kyle. As expected, his mother's memento protected him once more. His sights stayed on the trembling brambles above, where more projectiles caught the sunlight before they were fired. But this time Kyle was ready, parrying one so that it hit the bench he sat on earlier, and dodging the others so that they landed on the path he once treaded.

I can see them, Kyle thought, *though it's only last minute, I can see. There must be seven in all...* Five more darts zeroed in from various angles. Kyle's body was still sliding from the last maneuver, and there was no balance or time for any brand of elusion. Without options, he called upon his sugarcane again, sweeping away the darts in one swift motion, so that they bounced off the surrounding flora with dull thuds.

They're precise, too. Kyle noted the trajectory. His opponents had the aptitude to isolate his blind spots at the perfect moment; that last barrage being one example where they tried to hit from unorthodox angles. An effective strategy, had it not been for the sugarcane he possessed.

They had to be frustrated, seeing their darts thwarted by a mere piece of wood. Kyle heard a loud teeth-sucking sound when he parried the second barrage. "Stupse!"

There! The enemy revealed themselves, big mistake. As he sprinted towards the exposed canopy, another fleet of darts flanked him from the side. But his stride wouldn't be broken; ducking under the one on his right side, and hopping over the one from his left. Kyle was an agile lad. His reflexes polished even more since he gained knowledge of the paranormal. And as he bounded from trunk to trunk to reach the trees' summit, Kyle also demonstrated his might. *You can't escape!*

The sugarcane parted the bramble like a cloud, discarding branches and leaves … but no hidden bodies. *Not here?* From the corner of his eye Kyle saw some more rustling behind.

A thin black pipe protruded from the stirring bush and spat two darts in his direction. *Damn! Those bastards are moving?!* Kyle cursed his blunder, anchoring his arm on the nearest bough and swinging away from the missiles with great finesse.

Stupid. They wouldn't stay in one spot despite their cover… An error spawned from countless months of peace, but Kyle had learned his lesson. The rust was flaking off and his instincts yawned like the waking morn.

I think I figured out the bastards. Another rift spiraled towards him with the shooter's killing intent. Nevertheless, Kyle was prepared; clenching his weapon like a racket before a ball, his eyes fixed onto the gleaming silver, and then he swung hard with a fierce swipe.

Whap!

It was a satisfying sound, and as the dart was pushed along the same path it came, Kyle's eyes followed it with promise. The plan was simple, the timing superb.

"Ugh!" And it seemed successful too, as a petite, slender body flopped out of the canopy and unto the gravel. The foe donned a green body suit, with a black sash covering one eye, while the other lay bare with a dart lodged inside the socket. He would've blended in perfectly if it weren't for the bright scarlet spattering his uniform. Kyle inspected the shooter's pipe when he heard more whistles — allies of the fallen enemy.

I still got at least five more to take out. He sought cover near the abandoned Archive's building. *This is taking way too long!*

A shower of darts mangled what remained of the desolate structure. Time was running out for Kyle, along with his patience.

Damn it! I've gotta try something!

An object pierced through the storm of darts, homing onto one foe perched on the rooftop. *Brax!* There was an explosion of shattered glass, while two more bottles spun through the air at targets Kyle could not detect.

"What de hell?"

Screams and smashes adorned the air as the bottles drifted with deadly ambition. Thirty seconds? No, the slaughter lasted shorter than that. Footsteps broke the silence, causing Kyle to emerge from cover. Six corpses: each with shocked expressions and gaping wounds, and above them was a bandit with a scarf around his nose and a bottle case on his back.

"You…." Kyle said, while Sniper sucked his teeth.

"These bastards ain even put up much fight."

Kyle didn't meet Sniper on the best terms. Last year, when Kyle had some semblance of a normal life, he had an altercation with Sniper at a nightclub after spilling drink on his outfit. A normal mistake, but Sniper didn't agree, throwing a bottle at Kyle with lethal intent. The same lethal intent that sifted through the park minutes ago.

Kyle knew the hooligan was dangerous back then, and though Sniper rescued him from Bewitched Gully, the opinion hadn't changed.

"What are you doing here?"

Sniper rolled his eyes while tugging the scarf off his face. "Yuh ungrateful brute. Wha you mean, 'what I doing here?'

Saving you ass, dah's wha!"

Kyle was incredulous. "Why?"

Sniper sucked his teeth again. "Because you getting yuh ass cut again, that's why."

"I was handling myself."

"Oh, fuh real?" Sniper tossed the bottle into the air and caught it. Kyle maintained his battle stance. "It looked like you was struggling from a bunch uh soft men like dem. Yuh mean, you ain get nuh stronger since Bewitched Gully?"

"I'm fine." Kyle replied. "I told you I was handling it. Besides, you never bothered about my welfare before, so why do you care now?

"I don't."

Sniper tied the black scarf around his forehead, covering thin cornrows, and revealing a broad nose and a pout.

"Thanks." Kyle said.

"Dah easy," said Sniper.

"So … Do you know anything about these guys?"

"*Shadow Darts.*" Sniper said the words like a comprehensive definition, but the baffled look on Kyle's face proved otherwise. "It's a group that specializes in stealth, long-range combat and assassination. Dem does use blow darts, though; ain got nuh skill like the Pel-Tings."

The Pel-Ting Family of the East, a renowned organization within the island of Bimshire, especially among those involved with Dark Arcs. Their affinity for throwing objects with extreme precision had made them a name to be feared. But Sniper wasn't afraid when he spoke of them; his tone was more of disgust.

"Safe… Er… What's a Pel-Ting?" Kyle asked.

"Don't worry about dah." Sniper crouched on the ground like some sort of animal. Kyle thought he would start scratching his ears with his heel.

"Okay, so these Shadow guys, they specialize in assassination?" Sniper nodded and Kyle sighed, making his way towards the frayed remnants of a bench. "And here I thought they forgot about me."

"I get bore earlier this morning, too, so you ain de only one."

"Really?"

"Yeah, it was dem leader. He did weak, though." Sniper hopped up and started kicking out his legs. "After I tek care of him, de man gimme some very interesting information."

With that, he turned towards Kyle. His eyes (the same shade as the bottle in his hand) were focused right on the canewielder. "There's a mark out for my head, but that ain really nothing new, 'cause men does come after me all de time. However—" Sniper's diction became clear and astute, unlike the raucous Bajan he usually used. "—they're also after a guy who walks around with a sugarcane, and a Rasta with a cutlass. Now, what could they possibly want with you?"

Kyle didn't answer.

"And I just remember wunna men was in Bewitched Gully, too. A place that ain easy to enter in one piece, let alone leave. Why?"

"We were looking for something." Kyle finally responded.

"Like what?"

At that moment, Kyle opted to enlighten Sniper about last year's events. Highlighting the paranormal entities that came after his life, such as the dancing Shaggy Bears, the serial killer known as the Heart Man, along with everything he knew about the Dark Arcs. However, Kyle omitted the story behind his sugarcane, and the mistakes his mother made before passing away.

That was nobody's business but his alone.

"I shoulda guess you already familiar with de basics. Most men don't even know about de Gully, far less go inside." Sniper began pacing around. "How you get in anyway?"

"How did *you*?"

"I got my methods."

"There ya go." Kyle smiled. Sniper sucked his teeth.

"Wunna shoulda stand home, 'cause it only lead to more trouble."

"What do you mean?" Kyle couldn't imagine his situation any worse. With the debt he owed, the target on his back was large enough already.

"I mean, not only did you guys go into *Bewitched-Friggin-Gully* and make it out alive, but we also took down *Jamba* as well."

Jamba: the towering Mocajambe they encountered in that

accursed Gully last year. To call it a monstrosity would be a severe understatement. Its body was composed completely of wood, all two stories, and at its head was a mask that resembled the side of a small house with a giant nail placed at the top. Its weapon was a massive slab of concrete that Jamba wielded like a saber; one that stole large chunks of earth whenever it failed to hit its target. Kyle could still remember the polite boom from its voice, the burning purple glow from its eyes, and the roar of its giant weapon.

Sniper continued, "He was the Captain of the Mocajambes—the friggin *Captain*. I know the higher-ups catch a fit when he dead. Plus, the fact we manage to tek he out now draw unwanted attention from the wrong sorta people."

Kyle gave him a blank stare and Sniper retaliated with a growl. "We on the radar now, man. All uh we getting *noticed*, and I for one ain too please 'bout that."

"But aren't you used to it?" Kyle asked tentatively. "I mean, how is this any different from how it was before?"

"Oh, I see, Mr. Badass." Sniper had a mocking tone which Kyle didn't appreciate. "Look. You may think you see all that out there, right? But lemme tell yuh, dem got crueler people than a Heart Man and some monkeys, hear?"

"What do you mean?"

"Well, not like these men—bad example." Sniper saw Kyle focus on the cadavers, which were still scattered across the park grounds. Their lifeless eyes filled with shock and horror. "But dem got some people in this industry you ain gine be able to handle, and now that you in the spotlight, believe that they'll be coming after yuh."

"Don't worry. I can take care of myself." Kyle reassured himself more than Sniper.

"Not if you struggling with these lil' men."

"I wasn't struggling." Kyle contended, but deep down he was grateful that Sniper had arrived when he did. In fact, there was always this feeling that the ruffian knew more about the Dark Arcs than he was letting on. For starters, Sniper knew about the Shadow Darts, about how they fought and what they were after. Also, now that Kyle remembered, Sniper was the one who got them out of Bewitched Gully; the one who activated that strange bus stop with a mere piece of paper and made it act as some sort of teleportation device. Indeed, the ruffian was more experienced in obeah magic than he seemed. "Besides, how do you know so much about this stuff?"

Sniper was mute. Kyle turned around to face him, to look him straight in the eye, but he saw nothing but trees, buildings and bodies.

"Damn." Kyle hissed, and then gathered his things. The adrenaline had finally settled in his body, but his heart was still in staccato. Despite the battle's conclusion Kyle wasn't quite secure, he never was. And as long as his enemies were out there, he never will be.

Kyle walked away from the site, still glancing every other foot for the enemies' remains. He gave up after ten paces and continued on to the bus stop.

Then another notion came to mind. "Collins—Shit! Collins must have been attacked, too!"

Kyle rarely worried about the Rasta. Not only was he competent in battle, (Kyle could vouch for this after fighting alongside and even against him in the past), but Collins also had an upbeat attitude, no matter how dire the situation. Then again, that could've been the problem. Collins was too relaxed; totally ignoring everything they had seen before, and everything that was in store for them later on.

Kyle fished for his phone and sifted through the list of names on a modest green screen, his fingers trembling all the way.

Then he came across a name that he didn't want to see.

LIANNE

The word was printed in bold, black letters, and Kyle's fingers immediately stopped tapping when he saw it. His eyes loitered on it, anger and disappointment swelling up inside the longer he looked. His concern for Collins seconds ago had also disappeared, as he recalled the things that Lianne did. The way she always sent text messages to see if Kyle had gotten home all right. The way she saved a seat whenever he was late for class, (and that was often). The way she hogged down food whenever they sat down and ate together.

And the way she looked that night when she led them into Bewitched Gully to die.

Kyle dwelled on that last point, then he took a deep breath and deleted the number from its memory for good. Kyle wished that he could erase her from his own, but that just wasn't possible at the moment.

Kyle reached the sidewalk; the draft of passing cars brushing him as he strode towards the bus stop. All concerns about work had vanished, along with all concerns about his comrade's safety. Replacing them were excerpts from last year, when times were peaceful— weird— but still peaceful. When Kyle had some vague idea of who to trust. When overdue homework and unpaid bills were the worst of his problems. When he didn't have to live in constant fear for his life. Then again, it had always been like this and he knew it would never change—not the way things were now.

Smothered by these thoughts, Kyle felt a buzz tickle his leg. It was his phone.

"Oh yeah—almost forgot." The canewielder said. But fate wouldn't let him forget, and sure enough, another name was printed in black letters on that little green screen.

COLLINS

THE NEED TO PREPARE

The afternoon sun shone brighter in the countryside than in other parts of Bimshire. Under its light, a stray lizard scampered through the bushes in search of some shade. Eventually it would stumble upon a mahogany tree, but before it could get there, a large shoe blocked its path. That shoe belonged to Kyle Harding, who nearly stepped on the creature as he scampered down Molasses Drive to reach his home. Hurrying through the secluded gap, his steps upon the loose gravel below echoed amidst the surrounding trees. The neighborhood wasn't crowded; only ten houses separated by bush, kitchen gardens and other bits of greenery. There was a time when an eleventh house was in the Drive. It was the first home one came upon after disembarking, (as it was nearest to the bus stop.) A modest wooden building painted in a dingy green, and although Kyle never ventured inside it always provided him comfort. But that was due to the house's owner. "Granny…"

Rachel Pringle was an agent of the Dark Arcs, and as fate would have it, the one responsible for most of Kyle's problems. Every attempt on his life was crafted by her scheme; all to make sure Kyle repaid the debt owed to her employers. No, that wasn't totally true. Ms. Pringle acted out of jealousy and vengeance;

after all, Kyle was Veronica Harding's son. Needless to say, she didn't succeed. No matter what minion Ms. Pringle sent, Kyle Harding still managed to survive, and when he escaped Bewitched Gully he hadn't seen her since. Ms. Pringle disappeared along with her home, though the bus stop still remained (oh yes, The Powers that Be made sure of that), and as Kyle passed the abandoned lot he could only wonder where she was now, or whether she was plotting another assault.

Maybe it was her who sent those Shadow Darts?

The thought crossed his mind. And even though Ms. Pringle had vanished from everyone else's memory, (even the other neighbors), Kyle still believed she was there—watching and waiting for the right opportunity to strike. A whole year had passed since Bewitched Gully. What foul design was she planning over that break?

By the time Kyle reached his house, he'd already glossed over the telephone conversation from an hour before. Collins had a violent encounter of his own, where several adolescent assassins attacked him on a minivan.

"Wha? You get attack, too, B?" Collins asked.

"Yeah. And that Sniper guy said there are more enemies to come."

"Wait. You mean that drunk fella was there, too? Damn! We gotta talk, though. I rolling by your place in a couple hours. Look fuh me."

"Okay." And so, Kyle hurried home to meet the Rasta, (he didn't even bother going to work).

The Harding household was unchanged since his mother passed away. It was a concrete building painted in white and peach, with a varnished wooden gallery and a decorated roof with cherry-clay shingles. Kyle always thought it was bigger than he remembered as a child, but after discovering his mother was involved in magic, it became clear that it wasn't just his imagination.

Turning the key in his front door, Kyle wondered if his home was still safe, though deep down he knew that *safe* wasn't the best way to describe it. Gone were the days when flute music and tapping flooded his house at night. They had disappeared with the old witch Pringle.

"Hello?" Kyle called. "Guess nobody's home."

The place was the same way he left it this morning: with dirty dishes in the sink, the dining-room table cluttered, and the floor in need of a good sweep. Normally Mr. Beckles—his guardian—would've taken care of the mess, but he hadn't been spending much time in the house lately. He always had other errands to run, and today was no different as Kyle found a note on the table.

Gone to take care of some business. Will return later today—sorry about dinner.

L. Beckles

"Guess I gotta cook today." Kyle wasn't a bad cook; though he didn't fancy it very much, at least he wouldn't starve.

He checked the house before starting the meal, stopping first at Damien's bedroom. The boy was notorious for being untidy, but this, too, changed over the past year. Stepping in from the corridor, Kyle no longer tripped over stray shoes and books—everything was organized in neat little piles beside the dresser. The divan was made up, devoid of the dirty clothes that blanketed it before. Damien even mopped the dust from the room, giving it a nice pine scent. Although this change wasn't only limited to that bedroom, the owner changed somewhat as well. Damien was more active, no longer curling up under the cover on mornings, but waking up and dressing even before Kyle did. Damien didn't dawdle at his drills or chores either, focusing on doing each task efficiently.

It was like his little brother was another person.

"Ah well, better get to it." Kyle returned to the kitchen, jolting for a moment when he saw his mother's cadaver sprawled across the floor. Twelve years later and that night still haunted him. *Keep it together, Kyle. You got to be stronger than this,* he thought, before gathering the pots, pans and other things needed for the job, and trying his best to ignore his racing heartbeat. The stove was barely lit before a loud rapping came from the front door.

"Yo, Kyle! You home?!"

"Yeah." Kyle answered, not really caring if he heard him or not, and strode towards the entrance. On the other side an anxious Rasta stood—a stark antithesis of everything Damian Collins.

Collins, on the other hand, paused for moment. This was the first face-to-face meeting he had with the canewielder all year. Not much had changed. Kyle Harding was still lanky, reticent and owned a sugarcane. "Heh! You never put down that thing, do you?"

"Nope. Come in." Same old Kyle, not much for small talk.

Collins followed him inside, taking a seat on the living-room sofa while Kyle returned to the kitchen. The house had the familiar air about it, and although he'd visited a few times before, the place never lost its homely feel. As Collins inspected the couch and other furniture, he saw nicks and scratches that were probably left behind by a certain hyperactive child. "So, is the lil' guy around? Damien, right?"

"Yeah." Kyle wasn't surprised that he remembered his brother; after all, they both shared a first name. "He's not home, though. Think he still at school."

"Ah safe. You not worried about him being out by himself?" Kyle didn't answer, maybe he didn't know how. Collins cleared his throat and continued,

"Okay. So. Right. About what happen today—"

"There was another attempt on my life this morning." Kyle confirmed; just another day in the life of Kyle Harding. "According to Sniper, it was an assassination group known as Shadow Darts and—"

"Wait, that's the part I don't get. Sniper was there? Why?"

"He said he followed them after defeating their leader." Collins found that hard to believe, but it was just a small piece of a very confusing puzzle.

"Sighted. So he come and beat them off, then what happened?"

"Well…" Kyle broke off some macaroni and put it in the boiling pot of water. Most of what he knew how to cook started off with that. "He said there's gonna be more people coming after us in the future. Some of them dangerous—more dangerous than anything we've met before…."

Kyle lingered on that frightening thought; the Heart Man, Shaggy Bears, Gorilla Unit and Jamba—monsters from last year flickered in his mind. Collins couldn't fathom anyone more dangerous than what they already faced.

"Okay—but why are they after us?"

"Something about the spotlight being on us now that we escaped Bewitched Gully alive." Kyle said each word calmly, while emptying a can of corned beef into the warm frying pan.

"But that don't make any sense. I mean, how did they know what happened back then? And why is escaping the Gully such a big deal? Who are these people to attack us all de time without a proper reason?" The questions piled up, and Collins wanted to ask them for a very long time. He eyed Kyle, who was busy stirring the simmering corned beef; the salty aroma saturated the house. "You never did tell me what went down when we were separated either."

Ten minutes of Kyle draining the macaroni, adding it to the frying pan, seasoning with canned vegetables and herbs, passed before he answered. The mixture hissed under the heat, much like the rising tension in the room. "That's because you never asked."

"True." Collins recalled the aftermath of that night, the awkward silence as they dragged their battered bodies toward the parked car. Something happened while they were split up, something that scarred Kyle Harding deeper than any blade could. But back then Collins was too afraid to ask, this time was different. "I'm ready to know now."

"What are you doing? You should be home with your girl-friend. Exams done. Go out and party. This doesn't concern you."

"Heh…" Collins chuckled. "Can't believe you back with this again."

Kyle remained silent.

"We went through this before Bewitched Gully, B. My answer remains the same; the moment this shit started happening around me, it *became* my business. Hell, I get bore this morning, too! And I don't like the idea of having my ass hunted every five minute without some sort of explanation." The words were harsh, but Collins said them with his usual laid-back flair. Kyle faced him; he would've cracked a grin if it didn't reward the

Rasta's persistence.

"Fine then." Kyle sighed. Collins beamed. "I'm being targeted by a Practitioner named Ms. Rachel Pringle."

Collins recalled Practitioners were like wizard salesmen who traded magical favors for a fee. "Uh-Huh—Why?"

"She was once a neighbor of mine, friend of my mother's...." Kyle paused to empty the frying pan, and then continued with the discussion. He covered most of the details: the story about his sugarcane being a relic of the Dark Arcs, meaning that he now owed them for having it, and how every attempt on his life was orchestrated by Ms. Pringle so that she could claim it as proper payment. Kyle didn't mention his mother though, and he would've omitted Lianne's involvement if it wasn't so obvious.

"Oh wow. I didn't know alla that was gine on, B."

"Yeah." Kyle brushed off any sprout of pity and continued, "That's how it is. And now that you escaped with me, you're being targeted, too."

At that, Collins didn't respond; he could feel the cane-wielder's guilt.

"I'm sorry for dragging you into this. Whatever's going on here never concerned you. Just me and my—"

"Man, I already tell you it's my fault for following you in the first place." Collins remembered the first sparks of their friendship; on the night when they first encountered a Shaggy Bear and they fought side by side to survive it. Back then Kyle apologized, too, though he was injured far worse than Collins. "I guess I'm a bit too gypsy for my own good."

The living room was quiet as Kyle placed the pots into the kitchen sink. "Yeah, I guess you are."

Collins chuckled. "So, what you cooking?"

"Oh, just some One-Two-Three. Want some?"

"Nah, I good, man."

"Cool."

"So ... what's the plan now? What we gine do from here?"

"I don't know."

"Wow, that don't sound like you at all, B."

"What do you mean?"

"Last time you had more of a plan."

"Yeah, but that was when I had some idea what we're up against. But now we're completely in the dark… " Then Kyle remembered who gave that information in the first place—Lianne. "And look what happen when we follow that plan…"

"True." An ambush. The result was obvious, though Collins was stunned all the same. "So what we supposed to do? Wait for something to happen? 'Cause that idea ain sound too right."

"We don't have any other choice but to stay on guard and wait for these people or things to reveal themselves."

"Right." Collins sighed. This wasn't what he expected to hear after rushing over. "Anyway, I think I gine head out by Nadia now."

"Oh safe. How's she doing, by the way?" Kyle asked.

"She's good—had an exam this morning."

"Ah. How was it?"

"Okay, I guess. I rolling, though. Gine call you if I butt anything."

"Aight, man, you do that." Kyle escorted the Rasta to the door. "Wait, what happened to your car?"

"Oh. Nadia had to use it today—you know, because of the exam and all."

"Oh right."

"Yeah, man, so I 'pon de bus today." Collins said cheerfully, at least he was back to his old self. "Anyways. Later, B."

"Later."

They knocked fists before Collins walked toward the end of the gap, his dreadlocks disappearing within minutes. Kyle watched on after he'd lost sight of the Rasta, focusing on the beauty that would've been ignored on any other day. The green, yellow and burgundy crotons shone underneath the blazing sun, but the sight only reminded him of Bewitched Gully. *Damn…*

Kyle strolled back into his living room, looking around idly as the old clock ticked and the ceiling fan creaked. Waiting.

It would be an hour before Kyle heard someone step inside the verandah. He thought it for Collins, but the boney, middle-aged frame turned out to be Mr. Beckles.

"Oh, Kyle, you're home!" He sniffed the air and then made a humming sound. "And it smell like yuh start cooking, too!"

"I didn't expect you back so early, so I went ahead and start dinner." Kyle looked down at the two grocery bags in his hand. "That isn't a problem, nuh?"

"'Course not, yuh save me some trouble to tell the truth." Mr. Beckles examined the meal before serving himself a plate. "And I didn't expect to come home so early either, but my business didn't last as long as I thought."

"Oh…" Mr. Beckles tore through the dish with great relish, slurping up the pasta, much to Kyle's disgust. He always thought his guardian should have better table manners. "Hey. Can't you eat that any better?"

"Aww. But it tastes so good, I can't be worried about eating properly." Mr. Beckles guffawed before going to the pot for seconds. Kyle felt a burst of pride watching him enjoy the meal. "Maybe I should let you cook more often."

"I don't have enough time for that."

"Oh right, you were supposed to be at work all now. How comes you at home?"

"Oh…" Kyle teetered between telling him about the Shadow Darts or coming up with a lie. He went with the lie. "Something came up."

"Hmm? That isn't like you." Mr. Beckles inspected his ward, resting his fork on the plate. "Something like what?"

"Nothing really—" Kyle was accustomed to scrutiny, walking around with a sugarcane had always garnered unwanted attention. But the jeers of strangers couldn't compare to Mr. Beckles's probing gaze. "Just had this sudden urge to get home. Good thing, too, or not I wouldn't have made dinner, right?"

"Sure right!" Mr. Beckles took another forkful; by the look of his plate he was ready for another portion.

"You gotta leave some for Damien, too."

"Oh yes…."

Mr. Beckles was always a jovial person. As he chewed the last bits of supper, his face had a buoyant grin with wrinkles stretching around his eyes and mouth. But Mr. Beckles wasn't just a cheerful old man; he was a master in the art of Stick-licking. And the Harding boys were his pupils. It was then that Kyle had an idea.

"I want you to train me—again."

"Hmm?" The plate was clean by now, and Mr. Beckles was sipping the ginger beer that he'd brought home.

"I want to start back training sessions with you—if you don't mind."

"Oh? You really are full of surprises today, aincha, boy? You haven't asked me to spar in *years*, you sure everything's okay?"

"I'm sure—just feel like I've been slacking. If it's a problem I'll—"

"No no no. I'll spar with you if you want. Though I am a bit rusty, you might outdo me once we get started."

That statement was very far from the truth and Kyle knew it. "You've never fought me seriously. Not even once…"

"—Course I have."

"No, you haven't. I want you to fight me like you mean it, otherwise sparring is pointless."

"Hmm, would it?" Mr. Beckles scanned him again: the urgency in his demands was both unsettling and thrilling. If Kyle had asked at any other time Mr. Beckles would've refused, but something about the young man's resolve had enticed him to comply. "Okay then … I won't hold back during training. But there ain no going back once I get serious."

"I know." Kyle watched as the old man smiled and took another swig of his ginger beer.

Damien Harding came home exhausted. Now that school was over, his plans were simple: do homework, sleep, and maybe play a video game or two before anyone else came home. However, as soon as he entered the house, Damien heard clashes and grunts intrude from the backyard. It scared him. The last time Damien heard that noise, his home was under siege by a murderer with a glowing arm.

So it was with great caution that he eased through the living room, past the kitchen and towards the backdoor. Peeking through the louver, he saw two figures standing in the yard, one of which was the battered form of his brother. "Oh, it's just them training again."

Kyle and Mr. Beckles had been at it for the past week; though Damien had no clue what brought this on, and the sparring session sounded fiercer than usual.

"*Rah!*"

His brother's roar was punctuated by clashing weapons: the sugarcane in Kyle's hand and an ordinary practice stick in Mr. Beckles's. Against any normal opponent the sugarcane would've snapped the stick in two, but Mr. Beckles wasn't normal. Swinging hard and fast, the cane approached with a vicious intent, yet Mr. Beckles parried it with ease—taming its explosive power.

"Why am I not surprised...?" Kyle croaked. His body was drenched in sweat, with several scrapes along his arm and leg. "As strong as my offense is, it will always be neutralized by a strike from the right angle."

"Ah, so you realized!" The old man uttered with pride. "I've always admired your insight, Kyle. If it were a different time, you would've been regarded as a prodigy."

"Yeah right, and you're still not taking me seriously."

"I'm not?"

From what Damien saw he had to agree with his brother. Kyle looked battered, exhausted and spoke with heavy pants, while Mr. Beckles was still unblemished, relaxed, and kept his gaiety even in the heat of battle. It was always like this whenever the Harding boys sparred with their master. They'd fight their hearts out, push their bodies to the limit but in the end, they'd just wind up bruised and worn-out while Mr. Beckles had not even a bead of sweat on his brow.

"But I could swear I was pushing you pretty hard." Mr. Beckles said, as Kyle gasped for air.

"That ... isn't what I asked you to do...."

"Oh, it isn't?"

Kyle shook his head, and then resumed his defensive stance: one arm free, back-foot planted firmly on the ground, creating stability and power for the dominant arm to strike. These were the basics of Stick-licking, and seeing his pupil practice them so well made Mr. Beckles grin a little. "So, what it is that you want me to do, then?"

"Fight me properly."

Damien couldn't fathom his brother's request. Even if the old man was holding back, in Kyle's current state he wouldn't fare well if Mr. Beckles fought seriously. But the canewielder knew exactly what he wanted. Waiting around for an unknown threat was wasteful, but training with a known, skilled opponent was a better use of his time. The only catch was to force Mr. Beckles to treat this like a real fight, asking wasn't enough.

"So, what's to say I ain fighting you seriously now? Yuh look fairly break up to me…." Mr. Beckles said.

"That's not the point. You're supposed to be training me to protect myself, right? Well, fight me like you mean it, otherwise there's no point in sparring with you at all."

There was desperation in his pupil's voice. The kind of desperation he heard ten years ago, after Veronica Harding died. Mr. Beckles said, "Very well, then—"

And neither of the Harding boys had seen him since, that boney frame vanishing in the blink of an eye and reappearing right before Kyle's face. *Whack!* A flash of wood smacked against his cheek, knocking him off-balance before following up with another tap on his chin. It was fast, way too fast, but that was just what the canewielder expected—no—*wanted*.

His body filled with fresh pain as he fell, but Kyle was satisfied with this turn of events. These were the right conditions. If Kyle could handle this, then maybe he'd be ready for whatever comes next. He stumbled to his feet; a nasty lash came across his ribs just as he'd stood upright, making him reel again.

"What's the matter, Kyle? You asked me to go all out, and you expect me to *wait* until you resume your stance?" Mr. Beckles tapped his stick on the ground before dropping it full force at his student. However, the cane shielded the blow.

"Th-That's fine by me. Just keep it this way and I'll adjust." Kyle smiled, and so did his master. Damien, on the other hand, thought he was stark, raving mad.

Who in dem right mind would want that kinda punishment? He mulled it over as the session waged on for another half-hour. After which he was interrupted by a boisterous honking, which turned out to be a blue Toyota Runnex parked in the driveway.

"Yo, Kyle!"

"Ah!"

Damien recognized the cool-looking, dreadlocked guy who shared his first name. Excited, he wrenched open the door and waved in the gallery so that Collins could see him. And the Rasta did, returning the wave as he reached the steps.

"Gine on, lil man? Your brother home?"

"Yeah, he in de back." Damien replied, peeping inside the Runnex's tinted windows. "Bring any girls with yuh this time?"

"Wha?" Collins was so put off by the question that he tripped for a bit. "Oh. Nah, man. They ain with me today." Immediately, he remembered what was so interesting about the boy. Aside from the first name, Kyle's brother was small but fit for his age, and his umber eyes brimmed with interest much like the Rasta himself.

"Aww darn…."

"Don't worry. I'll bring them back once your brother decides to go out again." As Collins said it, Damien rolled his eyes.

"Like that'll happen…"

"How you mean?"

"My brother doesn't go out very often." The boy whispered. "He isn't cool like you."

"Oh, I wouldn't say that. Your bro could be pretty cool when he's ready." Collins beamed at him, but Damien wasn't convinced.

"Anyway, did you see my fro? I'm thinking of getting locks, are yours hard to manage?" Collins observed the ambitious afro which grew several inches from his scalp. It was flattering that the boy looked up to him, but Collins couldn't figure out why. Surely Kyle Harding made a better role model.

"Not really. You sure you want locks, though? I mean, you still in school and all…."

"True. I gine come up with an excuse by the time mine get your length."

Collins laughed, "By the time yours get as long as mine, you ain gine gotta worry about school."

"That's assuming I letting he grow locks at all." The phrase came from beyond the doorway, jolting the two in the verandah.

"Ah, Kyle, yuh home!" Collins saw the canewielder approaching them with a stern air and several bruises scattered over his skin. Despite his appearance, Kyle stood upright and didn't show any indications of pain. *Damn...*

"Wha you mean? I growing my hair in locks and that's that!" Damien barked, in which his brother retorted,

"Just because I ain carry you to de barber yet, doesn't mean I forget! Matter of fact, we gine tomorrow self!"

"Stupse!" The boy sucked his teeth before striding off to his room. Not accustomed to sibling quarrels, Collins fidgeted with his trident pendant.

"Sorry for encouraging him. He just asked me about them and I just started talking—"

"Nah, don't worry about it. That's the first normal conversation we've had in months." And for that, Kyle was grateful.

"Oh cool. So, what you been up to, man?" Kyle noticed he was staring at his cuts with great concern.

"I've just been sparring a bit."

"With *who*?" Collins asked incredulously. He'd been in plenty battles with Kyle before, and the canewielder was only this battered against the paranormal and the formidable. His opponent would have to be one of the two.

"You have a visitor, Kyle?" Mr. Beckles sauntered up from behind, and then focused his attention on the Rasta from last time. "Oh, it's you! Long time no see, Mister...?"

"Collins, sir." They shook hands, and Collins saw a stick resting in the old man's other arm. *Is he the guy Kyle was sparring with?*

"Right. Collins: the one with the cutlass in his shorts." Mr. Beckles focused on the outline under his grey shirt. "You ain had a chance to use that yet, I hope?"

Collins felt he shouldn't lie to this old man, so he kept as close to the truth without letting him know about their late-night activities. "Not recently."

"Ah, that's good. Young people shouldn't use violence unless necessary."

"Old people, neither—with all due respect."

"Hmm?"

"You use a weapon, and I'm guessing you taught Kyle how to use one as well." Collins concentrated on the way Mr. Beckles held the stick, his fingers gripping one end as it were a cutlass hilt.

Impressed that Collins noticed this minor detail, Mr. Beckles didn't insult him by denying it. Instead, he grinned, leading his guest into the house, "Good point. Well, don't just stand there. Come inside. D'you want something to drink?"

"Oh nah, I just come to shout Kyle. Hope I didn't disturb what you guys were doing…?"

"Yeah, you did." The canewielder answered bluntly. Kyle felt all his effort to provoke his master had gone to waste with this interruption.

"Oh, don't mind him. We can continue our spar some other time, couldn't we, Kyle?"

"Right … And you keep spoon-feeding me like before?" The other two took seats on the sofa, while Kyle leaned against the mahogany cabinet by the entrance. Collins couldn't tell if Kyle stood by choice or by injury. "Did you stop by for any particular reason? Any—" He glanced at Mr. Beckles, "—important meetings today?"

Collins understood what Kyle meant, and replied, "Nah, B, just wanted to see what you was up to. Was kinda relieved to see you weren't being idle."

The sight of the canewielder in diligent preparation showed he still had resolve. And that was what Collins needed right now: some resolve. Mr. Beckles fetched some mauby from the fridge and brought out three glasses to share the beverage. Handing Collins the bitter-sweet brew, he asked,

"May I see your cutlass a minute?"

"Huh?" Collins thought for a moment, drew the blade and handed it over.

The cutlass was finely crafted, both in design and practicality, with its edge catching the sunlight that poured through the window. Even Mr. Beckles had to admit, "Hmm… It's in good condition."

"I try to keep it that way."

Mr. Beckles lingered on the nicks and scratches on the blade, evidence from past skirmishes. Collins feared the discovery would open another discussion, but the old man just returned the weapon without query. "That's good. Yuh know, I met some people like you once."

"What?" The statement not only caught the Rasta's attention, but the canewielder's as well.

"Well, I'm assuming this isn't just an accessory. The proof is in the scratches, am I right?" Collins nodded. "Right. And there was a name we used to give people who fight with cutlasses— well— those who fight with them properly, that is."

"A name?" Collins felt his heart leap to his throat. Here it was, the reason for his journey into this underworld of magic and monsters, and it lay within the mind of this old man.

"Yes, there were called *Canecutters,* I think. Very spirited group, they were." As Mr. Beckles spoke, both looked at Kyle's sugarcane. Surely there wasn't a connection between the two … right?"

"Canecutters, nuh? So, are you saying that I'm one, too?"

"Perhaps. Assuming you know how to use that thing." Mr. Beckles chuckled. "Or it could just be coincidence."

"Do you know if they're still around? Canecutters, I mean?" asked Collins.

The old man thought for a bit, "Yuh know, there were a lot one time, and even back in my day you'd see dozens of them still roaming about." It was just like Collins remembered in his father's tales: a community of warriors who fought for justice and freedom. They weren't just fables, they were real! But what did his parents have in connection with them…? When Mr. Beckles continued, his hopes were quickly ebbed. "Nowadays, Canecutters are rare. In fact, you are the first I've seen in years, young man."

"Oh…?"

Kyle observed in silence. He was so engrossed in his own matters that he never suspected Collins's background, or that his master had any knowledge about it.

"I do remember one more Canecutter milling about, though. But I doubt you gine find he that easy."

"Please tell me. I'd really appreciate it." Kyle had never heard such sincerity in Collins's voice before. Or desperation.

"Even though I call him a Canecutter, he don't really look like one. For starters, he does be roaming 'bout the streets like a parrow—all homeless and what not. People used to call him *Father Hoe,* because he does always walk around with a hoe, offering to work people grounds for money."

Collins remembered the dingy old man from last week, who conned him out of ten dollars after dispatching those teenage assassins. "Are you sure this Father Hoe is a Canecutter … like me?

Mr. Beckles studied for a bit, and then with a grimace he replied, "Most definitely."

An hour passed since Collins had left the Harding household. After he learnt about the infamous Father Hoe, Kyle was anxious to get back to training —literally escorting Collins to the Runnex. It was a different side to the reclusive canewielder.

Reggae music blared from the speakers as he drove towards the south coast—Garrison Savannah to be exact. The Runnex pulled through a small gap with the race track on one side and the Bimshire National Museum on the other. Luckily there was no one around, so Collins parked in a clearing just beyond the aged, burgundy structures nearby.

It was late afternoon. The sun approached the border of the sea, dying the sky in light opal colors. Along the white barricade, Collins saw people jogging in pairs, while one or two others struggled to fly kites in the waning breeze. Collins walked around until he came to the site where he fought those adolescents. There was little to remind him of the encounter, a few scratches in the hardened soil, and maybe a red spot or two that baked under a week's worth of sunlight.

After thirty minutes Collins groaned, "Guess I shouldn't expect him to still be here."

"Expect who to still be here?" The polite drawl came from behind, and when Collins turned the parrow was standing there—beaming with tool in hand.

"Father Hoe!" The homeless man looked perplexed, which stretched the wrinkles on his face humorously.

"Who?"

"You—Didn't think I'd find you again."

"Oh? The same here, youngsta." Then Father Hoe out-stretched his hand. "Could ya spare me five dollars?"

"Huh? You can't be serious…"

"Please … It late, and I ain had nothing to eat since morning."

Collins contemplated for a moment. On any other day he would've refused, but this was a fellow Canecutter. "Here."

"Thanks, young fella. You a good lad, de Lord gine smile on you one day." Father Hoe started off in the opposite direction when Collins urged him to wait.

"Don't you remember me from last week? You bailed me out from a frig-up situation."

"Did I?" Father Hoe wore a grungy fedora, which he removed to scratch his scalp.

"Yeah—you know—it was six of them, all in caps and they used to dance?"

"Umm. Nope, still don't remember."

Is his memory that bad? It was a rational assumption, consid-ering Father Hoe had to be at least twenty years ahead of Mr. Beckles. "They were the ones who interrupted your hustle…?"

"Oh right!" Father Hoe exclaimed and Collins rolled his eyes. "I remember, fuh truth. That was a dangerous predicament I saved you from, nuh?" Father Hoe smelt the rising guilt in his mark and outstretched his hand again. Collins reluctantly conceded another five-dollar note.

"Anyway, how did you move so fast?"

"Dem was just moving too slow, dah's all." Father Hoe

replied before striding away from the pavilion. The parrow had extorted all he could from his mark, but Collins wouldn't let him escape so easily.

"Wait! Are you a Canecutter?" Father Hoe halted at the word. Collins asked again, "Are you… like me?"

"Sorry? Don't know what you mean." Then Collins drew his father's cutlass, slowly pointing the hilt as a non-aggressive gesture. Something about the weapon sparked Father Hoe's interest. Maybe it was the nicked blade or its craftsmanship, but when Father Hoe saw the sword, his demeanor changed. If only for a second, his ignorance disappeared and he became authoritative and all-knowing. "Can you use that thing?"

Collins nodded, but the parrow wanted to be sure. Dropping the hoe into the ground and then, in a motion too swift to register, flicked the blade so that several pebbles hurtled at Collins's face.

The cutlass reacted before Collins could think, slapping away the pebbles with a remarkable display of skill. Father Hoe nodded in approval.

"What the hell was that for?!"

"Do you have bus fare by any chance?"

"What? Why?" Collins grabbed his wallet but Father Hoe shook his head.

"No. We'll need to do some travelling, and I kinda low on bus fare at the moment."

"Oh. Well, I have my car parked not far from here."

"Good." Father Hoe straightened his fedora and then strode to where Collins had pointed. "You wun happen to know where St. Christophers is, nuh? It's down south."

"Err, I think so." Collins followed the parrow, unaware of his intentions. "You could always direct me if I gine the wrong way, though."

"That's right." Father Hoe stopped. "Maybe I should be following you, then?"

"Yeah, Pops." Collins then took the lead, bypassing the joggers who ignored them on their run, and soon the Runnex appeared under the shade of silk-cotton trees. The alarm beeped, then Father Hoe popped open the door and called shotgun for the seat upfront. Collins felt uneasy with the parrow on the upholstery, but at least Father Hoe didn't smell, as cinnamon flavored the air. *Nadia would so kill me if she knew about this…*

The engine purred, urging the Runnex through the lane encircling the Savannah and unto the main road towards Hastings. Traffic had doubled by then, as many commuters were either heading home from a tiresome day of work or going to various liming spots along the south coast to relax. Amidst the engine was the hum of a slow Reggae track, which would've been louder if Father Hoe hadn't complained that it hurt his ears. As Collins watched him tap his knee, he wondered if the parrow was indeed this fabled Canecutter. He didn't even have a cutlass which, as far as Collins knew, was a prerequisite for his family's fighting style. Still, Father Hoe's skills couldn't be overlooked…

They drove for forty minutes, traversing through the bustling streets of Oistins, the calm suburbia of Maxwell, and eventually the deserted roads of Enterprise which further led to the entrance of Long Beach. By now the sun's presence had dwindled, and the night was making plans to take its place.

"Ah, we're here!" Father Hoe hopped out of the Runnex just as it came to a halt. "Thanks very much for de lift, muh boy. Your folks mussy raised you well."

"Hey, wait up, Pops!" By the time Collins parked the car, Father Hoe was near the beach entrance. "I thought you were going to train me."

"What? At this time of de night? No, no, sonny. I just wanted some bus fare to get home, but the drop work just as good, I thank yuh." Again, he turned, and again Collins spoke,

"Please. I know this sounds crazy, and I can't even believe I asking this myself, but I need your help. Somebody tell me you're a legend… I don't know if that's true, but I do know I need to learn some of your skills. I think my life depends on it."

Darkness enveloped every stone, bush and pole around the area. But as dense as these shadows became, they couldn't overwhelm the glimmer in Collins's eyes. It was a sharp resolve that captured Father Hoe like a beacon in the night.

"Ten years. Dah's when last I see a scuffle like that in the open so. And 'pon a bus, no less! Tell me, boy, does this have to do with them youngsters that attack you the other day?"

"Yeah."

Father Hoe scratched his scalp again. "If you bring a snack box here tomorrow, we'll see what happens."

Collins was mystified.

"A snack box. You know: chicken, chips and a bun. Those are so expensive nowadays; near twenty dollars, can you believe that? But I ain had some in so long… "

"Are you serious?"

"Yup. Not the ones from Haloutte. Dem snack boxes don't got in nuttin. Get one from the shops that does actually feed yuh."

Father Hoe left, descending what seemed like a staircase leading towards the coastline. Assuming the snack-box deal was the agreement; Collins went home and returned the next morning with the meal. Long Beach looked different in sunlight. There weren't any buildings in the area, except for a lone shack surrounded by boulders. It wasn't popular either, as only one bench was on the entire coastline, and there was no formal lot to park on. Nevertheless, the Runnex halted at the entrance, and after ten minutes with no appearance from the parrow, Collins went down the stairwell from last night.

The morning light revealed a haphazard construction of old, dried-out plywood and concrete blocks for steps. It wobbled beneath his feet but Collins kept his balance. Surrounding him was an assortment of sea grape, button wood and other types of coastal vegetation which formed a makeshift tunnel for anyone who entered. Collins saw little through the thick leaves, and he wondered how Father Hoe managed at night.

After two flights the sound of crashing waves grew louder, and a breath of salt spray brushed his face upon clearing the thicket. As expected, the beach was deserted. No early morning swimmers, no joggers, no sunbathers, just an expanse of white sand, shrubbery and stray rocks—the sort of private shore tourists longed to enjoy.

"I wonder where Pops could be." The snack box in his arm was still warm, though Father Hoe would eat it hot or not.

Collins approached a field of dead palm leaves, with their trees leaning lazily in the breeze. A gentle incline stretched behind them, and as Collins regarded it, he noticed a small cavity. More like a cave or grotto, the work of limestone weathered by shifting tides over the years. "Maybe he's here."

Collins slid down the little slope leading inside, prickly burr seeds helping themselves to his ankles as he passed. Cursing and brushing off the primplers, he skipped several meters before noticing the change around him. It wasn't the shadows, since a nearby boulder blocked out the sun. Nor was it the primpler bush disappearing at his feet. No, the change occurred inside the cave. Where porous stone walls became smooth, lacquered wood and the ceiling of jagged teeth became burgundy shingles. In short, the grotto was a charming chattel house overlooking the beach.

"—the hell?" It engrossed Collins, in the same way Bewitched Gully did with its magical warmth. It was familiar yet frightening to see magic in front of his eyes, but Collins drew breath and urged forward. "Pops? Father Hoe? You there?"

"Ah boy, you manage to find muh." The parrow sauntered out from the doorway.

"What the hell? Is this your place?"

"Yep. Oh, is that my snack box?" Father Hoe pranced towards Collins like a child on Christmas morning, gaping at the container as if it were a coveted gift. "And it's Mapps, too? Bless you, muh boy!"

And he popped open the box, yanking out a barbequed drumstick and putting it in his mouth with frenzied delight. Collins would've been disgusted by his champs and smacks if Father Hoe's home wasn't so captivating. "So… lemme get this straight. You live here, but you walk around the street like you homeless?"

"Something like that—it's a personal preference yuh could say. *Mm!* These chips are heavenly. What's this barbecue sauce?" Father Hoe took several forkfuls of marinated fries and then lapped up his fingers. "Come on, we're not sticking around here."

"Huh? Why not?"

"There's a reason why de house was a cave in de first place." The parrow walked past him and led the way back to the coastline.

What Collins didn't see was an intricate pattern engraved on the boulders that formed the entrance, and along the sand, under the very same primpler bush he stepped through earlier. It was perhaps the craftsmanship of a brilliant Practitioner, one that made it possible for the parrow to live a secluded existence on this deserted beach.

"Sighted. So, we gine train now, then?"

"—this sauce is really something. Why don't those fast-food places have sauce…?" Father Hoe mused; you'd think the homeless weren't so picky about their meals.

"Pops—"

"Yes, yes, I gine sort you out now. Just hold on." Father Hoe sat on an old log. "Okay, draw your blade and show me what you got."

Collins was bemused so the parrow repeated, then he drew the cutlass from under his shirt and took his stance. "Now what? We gine spar?" The notion excited Collins, but Father Hoe snickered.

"Oh gosh, no, you might get yuhself killed if I did that."

"Right."

"Yes. Now it'll be a similar exercise as yesterday." He nibbled on the bun.

"Huh?" *Whack!* Without further notice, a stone was hurled at Collins's head. "Oh, this again?"

Two more came and they were slapped away by the cutlass. Collins noted the coconut trees planted along this section of the coast. Using his namesake, Father Hoe flicked some shells at Collins with an almost Pel-Ting level accuracy. He counted sixteen before Father Hoe ran out of ammo, all the while defending each of them from his critical points.

"Good, good." Breathing heavily, Collins watched as the parrow nibbled on the last chicken bone. His arm still throbbed from that last volley. "You're decent with your right. It's your dominant arm, yes?"

Collins nodded.

"I thought so. Well then, how 'bout we switch to the left arm?" And before Collins could even raise a query, more shells were hurled at him.

"O-ow!"

"Gotta come better than that." Father Hoe shook his head and continued the assault. Though Collins perceived the angle and range of each projectile, he felt awkward parrying from his left. Yet another glaring weakness which Father Hoe exploited.

They walked along the ABC Highway with purpose in their stride. There wasn't much activity on the road, rush hour had long past and only a couple vehicles trickled back and forth. However, it was one in particular they were looking for.

"It should be here soon, right?" said one of them: a young woman in her early twenties with a lean figure and a pretty face—though right now it wore an impatient frown.

"Yes." The other replied—a man in a white dashiki and a thick, red scarf around his nose.

"Best hurry up; know that we got other things to do!"

"Don't worry. We're right on schedule." He sifted through a cell phone until a middle-aged man came on the screen. "This is our target."

MARK JONES was the title under the image. He was an ordinary fellow—plump, unshaven, and with more jewelry around his neck than most women would wear. Mark had done frequent Dark Arcs dealings in the past and hadn't been up to date with the payments. There was more to his story but that was all the cell phone said, and all the two assassins needed to know. "Do you have his face memorized?"

"Yeah, yeah." She shrugged the question while monitoring traffic, only one or two cars passed by. "*The Mirror* working, yuh. It like um was worth de money, fuh truth."

The Mirror was a special device which created illusions for a specified area. It was mounted on the highway itself, covering a surface of ten meters across, twenty feet high. As she observed the row of lights bisecting the road and the line along the tarmac itself, she tried to locate the Mirror's exact position. But she saw nothing. This was the handiwork of a talented Practitioner after all, and if it was hidden from her experienced eye, then the ordinary driver had no chance of finding it. What the drivers did see was a highway packed with traffic from the other roundabout. It was only an illusion, but soon a real traffic jam began to form.

The only exception was one ZR van which was allowed through the Mirror without falling under the same spell. It was the exact vehicle they expected, with a white body and a long red stripe going along the centre.

"The target's here. Are you going to take care of it this time, or should I?" The man asked.

"I got this one." she replied, and slid down the incline to meet the van.

Mark Jones sat in the backseat with two alluring ladies on his lap. It was paradise: surrounded by the honeys, money in pocket, loud music in his speakers, and a clear getaway from the witch he owed.

"You could believe I get 'way, fuh truth?" he guffawed. "From now on is smooth sailing. Think I gine hit a hotel and enjoy some of de sweet life dem tourists does get. Right, girls?"

He caressed their curves while howling in laughter; the music no comparison to his mirth.

"But, Mark, you ain tell we how you get so much money?" one of the ladies asked, which also caught the driver's interest.

"Yeah, fuh real, when you gine spill the beans?"

"All in good time, people. All in good time." Mark sounded so confident that the driver peered behind to look him in the eye.

Big mistake. When the driver returned his gaze to the road, he saw an obstacle in front. It was a young woman, one of the assassins that awaited Mark Jones's arrival, though the driver couldn't have known that. She was just a crazy pedestrian who popped in the middle of the highway; an accident waiting to happen. Tires screeched as the ZR swerved away, but she stood her ground and drew what seemed like a giant slab of iron.

That was her weapon: a massive sword bound in chains which a girl of her size had no business wielding. Arching it with ease, she watched as the vehicle veered past. Inside, Mark saw her and for a horrifying few seconds he knew what the woman had come here to do. *Shi-!*

There was no time for regret. The gigantic blade was already in full swing and the van couldn't avoid its impact. *Wham!* The thick edge tore into the windshield and bisected the vehicle like a knife against salt bread. Running through metal, glass and leather, the sword also caught flesh and bone: the bodies of the passengers and Mark Jones—who watched in timeless dread as his torso was slashed.

Two frayed chunks rolled across the tarmac like pebbles upon water. Blood and meat leaked from the wreckage, the former of which dribbled from the corpses to the great chained blade—solidifying into crimson dollar bills before reaching the edge. *Ka-ching!* A chime from a cash register echoed at her feet.

"It's done." She said, while her partner joined the scene. He wasn't pleased.

"Six casualties for the life of one man; couldn't you at least be a bit more precise?"

She gave him the finger and then skulked away. The job was complete, to hell with everything else. The man shook his head in disappointment. "You don't have to be so rude, either."

But he expected as much from his companion, to the point of ignoring the curse words under her breath. The killers began to leave the gruesome scene when a soft mewling halted their stride. A cat with a thick, black coat slunk towards them with majestic strides. Captivating as it was, the man wasn't surprised to see it.

"Ah! Another job." He focused at its jaws, which had a cell phone tucked neatly between them.

"Fuh real? Who we got this time?" The woman asked, and her partner showed a glowing screen with two young men: a Rasta and a boy with a sugarcane in his grip.

"Looks like a couple of kids…."

News of the ABC Highway had spread throughout the island, though it was under the guise of a "serious car accident which resulted in six road fatalities." That was what authorities found, instead of the two chunks of metal and scattered body parts which the killers left behind. Headlines and photos surrounding the wreckage were posted in every available newspaper. Despite the horrific nature of the truth, the lie was just as dreadful.

The news didn't stop people from travelling to Malvern, St. John on that Sunday morning. The countryside in the southeast parish of Bimshire filled with long expanses of canefield, which would've been deserted on any other day except this one. For today was Rally day: when professional drivers from all around the country compete in contests of skill and dexterity. The lonesome secluded roads were perfect for competition, with its many arcs and bends meandering throughout the area.

Patrons gathered along hairpin turns and finish lines where most of the action took place. Big frame tents, white barricades, and sponsor flags were posted around the congregation, decorating the gentle green slopes with multi-colored majesty. Like ants around a hill, people settled near the placements, equipped with coolers, food trays, radios and portable chairs to catch a glimpse of their favorite cars and drivers as they sped by. Some people had to sit on a friend's shoulders to see anything, and as one girl grew comfortable, she was nearly knocked over by a passerby.

"Hey! Watch it!" She spat at a young girl who maneuvered through the throngs with ease.

Lianne wasn't interested in the road, her emerald eyes focused on the crowd of faces. She was enveloped in her search, disregarding the music in her ears, the sun beating on her shoulders, or the sandflies nipping at her ankles. Eventually, Lianne found her mark in a cluster assembled around a Pajero parked away from the road. It was clever to use the truck as a vantage point, some sitting on the hood or roof to get a better view. Lianne's mark was not among them though, instead she saw him resting on a patio chair with a plate of food in hand. His long, onyx hair shimmering in the sunlight, he glanced up at her before dipping a fork into his meal.

"You made it. I didn't peg you as a Rally Girl." His words were casual and friendly, but Lianne ignored them.

"I hope you've read the papers this morning."

"Nah, I not much of a paper guy."

"Six road fatalities on the ABC Highway, the biggest death toll via accident in the last decade. These people you brought in aren't very discreet, are they?"

"Nah, not really.... But they are thorough, I'll give 'em that." He took a forkful of rice and stew while Lianne berated him. She spoke urgently, though her voice was kept low for intended ears.

"Thorough? Their target was only one man, and they managed to turn it into a spectacle—"

"Yeah, Mark... We used to run the same van route back in the day, yuh know? Real cool fella." the man said.

"So cool, that you ordered his assassination?"

"Well, Mark was involved in severe tax fraud. I couldn't just let him off for skimping payments. I am the *Conductor,* after all...." Lianne stared into his face, indifferent to the man's beautiful features—his sable eyes or his smooth, bronze skin. If there was any remorse for his actions, she had yet to discover it.

"Sulemann. These killers you imported will only bring unwanted attention to the operation. Maybe you should try other options before—"

"Oh? What's the matter, *Ms. DeSilva*? You concerned about your friend?" Sulemann jeered, but he knew a line was crossed from the quiet fury in her eyes. Just as well, he liked to dance with death on occasion.

Scraping tires and revving engines punctuated the cheers and hollers of the nearby crowd. A decorated Impreza—Micey Bourne's car—had drifted along the U-turn with extraordinary flair, sending the spectators in a joyful uproar. But this noise couldn't penetrate the tension between Lianne and Sulemann. They would remain that way until the crowd settled down and excited banter filled the air again.

"I have no concerns for the Inheritor," Lianne began; to Sulemann's surprise she didn't acknowledge the use of her surname. "I'm more worried about the attention this unit will bring to the overall success of our—"

"Relax. Relax." Sulemann's mouth was full as he spoke. "You worry too much, Lianne. If you ain careful, you gine start breaking out from all the stress."

Her eyes narrowed.

"Everything's going according to plan."

"I hear you…." She leaned against the Pajero when another car wheeled around the corner. The crowd response was smaller than before; perhaps the driver wasn't as popular. "Are they informed of the target?"

"Yeah. The message get send right after they dispatch Jones." Sulemann took a swig from an oversized cup filled with rum. "They should make contact within the week at most."

"One week…."

"Yep. That's how much time your boy has to live." Lianne didn't react. There were no doubts about the assassins' ability or their lethal nature. However, if Lianne still harbored feelings for Kyle Harding, she didn't show it. "Hope he puts it to good use."

"Knowing Kyle, he probably is." A wry smirk peeled across her lips, much to Sulemann's surprise. "I'm going now—just make sure you keep these people under control."

"Heh. If anyone was listening, they'd think you weren't my subordinate, Lianne." He returned her grin, but when Lianne looked into Sulemann's eyes she felt the cruel authority seeping from his core. A malevolence so profound that it was a wonder he kept it hidden. Then again, that was precisely why Lianne followed him in the first place.

"They'd be mistaken." Lianne sauntered away from the Pajero, vanishing into the nearby crowd.

Sulemann finished his rice and stew and then took another gulp of rum. However, he didn't enjoy the meal, dejection ruined his palate. "Rest well, Mark…."

Collins had been training for days and already he was too fatigued to carry on. Father Hoe had bombarded him with coconuts, where the parrow got this unlimited supply was beyond Collins. However, along with his exhaustion, Collins noticed one thing: progress. Slowly but surely, he adjusted to his left; though his muscles and joints ached from the constant parrying. Not to mention the old wounds from ill-timed strikes.

Collins struggled to explain this to Nadia, who not only noticed her boyfriend's injuries but his early morning treks as well. *Man… I gine can't keep lying to her.* It was just another secret, and the more they grew the harder it became to reveal them.

Whack!

"Oww!"

"Pay attention, youngster." Father Hoe said, after a coconut struck Collins on the forehead. In his free hand was a fried drumstick, which came in a snack box from Eddie's snackette. It was the sixth restaurant Collins had brought him to sample, and as the days wore on Father Hoe demanded snack boxes from different restaurants to compare. "Yuh like you losing concentration."

"Sorry…." Collins rubbed his brow while the parrow resumed his barrage.

"Something on your mind, boy?"

"Um yeah… was just thinking about my girlfriend—Ow!" Another coconut landed in his gut, knocking the wind out of him. "What the hell, man!?"

"Just because yuh talking doesn't mean yuh shouldn't concentrate." Collins watched as the parrow stuffed some chips into his mouth. He had no energy to argue Father Hoe's point, so he just resumed his defensive stance.

"Right—uh—my girlfriend starting to wonder where I gine so early in the morning, and I was just studying what to tell her."

"Young love. Been a long time since I see that, lemme tell yuh. I was a village ram back in the day, yuh know?" Collins was incredulous. "Yeah, man, back when I had time for that nonsense. Not now, as you can tell by the way I live. On the bright side, though—"

Father Hoe tossed the shell with effort, forcing Collins to intercept with his cutlass. As the blade quivered, the parrow continued, "—you like yuh learning, so I wouldn't call this a waste."

Collins had to agree. He became so comfortable that it seemed like he was left-handed all his life. "I guess that's true."

"Yep! And you learn in a week, too. Very nice." Father Hoe went to his chicken wing while tossing the coconut shells on the sand. "Tell me sain, who trained you to use a cutlass?"

Collins was hesitant to answer. How much did this parrow know? Was it wise to tell him everything that happened in the past year? "I trained myself."

"Really?" Father Hoe rubbed the grease from his lips and examined Collins for a moment. "That's fairly impressive, having so much technique without any formal training."

Collins considered the term, "formal training". His only exposure to the martial art came from spying on his father in the wee hours of the morning. He remembered it being beautiful, surpassing anything he'd ever seen in his life. The form, speed and precision brought young Collins to the point of mimicry. It was a childhood game at first, pretending to be like his Dad—an invincible warrior who evaded an unseen enemy with great prowess. But play evolved into mania after his parents died. Collins obsessed over those movements, mirroring them so closely that maybe, just maybe, they could pass for the real thing.

"I mean learning all by yourself. You mussy some sorta genius, nuh?"

"Nah…" Collins wasn't worthy of the compliment; he had a long way to go.

"I guess we should move on to de next step, then."

"So, no more shells?" Collins asked, somewhat relieved his arm could be given time to rest.

"Yes, nuh? Believe it or not, I only agree to this thing because of the free lunch."

Oh, I believe you…, thought Collins.

"But as you is an interesting fella, I suppose we should get down to business."

"Business?" Collins repeated the word, while Father Hoe disappeared into his grotto and returned five minutes later with an ugly pair of blue slippers. Dropping them in the sand, the parrow said,

"Here—put these on."

"Why? I already have on a pair, see?" Collins pointed towards the burgundy Billabongs on his feet, which were stylish compared to the ones Father Hoe had offered.

"Less noise and put on de blasted things, nuh?"

"Fine…." Collins groaned, kicking off the fashionable reefs in exchange for tattered flip-flops. "Okay, they're on. Now what?"

"Come here. Lemme show you sain." Collins feared the sandals would unravel with every step, and when he came close, he saw several jewels in Father Hoe's palms. No, more like smooth, translucent stones that could easily be used as decoration. "Sea glass: formed from glass bottles thrown aimlessly into the water, and weathered down for years until it comes out like this. It's kinda like the ocean's reward for our lawlessness."

"Yeah…." Collins was mesmerized by the precious rocks, whose surface reflected a gentle glow on Father Hoe's creased hands. Then, with a sudden fling, the parrow sent the sea glass into the waves. "Hey!"

"I want you to retrieve all ten pieces for me." Collins was bemused, but Father Hoe continued, "And you better hurry since those are very dear trinkets to me. If I was to lose them, then I'd stop training you immediately."

"You serious?!" Collins heard no bluff in his words, scrambling into the area where he thought the sea glass had landed. But he noticed something peculiar when his feet touched the water.

They were heavy. At first, Collins thought his muscles struggled against the breaking waves, but that wasn't it. It felt like a hundred-pound weight was on his ankles. "What the hell?"

"I see you noticed the feature of those slippers." Father Hoe snickered. "Engraved on the straps are special patterns that control the resistance you receive upon touching a certain substance—in this case water. The sandals then become effective weights."

"Shite, man! Wha sorta messed-up training this is?" Collins hobbled until he fell completely into the sea.

"It's supposed to add five pounds for every five inches of water, but considering yuh location, it mussy weigh a ton right about now."

Father Hoe was right. Collins writhed around in the waves until he stood on two feet again—luckily, he was close enough to the shore to avoid drowning. "Pops... I can't do this."

"Why not?" Father Hoe watched as his student toiled in the waves, not an ounce of sympathy in his voice.

"I—Shit, man—I can't move!" Collins gasped and wriggled and twisted before he calmed down. Panic wasn't getting him anywhere. *Okay. Let me get this straight… These things are supposed to be weights, so like any other dumbbell I should focus my energy on my limbs—well, in this case, my feet."*

Collins tested this new approach, slowing his breathing and gathering energy around his calf muscles. After thirty minutes nothing happened. "Not working. I'm breathing right. I'm concentrating... So why isn't it working?" Despite his athletic physique, Collins wasn't a gym person. Other than drills he was a stranger to weight-lifting, but the error became clear after a while. *Posture! That's right, my body still ain position properly.*

He shifted his right foot (albeit with great difficulty) to stabilize his body. It took minutes to work, but as he strained his left foot budged forward in one solid step. "Bout time...." Collins grinned at the small accomplishment. "Hey! How I know the sea glass ain wash away already?"

"Oh, it won't." Father Hoe said. "They got on the same spell as the sandals, so when you find them they should weigh a ton, too."

"You serious?" But the parrow had already resumed his cleaning, leaving Collins to his trial.

As the hours went by the sky became a fiery orange, staining the waters below. The stones may have been brightly colored, but under the darkening waves Collins couldn't find them. "Damn! I gine end up being here all night."

Collins combed through the waters until they were deep black. By now Father Hoe had lit a bonfire which casted a golden glow along the shore. With a deep sigh, the parrow walked to Collins and said, "Look. This like it ain gine nowhere, so lemme tell you wha. If you could find one by the end of the night, I gine continue training you."

Collins didn't celebrate, his focus honed on the sea glass fragments below. He pushed his foot forward in clunky steps. If sight was no longer viable, he'd have to rely on weight. *The sea glass should be harder to lift up than the other rocks.*

Under this premise, Collins picked up shells, coral pieces and ordinary rocks scattered on the sandy bed. Until ten steps and thirty minutes later, he found something smooth, small and most importantly, "Heavy—I think I found one."

Collins wrapped his fingers around it, but he couldn't separate the object from the ground. He pulled, yanked and heaved, reigniting the burn in his muscles.

"Look, lemme sort you out before you give yuhself a hernia." Father Hoe poked his namesake into the ground and extracted the stone with ease. Collins was flabbergasted.

How much upper-body strength does this starved-out parrow have?

"Mussy alla them snack boxes." Father Hoe chuckled, almost like he read Collins's mind.

"Right...."

"By the way, as the training gone up, so has the fee. I gine need two snack boxes a day, each from different locations. And if them ain got chips, bring some macaroni pie." Father Hoe dried off the sea glass fragment and returned to the bonfire.

"Fine then. Wha 'bout these slippers, though? I supposed to keep these on all de time?"

"Not my good pair, boy!" the parrow barked. "Besides, they ain't much use to you outside the water anyway."

"Safe." Exhausted and broken, Collins lugged over to the shore with weighted steps. Yet another weakness had revealed itself.

"Hmm? You seem to be sulking, boy."

"Nah—just a bit tired." Collins shrugged off his depression with a laugh, and then posed a question of his own. "Hey, um... why do you live like this?"

"Like what?"

"You know: in hiding, away from people, as a parrow."

"—Because I like um. So wait, you got a problem with the way you live?" Collins mouthed a reply but Father Hoe continued, "Look. It's good to tek a break from people once in a while, especially when it in everyone best interest. But hey, this beach is mine. I could relax myself in my lil' private condo without nuh stress. Lord knows I deserve that."

Chuckling at the sentiment Father Hoe ventured into the cave, which transformed into a chattel house, and reverted into a cave once more. Collins ventured to his Runnex, with aching strides and the parrow's words in his mind. ...*When it's in everyone's best interest?*

...

Collins returned the next day with renewed motivation. Hobbling along the coast till sunset, he found only two more fragments: a neat, jade one in the afternoon and a dark auburn one in the late evening. On the following day he found another light amber piece, but was fruitless by nightfall. This continued for the rest of the week. After six bonfires and twelve snackboxes, he built a collection until only one more remained.

"Ah boy, yuh coming close to de finish line!" Father Hoe nibbled on a seasoned thigh.

In the sparkling waters beyond, an exhausted Collins trudged onward in search of that final fragment. His body ached so much that he could barely move on dry land, far less the dense waters. Still, Collins kept his attention on the rippling surface. "Damn it! Where de last one could be?"

Collins scoured on until his legs betrayed him, falling face-first into the water. Salt burned his throat and nostrils, but amidst the terror of drowning his palm touched a stray stone. One that, despite its small size, had the resistance of a boulder, *The last sea glass…*

The waves stifled his breaths as he tried to retrieve the stone. And if it weren't for the scrawny arms hoisting him to shore, Collins would've died right there.

"A big, hard-back boy like you collapsing in de sea? I guess young people ain't as strong as they used to be, nuh?"

"I'm… fine…" Collins coughed. His body was limp along the damp sand.

"You want some eddoes, dah's wha. But it look like we done for now."

"Bout time…."

"Like I work you too hard. All that weight training mussy tear some of your muscles, that's why you can't move so well." Father Hoe removed the sandals, and reached into his pockets for a small glass jar. "You gine have to rub some of this balm on your ligaments—got a lil' sain extra to make them heal quicker, but it should take a day or two."

"So, training done?"

"'Course not—gine got to do some shadow drills to get de blood pumping." A sadistic smirk clipped across Father Hoe's face.

For the rest of the week Collins did drills on his own. It was a familiar exercise, mimicking his father's movements; however, Collins also studied those of his recent foes. The Shaggy Bears, Heart Man, the teens, and even Kyle Harding became the enemy unseen. And as Collins slashed the air, he calculated every possible counter or evasion imaginable.

His muscles still ached in spite of their recovery, and a tingle flowed from heel to fingertip with every motion he made.

Almost like Collins no longer owned his body, and in some twisted way it allowed him to push without constraint.

On the third day of shadow training, when the sun was calm and the salty breeze blew strong, Collins grew tired of his situation. "Pops like he abandon me, yuh…"

Father Hoe was absent from his usual, dried-out log. But the parrow still made light work of every snack box, choosing to eat his meals at home rather than on the beach. "He mussy getting bored, too."

Collins was so engrossed in his unseen opponent that he failed to notice his audience nearby.

"That's an interesting way of using a cutlass."

"Huh?" The voice came from a young fellow stretching against a palm tree. *What the hell? How long he was standing there?*

The stranger had long, black dreadlocks that easily dwarfed Collins's as they stretched all the way to his lower back. He also donned a bright red T-shirt, a pair of dull cargo pants and heavy leather reefs. Yet, what really stood out were the young man's eyes, which were so stern that Collins flinched when he met them. Like caverns leading to a vehement black.

"No, I mean the way you wield the cutlass. I assume it's some type of martial art, which is odd considering how crude the weapon is."

"Am, boss… who are you?" Collins watched as the stranger spoke. His words betrayed by a stoic aura.

"Oh. Sorry. I'm Dario, pleased to meet you. And you are?" After minutes of silence he realized Collins wasn't going to answer, so he continued. "Mind if I join you for a bit?"

"Sorry, B. I kinda busy right now."

"Oh dear, you sure? I was hoping to duel a Canecutter for once in my life."

How does he know about the Canecutters? Although the question rang in his head, he showed no reaction towards Dario. Feign ignorance: that was his best option.

"I heard they were pretty skilled back in the day, but you don't really see any stirring around now."

"Puh!" Collins grunted, mostly out of jest than provocation. He remembered saying similar words to Kyle Harding last year. If Collins knew how ridiculous he sounded at the time, he wouldn't have issued the challenge either. "What you feel this is? Some kinda kungfu movie?"

Dario grinned and then slapped the tree trunk. The blow sent one of the palm leaves down until it landed neatly in his slender hands. The act left Collins confused, and somewhat intimidated.

"I ain got time for this, man...."

"I know. But I'm coming anyway." Dario disappeared from beside the tree, and reappeared right in front of Collins, palm poised and ready to strike.

F-Fast! He didn't have time to study the attack; his cutlass just rose to meet the leaf rushing towards him.

Fwish!

The blow sent Collins back despite his guard. It was amazing such force came from an ordinary palm leaf. And it was ordinary, plucked before his very eyes and without any magical influence, unlike Kyle Harding's sugarcane. Confident in this fact, Collins asked, "Hey. You sure you wanna use that thing? One strike from this cutlass and it ain gine be nuh good."

"Don't worry. You won't be attacking." A small eruption of sand came from where he stood, and sure enough, Dario was right beside Collins again.

"Shit!" This time he wasn't allowed to counterattack, and the lash across his back pealed throughout the deserted shore. *Thwack!* The palm leaf felt more like a steel belt, but Collins recovered, hopping away to create some distance.

"Hmm. You're pretty quick, Canecutter." Dario resumed his attack; again, Collins couldn't see where the next blow came from, nor was he able to prevent it. Another flicker of green whipped against his cheek, his arm, and his leg.

Crap! He's too fast! Okay... just calm down. Study the opponent. There must be something to his speed. Collins urged himself to think, but he found no solution. Blood drummed on his temples in frenzied beats. *First, this guy's pretty agile. Even on the unstable sand he can move comfortably without slipping, unlike me.*

This point was evidenced by Collins's counter swipe, which was easily sidestepped and returned across his chest. *Plus, the wind is pretty strong here, and this man fighting with a palm leaf. So, he should be meeting a lot of air resistance every time he swings it around—making it impractical to use.*

But Dario showed no hassles with this weapon. Wielding it like a Bo-staff, he poked, slashed, and whipped with so much speed and finesse that Collins could only register the blurry silhouette writhing towards him. *Either my theory is wrong... or this guy got some insane upper-body strength! Just like Pops!*

There were no other options; Collins had to parry that palm leaf. But how could he parry what he could not see? Every attempt was fruitless, with the blade hitting air or a stray bristle. And, as if he knew the tactic, Dario deflected the cutlass and lashed Collins's wrists.

A fierce agony nipped his hand but Collins endured, grabbing hold of the palm leaf with his free arm. *Got it! Now I gine cut it in two!*

"Useless." Dario uttered, and twisted his weapon so that the bristles grated Collins's fingers. Curses filled the air as the palm leaf flicked sand into the Rasta's eyes.

Collins howled; the burn engulfing his body as he was flogged. Blind agony fizzled into numbness until he collapsed on the beach.

Whap!

"I guess this is the most I'll get out of you. A bit disappointing." Dario chucked the palm leaf aside. "You better improve; otherwise, your death won't be entertaining next time we meet."

Dario ambled past him and disappeared along the deserted coastline. The sun blazed overhead, but Collins couldn't feel it. His body was too inundated with pain to register anything else.

What... What the hell just happened...? Did I just get beat? Nah... that couldn't happen. Not after so much hard work... That would have to be a joke...

The blue sky blurred into blackness and he surrendered to the fatigue. But as Collins passed out, a cheerful drawl filled his ears.

"Cha boy. As I just finish patching you up, yuh gone back and get wounded again?"

Collins woke in a bedroom that wasn't his own. The wooden walls were painted in bright saffron, and the windows draped in off-white curtains to match. On his divan were sheets with quirky yellow-and-red plaid patterns, and everything else, from the dressers to the wardrobe, was organized tidily. Indeed, very different from his own bedroom.

"I'm alive?" The pounding in his head confirmed this fact, and as he rose a minty scent itched his nose and a cooling sensation came off his skin.

"Ah! I see you're finally awake." Father Hoe sauntered in with a damp towel in his hands. "You were out fuh half the day. Here—put it on your head."

Collins did as he said. "Shit! This is *cold!*"

"Less noise. This here gine relax you muscles, as you get brek up. Multiple lacerations, swelling—is like you get beat with a belt or something."

"A palm leaf." Collins said, as if the notion wasn't ridiculous. Then again, he did face a sugarcane last year. "The guy had a palm leaf."

"Wow, that's a new one. A *normal* palm leaf, nuh?" Father Hoe asked as if he expected something else, but the nod from Collins refuted his assumption. "And a palm leaf lick you up so? Its owner mussy very skilled."

Collins went silent. It wasn't just skill; Dario had a speed which surpassed anything Collins had ever seen before. Faster than the Gorilla Unit or the Shaggy Bears…

"Yeah. He was."

"So, this is why you was so anxious fuh training, nuh?" Father Hoe's question snapped Collins from his stupor, but he didn't respond. "Yuh know, as your life depend on it or what not."

The hush was disrupted only by the crashing waves and the sea breeze pouring in from the windows. Collins began to speak, but he was cut short by the parrow. "I sure you have yuh reasons for keeping quiet, but it clear that you running outta time."

"Yeah. Seems so."

You better improve; otherwise, your death won't be entertaining next time we meet.

For the first time in a year, Collins was afraid. The enemy had revealed himself, and he was on a different level. "We gine have to step up my training some more."

"I agree." Father Hoe started, "But unfortunately your body can't handle anything more. For one, your muscles so frig up from weight training, not to mention these fresh injuries."

Collins tried to stand but felt a great stiffness in his limbs. "Shit…"

"We gine have to take a break, at least for a couple days so you can properly heal."

"What? Pops, I gotta get—"

"If you push now you could as well forget about fighting—you'll barely be able to walk." And just then Collins stopped fidgeting at that horrific notion. Weakness and disability were two different matters.

"Fine."

"Good. Now you welcome to stay, but I sure you got a little lady at home that worried 'bout yuh."

Crap… Nadia! To be honest, Collins had forgotten his girlfriend this past week. "Guess I'll be going, then."

"Driving gine be hard in your condition, but I got something to tek care of that. Hold on."

Father Hoe sifted through the cabinet, where a number of trinkets lay scattered on the shelves, including a plastic bag which had a little brown object with white crystals on top. "A tamarind ball?"

Collins inspected the morsel while Father Hoe closed the dresser. "Nibble that on your way home. It should dull the pain long enough for you to drive."

"But if it numbs the pain, maybe I could—"

"If you exert your limbs anymore you won't be able to use 'em. Is that what you want?" He took the Rasta's silence as a

No, and then strolled out of the bedroom. "Now hurry up and go home. The sooner you rest, the sooner you could return and train."

"Okay." Collins replied hollowly while biting on the tamarind ball. "This tastes like crap, by the way."

"Sorry— not really the best cook but it gets the job done." Father Hoe snickered, but Collins just shook his head and stumbled out of the cave-hidden house, along the deserted shore, up the bushy staircase, and into the Runnex waiting by the entrance. All the while he sucked on the morsel, not enjoying it in the least. A typical tamarind ball had a sweet-salty taste but this was bitter-sour. For the twenty minutes it took to limp towards his car, Collins ignored the pain, like a distant itch to scratch later.

Well, the pain gine away fuh now… Collins turned the ignition, and with a great degree of discomfort, he stamped the gas pedal and wheeled the Runnex down the road. Though the trip was short, his thoughts made it seem like he travelled for hours.

How did he move so fast? How was he wielding a palm leaf so good? Why couldn't I hit him? Why wasn't I faster? Each query pounded his brain along with images from the last battle. He replayed them over and over in an attempt to learn something new—but it was useless.

"Shit!" Collins honked at an overtaking car. He rarely cursed, but a few obscenities were hurled at the other driver. The rage made his head throb, and Collins had to stop at the next roundabout to calm himself. "Woah… Gotta chill yuh heart, Damian. Yuh losing it."

He took a deep breath, inhaling the cinnamon air inside, and then switched on the radio so that soothing reggae music oozed from the speakers. Until now Collins never realized how calming the car was, but he was thankful all the same.

The distraction ended when he pulled up to his house. As Collins strolled past the mess in his bedroom, he questioned the circumstances of his defeat. Unlike the Baku or the monstrosities of Bewitched Gully, Dario was just a man. There was no magic behind his skills, or a blatant connection to the Dark Arcs.

"There's gotta be some hidden trick to it." Collins muttered;

his face to the ceiling above.

"Something I couldn't see, like magic shoes or… " Perish the thought. Excuses won't change the result or help him improve.

Outside was black by the midnight hour, and on his telephone, Collins saw blinking white lights: Nadia's unanswered messages. "I guess I should call her."

But Collins couldn't dial the number. His mind was too scattered with Dario's attacks, and he wasn't in the mood for Nadia's rants right now.

When Collins blinked it was dawn. By now, the tamarind ball's effect had dissipated and a fresh numbness gripped his body once more. Movement was out of the question, as he had to crawl to the toilet to pee. "Damn it, Pops! I thought this was supposed to make me feel better."

He wished for a bottle of that Noni-Apple juice Sniper gave him once. It may have tasted like piss, but at least he would be fully healed by now. "Look, I gotta get up."

Collins didn't rise until outside was orange again and more blinking lights were on his phone. "Crap. I should really give her a call."

His fingers trembled as he slid them over the screen. Collins knew he wasn't the best boyfriend right now, Nadia deserved better. And when he heard the soft, raspy "Hello?" on the other line, he regretted not calling sooner.

"Hey, Nadia."

"Oh. It's you, Damian." There was no anger in her voice, or joy. "Yuh finally decide to call."

"Yeah, I was kinda busy lately. Sorry about—"

"Busy, nuh? I hear you." Collins knew Nadia was rolling her eyes. "I wonder what you so busy doing?"

For a moment Collins wanted to tell her everything, to bring her into his world full of violence and obeah magic. He changed his mind.

"Who is she?"

Collins gaped at the receiver. "Who is who?"

"De woman you cheating with, nuh?" Nadia unleashed her confined fury. "I know nuff girls does be all over you, so don't bullshit me, okay, Damian?"

Collins felt his chest sink. Had he ignored her so long that she was brought to this point? He could only imagine those doubts Nadia harbored behind the missed calls and late nights. "Nadia… nothing like that gine on. Really. You don't have to worry about—"

"Oh, I ain worried. I know I'm too good for you, and you would have to be a Johnny to pass all of this up!"

Collins grinned; at least she wasn't that angry. "Come on. Gimme more credit than that."

"Good!"

"You pouting?"

"No." She giggled, and he joined her. "That don't mean that I forgive you, though."

"I know and I'm sorry—real ting." Accepting the sincerity in his voice, Nadia continued the conversation in good spirits. She updated Collins on everything he missed during the week: the gossip, the pictures, the songs—all of which escaped him. Nadia's happiness was all that mattered.

"You sure you okay?" she asked.

"Yeah, I'm good. Hey, how about we hang tonight?"

"Huh?"

"I mean, we ain see each other in a while." Collins assumed that was what his girlfriend wanted, but Nadia suspected naughtier motives.

"Just so you know you're not getting laid tonight."

Damn. "Nah, I didn't mean so." Collins laughed.

"I was supposed to hang with Charlene tonight anyway."

"Wait, she back in de island?" Collins hadn't seen Charlene in over a year, not since she returned to her home country, San Lucia. Come to think of it, someone else had missed her, too…. "I gine pass through anyway, and drag along Kyle to keep she company."

"Okay. Pick me up at eight, then?"

"Nuh problem. By the way, where you gals thinking of going?"

"The movies…?" Kyle didn't expect to hear this when he answered Collins's call.

"Come on, B. If you train too hard you gine wear yourself out."

"Idiot! Don't you understand the situation?!" Kyle barked so loud that it caught the attention of everyone in the house: Mr. Beckles in the backyard and Damien in his bedroom. "We don't have time for movies."

"I get it, man, but—"

"No. I don't think you get it." Kyle brought his voice towards a whisper. "We don't know how dangerous these guys are, or when they'll attack. That's why we have to spend every moment preparing while we still can."

"Believe me, I know the kinda danger we in." The Rasta's tone made Kyle stir.

"Wait. What do you mean by that?"

"Come and I'll let you know."

"Would you stop playing games already?

"Trust me. This gine be worth your while."

"Fine…" Kyle finally surrendered, too exhausted to argue anymore. "By the way, did you find him? That Canecutter guy?"

"Oh, Pops? Yeah, I found him."

"Oh, good." Kyle uttered with a bit of relief, at least Collins didn't waste the last couple days. "So, what's he like?"

"Stubborn, bizarre, brutal, sarcastic, crafty, lickerish—"

"Lickerish?" Kyle asked.

"Yeah. Man con me outta twenty-five snack boxes, B!"

"Oh. He sounds—err—interesting." Kyle listened on, bemused by the agreement Collins made with the parrow or the methods of his preparation. But after ten minutes of ranting, Collins concluded by saying,

"He's a good guy, though. We could trust him, I think."

"Cool. You think so? I mean, you haven't told him anything

but he's still training you?"

"Nah. I ain tell he nothing. What about you? Does Mr. Beckles know?"

"Not sure." At the back of his mind, Kyle suspected that his master knew more than he was letting on. Collins felt the same, especially after spending a week with Father Hoe.

"Ah well, I gine and get ready. The show at nine, by the way."

"That fairly late, though." Kyle said, recalling he had no transportation of his own.

"Don't worry, B. You know I got you covered. I'd pick you up again but I gine be short on time."

"Fine. I'll be there." Kyle agreed, and upon ending the call he couldn't help second guessing his decision.

In the backyard, Mr. Beckles squatted next to a wooden dummy which was used for practicing strikes. Kyle saw no fatigue in his master, and even though they were training from early morning, Kyle couldn't push him at all.

"So you gine out tonight?" Mr. Beckles hopped up and held his thighs like they were catching cramp.

"You shouldn't listen to other people's conversations."

"Oh sorry. But de house so small, yuh see."

"Right." Kyle brandished his sugarcane again, adopting his stance to resume their duel.

"You sure you wanna continue?" Mr. Beckles scrutinized his student, who wasn't in the best physical condition. "Fractured arm, dislocated shoulder, four cracked ribs, lacerations on—"

"I'm fine."

"Nonsense. As your teacher I suggesting that you should rest, but as your opponent I inclined to finish you off." Kyle took pride in that statement, but he wouldn't relent. Not when he was still conscious.

"I said I'm fine." Kyle thrust his cane at Mr. Beckles's torso; his speed not ebbed in the least. However the strike was evaded, and Mr. Beckles punished him by opening every wound on Kyle's frame.

"Ack!" Kyle collapsed on the floor.

"Oh? Why you surprised that I exploited your injuries? You asked for a real fight, remember?"

"I know. I know…" Kyle strained to his feet, until Mr. Beckles guided him towards the training dummy for support. "Exploit all available weaknesses—the basics of combat, right?" Suddenly Kyle's grip on the old man's arm tightened, the sugarcane lashing out at the defenseless master.

Crack!

But even that attack was thwarted by Mr. Beckles. "Right. You got anything else up yuh sleeve?"

"No…."

"Good." Mr. Beckles smiled, and again (albeit with more caution) lifted his student who was scowling at his discarded sugarcane. "Now how about going to the movies, huh?"

"Tch! I'm not tired—"

"But I am." Mr. Beckles brushed a minor crinkle from his shirt. "Besides, I have other errands to attend to. I'll be back to check up on Damien, though."

"I don't need checking up on." The voice came from the back steps where Damien sat. "And you need to get out de house, fuh real."

"Wait, why are you taking his side?" Kyle asked, but Damien circumvented the question.

"Because I tired uh having a lame brother who doesn't go out clubbing like other guys his age."

"Don't you have some homework to do?"

"Nope. Already finished." Damien said, and for once Kyle wished his brother wasn't so smart. Mr. Beckles, on the other hand, saw this as the perfect diversion.

"Seeing that the mood has changed, I better get ready."

"But—"

"You should give them clothes in your closet some more air, 'fore they catch mildew."

"Yeah, Kyle, try and wear something proper this time. Otherwise, Collins gine take all the girls." Damien muttered. Though he disapproved of such behavior, Kyle was relieved that his brother acted like his old self. When he approached the back door, Damien asked,

"Say, Kyle, you've been training a lot lately, how come?"

"What do you mean? I always try to brush up my skills once

in a while."

Damien knew Kyle was lying but he couldn't understand why. There was something behind these sparring sessions. Something urgent. Something dire.

"I was just a lil rusty, that's all." Kyle reassured him, but Mr. Beckles chimed in.

"Want help sorting out yuh outfit?"

"Nah, I'm good. Not like I gine want your fashion sense anyway." Kyle said.

"How you mean? I'll have you know I does be dapper when I ready!" Mr. Beckles huffed and Kyle smirked, making his way towards the shower to bathe and dress—a process that took forty minutes.

Kyle emerged from his room, bedecked in a fresh blue-and-white polo shirt, jeans and matching sneakers.

"Hear yuh! Kyle, you could still do a ting." Mr. Beckles whistled. Damien glanced at his brother with moderate interest.

"Yeah, you actually look decent. Not 'pon Collins's level, though."

"Gee…Thanks." Kyle rolled his eyes before regarding Damien. "But I'm still not comfortable leaving you home by yourself."

"I'll be fine."

"No, you're not!" Kyle paused, surprised much like Damien at his own exclamation. Déjà vu. His mother had reacted this way once upon a time, and though Kyle never took heed as a child, as an adult he was well aware of the dangers of the night.

"Don't worry. My plans got canceled anyhow." Mr. Beckles said, evaporating Kyle's fears.

"Okay. Well, if you don't mind."

"Nope, it's okay. You should hurry up and go 'fore the bus leave you. It's almost six-thirty."

"Oh right. Aight, I'm going." He rubbed Damien's untidy head, an action that the boy hated—most of all now. When his brother returned the farewell, Kyle took up his sugarcane and went through the front door.

As soon as he reached the top of the hill, a transport board bus lumbered towards him with the words BRIDGETOWN in bright orange neon. As he boarded it, Kyle peered at the spot where Ms. Pringle lived. Bush had covered the plot as if the witch's home had never existed. But Kyle knew better, and though everyone else had forgotten about her, Ms. Pringle's malice was entrenched in his memory.

These thoughts spanned two bus rides and an hour, until Kyle saw the towering white building of the movie theatre. Olympus Theatres was a separate part of Sheraton Centre, situated outside the main compound to accommodate patrons. As Kyle strolled along the street, where numerous cars trudged toward the car park, he heard a familiar voice utter his name.

"Kyle!" Before he could turn properly a soft, citrus-smelling body was pressed against his chest. Looking down, Kyle saw a head of black jheri curls and two large, gold hoop earrings. Lianne was his first guess, but then the girl peered up and grinned.

"Charlene?"

"You remembered!" And her embrace tightened, squeezing the breath out of Kyle.

"When did you come back?"

"I see wunna doing the tearful reunion." Collins sauntered from behind with Nadia under his arm: him in a black T-shirt and khaki three-quarters, and her in a simple skirt and blouse.

"Wait, you knew about this?!"

"I told you it would be worth your while, right?" The Rasta grinned along with the other girls, but Kyle was too dumbfounded to respond.

"I come in last week, but I didn't have your number so I couldn't call. And you ain even keep in touch…." Charlene frowned; an act Kyle was entirely unprepared to handle.

"Sorry. We don't have a computer at our place, so I couldn't get online."

Collins snickered at the effort and Kyle felt his cheeks rise. "I woulda never picture you as the shy type, B."

"Less noise." Kyle muttered, but the Rasta ignored him and placed a piece of paper in his hands.

"Here, I buy you ticket already. You owe me fifteen bucks."

"Oh thanks."

"We got half-hour to kill, so could as well walk 'bout." The girls approved the idea, Charlene in particular latching onto

Kyle's arm.

The group entered the mall from an adjacent doorway, where they were greeted with a clothing outlet which caught the girls' attention. This was the first of many boutiques inside the compound, each one varying in apparel and accessories for man, woman and child. And the ladies traversed every one, scouring through blouses, skirts and even lingerie, much to Kyle's embarrassment and Collins's pleasure. In fact, the Rasta was at ease in this environment, poking fun at the various mannequins on display, skylarking amongst the television screens, sampling music from the record stores, buying caramel nuts from the vendors—all the while greeting any familiar face he came across (which turned out to be many). Kyle had forgotten how popular Collins was, until many passersby gave him a quick hello. In contrast Kyle only garnered stares from his sugarcane, with Charlene distracting the onlookers on occasion.

When the group entered a perfume parlor, and Collins guided Nadia away to sample some scents, Kyle took the opportunity to appraise the young lady. Dressed in a baby blue blouse and white leggings, Charlene caused many passersby to lose their stride. However, Kyle only focused on one feature,

"Your hair, the style's different."

"Oh, you noticed? Thanks." Charlene beamed, and then went into detail about the many different hairstyles she experimented with throughout the year. Then she talked about her stay in San Lucia, glossing over facets like her internship at some company, her countryside home, and the numerous hotspots which Charlene promised to carry Kyle whenever he visited.

"Aye, lovebirds, movie start ten minutes ago. Lewwe roll." Collins said.

And so they went; up the series of ramps, past the custodians (Kyle having to hide his sugarcane down his pants leg), and into the dark theatre. Kyle ignored the film, preoccupied by the jheri-curled head resting on his shoulder, and the pineapple aroma filling his nose. It was nice. Better than the blood and sweat he knew for the past week.

"That movie was soooo good!" Nadia lauded, as they strolled back into the main lounge.

"Yeah, boy, that main girl was hot as france, too. Ow!" Collins said to his detriment, as Nadia pitched a slap across his shoulder. Though in jest, the blow landed on a healing wound, exploding his shoulder with pain.

"Oh gosh, you okay?"

"You like you don't know your own strength." Collins smiled, coercing her to rub the same shoulder in apology.

Kyle and Charlene were oblivious to the commotion ahead, too entangled in each other's presence to acknowledge anything else. Not the queue of people waiting by the booths for popcorn, not the incoming patrons on their way to see the next film, not the mural of movie posters pasted on the wall, none of it caught their attention. Kyle was only granted liberty when Nadia dragged Charlene to the bathroom.

"Wunna look too sweet." Collins had a perverted glint in his eye that Kyle didn't like.

"You too, despite your injuries."

"Ah, so you noticed…"

"Of course I did. You been limping ever since you arrived, and that slap Nadia gave you was on a fresh wound." Kyle announced systematically.

"Cha. I was trying to hide it, too. Guess Charlene ain distract you enough."

"Is that why you brought her?"

"Nah, man, that was just good timing on she part." Though Collins smiled, Kyle didn't believe him.

"So, I assume you didn't get those from training."

"Well, not all." He saw the canewielder frown at him expectantly and continued, "But yeah, I think I meet the enemy a couple days ago." Collins then recapped the entire incident, highlighting the way Dario looked, the weapon he used, and his astonishing speed. "—B, I couldn't even see him. He was *that* fast."

"…And he let you go?"

"Yeah. I dunno why, but most likely he gine popup sooner or later."

Kyle furrowed his brow after hearing the news. "I guess we should keep on the lookout, then." That was the smartest choice, though it wasn't any different from how he spent the past ten years. The two were quiet afterwards, careful not to whip themselves into a panic.

"Why the serious faces?" Charlene harped as she returned with Nadia.

"Yeah, wunna look like somebody just died."

"Nah. Kyle was just wondering what taking y'all so long in the bathroom."

"Hey!" Kyle would've slapped him but Nadia got to Collins first, disregarding how much it hurt him last time.

"Aww, sorry we took so long. We were having a girl talk." Charlene giggled and seized Kyle's arm once more, but the effect wasn't the same. No longer was he transported to a peaceful world, but one filled with risk and peril: his world. As they walked down the ramp and into the lobby, where carefree teenagers discussed the film they've just seen, Kyle couldn't help but feel isolated. He was an island in a sea of oblivion, and his only visitor was Collins. "Umm, you good?"

"Yeah."

"'Cause you seem like you're lost about something."

Kyle hadn't noticed that he'd been in a daze, or that he was strolling past the car park and not listening to the girl on his arm. Charlene didn't complain, though. She knew Kyle had his secrets, and respected them enough not to pry.

"Nah, I'm fine—oof!" The couple ahead came to a complete halt, with Kyle bumping into Collins's back.

Two individuals had emerged, and by their appearance they didn't seem the least bit normal. On the right a young woman: who under any other circumstance would be very attractive. Her body was shapely but tall and slender, though you couldn't see from her baggy, distressed jeans and oversized shirt. And her pretty features were twisted by a vicious scowl. On the left: a man in a white dashiki looked the total opposite; calm and reserved but with a treacherous air about him. In fact, the pair had a profound thirst for slaughter similar to the Heart Man, or perhaps even greater.

Collins felt it too, squeezing Nadia's hand so hard that she hollered, "Oww! What de hell, Damian? Is something wrong?"

"Nadia, I want you to listen to me carefully…." His voice was different from anything she heard before: austere and alarmed. "Take Charlene and get as far away from here as you can."

"What you talking about?" Her voice was shaky. Confused. Collins repeated the words again—albeit sharper.

"I think it's best to do as he says." Kyle strode forward, sugarcane drawn in a way the girls had never seen— as if it were a weapon. He, too, was cold and somber, much unlike his usual reticence.

"But—" Nadia couldn't fathom the situation at all. Who were these people? And why were the guys so concerned about them? Nothing was clear except that something was wrong—very wrong.

"Come, girl, I think Damian's right; we better go around and wait by the car." Charlene guided her away from the scene, while regarding the unknown duo with discerning eyes.

"Don't worry, we won't be long." Collins reassured her, but knowing his girlfriend that wasn't enough.

"Be careful, okay, guys? We'll be back with help soon." Charlene kept her gaze upon Kyle, who didn't even seem to notice her now that the enemy had arrived. Collins nodded in reply, though he feared the authorities could do nothing to help (assuming they got there in time).

It wasn't until the ladies left that Collins drew a cutlass from under his shirt, adopting his fighting stance much like the cane-wielder next to him. Silence reigned supreme. No cars, no music, and the lights flickered ominously about the lot. Then the robed man stepped forward.

"Evening, gentlemen. Judging from your response, I assume you know that we're here to claim your lives." His words were frigid but polite.

"Assassins, right?" Kyle asked, though he'd never heard of assassins who faced their target head on and announced their intentions up front. Either they were stupid or had great confidence in their abilities.

"You're not afraid— that's good. How about you, Canecutter? Have you gotten stronger?"

"*You!*"

"You know this guy?" Kyle saw the fear in Collins; this must have been the man who attacked him earlier.

"Remember the guy with the palm leaf I tell you about? That's him." Collins confirmed, but he hardly believed it himself. Dario was a different man than before; his aura dark and intimidating.

"I'm glad you remembered me. That means you took my words to heart."

"Hear wha gine on! Wunna could cut de chitchat and lewwe do this thing?!" The girl barked, but what really stopped the conversation was the heavy object hitting the ground.

What the hell? Is that a sword?! It was a wonder Kyle never saw it until now. The object was several feet taller than the woman, just over her breadth, and from the thud it was many times her body weight. *A palm leaf and a gigantic sword… Who the hell are these people?*

"Please forgive my colleague. She's always been rather impetuous and doesn't understand the meaning of restraint." At this the girl cursed while Dario continued, "You may've heard of the incident up ABC Highway last week."

Kyle recalled the newspaper headlines. "Two car collision, six people died… that was you?"

"As I said: no restraint." They watched as Dario shook his head, eager for a chance to launch a preemptive strike. "Though in my own way, I'm not much different either."

Dario reflected on a prior job, when he himself cut down a room of targets with his palm leaf. It was concise, yet brutal, as their blood smeared in long strokes along the walls. At least their deaths were quick, as the last thing they saw were Dario and his palm leaf writhing through them like a serpent.

"Why you always gotta be talking out we business? I did like you better when you was quiet." The girl sucked her teeth, so that it echoed along the buildings and the empty lot.

"I owe them this much. Marks such as these are perfect for our last kill. I'm especially impressed that they defeated Jamba."

Kyle considered Sniper's warning; Bewitched Gully *did* put them on the radar. But the girl wasn't impressed, spitting on the sidewalk before she spoke.

"So wha? Feel I give a shit that dem beat he? Jamba was a soft bitch anyway!"

Are you friggin serious? Collins remembered that monster in Bewitched Gully. Like one of hell's generals, the Mocajambe tore up the forest as if it were mere cerasee bush. It was a miracle that they survived.

"Jamba was a captain. Weak as he was, that still held some merit." Dario reached behind his shoulders for something lapped in cloth (presumably a palm leaf). "That is why this mark is so interesting. They may be meaningful kills for once."

"Frig this! Enough talk!" And as she shouted, the girl appeared one foot away from Kyle with her weapon held high. Now that it was close, he noted the many chains and seals wrapped around the immense blade, barely keeping the brimming bloodlust within.

"Shit!" She was fast, but the sugarcane would reach her in time. Whether it would break was a bigger concern.

Whack! The sound rang in the air, though it wasn't caused by metal upon wood. Seconds before the girl swung her sword, a rock jetted to her temple with fatal speed and accuracy. It was only a last-minute shielding with the blade's hilt that saved her from harm.

"Ah, *Pick-out*, I didn't know you were involved in this as well." Dario spoke to a man sitting on a nearby rooftop. He was short, muscular, with a bottle case strapped across his back and a black bandana across his face.

"Sniper." Kyle uttered with surprising relief. But Sniper didn't pay him or Collins any attention, addressing the two assassins instead.

"Nah, not really. Just hear that two uh wunna was 'bout de place and decide to tag along. *Cutup. Headgone.*"

The names were ridiculous but Collins didn't dare snicker; the tension among these killers rising with every breath.

"Puh! Yuh really got some nerve showing your pissy face in front we again, Pickout!"

"Cha, Rasheda. I see you still don't keep nuh lid on that mouth."

"Don't be calling my name, yuh bastard!" The girl barked,

and Sniper with a jeering tone replied,

"Oh sorry—Headgone—better?"

So, she's Headgone … that must mean the other one is Cutup. Collins was too enthralled by the conversation to move. *Why does that drunkard know these guys?*

"Pickout, if you aren't involved with these two, then why are you here?" Dario's polite tongue slowly eroded into hostility. "Depending on your answer, you might not make it out alive."

"Dah's assuming you could get me kill." Sniper reached for his bottle case, wary not to alert the two killers of his action. But before he could wrap his grip around a bottle's neck, Dario had sprinted twenty meters, vaulted up the two-story building, and was upon him with blurring red scarf and bandaged weapon—all in a blink of an eye. "Frig!"

"That's it. That's the insane speed I was talking about." Collins observed as Sniper evaded the swathed weapon, but by now Headgone had joined in the fray, her massive sword held high like a guillotine…

BRAM!

The impact took a huge chunk from the building, but Sniper was unscathed. "Cha, Cutup, you still quick as hell. I could barely keep up wid yuh." He ignored the girl's monstrous attack, grabbed the rocks that were cast airborne as a result, and chucked them at his two assailants.

"I still feel like you're taking us lightly, Pickout." Dario swatted the stones like common houseflies.

"Nah believe me, B. I'm taking you *very* seriously." Sniper zipped down the side of the building and brought the battle back to lower ground. With exceptional acrobatics he dodged the two killers, but every time he reached for his bottle case a blade or a palm leaf would interrupt him. *Damn! They won't let me use my Bottles!*

Kyle and Collins watched in awe as the fight raged on. It was clear the combatants were beyond their level; running along walls, skipping across vehicles, all in a culmination of hazes and eruptions. Even with Kyle's eyes (which were accustomed to Mr. Beckles's speed), he found it difficult to spot the split-second tactics being displayed. For instance, when Headgone's massive sword was parried by Sniper's bottle case as she swiped at him, or when Cutup's bandaged weapon slapped his arm before Sniper could properly fling any rocks (let alone his bottles).

"Wow…" Collins, on the other hand, caught none of this, even though he'd faced Cutup once before. Only the obvious details became open to him, like when Headgone's missed strike rendered an abandoned Honda Civic in two. "These guys are completely out of our league."

"Maybe." Kyle muttered, drinking all the knowledge he could. It was simple for the most part. Cutup was fast and delicate, while Headgone was wild and devastating, and as far as weapons went, he'd have to face them to get a good estimate, but the girl's massive sword should be heavy and slow to wield while the palm leaf should be swift (despite its wind resistance). "They're strong, though."

They both believed that fact, but aside from their extraordinary skills there was nothing magical about these assassins. They were only human. So why were Kyle and Collins afraid?

Dario stopped in his tracks and beckoned his partner to do the same—something she wasn't pleased about. "Wha happen, man?!"

"I believe our targets are examining our abilities."

"So wha? Let dem watch. It ain like dem could stop we anyway." Headgone growled, but she was interrupted by a Bomber Bottle hurtling her way.

BOOM!

A bubble of flames detonated in the car park, attracting the patrons still on the compound at this late hour. But as the saffron glow and billowing debris subsided, the assassins stood unscathed from the blast. Sniper crouched a few feet away from them.

"Your speed was never a joke, Cutup…"

Dario brushed the soot off his robes and weapon. "I could say the same about your ammunition." His mood was more polite now; hostility was no longer necessary since the battle had an unwelcomed audience. "This may be the time to take our leave."

"You Sonnava—Wait. What?" Headgone barked, from the grip around her sword it was clear she wasn't ready to leave.

"Mekking sport! I now getting start—"

"The situation's changed now that we have spectators and a third party has intervened. Besides, there are other matters to attend to."

"You sure it ain 'cause you're scared, Cutup?" Sniper prodded with another bottle twirling in hand. "Being in public never stop you before, especially up at ABC Highway."

"You should know better than to provoke me, Pickout." Collins felt an unrefined bloodlust leaking above Dario's scarf. It was just like Long Beach, the blackness behind cold pupils and a civil tongue.

"Just saying."

"Tch! I really wanna kill him." Headgone sheathed her oversized sword with disgust.

"Now is not the time." Dario told her before turning towards Sniper. "But if we meet again, Pickout, you really will be killed."

Collins flinched at the warning, but Sniper was nonchalant. "No problem. We just won't meet, dah's all."

"Fair enough." And with a waft of debris the pair vanished from the scene, leaving behind a crater, frayed vehicles, and several flabbergasted onlookers. Collins breathed a sigh of relief, but Kyle wasn't assured, sprinting towards the vacant combat zone.

"Okay, what was that just now? And how do you know those people?"

"Huh? Oh, wunna was still here? I forget yuh…." Sniper took another bottle from his case, apparently an ordinary one since he drank from it.

"Cut the crap, Sniper. I want explanations." Kyle demanded.

"Yeah, B." Collins added. "Inform de men."

The number of spectators had risen with sirens blaring in the distance. After the explosion, someone had called the authorities and they responded with unusual punctuality. As Collins listened he felt a buzzing in his pocket, Nadia's name came up in bold letters with this being the seventh call. "Shit! I forget about de girls."

"Sounds like yuh got bigger priorities." Sniper tossed the bottle one side.

"No, we don't. Now are you gonna keep wasting our time, or are you gonna tell us what's going on?" Sniper glared at Kyle. Only the courtesy of past comrades stopped him from cracking the canewielder's head.

"Fine. You guys sure know how to thank a fella. *Tch.*"

"Sorry. Thank you." Kyle said. Sniper pouted while Collins hung up the phone with discomfort.

"All right, the girls are okay. Though Nadia fairly pissed at me…."

"That's good to hear." Kyle replied, guilty that he had forgotten about Charlene.

"I tell them to head home without us, but she still want an explanation." They both looked expectantly at Sniper who was already on another beer.

"What? All right, since wunna ain plan on letting this go, I could as well explain." Red and blue hues touched their faces and stained the dark sky, while police wheeled unto the scene. "But we can't stand around here. You all got somewhere to go?"

"Amm…" Collins considered the time. It was well after midnight, and as public transport had retired for the night, it was impossible to get home without a car. Despite this quandary, Kyle replied,

"No. We don't."

"Hey, but—"

"Lewee get from 'bout here, then." Sniper walked down the lot, away from Sheraton Centre and towards the vacant main road. When a bus stop appeared several paces later Kyle and Collins assumed they were about to use a more paranormal means of transport, but Sniper just kept his stride. He didn't reach in his pockets for that suspicious piece of paper, and the bus stop remained normal, save for the odd flicker that occurred every time Kyle came close. Eventually they came to Vauxhall. Amidst the cluster of homes was the faint whisper of sirens, but that was the only sign of the commotion up Sheraton Centre. Sniper stopped at a tamarind tree, where a streetlight glowed strong and a large discarded drum rested underneath.

"Here looks good enough." He sat on the drum while Kyle and Collins took anxious glances around the neighborhood.

"Right, so explain your relationship with those people."

"Man, you don't waste time, nuh?" Sniper took another swig, and Collins made a chair from a mossy stack of bricks. "Wunna men ever hear of *The Gulf*?"

"The… Gulf? No."

"Seriously? Layer's Gap? Ten years back?" There was still silence so Sniper elaborated. "It was a big warzone in the country, dah's why people nicknamed it, 'The Gulf'? Geez. Wunna don't read the news?"

"No. I was studying other things at nine." Kyle replied.

"Yeah, I was never interested in that stuff." added Collins.

"Safe. Well, yeah, that's how we know each other. We are the *Children of the Gulf* … also known as *Gulfsyde*."

Layer's Gap, St. George was a peaceful countryside neighborhood. Everyone lived close with one another. If you wanted to borrow a spoonful of salt you could go next door and ask, and no thief would dare steal from a house that was monitored constantly by a concerned neighbor. It was a safe community, and this is exactly why Justin frowned with such tedium when he saw the black- and-white sign.

"Man, this place look boring."

As he walked down the hillside entrance of the district, Justin knew he wouldn't be staying long. The humble houses huddled along the road with nets of bush and lianas gathering on their walls. The cracked streets filled with residents going about their daily business, while stealing glances at this newcomer entering their village. Even the sandflies circling hungrily around his feet made Justin sour.

"Tch! I thirsty, though." He reached into the bottle case holstered on his back and sucked his teeth when he found it bare. Luckily, a rum shop meager enough to match the surroundings appeared on his right. With several drink posters on the walls, and an array of bottles lined out behind the bartender, there was no question about what was served here. "Yo! Pass me two beers dey."

A stout old man fetched them, but hesitated before putting them down. "…How old are you, son?"

It was clear that Justin was still a boy; no stubble, creases or scars despite his strapping physique. "I at drinking age, now hand them off."

"Look like fifteen to me." A chuckle came from the other end of the bar, where another young man with an afro that would put Damien's to shame was sitting.

"I'm sixteen, yuh idiot!"

"Funny, last time I check de drinking age was eighteen. So, dah mean you still underage." The youngster said, with each retort slowly eroding Justin's temperament.

"Why you don't go and comb yuh hair, instead of jucking you mouth in people business?" asked Justin, who ignored the knots on his own head in dire need of a brush.

"I don't have to comb my hair. I like it this way."

"Puh! You look like a fowl cock." Justin spat. "And you shouldn't give me any gripe. You look de same age as me."

"I'm nineteen, well above the drinking age." He smiled, and Justin sucked his teeth again.

"Look, hurry up and gimme de drinks, man. Before I lose my patience…" And at this Justin rubbed his finger against an empty bottle standing innocently on the counter. An ordinary item to be sure, but that was only in ordinary hands, and a Pel-Ting's hands were anything but that.

"No need to get antsy." To everyone's surprise, the fellow had moved five seats and sat right beside Justin—all without a rattle of the stool leg. "Give him the drinks, Aussie."

The bartender complied, though it took long for Justin to pick up the bottles in light of his thirst.

"Yeah… Like yuh know!" Justin huffed, but he was shaken. *How did he get there so fast?* The question pounded his mind but Justin ignored it, swilling one drink and moving on to the next. "Feh! Enough of this shit."

He said at last, and then with a slap on the counter, Justin rose from his seat and stormed out the door.

"Hey! You didn't pay for those!" The bartender called but

Justin didn't listen, skulking up the gap with livid stomps.

"I now come here and I getting gripes already? Joke!" He'd seen enough. He wanted to leave, but one thing that diverted Justin's ire was the youngster's movement back at the bar. In all his years Justin had never witnessed anything like it. But he would have to meet that loudmouth some other time, away from this lowly village. Justin finished the second bottle upon reaching the outskirts, and aimlessly tossed it aside.

"Ow!" The shout came from his right, where a couple red-clad hooligans had crouched along the sidewalk; a clutter of shattered glass at their feet. "What de rangate!?"

"Whoops." Justin shrugged, pissing off the trio even more.

"You bastard!" said the one with blood trickling down his brow—the bottle's inadvertent target.

"Not my fault you was in de way." The last straw. That flagrant disrespect, even in the face of his own mistake, would anger anyone let alone a couple of short-tempered hoodlums. Spouting *rassgates* and *cunnys* and *fucks*, each hoodlum revealed several firearms tucked inside their pants.

"Oh, you don't even *know* how much you frig up just now."

"What? You feel I frighten fuh guns?" Under any other circumstance, Justin would've killed them before they could even draw. But as he reached into his bottle case, he suddenly remembered that it was bare. *Shit! I ain got nuh bottles!*

Panic invaded, but Justin wouldn't let it show. He scoured his surroundings for projectiles; two feet away were two small stones—the perfect ammo. So, with a swift dive, Justin scooped them up and flung them at his attackers; one landing on a hooligan's wrist just as he was about to fire, and one breaking against another's brow. Two were down within seconds, but the survivor still had a loaded gun at Justin.

Crap.

Eyes glinting, the hoodlum savored the sweet helplessness of his victim. The hammer cocked, the barrel directed, he stared down at Justin with victory on his mind. But he wouldn't pull the trigger, as a sharp pain stabbed his neck and his eyes blurred into blackness.

Whack!

"I didn't need your help, you know." Justin looked beyond the unconscious body and saw the youngster from the bar.

"I figured." He smirked as Justin dusted himself off. "Still, it would be bad if you died without paying for those two drinks."

"Heh! So that's why you came?"

"Yup."

"Cha, that's too bad, 'cause I ain giving no money to that bar." Justin looked down to see the guy with his arm outstretched.

"Well, that's okay, you could just pay me."

"Like that gine happen." Justin resumed his trek up the hill, but after a couple steps he asked, "You gine keep following me, nuh?"

"Yup." And so, the youngster did; both passing the same row of houses with the same inhabitants who peeped at Justin when he first arrived. Only this time they were more suspicious, as they wondered why the youngster was accompanying him now. Noting their faces, Justin asked,

"What do they call you, loudmouth?"

"Name's Glenn. Yours?"

"…Justin." Justin was reluctant to share his real name with strangers.

"So, Justin, what brings you to this village?"

"Nuttin really. Just wandering."

"You 'pon some sorta rum-shop crawl? Sampling drinks all across the country?" Glenn snickered.

"No, yuh poppit! I just stop in there for a drink, which I nearly ain get because of you!"

"Well, you are underage…"

"So are you!" Justin grunted.

"I'm nineteen, remember?"

"Right. Yuh lucky you bail me out back then, otherwise I woulda crack you head by now." Justin gave the most ferocious glare he could muster, but Glenn just grinned in return.

"Good thing I bail you out, then." Though there was no sarcasm in the words, Justin still felt belittled by them. But he wouldn't attack Glenn. Perhaps it was the speed at the bar, or the blithe response to Justin's threats. "So, if you're just a drifter that means you don't have a place to sleep."

"I does mek do when I ready." Despite being a parrow, Justin had his pride.

"Cha. You could always crash by my place, if you want."

"Sorry, big man. I don't bat for that team."

"Nah not so. I ain like that either. I mean, I have an extra room."

"Even so, I ain bout that life, you unstaan?" Justin puffed out his chest like a ghetto peacock.

"Fair enough. I guess you should be fine even if you got a mark on your head now."

"Dem men part of a gang?" Justin recalled the red colors, a uniform among most low-level thugs in Bimshire.

"Yeah. Over de Wall has been growing in numbers lately."

"Really? Never heard of 'em."

"Yeah, well. I been seeing them around the village from time to time. Watch youself, though. Might not always got rocks around when them come." Glenn chuckled.

"Even if them come by the hundreds, them gine get wash off. Don't worry." Justin was intrigued. Trouble often found him when he least expected, but then he was never one to avoid it. "I barely want them pass back."

By then the hoodlums had disappeared, probably gone to lick their wounds, though Glenn thought different. "You might not gotta wait long. Them gine come back."

Justin contemplated for a bit. He had no place to be, and Glenn was offering room and board. "Yow, you got any food?"

"Uh… I think so."

"Good, 'cause I starving." Justin followed his host back down the gap.

"So, where did you live before?" Glenn asked. Anyone in the Dark Arcs trade knew what lay in the eastern parish of St. Philip. And though Glenn probably knew nothing of the Pel-Ting family, Justin didn't want to risk sharing his history.

"Up in St. Thomas—you know— inland."

"Near Welchman Hall?"

"Yeah." If Glenn suspected his lie, he didn't show it. They walked past an old vendor who was busy setting up her coal pot.

"Hey, Betty." Glenn greeted. "How you doing this evening?"

"I'm fine, youngin. How you doing?" The old woman gave a crinkled smile at Justin who paid her no attention.

"I'm good, you know how it is." Glenn replied. And with a wave they continued on, passing more houses and their inhabitants—including one curious lad with long dreadlocks who was raking his backyard with a dried palm leaf. "Yo! Wha gine on?"

He didn't respond, too absorbed in the dead leaves, rotten fruit, and bits of pebble scattered on the ground.

"That's Dario; he doesn't say much from what I know."

"Wha happen? He can't afford a rake?" Justin scoffed, though the dreadlocked boy ignored him and was fully engrossed in his task. "Tch! Whatever…."

Glenn giggled and led him further down the street. Beyond them were houses slightly newer than the rest, with painted verandahs flanked by multicolored croton plants and white lattices. Justin wondered if any belonged to Glenn, but before he could ask a loud bark came from behind.

"Bout time you show up!"

A young girl stood with her arms folded, lips pursed, and feet tapping the ground in avid impatience. Justin would've found her attractive, with her shapely figure and her beautiful features, but as he listened to the girl's irate tongue, he grew more annoyed. Glenn greeted her like any other passerby. "Hey, Rasheda, you were looking for me?"

"Yeah. And wipe that look off your face, it ain nothing so!" Justin turned to see Glenn feigning innocence—at least he understood how irritating that was.

"So, what you wanted?"

The girl tramped over and shoved a plastic bag in Glenn's hand. Justin noted the outline of a food container.

"Here! Aunty send this fuh you."

"Wow. Tell her thanks fuh me. How she feeling, by the way?" Rasheda's family consisted of one old woman who had a hand around the knob of death's door. On good days she walked around with aches and coughs. On bad days she was curled up in bed struggling to get up. This was a good day.

"She's okay for now." Rasheda said. She, like her great-aunt, didn't want anyone worrying about her well-being.

"That's good to hear. And what about you?" Glenn smiled at her, but they were both interrupted when Justin snatched the bag and started rummaging through.

"Hey! Wha' the hell you think you're doing?!" Rasheda snarled at this strange boy opening up the Styrofoam container and drooling over the contents inside.

"What? I hungry." Justin said simply with a forkful of chips in his hand.

"Uh … Sorry. This is Justin, he now come here from St. Thomas." Glenn thought it best to introduce him before things got out of hand, but it was too late. Justin and Rasheda were already scowling at each other. "He's staying at me for a while."

"Really? I ain know you were the type to take in strays."

"I was a stray myself not too long ago, remember?" Rasheda's surprise evolved into disgrace, as she recalled when Glenn first came to Layer's Gap—staying at her place before he eventually got his own.

"This food ain too bad at all, boy. You Aunty planning to cook again?" Justin had worked his way to the fried dolphin and Rasheda relapsed into her glower.

"Whatever. Well, good luck with this one. I gine home." She puckered her brow at Justin, and skulked past Glenn who was waving goodbye.

"Look like you got girl trouble."

"No, she's not my girl. We're not like that."

"Oh safe, you probably dodge a bullet then." Justin indulged in the meal that wasn't intended for him. "—though if she could cook half as good as her Aunty you might miss out after-all."

Glenn grinned, and then went ahead to the outskirts of the village. Eventually they stopped at a cart road which led to a modest brown-and-white cottage wrapped by a small forest of trees. The foundation was high, and the house was buttressed by several wooden beams which were still sturdy despite their age. And the house was old, not as old as some of the others in the village, but still well-maintained. As Justin entered the living room, he kicked off his boots for fear of dirtying the burgundy carpet.

"Man got a pretty sweet place here."

"I do all right," Glenn said, while making a sweep of the house. It was odd for the average homeowner to do this, but for a drifter like Justin it made perfect sense. There were four chambers in the house. The longest one forming the dining and living room plus the kitchen, while a bathroom and two bedrooms remained. He pointed to the one on the right, "This one over here is yours. I ain get a chance to make it up, though."

"Cool." He wasn't prepared for guests and that brought Justin some comfort. At least Glenn wasn't the sort that picked up random strangers off the street.

"So, what do you do? I mean, before you started wandering about?" It was obvious that Justin didn't want to answer it, most drifters never do, but even Glenn had to admit it was weird for a sixteen-year-old to be walking about without a school or a job—especially in Bimshire.

"Well, I done school a while back and I didn't feel like staying home, so here I am." Justin said. "What about you?"

Glenn was surprised by his courtesy. "I—uh—used to do some freelance work up till recently. But I took a break from that."

"You must be doing pretty good if you living alone."

"I guess, but I didn't buy this house and I only pay the bills."

"So, you haven't been here that long either?" Justin was past the halfway point in the meal, realizing this Glenn retrieved the Styrofoam container from him.

"I think it was two years since I first came. Though I only had this house like a year now—was staying at Rasheda's before." As he got a fork he saw Justin leer.

"Heh! That must've been something else, nuh?"

"Err… not really. You seen how she is already. No one gets close." Glenn gave a wry smile and sighed, like a parent accepting their unruly child for what it was.

"I realize. Welp. I getting tired, feel I gine hold some sleep now." Justin realized that he wasn't getting any more food for the night, and helped himself to a glass of mauby that Glenn brought from the kitchen. "Is here you say that de bedroom is, right?"

"Yeah, just through there." He pointed beyond Justin's back which still had the bottle case strapped to it. "By the way, I've been wondering since I first saw you. Do you always walk around with that thing?"

"What thing?" Justin knew exactly what he meant. Everyone was attracted to his bottle case at some point, whether it was out of fear or bewilderment. Nevertheless, Glenn read his reaction and chose not to push further.

"…Nevermind. Sleep well."

"Yeah." Justin muttered and slipped into the bedroom. It was modest, with cramped walls and a single, uncovered divan. Still, for someone who had planned to sleep under the cellar of some random house, it was perfect. And as his head landed against the bed Justin dozed off, not realizing how tired he'd been after wandering for two whole days.

Rasheda's day went like any other: she woke up, cooked, cleaned up her Aunty, went off to her classes, shopped, and then slogged through rush-hour traffic in a cramped minivan while returning home. She was stressed, temperamental even, so as Rasheda plodded down the road with a handful of shopping bags, the last thing she wanted to see were a bunch of rowdy thugs ahead of her.

"Great." She hissed, and quickened her gait upon approach. She wasn't afraid. They were more of a nuisance than a threat, but even that was too much for her to handle right now.

"Psst! My friend!" And so, it began as soon as the first hoodlum laid eyes on her. Rasheda knew she had an athletic body; long legs with full thighs, slender arms, tight stomach, and contours that matched her frame and weren't out of place. In short, she was appealing to the average Bimshire man. And with a twisted attempt at flattery, the group began to howl at her like she was some sort of farm animal. This did not bode well for Rasheda's temper. "You look ripe, yuh!"

Rasheda flouted the remark but that didn't stop them, nor did she stop walking.

"You got a boyfriend? Want one?" She rolled her eyes at the question.

"Dem bags look heavy. Lemme help yuh." Then bother evolved into threat. One of the hoodlums had invaded her personal space, grabbing at the grocery bag in her hand.

"Hey, back off!" She growled, and the fellow raised his palms in apology.

"My bad, my bad. I was just helping yuh, miss. Hey, are you far from here?"

Rasheda didn't answer. There was no way she'd tell a criminal where she lived, lest she suffered the nasty consequences later.

"Yo! So you gine just ignore me when I talking to you?" The hoodlum roared. It was strange that they hadn't given up when she passed them by.

That was when she noticed they weren't ordinary thugs. Red decorated their wardrobe: red scarves, red shirts, red shoes, red to mark their allegiance to Over de Wall. *Damn…*

Rasheda had seen them loitering around the neighborhood before, but not in such numbers—at least ten of them were there. "You like you is a rude one, though!"

"Nah, I like them so. Nice and feisty." It came from a thug who had a bandage around his head. The same one that met Justin's bottle last week.

Rasheda backed away. There was still no fear, nor blind courage. She needed to create some distance without alarming them, catch them off-guard somehow. But she couldn't run, not when Over de Wall had firearms. Chances are a bullet would pierce her before she got ten meters away, though they intended to molest her, not kill her. "I said, back off!"

The only choice left was to attack. Even if it was downright suicidal, she would have to try. Slowly reaching under her blouse Rasheda snapped at them, but they only guffawed and did the same. "What you gine do, little lady? Fight back? All ten of us?"

They jeered, drawing several guns which twinkled menacingly in the setting sun. Berettas, Glocks, even a couple Smith & Wessons were among the weaponry they had. Rasheda knew nothing of guns, but she thought of an action film when she saw the hoodlums. "You think I frighten fuh wunna? Come at me if you's a man, then!"

She was a rabid dog bearing her fangs. Secure in their numbers and firepower they stalked forward, a mischievous leer in their eyes.

"Wow… All these men fuh just one girl?" Glenn ambled onto the scene with the same carefree air that often pissed Rasheda off.

"Frig off, boy." One of them said, but his injured comrade remembered him clearly.

"That's him! He's one of the guys from the other day!"

Glenn observed the fellow pointing at him. "Um. Do I know you?"

"You bastard! You and that bottle-case fella knock we out the other day!"

"Oh right. How you doing, then? Feeling better?" The atmosphere had changed completely, with most of the tension focused on Glenn.

"So, this is the guy who brek you up so?" The first one to speak, the leader of this bunch, was a gruff man in his late twenties who had a lifetime of lawlessness behind him. "He don't look like nuttin much, but at least you show yuhself now. We gine teach you good what happens when you mess with Over de Wall."

Glenn sauntered to Rasheda's side; his eyes affixed on them.

"So, that's why you're here? To avenge your friend?"

"To uphold our name." The leader said firmly, their priority had changed and the fun and games were over. He revealed two semi-automatic pistols, again there was no rush as his quarry were unarmed.

"Fair enough." Rasheda didn't know what Glenn was thinking, he was only going to get himself killed on her account. But when she turned Glenn wasn't there; he was already in the middle of the throng.

"Argh!" The leader howled as blood trickled down his arm. A fork had been driven into the middle joint so that it couldn't bend—Glenn's handiwork. The leader tried to move the other arm, but it was instantly paralyzed by the same fork penetrating his arm pit. "S-Sonnava—"

"I imagine you in alotta pain right now since I just stab the Brachial Plexus. Don't worry. I ain gine judge if you scream…."

"S-S-Shoot him!" The other nine snapped out of their shock and scrambled to their weapons, but they were too late. Glenn was already in motion while they still fumbled. The hollow thunks of the fork tearing into flesh filled the area, and Rasheda could only watch on as he slipped through the foes. He aimed for the non-vitals too, choosing to immobilize rather than kill the hoodlums. Rasheda noticed carmine streaks coming from their ankles, wrists, fingers, but nothing too serious like the throat or chest.

"*GAH!*" Only two remained, about twenty feet apart, and Glenn still had his single fork. The problem lay in their motives. If he attacked the one closest to him that would leave the other one open to fire—worst case he would hit Rasheda, and that couldn't be allowed.

Crap! He had to act fast, but to his surprise Rasheda had drawn a weapon of her own—a dull machete which she slapped into the nearest hoodlum. Problem solved. Glenn plunged the fork into his opponent's thumb so he couldn't pull the trigger, and then gave a swift blow to the head to knock him out.

"Okay, when did you start walking around with that?"

"Why? What's it to you?"

"It's a weapon. How do you feel your Aunt—"

"I could take care of myself." Rasheda flared. "I d'ain need your help just now. I coulda handle them."

"Fair enough." Glenn was more alarmed by her sword than her insult. Then after a long silence, Rasheda said,

"Thanks."

"You don't have to do everything yourself, yuh know." Glenn sighed.

"What you mean?"

"You always try to do everything on your own. Like you feel help does mek you look weak or something." Rasheda would've cursed him for his 'holier than thou' words, but this time she just listened. Glenn suspected she was still tense from the encounter. "I get it. You's an independent woman. But not every helping hand is out to get you."

"So, you think I gine wait around and depend 'pon a man?"

"…I guess not." Glenn replied.

Silence returned. Then Rasheda asked, "So why those guys was cross here?"

"We had a lil' quarrel with them last week. Not as bad as just now, though."

"We?"

"Yeah. Me and Justin." Rasheda rolled her eyes, the drifter stirring trouble again—of course.

"I hope wunna know what you doing. Over de Wall ain easy."

"But you had it covered just now, though." Glenn chuckled.

"I was only defending myself!"

They looked over at the spot where they left the bodies. They were gone, probably gone to warn the others, and Glenn surmised the worst was yet to come.

"Oh, by the way, I bring back the dishes from the other day." He said while grabbing one of her shopping bags and offering to walk her home. Rasheda didn't complain.

"Aight, but keep de fork. I doubt we gine be eating with that after today…." Rasheda muttered and skipped ahead.

Wesley Broome Primary was a respectable school once upon a time; enrolling children who couldn't afford to travel to the city or to pay for more private institutions. But as times changed, and parents started affording "better" primary schools, Wesley Broome lost students until there were none left to support it. For ten years it had been closed down, with its yellow stone walls now ramshackle and its shingled roofs on the verge of collapse. Its few classrooms were deserted, while tables and benches became silage for wood ants and termites. However, the building was still intact. Many proposed refurbishing the school under a different name, so as to benefit more of Bimshire's youth, but that didn't come to pass—or rather—it wasn't allowed.

For Wesley Broome was occupied by someone else. Someone who preferred graffiti, posters, and obscenities on the same playgrounds children had frolicked years before. Someone whose lawlessness met and bred, until it spilled over into the public eye. Someone who dyed the school in blood-red: the same colors that would stain Bimshire soon. Someone named Over de Wall.

The state had abandoned Wesley Broome by then. As far as they were concerned, it was just an old building rummaged by vandals. Over de Wall was more than that, though. With a legion of two hundred strong, they engaged in crimes from larceny and vandalism to assault and drug trafficking. They were a formidable militia, whose purpose surpassed that of any other gang in the island.

In the past month they raided several post-office branches, in an effort to confiscate any motorbikes the couriers used. They didn't care about money or valuables. What they wanted was efficient transport that enabled them to make easier strikes and escapes. A higher goal. This was what separated Over de Wall from the others, and soon their influence extended from St. George to the neighboring parish of St. John.

At the helm of this militia was Mix Drink; a name that spread across the island in infamy as well as discreet ridicule. Alvin Hunte (his name given at birth) was unlike most gang leaders, just as Over de Wall was unlike most other gangs. He didn't command his forces with fear or intimidation, reserving those for *enemies of the cause*. The only thing he shared with them was his appearance—the man was undoubtedly a hooligan.

As he lounged on the old stage, which was once a podium for morning assembly, Mix Drink resembled a scruffy king settling on his throne. In a mesh vest with columns of red, yellow and green (the Rastafarian colors), a patchy pair of jeans, and some working boots, one wouldn't believe he was charismatic enough to inspire hundreds. But as he held a bag of dried green leaves up to his nose, there was no one in that school hall who doubted his authority.

"This like um is good stuff, though." Mix Drink took another whiff and returned it to the jittery underling before him. "How much of de shipment come in last night?"

"About ten kilos, sir."

"Thirteen." The correction came from a young lass who marched across the stage with as much clout as Mix Drink himself. "I dunno why we keep you around if you can't even count right."

"Go easy on de man, Kamilah . He never finish school."

"That ain de point, Alvin." Kamilah was the only person in Over de Wall who could call Mix Drink by name and still keep her tongue. No one else would even risk it. But it was different with her—it always was. "You need to keep useful people around you, otherwise you ain gine get nuh further."

By now the underling was trembling. Sure, he feared his leader; as indulgent as he was, Mix Drink could still be ruthless when the time came. But Kamilah was different. She was intolerant, unforgiving, and demanded the greatest performance at all times; the perfect lieutenant for Over de Wall's army.

"So wha I supposed to do?" Mix Drink asked, "Kill he to set an example? That ain my way."

"Want me to do it?" Kamilah drew a revolver and pointed it at the underling so that he whimpered. The weapon itself was polished. A Winchester 97 without a spot of rust on the barrel, and unlike most people who thought it troublesome to wield, Kamilah often found great use for it. Like last night, for example.

"I say don't kill him." Mix Drink didn't stress the words, but it was enough to make her holster the firearm. "Every man in Over de Wall counts. We do for ourselves and no one else. Remember that."

"T-Thank you, boss!"

"But that don't mean you should slack off, you know, Mackie?"

"Y-Yes I know, boss!" Mackie stammered.

"A bare waste of space." Kamilah sighed as Mackie scampered away. "Still say you shoulda killed him."

"Maybe. But he's a good man, just a bit clumsy." Mix Drink

shrugged and stuffed some dried leaves into his pocket. "Besides, I ain want you killing unless you have to. And now ain de time."

In the hush that followed, Kamilah unwrapped a sugar daddy (baked flour sticks with frosting on top) and shoved it into her mouth. Mix Drink had the impression of a fourteen-year-old girl instead of his best lieutenant.

"You back with them sweets again? I thought you d'ain like them."

"I don't."

"Then why you does be eating them?" Mix Drink had been with her for the past six years, and on every day Kamilah would nibble a sugar daddy. He didn't understand it. But then there were many things he didn't understand about Kamilah, other than her efficiency with a gun.

"It's for luck." Kamilah replied.

"Luck?" Mix Drink grunted. "You don't need no luck, girl. Jah will always see the righteous through, unstaan?"

"There ain no Jah. Not for me. Not for them. Not for this world, that's for damn sure." Kamilah's words were somber and Mix Drink took no offense; turning on the large Boombox beside his chair so that melodic moans oozed forth throughout the hall. Mix Drink didn't fancy himself a religious man, but lately he felt like a righteous one.

"I feel Jah does like to test loyalty. Take Sizzla here so. Man does sing 'bout the plight of the poor people and expose the corrupt Babylon system fuh what it really is."

Some don't care their heart is like ice
After kill another them rejoice but I'm
Holding firm.

And Mix Drink chanted along with the chorus, much to the amusement of several subordinates around the hall.

"See that there? That is de message that Babylon trying to hide from de public. Jah's message. Is just another way for them to maintain power. And we, as the righteous hand of Jah, are just more messengers."

Kamilah didn't notice the gathering that formed around this speech. As Mix Drink took to the podium and declared his words, there was a tumultuous applause in response. It was this motivational stimulus that ensnared all who followed him. In a different life, Alvin Hunte would've been an amazing politician.

"'Cause the corrupt got to hear from the poor people, correct?!" Mix Drink bellowed over the music. "And Over de Wall gine show Babylon just what the poor could do when we ready!"

Everyone howled; glass bottles were thrown at the walls, boots stamped the floor, and gunshots echoed in the air. Kamilah shuddered at the scene, for in this moment she was reminded of the fearsome nature of their army.

Then the commotion dissipated.

"Cha boy, look like I missing the action, yuh." A merry voice punctured the noise, and as Kamilah looked on, she realized it didn't belong to any hooligan. The man was tidy—too tidy for these parts—in a white dress shirt complete with black tie and black slacks. The crowd separated in silence as he passed through, each person eyeballing his pretty features: long, sleek, onyx hair and amicable grin, with great prudence. "Oh wait… don't let me interrupt."

"Nah, nah…." Mix Drink said, his tongue losing some of its zest. "We just ain expect you today, dah's all."

"Oh sorry. I got a bad habit uh showing up unannounced." The man rubbed his head in apology. "It's bad for business, but then again it helps to keep clients on dem toes."

"Yeah, yeah—well come forward, man." Mix Drink signaled for another chair. Kamilah thought he was acting strange. Mix Drink wasn't the sort to fuss over a guest; if anything, he would regard the person with equal ground and respect. But now he seemed almost subservient. It was only when the guest strode before her that Kamilah understood why.

Oh… It's this guy.

"I see you looking as lovely as always, Miss…" He didn't recall her name. "How you doing?"

Kamilah's first instinct was to blow his head off, but her hand remained on the holster. She wouldn't risk it with him. "Fine."

"Good to hear! So, Mix Drink, yuh cool, too?"

"I good, Sulemann." Mix Drink paused and looked around the hall, which everyone took as a cue to leave since they filed through the numerous doors. Kamilah would've moved too if

Mix Drink hadn't touched her arm and gestured to stay close. "So wha bring you to my yard?"

Sulemann turned his eyes to the ceiling. "Well, no reason, really. Just came to check up on our *little friend.*"

Kamilah swallowed hard, while Mix Drink nodded to the guest. "Oh, I hear yuh. Hold on a sec, lemme get it."

"*Him.*" Sulemann corrected. "He's a 'him'."

"Right … Him. Be right back." Mix Drink couldn't trust a subordinate with the item in question—too sensitive—so he ducked through the sprawling burgundy tapestry behind the stage. Ten feet, that was the furthest he allowed it from his eye.

Kamilah knew what it was before it came into view; a crudely crafted doll about ten inches tall, with a cherry-oak polish and basic design. It resembled a toy with cute cylindrical limbs, a little paintbrush in hand, and dots on its square head to represent a face. However, the doll was moving—*alive*; loafing in Mix Drink's hand as he brought it over. To be honest, it disturbed Kamilah. This creature they called a *Baku.*

"How you doing, lil' guy?" Sulemann whispered, but the Baku didn't acknowledge him. "You look well."

"It bounds to look well. That thing's been taking one-eighth of my product, man." And as Mix Drink spoke the doll stood up, outstretched one tiny arm, and demanded with a high-pitched voice,

"Payment!"

Kamilah shuddered at the command; yet another thing she didn't like about the doll. From the time Mix Drink acquired the Baku it made those incessant, prudish demands as per the following instructions.

Give the Baku what it asks,
and it will give you what you need.
But if you fail, it'll have your tail.
These simple words you best heed.

They heeded those words, providing the Baku exactly what it asked for—like clockwork. Following the routine, Mix Drink pulled out a hefty bag of dried Sinse leaves and gave it to the Baku, who had already conjured a long roll of paper to wrap the leaves inside. A-H-H… It wrote the letters in smoke as it exhaled, and while Kamilah caught the bitter smell she remembered that the doll was intoxicated not exhausted.

"Yuh see? De ting greedy as hell; that was its fifth blunt in an hour. Man, if we keep on like this, we ain gine got no herb to sell 'pon the street."

"Unfortunate as that may be, I don't think it's wise to stop catering to the lil' fella. We wouldn't want any more tragedies to happen just because you being stingy."

Tragedies…? Kamilah loitered over the word.

"Wha that supposed to mean?" Mix Drink asked.

"Just mean that you ain gine like the consequences. Trust me." Sulemann's words didn't sound like a threat, more like a precaution.

But if you fail, it'll have your tail.

"Well, whatever. I ain complaining. This little fella serve we real well." Mix Drink spoke with the utmost sincerity. The way he understood it, Bakus could grant any tangible request in exchange for something it liked. In this case it was armaments for Sinse leaves. A simple deal, really; one that catapulted Over de Wall from a backyard gang to a force that rivaled local military. Things were possible now. "Why you help us out in de first place, though?"

"—because we all want similar things." Sulemann replied.

"Fair enough."

They discussed other issues afterwards: like the amount of Sinse being imported into the country, how much items the Baku had conjured since his last visit, and how frequent were these requests. All the while, the doll took long drafts from the oblong cigarette, blowing billows of smoke with pleasure-filled sighs. Kamilah had enough of it: that intoxicating scent, that lazy, walking doll, and this visitor with his deceptive smile. She was about to interrupt when someone beat her to the punch.

"Boss! Boss!" An underling stumbled into the hall with lumbering steps and blood trickling down his leg. Mix Drink would've scolded him with a bullet to the other leg, but he was in good spirits.

"What is it?"

"W-We got problems!" Another one entered, with blood

blotching around his armpit and a twitching arm. Soon they were followed by three others who were just as battered.

"Who did this?" Mix Drink asked; his voice calm because of Sulemann's presence.

Then the group explained the situation, detailing the young man with an afro and the boy with a bottle case strapped across his back. Of course, they understated the degree of their defeat, creating injuries which they inflicted on Glenn and Justin, and disregarding Rasheda's involvement altogether. But Kamilah knew Mix Drink was still livid.

"Cha, fella, looks like you have some matters to attend to." Sulemann shook his head and clicked his tongue.

"Sorry about this, but I gine gotta cut the meeting short."

"No worries. I had other business to take care of anyway." Sulemann grinned. "Ambitious people like us can never find time to relax. Yuh know?"

"Yeah." They both rose from their seats, with the Baku stirring from his stupor and grumbling at the two. "We gine gotta meet later."

"Let's." They shook hands, Sulemann had a firm grip despite his dandy appearance. "I hope everything work out, and remember what I say about being stingy. I'm afraid this lil' guy is a much harsher business associate than I am." And with that he patted the doll's head, smiled at Kamilah and ambled down the stage, past the tattered group and through the gaping exits of the hall.

"I don't like that guy." Kamilah said frankly.

"Me either. Can't trust him nuh further than I can spit, but we need him around."

"Why? Just because he can give us weird creatures like that *thing*?" She pointed at the Baku who was still rubbing its dotted eyes.

"Yes. You see what it can do. With this Baku at our side, we can take this entire nation by force. Just another gift from Jah to do his work, yuh sight?" Kamilah didn't answer but she knew it was true. Over de Wall had conquered rural Bimshire within a year; decimating rival gangs, police, and even the Bimshire Defence Force with sheer firepower alone. Authorities assumed illegal smuggling or hidden arms manufacturing were the source of their artillery. But the truth could only be determined by an insane mind. "Now about these men…"

A wounded hooligan stumbled forward in anticipation. "Yes, boss."

"The propuh thing to do is send a few more men to tek care of them. But I kinda antsy and I feel is time we make a statement." His voice boomed over the hall, and as he picked up the Baku, files of red shirts began to stream inside. "'Cause these men like dem taking the name of Over de Wall too lightly, boah!"

"It's true!" Another chimed in.

The hall observed their leader as he retrieved the wooden doll, which turned its block head and asked the fundamental question: "What yuh want?"

"Guns. Nuff guns." Mix Drink demanded and the Baku obliged, creating bolts, springs, hammers, bullets, frames of various shapes and sizes—all to form the artillery they needed. Consecrating the hall in a pinkish light, the doll littered the floor with every available type of firearm. His minions goggled at the conjured, scrambling for each weapon like kids in a candy store. Some tested out their new toys, firing a couple rounds into the ceiling several meters above.

"Haha! This is great!" They exclaimed.

"Yuh welcome!" The Baku yawned and went back to finishing off its blunted cigar. Kamilah regarded the wooden doll with utter disgust. This was unnatural. Nothing on this earth should be able to summon an entire shipload of guns out of thin air.

"What yuh waiting for, Kamilah? Restock yuhself 'cause we gine to war soon from now." Mix Drink fetched a belt full of bullets like the ones from the Desperado westerns.

"If this is the work of Jah… I want no part of it." She reluctantly placed rounds in the barrel of her Winchester.

"That's okay. You don't have to believe in him. Once you fight for me—for the cause—then it's all good." Mix Drink fired a shot for silence.

"These men feel this is a joke! Attacking one of ours and expect it to done so? Nah… they got to go! The upstarts, the Babylon, every onna dem need a bullet in the ass like the bold-faced dogs they really are!"

Affirming howls filled the air along with more gunshots. Mix Drink continued, "To show we ain friggin 'round. Over de Wall gine burn this whole island down, starting with this pissy village!" His soldiers loved the idea, like scavengers chomping at the bit for more chaos. More bloodshed. It was okay if they didn't care about the cause. About the change they would bring to this country. As long as they wreaked havoc in his name, Mix Drink was satisfied. He sat back on his throne, listening to the chorus before him.

"We gine pop dem off!"

"We gine pop dem off!"

"We gine put we A-Ks Over de Wall!"

Justin had monotonous mornings ever since he stayed at Glenn's house. He woke at midday, as he had no job, school, or any other obligations to attend to. But whenever he rose, Glenn would have a list of tasks to do around the house.

"I don't do chores, big man…." Justin regarded the dishes in the sink.

"Well, you are eating here for free." Glenn replied. Justin was not obligated to pay rent for his lodging, Glenn wouldn't allow it. However, that hadn't stopped him from cajoling his guest from time to time.

"But dishes, big man? Why you don't ask you girl to do 'em?" Justin groaned as he started scrubbing a dirty plate.

"I doubt I could get Rasheda to do dishes fuh me." Glenn chuckled at the thought.

"Man, most girls does only get on antsy to fellas dem like. Trust me, I know these things."

"… Oh really?"

"Yeaz, man. I used to got the girls lick up back home. And

your girl, man, she cute fuh truth, but she attitude just ain for me."

"Don't worry, I think she ain too fond of you either." Glenn snickered, but Justin wasn't amused.

"Man, frig this!"

"Wow, wunna people does got some tempers, boy."

"… Just gimme something else to do besides dishes, nuh?" Justin grumbled while stifling the urge to throw the plate at his host.

"Hmm. I guess the bush want trimming from 'gainst de road and the guttering want clearing, too. But that a bit high, I could handle—"

"De guttering sound good. Lemme do that!" Justin dashed through the back door. Glenn was surprised at how fast he volunteered, as the task was troublesome due to its height, however, as Justin bounded the mango tree like a monkey and landed on the roof in less than a breath, Glenn understood why.

"Guess you got it covered, then?"

"Yeah, man … But what I supposed to clean de gutters with?" Justin asked awkwardly. He hadn't given the errand much thought outside being an alternative to cleaning pots and pans. Glenn shook his head before handing him some gloves, a small broom, and a bag for him to use. The task lasted hours, with Justin having to shimmy along the edges to scrape dry leaves, seeds, and any other debris. "Cawblen. Country does got yuh house stink if you not careful."

Justin mopped his brow; the sky, dimmed in a dense orange, rewarded him with its glow.

"Yow! You done up there?" Glenn called. He completed the other chores in the time Justin took for his one.

"Yeah, man, I done." Justin said, disregarding the stack of leaves in front of him.

"Cool, I gine and get some roast corn. Wanna come?" As Glenn posed the question, Justin was off the roof and on to the muddy earth below. "Guess that's a yes, then?"

"Done know. Though roast corn ain my thing." Another alternative to work which Justin gladly accepted.

Evenings in Layer's Gap bustled with activity. Children,

recently freed from school, were now frolicking in the middle of the road; playing games like Doggie Doggie Step Right Out, Red Light, Green Light, Stickie, and many other childhood pastimes. Those not in the road had taken to a park in the western part of the village. Quaint like the rest of the district, the park was crafted using crude materials: like planks of wood and rope to make swings from golden-apple trees, barrels and pipes for sea-saws and slides, old tires and rocks painted to garnish the surroundings—all of which were enjoyed by the residents. Glenn even said Layer's Gap had gained national renown for having the best community park on the island, but Justin never had an interest in such things.

Older folk took to the pasture, where two separate games of football and cricket were played on a pitch so small that both sets of players often overlapped. Ahead of Justin was an intense road-tennis match, which was forced to pause when a delivery truck drove through. "Rangate, man!" bellowed one of the players who was on match point.

"Out here does be different 'pon evenings, yuh…." Justin said.

"Most people does come out and do dem thing. Don't even talk 'bout weekends." Glenn hailed the group as he passed by, and continued to do so for the remainder of the trek.

"Why you greeting people and dem ain answering you back, man? You look like a chump."

"Better to be a chump than unmannerly." Glenn replied, and though the notion was naïve Justin didn't argue.

They eventually approached a familiar house, where the dreadlocked boy was busy sweeping his front yard with a palm leaf. Justin indulged Glenn by nodding at the boy, but when he was ignored Justin snarled, "Man ain even looking at me."

"That's because you ain saying nothing," Glenn chuckled over sucking teeth. "Yo, Dario. Wha gine on?"

The dreadlocked boy didn't respond immediately, too preoccupied with the stones at his feet. When Dario did acknowledge the two, Justin realized why he wasn't noticed before. Dario had thick, black dreadlocks which draped over his face and hid his eyes. People speculated whether he saw beyond his hair, but the question was answered when Dario replied,

"I just here. What about you?" His voice was soft and muffled, almost like he struggled to enunciate his words.

"Man, I good—just here rolling with my boy." Glenn pointed a thumb at Justin but Dario didn't react—an act that annoyed Justin even more.

Is this guy an invalid or something?

"Okay. Well. I going in soon before it get too dark." He ran the palm leaf over the ground once more for good measure, flicking specs of dirt over Justin's boot in the process. "Oh. Sorry." Dario said, but Justin was about to erupt.

"Man, that okay. No harm done, right?" Glenn intervened.

"The hell you say? These Timbs ain cheap!" Justin barked.

"Why wunna don't leave the boy alone, though?!" Rasheda strode to the group with parcels in hand. The stress from a hard day still showed on her.

"No, they weren't doing any—" Dario began before he was interrupted by the other two.

"He good. We was just checking how he doing."

"Aight then. It ain like the man is a child." Justin patted Dario's shoulder so hard that he rocked with each touch.

"You can't see that he ain comfortable with wunna?" Rasheda rushed over, for some reason the girl often took a protective approach to Dario.

"Really, Rasheda. It's okay. I was just leaving." Dario murmured. All these strange eyes made him uncomfortable. He had to get away.

"And you, too! Always hiding away in de house and only coming out to sweep de yard. You in de country, man! Try and get some fresh air!" Rasheda flailed her arms in the same way a mother would when scolding her child.

"S-Sorry…" Dario bleated.

"You! For a loudmouth she got a point." Justin concurred.

"Who you calling a loudmouth, yuh poppit?!" Rasheda then rounded on Justin, and the quarrel began attracting any passersby close enough to hear it.

"I agree though, Dario, you really need to get out. But I can't fault a fella for wanting his space." Glenn added, noting Rasheda's stunned expression. "Anyway, we gine for some roast corn, you wanna come for some?"

Dario considered for a moment, and then shook his head along with his flowing dreadlocks. "No. It's okay. I really need to be getting back."

"Ah well, suit yourself, then." Glenn grinned.

"I hope wunna ain plan to work that woman too hard!" Rasheda sucked her teeth and then tugged the stuffed bag in her hand. "I see she order real corn from the market this evening. Aunty send down some stuff, too."

"That mean she gine get good business tonight." Glenn laughed.

"Not from me." Justin huffed, turning a scornful chin to the groceries and then at the timid Dario who, although awkward, didn't coil under his gaze. His eyes meeting Justin's through a thicket of dreadlocks.

"Well, you ain gotta come, then." Rasheda growled. "Nobody ain even invite you!"

Justin sucked his teeth, but before he said anything Glenn kept things civil once more. "I did. Anyway, Dario, we gine catch up later. Go and do your thing, man."

From the grin on his thin lips, Glenn could tell Dario was relieved by the farewell. "Thank you. I'll see you guys later, then."

"Get in good, Dario." Rasheda added, though she knew the statement made little sense as his front door was just a few steps away. They all watched as he entered a paltry grey cottage fashioned with rundown white trimmings from yesteryear—both elegant and derelict. Glenn thought he worked hard to keep his house in order, but it was nothing compared to Dario's day to day labors. The moss and lianas that would normally cover a building this age were constantly scrubbed away, and the windows (which were always tightly shut) didn't have a smudge of mildew on them. Rasheda always wondered who else lived in there with him, as it was the only house in the neighborhood that onlookers couldn't peep into.

"That boy need a life…" Justin grumbled, which then tempted the girl's retort.

"He got more than you, at least he ain lodging at some

stranger's place. Part you come from anyway?" Rasheda was about to unleash more words when Glenn grabbed hold of her groceries. "Wait, wha you doing?!"

"They look heavy."

"I can han—fine, whatever." She surrendered them without much complaint, recalling Glenn's words from the other day.

The trio then set off down the road, Justin trailing behind the would-be couple who were busy chatting about something or the other. Throughout the trek, he couldn't dismiss the discomfort he felt. He didn't belong here. Not in a cheerful little village, with affable neighbors like the ones lounging on the sidewalk with barbequed food in hand, melodious music in ear, or an amusing piece of gossip in tongue. It was too hospitable for him. Too down-to-earth, much like Glenn who was offering him room and board. Even Rasheda, with her boorish behavior, was still friendlier than the apathetic people he grew up with. After all, she cared enough to curse him in the first place.

Harboring these notions, Justin stumbled into the two in front.

"Aye! You daydreaming or what?" Rasheda snapped.

"Sorry."

"For real, though. You was kinda quiet ever sense we left Dario. If you don't want nuh roast corn I could always buy you sain else, yuh know." Glenn said.

"So, wait? He don't work? Why you gotta be buying food fuh he?" The question sparked another quarrel until they were interrupted by a polite drawl.

"Oh dear. De young people suh miserable this late in de evening?" Justin looked beyond them, where an old hawker sat by a large black coalpot. "Yuh would swear you all was married for years, de way wunna carrying on." She smiled. The creases in her brown skin stretched and curled.

"Marry to who?!" Rasheda exclaimed, scandalized by the remark. Glenn dipped a couple fingers into his wild afro and scratched the back of his head.

"Nah, Betty. It ain nothing like that."

"Oh sorry, I misunderstand. I thought you all were... Oh dear. Sorry if I made you uncomfortable, hear, boy?"

"Wait, so why should he be uncomfortable? I'm a great

catch!" Rasheda said, affronted.

"You mean somebody would catch something if they hang around you." Justin added, and Rasheda rounded on him with Glenn struggling to hold her back. In all the commotion, Betty peeped at this strange young man with the bottle case on his back.

"Hello there, youngster. I never see you around these parts yet."

Justin pushed out his lips. He didn't need to explain himself to this old woman he just met. Noticing this, Glenn chimed,

"This is my boy from St. Thomas. He staying by me for a while, just for a visit."

"Oh okay. So, yuh liking the village so far, young man?" That melodious drawl was too much for Justin to resist.

"It aight. Can't complain."

"That's good, and now yuh out having a good time with the other young people."

"You know how it is, Betty." Glenn leaned over the pot, drooling at the two blackened cobs above the blazing coals. The air had a sweet, smoky flavor which made mouths water. "So… you soon done?"

Rasheda slapped his arm. "You! Why you don't hold on, though?"

"That is no problem, deary." Betty prodded the cobs with a long metal rod. "These two soon done. Just hold on fuh a bit, right?" She then regarded Justin, who wasn't showing any interest in what she was cooking. "And you want me to put one for you, too?"

"Nah, I good." Justin grunted, but like a good vendor Betty didn't take offense.

"Oh. A strapping fella like you mussy want something more filling, right?" Justin nodded, now she was speaking his language. He peered at the other stalls, where the smell of barbeque meats filtered throughout the street. "Oh dear, and I ain even got no more pigtail to offer yuh. Though I could guarantee my corn just as sweet." Betty stirred the pot with confidence, so that a few pops rang from the cobs. There was a brief moment when Justin felt inclined to believe her, but he refused the offer once again.

"That's okay, I gine just take his share." Glenn added, and he paid the hawker with a couple dollar bills, securing the cobs with relish, while Rasheda patiently waited until hers were complete.

"So, how your Aunty doing, sweet girl?" Betty asked.

"She doing okay, you know. Still wouldn't keep off she feet if yuh pay she." Rasheda shook her head, but Betty clapped her hands and laughed.

"That sound just like Yvette, fuh truth. She was never one to stay quiet atall." The relationship between this old hawker and her great aunt was never known to Rasheda. All Aunty ever said was that Betty was an old acquaintance from back in the day, while Betty would say, "Yuh know, she was always one of my favorite clients."

"Really?" As far as Rasheda knew her Aunty hated roast corn.

"Yes. She was a good customer, even when I had my slow days." Betty mused, and smiled secretly to herself. Her mind travelling to busier times.

"I ain doubt you, Betty." Glenn smacked as he spoke. "With corn so good, I'd be yuh favorite customer, too."

"You! Try and finish eat and stop talking, do!" Rasheda slapped his arm again.

"Boy, you remind me of another friend of mine; though he like roast corn more than you." Betty cackled. "You sure you ain want none, youngster?"

"Nah, I sure." Justin said, making it a cue for them to leave.

"Okay then. Well enjoy de rest of yuh evening, hear, dearies?"

"You too, Betty." Glenn and Rasheda said simultaneously. They both felt guilty but Betty took no offense. As she watched the young trio amble down the road, she lingered on the one with a bottle case on his back.

"Hmm. Another interesting fella I get to meet today...."

Dario closed the front door as soon as he entered. A minute had passed since he left the others outside but he still felt a twinge of regret. Perhaps he should've accepted their offer and joined them for an evening on the gap? Surely eating barbeque, listening to music and lounging with neighbors was better than staying home. Turning on the lights, Dario recognized his only company: some dingy curtains which perfectly accentuated the squalid furniture. Porcelain ducks, swans, dogs, gentlemen and ladies greeted Dario as he walked by, and on the walls were paintings of scenic vistas which he often ignored aside from dusting their frames. An empty home by all accounts, though Dario didn't believe he was alone.

A certain presence filled this house. Stern and cruel, it seeped from the walls as he traversed the narrow chamber, just beyond the kitchen, past the bathroom and down the short corridor. Dario turned the knob and the door creaked open, like a hollow invite to some sacred place. The scent of stale air, incense and mildew bore down on him like the master's hand itself.

As nightfall approached, the room was dark without having to draw in the thick drapes. Dario didn't turn on the lights. He just eased towards the dresser where several trinkets lay scattered: a lighter, a chain made of chunky wooden beads, a long red scarf with matching head-tie and a jar containing long, thin sticks covered in foil—the latter of which Dario picked up and burned with the lighter. The sweet smoke masked the stagnant air, if only for a short while.

Next to the dresser was a bed that hadn't been slept in for years, with rumpled sheets and pillows resting askew. The entire room was undisturbed, aside from the sticks of incense Dario burned every day. He wouldn't dare derange any more than that. Dario turned towards the dresser again, which resembled a shrine more than anything else. A discolored image of an old man patting a quiet boy formed the centerpiece.

"Everything seems to be in order." Dario muttered to an invisible ear.

Rage burbled in his chest as he stared at the picture. Why must he continue to do these menial tasks? Four years, that was the last time they mattered. And though Dario longed to leave this place, he wouldn't. For his master was a cruel man. A cruel man, indeed.

"The yard's done." Dario said to the pillow. "Five hundred sweeps just like you asked, and not a leaf or seed on the ground."

Dario was diligent in his dues. He cleaned every day, knowing every nook and cranny and how much dust was in between them. With any luck the master would be satisfied with his toil, and Dario would have the perfect opportunity to… No, that won't work. It never does.

A loud pop interrupted his thoughts. Dario didn't flinch. He'd spent too many years learning not to. Instead, he wondered what caused it, and after a short search, Dario found a hole in the wall with smoke meandering from the bullet lodged within.

It was odd. The smell of gunpowder overwhelmed the incense, and his ears rang from the piercing sound. Soon Dario would drown in this fresh sensation as the house became flooded with it. Bullets crashed through hollow boards and weathered glass windows, riddling the house with holes. And instead of ducking for dear life, Dario marveled at the violence around him.

"W-What's going on?" Dario shimmied along the floor with the speed of a mongoose, amidst the bangs and crashes blaring above. Wood and glass rained on his skin, each fragment bringing more discomfort than the last. But Dario ignored it, his heart steady since the ordeal began. That is, until he returned to the bedroom…

BOOM!

A wave of smoke and rubble and flame had poured from the chamber, knocking Dario on his back. When the blur in his eyes subsided, he found a gaping hole bitten into the wall, and the divan and dresser now in pieces. The destruction before him was unreal; like a scene from the television he rarely watched.

He skulked to his feet, peering through the hole in the wall.

Amongst the darkening blue and the orange flares, Dario saw streaks of red passing by. Persons clad in scarlet entered from all sides. The five that he could see rode terrain motorcycles, while the others rode ordinary bikes like bandits raiding a defenseless village.

His neighbors scrambled for refuge but all didn't make it in time. A young couple was gunned down while taking flight behind a garbage can. One middle-aged man was perforated with an array of bullets so that splotches of blood came from his chest. A child met a spray of shrapnel on his way to a road-tennis match, his body and racket shredded apart. These were just the few casualties Dario could see, and dozens more had gathered where he couldn't. Screams interrupted shots and detonations but at least they were evidence of life.

Dario observed the bedlam; burning each act of violence into his mind. He wasn't a stranger to slaughter, not after everything he experienced as a child. But this was different. It was wild. It was random. It was hell, but a different version of the hell he knew.

At his feet was the portrait he despised; its edges singed by the earlier explosion. Dario imagined the punishment he would suffer when his master finally returned. But he wasn't afraid. In the madness around him Dario saw escape, opportunity.

Then, as if attracted to his excitement, a hooligan appeared from his side with an AK-47 aiming gleefully at Dario. It was the last thing he'd ever do. Before the trigger was even pulled, Dario slithered to his palm leaf and lashed the enemy across the torso. The blow was so harsh that bits of skin and fabric were torn off by the bristles.

Something had awakened inside Dario. Perhaps it was roused long ago and only now able to roam free?

Either way it was escape. Opportunity.

The environment had suddenly become very familiar for Justin. That rotten, sulfuric scent of gunpowder mixed with the fragrance of boiling blood and burning flesh. It was the smell of conflict—the flavor of turmoil. Justin never expected it to surface in this quaint little village. Layer's Gap had been transformed into a war zone. As he took cover behind a nearby house, billows of smoke caught his eye along with the red shadows that blurred through them. The food stalls were over-turned, pots of half-cooked food and grease were scattered on the ground, and their owners were long gone. Those buildings still intact were rife with bullet holes, and embers cracked at their doorstep. No one was hurt, at least not the ones closest to him. Several patrons huddled behind a snow-cone cart. An unexpected choice for cover, but fear often made people do unexpected things. Justin knew this well, though there were few like him who didn't seem afraid. Cautious, but not afraid.

At his side, Rasheda and Betty had taken refuge under some steps, the former too worried about the old woman's safety to fear for her own. "Hey, you okay?"

"Yes, child, I good." Betty rummaged through her belongings to make sure everything was intact. "Wha 'bout you? You like yuh get scratch…."

She regarded the scrape on Rasheda's shoulder; a result of her reckless attempt to save Betty from harm. "I'm fine, this ain nothing."

The wound wasn't serious, just a peel of flesh with blotches of red seeping through the pink. "Even so, a young girl like you with beautiful skin shouldn't have marks like this. Don't you agree?"

"That don't matter right now!" Rasheda barked but Betty wouldn't listen, reaching into her pot for a jar of scarlet powder.

"Here, this is cayenne—rub some of this 'pon the scratch.

And don't say no, neither!" Betty's tone quelled any objection Rasheda had. It felt like a fresh wound was seared into her, but to Rasheda's surprise the skin had healed within seconds. "See? It working already!"

"How?" Rasheda was dumbfounded.

Justin was taken aback, too. It had been ages since he saw the cayenne remedy, and he didn't expect anyone in Layer's Gap to have it. But that wasn't important now. "So, who attacking we?"

"Over de Wall."

Justin barely recognized Glenn's voice; it lacked the casual chime that often annoyed him. It was cold. Bitter. And as Glenn strode forward, Justin recalled what intimidated him back at the bar. It wasn't a matter of skill or speed, but the killing intent behind them.

"Dem finally gone and done it…." Glenn remarked, as revving motors and roaring gunfire hinted at the butchery beyond. Justin watched him closely. Would Glenn be comfortable in this environment? Or would he cower like the others?

Glenn continued forward, glancing around until he found an ice pick on an abandoned stall. Just what he needed: something sharp. And like clockwork a troupe of motorcycles wheeled onto the scene, scavenging for leftovers from the first raid. At first, they were delighted by the find: some adolescents and a few elderly—easy food for their high-powered weapons. However, they soon discovered their mistake.

"*Ack!*" The ice pick punctured the first one's throat, seconds after laying eyes on Glenn. A nasty blow. The kind he promised to never do again, but that was until the enemy spilled blood on his home.

"Frig! Part he come from now?" One rider screamed as his comrade wriggled in the dirt. "And he tek out Gibson, too?!"

The quarry was dangerous. The thought was fresh in his mind when the ice pick impaled his wrist, then his jaw.

A foul squelch came from Glenn's victim as he flew off the bike. It even masked the cries from the fleeing villagers in the distance. "Shit! Men, shoot he! Shoot de bastard!"

Even with ample artillery they were ill-equipped to handle Glenn, as their effort to "shoot the bastard" ended with an ice pick to the chest, eye or ear. Four more remained, circling around the perimeter to examine the threat. There was reason in this approach. Keep mobile. Glenn wouldn't be able to catch them then. They were wrong.

Clank! The ice pick was shoved into the rotary of one motorcycle wheel, toppling it over.

"Frig!" The rider, now cycle-less, scrambled for his gun and fired off random shots to hit two of his comrades.

"Fools. You are so fussy when using guns on innocent people, but when facing an actual opponent, you scuffle around like ants?" Glenn retrieved his ice pick and marched towards the defenseless hooligan. "You disgust me…."

His words teemed with bloodlust. He wanted to slay them all. Even if an ice pick was his only weapon, Justin believed Glenn had the intent and the ability to do so. And he was not alone in this belief.

"Glenn…?" Rasheda felt it too: that rich, murderous aura. For the first time, she saw the annoying boy from down the road as a killer—as his true self. Justin almost pitied her for not realizing until now.

Everyone else was stunned into silence, with the exception of the hooligan whimpering beneath Glenn's gaze. Justin thought he could hear Glenn's internal cogs turning as he considered sparing the enemy. His grip around the bloody ice pick: unwavering and cold. But in this hesitation, the hooligan cocked the hammer of his gun…

Crack!

None saw the motion of Justin's arm or the rock flung at the enemy's forehead. "Don't even try it. I ain as forgiving as my boy here."

"Who says I'm forgiving?" Glenn replied, as more motorcycles sped from the other side of the gap. "…Backup?"

Was everyone's first assumption, but from the frantic way the bikes zipped around they seemed to be escaping something rather than bringing reinforcement. It wasn't long before the pursuer appeared as a green blur darting across the street. Justin thought it was a giant snake, thrashing the bodies of metal and flesh like they were standing still. Only when the serpent stopped, Dario emerged with a bloody palm leaf in hand.

"De hell?" Justin asked as he goggled at the quiet invalid. "The man outrun two motorcycles?"

Dario was puzzled by the assembly at the end of the street. "What are you guys doing here? It's dangerous."

The question made Glenn snigger, dispelling the previous tension. "We know, but you don't have to worry about us. Everything already covered."

"Cool." Dario saw eight dead bodies scattered along the pavement with multiple disheveled motorcycles. There was no alarm in his eyes, which skimmed over to Rasheda and Betty.

"How 'bout you, man? You good?" Glenn asked, noting that Dario had no wounds.

"Yes I am. But my house is destroyed…." Dario sighed, in a way that showed more joy than sorrow. Down the street from whence the riders came, Justin noted one or two bodies lying on the ground. It was another familiar sight for him, aside from the state of the cadavers. Their skin was shaven off, as if by coarse sandpaper, and when Justin walked beyond Dario's palm leaf he counted at least twenty bodies.

"What the rass…?" How one man did this with such a weapon, Justin didn't know. But he had seen stranger things in his time.

"Cha, man, sorry to hear." Glenn said, as the remaining hooligan tried to slither away. The ice pick twirled between his fingers, delicate and deadly. "Part you think you gine? I decided not to kill you, but that don't mean I gine let you go either."

"Ha! You think I wanna run away? I already know I gine dead!"

"Ah. I see." The bravado moved Glenn a little, though he knew the hooligan couldn't return to his leader without consequence. Still, something was off…

"But if yuh feel I gine help you, yuh lie! Fire 'pon informer. *Hail Over de Wall!*" There was a click and the clatter of a grenade pin. Glenn lodged the ice pick in the hooligan's hand but the explosive vest was already armed.

"Shit!" Glenn darted back, Justin somersaulted away, Rasheda and Betty huddled further into the cellar while Dario just stood his ground.

BOOM!

Over de Wall's tenacity came in smoke and flame. Mulch was all that remained. "He sacrificed himself rather than be held hostage."

The act shocked him, not because of its gruesome nature but as a testament to their loyalty. Over de Wall wasn't just a gaggle of thugs. They were organized. Driven. Two qualities that Glenn thought were very dangerous in hostile groups.

"Bah—Dumbass!" Justin scoffed, kicking off a pinkish clump that landed on his boot. "All he do was pelt way he life."

The frenzied roar of motorcycle engines and wild gunfire disappeared from the air. "Did they retreat?"

Dario assumed as there were no opponents aiming at him. Justin hopped to a nearby rooftop and saw streams of dust exiting the street. "Yeah, um look so."

"Thank goodness!" Betty emerged from the cellar with Rasheda at her hem. Brushing the apron over her long skirt, the old hawker asked, "Nobody ain hurt, nuh?"

"Well, no one here at least." Glenn uttered as throngs of injured sprinkled the street. Even though the worst was over, Over de Wall did considerable damage to the village.

"Cheese on bread! It's like de Defence Force come up in here or something!" Rasheda exclaimed, as her favourite variety shop was reduced to a few smoldering boards and blocks.

"This is terrible. Absolutely terrible…." Betty regarded the same building. "That was Ms. Boxhill place. Oh Lawd, for this to happen." And as she listened to the hawker's commiserations, a notion entered Rasheda's mind.

"Crap! Aunty!" Rasheda bolted down the street with Glenn hot on her heels. *If anything happened to her…* She raced along with her thoughts, passing mutilated houses, singed crotons and burning lattices. In her wake, dozens of people limped across the street in an effort to reach their loved ones, some of them were too injured to even move, but Rasheda ignored them and bore through a garden as a shortcut to her walkway. *Please let her be all right…*

She finally reached her verandah, skipping up the unpainted wooden steps and opening the galvanized door. The house looked fine from the outside, save for broken windows and burn marks on the delicate yellow-painted walls. Her chest pounded when she gripped the cold knob, and it was only when Glenn patted her shoulder that Rasheda managed to turn it.

The rug was hazardous, with broken glass and capsized furniture impeding her trek through the front house. But Rasheda continued on, every step more careless than the last, because the further she ventured into her home the closer her nightmares turned to reality. Glenn understood her fear. As he saw several gouges along the floor and ceiling, he had to believe a vicious scuffle happened there. Then Rasheda shoved open the door to her Aunty's room and speculation became certainty. The familiar sour of blood filled Glenn's nostrils, and he noted the scarlet smeared on the walls.

Shit… Glenn avoided the bed for fear of what might be seen. Instead, he found a severed foot next to the closet, and a set of fingers on an empty barrel serving as a dresser. Glenn only looked up when he heard Rasheda shout,

"Aunty!" The old woman was lying with her back against the divan and her limbs sprawled slapdash away from her body. Sandwiching her thin frame were two other cadavers, who seemed to have fallen after suffering one final attack from their quarry.

At least she fought until the bitter end… Was what Glenn assumed until…

"Aye. What yuh keeping suh much noise for, girl-child?" Yvette spoke with an exhausted tone, but that was more than enough for her great-niece who bounded forward to make sure she was all right.

"You alive!"

"'Course I am." Yvette coughed. It was clear she just scraped by the ordeal.

"What happened?" Glenn asked, as he helped her away from the two corpses on her side.

"I don't know. One minute I was mekking tea, and the next I hear gunshots and these three people come in de house."

"Three?" He asked, but then saw the severed head rolling on the window sill. "Oh."

"I had to defend muhself, you see. Cut dem down or lose my life—heh—can't believe these old bones still got lil' moves left." She hacked and Rasheda patted her back to clear her windpipe. Glenn noticed that Rasheda was trembling herself.

"Aunty, we gotta hurry up and get you outta these bloody clothes."

"Yuh right. But tell muh, wha 'bout the rest? How everybody else doing?"

Silence followed.

"It's pretty bad. A good set of people get injured and who knows how many get kill." Speaking of which, Glenn thought that someone should've notified the authorities by now. But he heard nothing. Not one siren filled his ears and he couldn't figure out why.

"I see…. Wait! My tea! I still ain drink none fuh de evening!" Yvette struggled to her feet but Rasheda wouldn't have it.

"Forget de blasted tea, nuh?! You near loss you life, try and rest yuhself!"

"Oh dear. Looks like yuh had quite a commotion, Yvette." Betty entered the front house, appraising the shambles.

"Yeah, Betty, you could say so. And, no, I'm fine, they ain get to lay a hand 'pon me." Yvette said, as the hawker retrieved the cayenne from her bosom.

"Okay, but I can't say de same for yuh house, though." Betty searched in vain for someplace to sit but most of the furniture was busted. "I guess we could tek care uh that later."

She winked at Yvette, who simply frowned and said, "Sure, but first get me some tea, nuh? 'Fore I catch air in muh stomach."

One cup of tea. Three times a day. It was Yvette's only routine and she wouldn't break it today. Not today at all. She deserved that much. Glenn appreciated this fact, and he knew it brought some relief to Rasheda.

"*Stupse*. Now the place get boring again." Justin sucked his teeth from the verandah ledge.

Rasheda was incredulous as she scooped spoonfuls of sugar into several cups. But Glenn was more pardoning, "What's the situation out there."

"Yuh neighborhood well frig-up, boy. A lotta houses burn

down and some people hurt, but I think only five people actually dead." Small numbers in his opinion, but Justin saw the devil in Glenn's eyes. "Dario went back to check on his, so he say. Weird fella."

Glenn stalked out of the room. His mind engorged with disturbing notions about the future of his home. And the one that struck him the most,

This gine happen again. And it gine happen real soon…

Chaos reigned at the District D Police Department. There were more car accidents throughout the parish (though none as bad as the one on the ABC Highway several years later.) Petty crimes were rampant, with a few gas stations and convenience stores being robbed, and even a small bank being held at gunpoint in the middle of the day. Business as usual for dispatch operators; that is, compared to the more bizarre calls they received.

Darryl Carter noted another strange report on the call-in line. Gunshots. Explosions. Bandits in red rampaging through the streets. Darryl believed it was pure fiction, but from the distress in their voices he swore that terrorists were on the island.

"I'm sorry, sir, can you repeat that?"

"Uh say de men pelting grenades 'bout de place now. And I just watch muh neighbor get gundown!"

Darryl gawked at the receiver, processing the information, but the silence was broken by a hysterical plea from the other line.

"When wunna gine hurry up and come up hey, man?! Alla we getting kill 'bout hey!"

"O-Okay, sir. We'll send someone shortly to investigate." Darryl recited.

"We ain want somebody! We want de friggin Defense Force! Come quick, nuh!"

"Okay, sir, just remain calm and—" There was a click and the receiver went dead. Darryl was bewildered. He couldn't get the caller's name or location, but there was no need as he knew the place of interest.

"Layer's Gap again?" His colleague asked.

"Yeah…." Darryl sighed, jotting down the information on a notepad. "This would make the third time today and mussy the hundredth time this month."

"Guess you should tell de Superintendent." A pointless suggestion. First, they'd inform the nearest units of a disturbance around that district. Then, after the units investigated the area, they'd find nothing. No explosions. No gunshots. It was like the place known as Layer's Gap never existed.

"But that ain gine do nuh good." Darryl muttered on his way to the Superintendent, giving a detailed report of the phone call and the location.

"I already tell you that is a waste of time." A hoarse, exhausted voice came from behind a large stack of folders. "Those Layer's Gap calls are nothing but pranks. Hoaxes."

"You feel so?" Darryl asked. "They sounded really distressed, sir. I even hear an explosion in the background…."

"So how come when our officers arrived at the scene, there wasn't a broken window to be found?" This time a face with stubble cheeks and thick-rimmed glasses scowled at him, but Darryl pressed on.

"There gotta be some explanation."

"Well, that would have to be left unsolved, 'cause right now we up to we ears in reports— legitimate ones." He added when he noticed Darryl about to interject. "Like that robbery at Shell, Holetown this morning."

"Yes, I sent you that report, sir." The Superintendent mopped his brow wearily without reply. "But I still feel—"

"That's enough, Carter!" The Superintendent barked with a stern finality that silenced Darryl at once. He had overstepped his bounds, and without another word he returned to his post and awaited the next distress call from Layer's Gap.

"Why won't he listen?" He muttered while traversing the corridor. It was true that the department had its hands full with rising crime rates, and the investigations in that village were futile. But still…

"Watch where you're going." Darryl bumped into a dapper gentleman striding in the opposite direction. Clad in an expensive grey suit, he glared at Darryl without stopping his gait.

Judging from the court robes on his arm, Darryl guessed he was an attorney—a member of the Queen's Council to be exact. Darryl waited a minute, then followed the gentleman's trail until it stopped at the office he left minutes ago. "…The Superintendent?"

He contemplated over the black plaque on the door. Darryl was never inclined to eavesdrop, but curiosity got the better of him. Pressing his ear against the wood, he listened to the muffled voices on the other side, recognizing the Superintendent in an instant.

"You see wha you got me dealing with!?"

"I have no idea what you mean, Superintendent Taylor? As far as I know, we had no direct hand in the rising criminal activity that's afflicting this area of Bim—"

"Don't play nuh word games with me, Pilgrim. We not in nuh blasted courtroom! You know what dem calling Layer's Gap now? *The Gulf!*"

Darryl drew breath.

"Yes, it's a very crude name given by its inhabitants." Pilgrim said; his tone calm and condescending.

"Got people thinking that up dey is some sorta warzone!" There was a clatter from the other side. Superintendent Taylor had slapped some files off his desk in frustration.

"A warzone is accurate … but you needn't worry about those rumors. We have them under control, much like the ongoing conflict in Layer's Gap."

"I does gotta worry. This whole situation threatening the integrity of the Royal Bimshire Police Force." The declaration made Darryl swallow hard. This was more serious than he imagined. Taylor continued, "And only because of that Over de Wall gang… How did they get so much artillery? It's like we getting invade by the States or something!"

"That is a consequence you should attribute to your present Commissioner." There was a leer behind Pilgrim's words that pervaded the door between him and Darryl. "All of this could've easily been avoided if he was just obedient like his predecessors. But all newcomers must have something to prove."

There was a hush, and Darryl pictured Taylor rubbing his brow from the stress.

"An ordinary upstart who believes he can change things, because of some position in a meaningless hierarchy. *The Fool.*" The scraping of furniture and the slow pound of footsteps, Taylor had risen from his seat. "...Seems like you also forgot the true authority in this country, Superintendent."

Taylor bit his tongue and then a hollow plop signaled his defeat. "No. I ain forget."

"Good." Pilgrim replied. "So stop fretting and play your role. Everything will pan out in due time."

Darryl's mind raced with conspiracies that threatened the government and the country. This couldn't be real. Could it? He was so entranced that he didn't notice the snow–white cat slinking around his ankles. Its purr piercing the muted air. *When did that get here?*

"It appears we have an eavesdropper in our midst." Pilgrim announced after a mewling came from the other side of the wall. Then the door popped open, revealing the two inside; Taylor horrified that someone overheard his conversation, and Pilgrim stroking a large black cat that blended in perfectly with those court robes on its owner's arm. "You know what they say about curiosity and cats."

Fear stabbed Darryl's chest and throat as he met Pilgrim's gaze; a pure malevolence that was mirrored by the onyx feline on his arm.

Run. Before the idea could form, a burn pierced his back, making his body limp and heavy.

Darryl didn't understand what just happened. How, in a matter of minutes, his life would end in this lonely corridor. Unheard by anyone save the two staring down at him.

"You... You didn't have to kill him. He was a good lad... I

could've—" Taylor sputtered.

"Incompetence: that is the biggest affliction of this country. And this department, too, from the looks of it." Pilgrim rose; the two felines striding at his heel before climbing his shoulders—their rightful place. "If you are worried about the mess, it will be cleaned momentarily. As for the demonstration, we will leave that up to the Commissioner. Good day."

The office door swung to a close while Taylor remained in silence. Darryl Carter's body probably still lay on the floor, or perhaps it was dealt with as Pilgrim promised. Spick-and-span as usual. If only Superintendent Taylor's problems could do the same.

"What did I get myself into, nuh?"

It had been months since the premier attack on Layer's Gap, and things were starkly different from when Justin first arrived. The chattel houses that lined the streets were reduced to smoldering blocks of rubble, along with the fruit trees that once provided shade for those who liked to lime on the block. The roads where vendors gathered to sell their food on weekends were now riddled with holes and craters. The fields, like the trees, were blackened and scorched, making it impractical as farming ground or cricket pitch. The community park, which was once the pride of the district, was no more. The makeshift swings, seesaws, and slides reduced into crude forms of burning rubber, wood and stone, unavailable to the dozens of kids who utilized it.

Not that there was anyone around.

Perhaps the biggest change in Layer's Gap was the emptiness. Villagers no longer roamed about on their errands, or stayed outside catching up on the times. Instead, the few who survived the daily onslaughts from Over de Wall were huddled down the safest spots they could find. Places such as abandoned outhouses and barn cellars which only housed livestock before. Or in the basements of the few houses intact, like Rasheda's, where several persons (some she hardly knew herself) had taken refuge. Glenn's home also survived, though it was more of a base than a sanctuary. In the midst of this warzone, which was now aptly called *"The Gulf,"* a legend was born. Where a handful of children had successfully protected the village from total devastation.

Gulfsyde brought salvation to Layer's gap when nobody else could. Notorious among friend and foe alike, they survived grueling assaults against all odds. Those that made it back to Wesley Broome recalled the horrors of their failed raids. Of *Cutup* who slashed their comrades with a palm leaf, *Juckup* who stabbed them with forks and ice picks, and *Pickout* who wore a bottle case on his back and could knock you out from meters away.

"I kinda like dah name—*Pickout*—that sound hard, boy!" Justin lay atop Glenn's roof. It was a familiar post, since he often spent time surveying the distance for approaching enemies.

Glenn sighed. He was on the step organizing various screwdrivers, scissors, drill bits, nails—tools for his destructive trade. "Don't tell me you catching on that stuff, too?"

"Man, yeah, I like um. You should too, *Juckup*." Justin teased.

"Geez…" The titles had spread so far that villagers had taken to using them instead of their real names. As people gathered around the house, they greeted the boys by their aliases, to which Glenn replied in a bother. "You don't have to call me that, yuh know."

But they didn't listen. They felt proud of their heroes, like fables to tell their kids at night. This is what troubled Glenn the most. He didn't see himself as someone deserving of their adulation. Not with the things he had done.

"Oh, there yuh are, Cutup!" Justin cheered as Dario strolled through the doorway with his legendary palm leaf. Of course, the dreadlocked boy knew nothing about the rumors, so he just looked up at Justin with a puzzled frown and continued onward to the living room.

"Anyway, lemme hear what wunna find." Glenn said as soon as everyone had congregated inside. During the past months the village had assembled any able-bodied men to take up arms and defend themselves. It was a cumbersome task, considering that no one had the firepower or skills to be of much use. Still, the volunteers had important functions such as making sure civilians were secure during a strike and gathering information on the village's state. For a rag-tag bunch they were moderately efficient, though that was due to the strength of the famed three.

"Well, we still holding up." One volunteer muttered; it was clear that he held his doubts. Another added with more fervor though,

"Yeah. We good as long as we got you all here!" Evidently, he believed in his heroes, but Justin didn't believe. He knew his own abilities, and there was no way he, Glenn, or Dario could be everywhere at once.

"I haven't seen Over de Wall lately either." Dario said eerily; after his house was destroyed the dreadlocked boy made it his business to track any enemy near the village. What he did when he found them, only his palm leaf knew.

"And de other gangs that 'bout the place might be getting restless." Justin added from above. Glenn didn't think the drifter knew anything about gang culture in Bimshire, but it was a worthy guess.

"Safe. So, fuh right now we got a little downtime, right?" The comment quelled the villagers' anxiety, which was Glenn's intent. "Then we should mek sure that the farms and water stores still in good shape, along with the safe houses."

The volunteers assented with enthusiasm and filed outside to complete said tasks. But just as the last person disappeared behind the door, Glenn's expression turned grim. "This isn't good, guys."

"How yuh mean?" Justin asked from the ceiling.

"We can't hold out much longer. Resources running low ever since Over de Wall attacking the farms and water stores when dem strike. And we getting too many casualties, I gine gotta stop them from volunteering soon…."

"Well, it should only be a matter of time before—"

"—Help arrives?" Glenn interrupted Dario's suggestion, even though it was one of the rare times which he spoke. "—Been months since this start and not one cop come to investigate. Not only dem but garbage men, post men, not even a stray car ain pass through here. It's like the rest of the country forget we exist."

There was silence after this point. It wasn't like the three had anyone else to contact right away, but they were certain that the other villagers had family in other parishes they longed to reach. And though many have tried to leave the district, *something* prevented them from doing so. An enchantment of some kind which blocked passage beyond a certain point. Justin's best guess was obeah magic, but he knew nothing about the art outside the products it made.

"So wha's de plan, then?" Justin chimed from above.

"We gine gotta stop waiting for them to come and launch an offensive. You know, turn de tables." Glenn's proposal was well-received as bangs and howls came from the rooftop.

"That's what I talking 'bout, man!"

"But we don't know where their base is." Dario brought another hush to the room. Justin, in particular, could be heard sucking his teeth through the ceiling.

"Yeah, you right, and last time we try extracting one fuh information…" Glenn recalled that last hooligan's resolve. "We just gotta try harder next time we catch one."

But it was harder to corner the enemy in one-on-one combat. After several defeats, the gang switched to a much safer and effective form of assault, where they utilized far-ranged bombs rather than riding into the village. Thus, instead of red blurring through the streets, the residents of Layer's Gap only saw the incandescent bursts of missile fire. Justin often neutralized them with his uncanny throwing skill and accuracy, but some rockets still got through. After all, he couldn't be everywhere at once.

Examining the billows where his missed shots landed, Justin saw a familiar sight. A small flicker of orange cutting across the span of grey above, with a roar like it tore the fabric of the sky itself.

"Shite. Men, like we ain gotta wait long for another attack!"

Justin skipped across the houses, for his plan would require close proximity.

He yanked a particular bottle from his case; one that countered the rockets before. His eyes fixed on the approaching line of flame, Justin calculated the direction, interfering wind-speeds and distance for a few fleeting seconds before hurtling the bottle like a grenade.

Boom!

A fiery bubble signaled success, while the explosions behind his back showed failure. "Frig…"

"Don't mind that!" Glenn said, darting away from the fresh plumes of smoke. "Take care of things here! I gine and see if I can find where they're firing from."

"Huh?" And as Justin saw Dario's dreadlocks scuttling past him, he knew that the location of Over de Wall was priority right now. "Aight. But I only got eight bottles on me, hear!?"

Glenn nodded, taking careful note of that piece of information. Eight bottles meant that he could only stop eight more missiles before running out—leaving Layer's Gap open to complete oblivion. For sure the stakes had risen now. And to make things worse he had to work under a time limit. Where were they attacking from? He looked to the north-east where the first missile was fired. Dario must've known more, since he parted ways upon reaching the community park's remains.

From wha I remember, a projectile of that caliber can only travel from a maximum distance of two hundred meters, if there ain no crosswinds to offset it…

Glenn calculated while he ran, but two explosions behind his ear broke his concentration. *Shit. I'm losing time!*

He was near the outskirts now; greeted by breadfruit and tamarind trees before reaching the main road. Glenn suspected foul play had kept outsiders away from Layer's Gap, but he never had time to mull it over before. Sprinting past the main road, he couldn't ignore the few cars driving by, oblivious to the carnage mere meters away.

The third explosion went off. Then the fourth.

Gotta take into account the angle them come from, too. More vertical than lateral, which means they must have fired from a high vantage point. Glenn inspected the sky once more, barely catching the residual streaks from the first missile launch. They indeed came in a straight diagonal line from the highest place Glenn could think of. A steep incline which led to an abandoned mechanic shop on the opposite side of the village, where the few people who could afford cars would get their vehicles fixed, along with other motorized items and tools. However, after business went sour the owner left the shop to ruin, and now it was reduced to a pseudo bird's nest where the enemy could plan their strikes from a secure location.

Bang-Bang!

Gunshots verified his suspicions, as Glenn forfeited the element of surprise when he entered the grounds. *Found ya...*

But this wasn't a problem for the youngster, who skirted the stray bullets easily with quick sidesteps and slides. About seven shots were fired by the time he vaulted a run-down pickup truck, ducked under a rusty old tractor engine, hurdled over several metalwork stations, and pounced on the defenseless hooligans cowering in the main workshop.

"Rassgate!" One cried in terror as he saw the bloodthirsty expression on Glenn's face. It was too late to run far less shoot at this agile threat, and within moments they were smote with a pair of pliers which Glenn yanked out of nowhere.

"Gah!" Another one yelped; Glenn taking care not to deal any lethal blows but focusing on the joints within their limbs, rendering each one immobile. It was swift yet deeply agonizing as the pliers struck the most sensitive nerves, and for added measure, Glenn disarmed the explosive garters around their waists.

"Good. Now we won't have you doing something troublesome like dying too soon." his voice cold yet mocking. It was an air of cruelty few had the displeasure of witnessing. "For starters, you gine tell me about your headquarters."

"Frig you, yuh cunny! We ain telling you *shite!*" One bellowed, despite the damp spot in his pants. But Glenn remained clear, speaking in the plainest English so that there was no misunderstanding.

"Oh, I beg to differ. Seeing we at a place where my objective will be easier." They followed his eyes as he scoured the workshop, lingering purposely on the sharpest, most jagged objects in the shed. "So, I know for a fact that I gine mek at least one of you talk before I done. It's only a matter of how much pain wunna could take. And I am a patient man…"

Although Over de Wall was armed like soldiers, most of them lacked the training and discipline that the true military would have. And even if they feigned bravery upon Glenn's approach, they couldn't help but tremble. After all they were only hooligans, accustomed to petty crimes, vandalism and lawlessness. To hell with Mix Drink or the cause. One gangster saw his death five minutes in, a long torment that would endure until his last heartbeat. He didn't sign up for that, and soon he sputtered,

"W–W–Wait! I gine talk! I gine talk…"

"Talk then." Glenn said expectantly.

And the captive talked, oh yes, he did. He told Glenn not only of the Wesley Broome Primary headquarters, but of Over de Wall's inner workings as well. Like the mysterious source of all their weaponry, the number of gang members in total, and the person in complete command of them all.

"…Mix Drink, huh?" Glenn considered the name; its ridiculousness wasn't unlike his own alias. *So he's the general of this militia.*

"Yeah, and he bodyguard, Kamilah—*frig!* She gine kill we if she find out we inform 'pon de men!"

"Speak fuh yuhself, I ain tell he nuttin!"

"Feel she gine care? She gine kill all uh we just for talkin!"

A frantic quarrel was sparked at the sound of her name; apparently, they found Kamilah more fearsome than the commander himself. Glenn noted it, and then silenced the argument by stabbing the table with his pliers. "I suppose it would be a bigger punishment to let you go rather than deal with you myself."

They quivered at the thought, much to Glenn's pleasure. Leaving them maimed and terrified, Glenn disarmed the RPGs and other explosives before exiting. There was silence in the distance too; no eruptions or smoke, which meant that Dario had also found the other location.

"Good… we clear fuh now." It was with this small victory

that Glenn slid down to the village. However, he was well aware of the feat ahead and the task that needed to be done.

"Wesley Broome Primary, nuh? So, de men tek control of a whole school? That fairly sick, though." Justin remarked from the rooftop. After securing the village, Glenn had gathered Dario and Justin and told them everything the enemy confessed.

"It was taken over sometime back, and them got so much control that the police can't make them move out." Glenn added.

"So... What do you plan to do now?" Dario asked. Unfortunately, his palm leaf spoke more than the enemies he encountered.

"It obvious, big man! We gine storm dah school and mashup de place!" Justin grew tired of sniping stray missiles instead of human skulls, so the notion excited him most of all.

"That's the plan... but these men number in the hundreds. And even though we tek care of a good set over the months, it's still safe to say that they far outnumber us. I mean, it's only three uh we..."

"Four." A voice came from around the corner, and as everyone turned, they saw Rasheda glowering at them with her deep, brown eyes. "I'm coming with you."

"Coming where?"

"Stop playing de fool, Glenn. You just say that you need extra help if wunna gine to their headquarters. And I can fight so—"

"Absolutely not." Glenn said.

"Last time I check I ain need your permission to do anything."

"It's not safe." Glenn continued.

"For the others, yeah, but you know well enough that I could fight, Glenn. You just—" But then she was cut short by sudden, sharp squalls grazing all around her body. They only lasted for an instant, in which Glenn vanished from before her and appeared behind with a scissors at her torso. When Rasheda drew breath, she saw her clothes unravel: the sleeve, collar, the hem of her blouse, the tabs around her pants, all split apart with miniscule precision. A chill slithered down her neck as she regarded the sharpened edge of Glenn's scissors.

"We up against scores of men, armed to the teeth with Lord knows how much weaponry. How you think you gine fare under a shower of bullets, if you can't even see me?" Rasheda glared at Glenn, swallowing her words but not the point he was trying to make. She would not back down.

Silence pervaded through the room as the two locked eyes for several minutes. Then Justin broke it,

"Hey, come on now, man, that ain fair." Glenn didn't look around at him, neither did Rasheda. "Testing out her ability against *your* skills?"

"I'm just showing her what it gine be like out there." Glenn replied with an odd bit of defensiveness.

"More than dah, if you ask me." Justin snorted, and Glenn glowered at him in a way that said,

But no one asked you.

Dario in the midst of the discussion just watched Rasheda, enthralled by the girl's determination and courage. He'd never seen her as someone who needed protection, mostly because she was always the first to bolster him in times of need. Then in a phrase that, despite its meekness, served to grasp everyone's attention, he said, "I agree."

"Huh?" Rasheda was the first to utter.

"I… I think that if Rasheda wants to fight, she should fight." Dario stammered under Glenn's concentrated gaze. "I mean, it's her home too…."

"Aight then!" Justin jumped up, seeing eye to eye with the soft-spoken Rasta for once. "Look—"

He then flung a couple stones in Rasheda's direction. There was less than a second to react, and she was exposed.

Clang!

In one motion a cutlass swatted down the three rocks, Rasheda's arm outstretched but her eyes still affixed to Glenn's stern face. Dario was agape, while Justin whistled in amusement.

"Look like you underestimate yuh girl."

Glenn frowned at her resilient stance, but then noted that Rasheda's weapon arm was still quivering from the sudden movement. It was manifest that she exerted her muscles with the maneuver. "You right. I don't need to give you permission, 'cause you gine come anyway."

"Once you know, poppit." Rasheda replied, and Glenn gave a wry grin.

"Good. Now all uh that settle, what's de plan?" Justin skipped to ground level expecting a briefing, and he wasn't disappointed when his boots touched the earth.

Glenn went into express detail about his plan to infiltrate the primary-school fortress. Knowing the general layout and numbers that resided in the base, he was able to formulate the plot, albeit under a short space of time—only three hours had passed since he interrogated those thugs. There were still many variables; Glenn hadn't seen the fortress himself so the layout wasn't accurate, and of course there was the inexhaustible munitions provided by a peculiar wooden doll.

"We gine got to move soon though, so you all should prepare accordingly." Glenn concluded.

"Why so soon?" Dario inquired, not wanting to leave the village so suddenly. Baby steps on the road to freedom.

"I didn't kill those guys, so it should only be a matter of time before they return to their base. Four to five hours if them crawl fast enough…"

"So why de hell you let them—" Justin began, but Dario waved it off and made his way back to the main roads of the neighborhood—presumably to the ruins of his home.

"We'll meet back here in an hour!" Glenn called after him. From the barely discernible nod Dario gave it was assumed that he noted it. Rasheda walked away without another word.

"Cha boy, you in de hot seat tonight." Justin remarked. He was the only one who didn't have a place to go or things to prepare.

"Well, I ain mind that. Better me in there than she in a coffin." Glenn then turned to Justin and asked, almost like he was waiting until they both were alone. "Question: why are you involved in this? I mean, not that I don't appreciate yuh help, but this ain your village."

"I dunno. I just doing it to cure my boredom, I guess." His answer made Glenn snort.

"That sound like something you'd do, fuh truth."

"Heh. You mek it sound like you know me, yuh bastard."

"But I feel I do know you, *Pel-Ting*." The title made Justin stop in his tracks, his demeanor switching from blithe laziness to taut hostility. "I'm right, nuh? You are a member of the Pel-Ting Family of the East."

"So, what if I am?" Justin's dialect vanished as he turned to face Glenn. His hands sliding towards his back, to the bottle case fastened behind it.

"Nah, don't get me wrong. I ain got nothing against de Pel-Tings. Just that case you wearing along with your marksmanship… Well, it was more than a lucky guess, I mean." Glenn grinned, but Justin didn't ease his air in the least.

"I don't roll wid them anymore."

"That does never matter once you got de same skills." Glenn was right. The Pel-Tings had so many enemies that even the skills alone sparked apprehension and fear. "Though it's good we mek an ally out of you, since you could make the mission a lil' easier."

"How you mean?" And at this Glenn disappeared into the yard, but before Justin could properly follow, he was blinded by a rich violet light. Once that glow had cleared, Glenn emerged with two bottle cases in hand, with the seals plastered around them as they emitted a faint purple flush.

"You use these, right?" Glenn eventually asked. "*Bomber Bottles*? That's how you were countering the missiles before they hit the village, nuh?"

"Yeah…" *How did he know?* Was one question that filled Justin's mind. The other was: How did he manage to get a hold of more ammunition? As far as Justin knew there weren't any Practitioners around to purchase them from. Yet these queries evaporated the moment Glenn thrust both cases in Justin's direction.

"Here. You'll have more use for these than me."

"Thanks." Justin grunted while inspecting the bottles; there were twenty-four of them in all— more than enough to topple an entire fortress.

"Nuh problem. They were catching dust out here anyway. I shoulda give you them sooner, to be honest. But I had to mek sure I could trust you." Glenn beamed and then went back into the house. It was only when the side door was open that Justin snapped back to his senses.

"How you manage to get these?"

"Oh. Well, I know some people." Glenn said vaguely, and left Justin outside to ponder what exactly he meant by the phrase.

…

An hour later, Glenn heard a rapping on his front door. Thinking it was Justin again he bellowed, "Don't worry about where I get de things from, I tell yuh—Oh…" But upon opening it, he saw none other than Rasheda's slender frame standing at his doorstep. Her face was fixed with the same indignant pout she left with earlier. "Er. Hey. You're early."

Glenn blurted out, forgetting that this was the assigned meeting time. Rasheda sucked her teeth and strode to the verandah lattice, arms folded as she leaned against the wooden rail.

"Guess you're still mad at me, nuh?"

"Wha you think?"

"Sorry but I had to…" Glenn began, but the girl just grunted and looked the other way. "Why you gotta be so hardears all de time? I know you Aunty was teaching you from young, but this is the real thing. Nobody gine be holding your hand and easing up offa you. A battle don't work so."

"You come here two years ago, so stop acting like you know 'bout me." Rasheda's words were cold, but true. He knew nothing about her, and she knew nothing about him. Glenn sighed.

"I know that you've never taken a life before—that's enough." Rasheda fell silent. "And in a battle like this killing gine be a requisite."

In this moment it became clear just what Glenn was protecting her from: that profound burden that one must bear during battle. Rasheda witnessed so much death since the raids began. Familiar faces snatched away in an instant, without a second thought; by Over de Wall, by Glenn and the others. She never considered the weight of the act. Rasheda just knew that she wanted to do something because she had the ability, and in her mind doing nothing was an even bigger crime. Curse Glenn for complicating the issue with notions of morality.

"Look. Your Aunty trained you to defend yourself from harm, and to pass down the rituals which she learned through generations, but I feel she never intended you to go out just for the sake of killing."

"But you acting like wunna gine just to murder them."

"That's exactly what we gine do. Over de Wall got to get taken out for this village to survive. They won't back down otherwise; it's become too personal for them." He was exhausted, and hadn't taken any time to rest or gather his energy. "Please try to understand."

"I do, you idiot…" He heard her say, before feeling fingers running through the mat of his hair.

"Huh? What are you—"

"You know you ain a bad looking fella…" Rasheda cooed strangely. "If only you would tidy up this bush from yuh head. You wouldn't look so prickle."

Glenn then felt a great tug at the root of his hair, which made him squelch in discomfort. "Ow—wait, you plaiting my hair, fuh truth? We ain got time"

"Just hold still—I gine be done in ten minutes. Besides, you ain gine up there without looking your best, right?" Rasheda yanked again, Glenn could tell she was enjoying this a bit too much, though some part of him wondered how he would look with his hair plaited. He found himself lying comfortably against her leg as she squatted behind him. Aside from the stinging on his skull Glenn was rather cozy there, taking in the murky evening and the cool breeze which had the slight aroma of rotten eggs. Sulphur. Even if he tried to forget the upcoming ordeal, that scent proved to be a potent reminder.

"Back in the day, I remember fantasizing about times like this. You know, when I could just be lazy and cool out. Without a care in the world."

"You sound like an old man."

"Well, I had to grow up early." Glenn laughed. "Ain had

a choice in the matter either. It was between that and getting lick down while you slept. And the only body I could blame was myself for not being on point. That's what it was like back home. Keep alert or die skylarking."

There was another tug; each strand of hair pulling on his skin. Glenn was aware of it, as much as he was aware of Rasheda's beating heart, or the slow, silent breaths she took.

"You don't know how good you got it. Like, this is strange to you. The explosions and guns and killing and shit. Like I can tell this is strange, even now. But to me this is just the same old, same old. It's almost nostalgic…." Glenn mused.

"Where you come from?" Rasheda asked after a moment's pause.

"I gine tell you one day. When we got time and we ain gotta worry about nothing. Well, when we gotta worry about less."

Somewhere in the village a child was crying. Whether it was hungry, agitated or scared, they didn't know. But the sound jolted them, reminded them of all they stood to lose.

"I had to become a person I wasn't very proud of. Anything else and that was that. For a time, I thought that was all I could be. It was all I knew. Now I've made peace with him, because he saved my tail more than I could count. He's necessary. But you different, you see? You don't have to become that person. You don't have to be stained by it, like I have."

"So, what you feel I should do?" Rasheda asked, her words came out in a whisper. Quiet but strong. "You think it better to keep hiding in a cellar and pray for the worst to be over? To stand by when you risking everything? No. I won't do it, Glenn."

Her fingers sprung away from his head.

"There. All done." Rasheda announced, and when Glenn rubbed his skull he felt the thick rows of hair going all the way towards his neck. "I couldn't do them so thin in such a short space uh time" *Since you got nuff hair and all.*

"Wow. It feels tidy." Glenn continued to caress, not accustomed to the wind brushing his scalp so directly.

"Yuh welcome. Now you finally look decent for once." She had already risen from the step, forcing Glenn to scramble from the sudden movement.

"Listen, Rasheda, I—"

Clasping her hands against the sides of his face, she gazed into him with rich auburn, her lips growing closer, her breath tickling his nostrils. Rasheda remained there for many minutes, but to Glenn it seemed longer. What was it in her eyes that bothered him so? Resentment? Fear? Pity?

"I know." Rasheda said.

Naïve. You are too damn naïve, Rasheda. Glenn wanted to say, but he simply held onto her. If she couldn't be stopped by his words, then he would have to protect her with his skills. Just another thing to consider on this sortie tonight. *No pressure.*

"Ahem. Aight, lovebirds, we really ain got all night." Justin's intrusion sent the two reeling away from each other.

"H-How long you was there for?" Rasheda barked at the giggling ruffian, but then she felt mortified when she saw Dario's dreadlocked form standing beside him with an uncomfortable fidget.

"From 'bout de time you start plaiting he hair. Um look tight, though." Justin said with a matter-of-fact tone.

"Thanks, man. I like um, too." Glenn replied with great amusement, which only served to piss off Rasheda more.

"Why you acting so carefree for?!"

"What? I notice them when you start 'pon my hair too, but you wouldn't listen when I say—"

Rasheda sucked her teeth.

"…Anyway, guys, wunna ready?" He asked with a hop, judging from their appearances he could tell that they were. They didn't look any different physically; aside from Justin who now had two bottle cases strapped end-on-end across his back, giving him the bearing of some sort of tortoise. Dario brought his trusty palm leaf and nothing else. Glenn figured he took the hour to gather the resolve to leave the village and embark on this mission. And lastly, Rasheda, who stood beside him with a cutlass tucked neatly in a leather scabbard across her hip. Glenn had to get accustomed to her being armed and dangerous, but he couldn't deny the steely determination etched in her face.

"Yeah, we ready." Her tone was firm and unwavering.

"So, this is it, nuh? No big speech, no farewell party, no

parade, not even a last drink?" Justin groaned. He didn't know why; after all there was never such pomp when he set off to sorties in the past, and he shouldn't have come to expect any now. Nevertheless, Glenn responded with a grave,

"Nope."

And then took out a bandana and wrapped it across his face so that it covered his lips and nose like some sort of bandit. It was the first time he'd done it since the Over de Wall attacks began, but the gesture did signify one thing: he was going to fight seriously. With callous eyes peaking over the scarf and a matching intensity in his voice, Glenn gave his first command of the evening.

"Let's go."

Kamilah organized the parts on the counter. Every barrel, clip, spring, screw and bullet, assorted and aligned to the weapon they belonged. Meticulous work, but it calmed her, to the point of doing it every day. Kamilah regarded each gun with care, not as tools but as souvenirs of past experiences. Like the M 37 shotgun she just assembled. A powerful weapon, retrieved during a morning raid in St. Lucy; its wielder was a desperate man but Kamilah respected that and the weapon. A similar story for the Berettas, AK–47, and every other firearm she possessed. Spoils of war. Earned not given, unlike the creations of that accursed doll. And one particular gun, the gift from *him…*

Kamilah was lost in thought, polishing and reassembling her guns with automatic efficiency. "Done." The first ritual was complete. Now for the second part. After she placed the weapons in holsters, Kamilah retrieved some sugar daddies from her case. She squinted at the sweet taste. She had never grown to like it, and part of her wished she didn't accept it back then.

"Hey… You like sugar daddies, kid? They're my favorite. Come.

They'll help you feel better."

Kamilah should've refused, but she couldn't speak at the time. The whizzing bullets and blaring gunfire had silenced her. The second ritual was complete, and as Kamilah exited her chambers—an empty classroom with only one table—she believed the day would get better. After all, luck was all she needed in this world. Then…

"Idiots!" Her voice boomed throughout the old school hall and made everyone inside flinch—even Mix Drink. Kamilah marched towards the three who returned. They were mutilated, thoroughly so, as if by the sadistic blade of some unknown demon. No, not unknown. Kamilah was aware of the culprit. She had heard the name for months now. And though these three tried to warn of Gulfsyde's approach, they still couldn't be forgiven. They divulged information about the base, and they dared to return in such a battered state. A lesion on the pride of Over de Wall. By all rights, Kamilah should've killed them on the spot, but they weren't worth the bullets.

"Lemme get this straight." Mix Drink paced across the stage, his air was that of a general addressing his troops: authoritative and intimidating. He wasn't nearly as livid as his petite lieutenant. "You said you got ambushed by one of dem villagers—"

"Y-Yes, boss. It was Juckup! He more than de rumors say—de man fast as hell!" One of the three bellowed, but Kamilah interrupted,

"I thought Cutup was the fast one. You know—the one with the palm leaf?"

"Man, no! Juckup fast too, and he tek we out with a pair of pliers!" Despite the validity of these claims (and the wounds to prove them), their audience was skeptical. Still the hooligans pressed on, "Is de truth I tell yuh!"

"Puh!" Kamilah scoffed and threw up her hands in disbelief. Mere stories, that's all they were. And yet Gulfsyde formed the main bulwark of Layer's Gap's defense, and a particular thorn in Over de Wall's side. "I barely feel wunna making this up."

"W-We're not! Fuh real!" They protested.

"I can't take de word of lowlifes who just happen to join when we on top." And at this the crowd stirred.

As a result of Over de Wall's dominance, other rival gangs began to fizzle out because of fear or direct takeover, and the strays who were left behind decided to join Over de Wall. Their reasons varied; many wanted to be a part of the gang that would eventually overthrow the country, some just wanted money, others wanted random havoc, and there were even the few who pined for a place to belong. All the same Mix Drink welcomed everyone, as long as his force grew for the cause and the people. But this created multiple rifts in the gang, as the oldest members began to resent the newcomers, and vice versa. It was this can of worms which Kamilah had just opened, and it was only when Mix Drink took his seat and waved his hand that order returned to the school hall.

"None of that matter right now. Once you in Over de Wall, that's de end of that. We ain 'bout nuh segregation in this gang. That is a Babylon ting!" Mix Drink took a drag from a cigarette blunt, and the little wooden doll on his lap did the same. "But you know what wunna do wasn't right."

"We know, boss, and we sorr—" *Bang!* Silenced by a bullet to the head, the entire hall followed suit as the two remaining thugs awaited their punishment.

"I know wunna sorry but, you know the law of Over de Wall, right?" And with a reluctant tongue one of them answered,

"…Never inform 'pon de men."

"Once you know." Mix Drink pulled the trigger twice more. The only living beings on stage were him, Kamilah and the doll, while his audience was too thunderstruck to voice any objection.

"I could've done that, you know." Kamilah said, breaking the hush a couple moments later. "You didn't have to—"

"Yeah, I did. I can't be leading de men without getting my hands dirty. That is a Babylon act, too." He took another drag from his blunt and then got to his feet. "As wunna now hear de enemy on dem way. Men coming into we yard to challenge we 'cause dem feel we soft. And you done know we can't let that happen."

There were murmurs around the hall as their fears were coming to fruition. Like frightened ants stirring in their nest, they waited for the demons of Layer's Gap to arrive. But this wasn't his army. This wasn't the force he had groomed and pruned after so many years. Too scared. Too frantic. Far from what he needed to conquer Bimshire, let alone change it. Mix Drink locked eyes with the closest of the lot; he was whimpering like a red-clad pup about to be put asleep. Then Mix Drink roared,

"We gine show dem Over de Wall ain nuttin to fuck with!" And with that a great violet light filled the stage, and once dissipated, all forms of artillery had littered it. Picking up an M 16 and spreading his arms in invitation to his subordinates, Mix Drink called, "Now who ready to washoff these men?!"

That did it.

A tumult surged through the hall, as nearly one hundred scarlet-clad hooligans howled in reply. His minions. His pawns. Every one of them cascading Mix Drink with glorious praise. He bathed in their applause, drank it, and grew stronger. It won't be long now until this power reached the whole of Bimshire. And as long as he had Jah's blessing, he would be able to break this corrupt system once and for all. This system that keeps everyone under its heel poor and powerless. Like roaches. Well, Mix Drink knew who the real roaches were, and soon he'll be squashing them himself. He paid his dues in blood for that purpose.

It was in the midst of this celebration and gathering of arms that something exploded in the distance. The blast rattled the windows and flooded the air with dust.

"They're here." Kamilah declared as more blasts roared from beyond. The rest of the hall began to panic but she expected as much. Kamilah always does. "Good, that saves me the trouble of hunting them down myself."

"Need anything?" Mix Drink asked, gesturing towards the dwindling stack of guns. But she shook her head in reply.

"I'm good with what I have. If I can't finish them with that, then I have no business guarding you."

"Don't say that, yuh. I would still keep you around." Mix Drink took one last draught before extinguishing the cigarette under his heel. Like the roaches to come.

"Idiot, you too kind." Kamilah smiled honestly, before venturing off the stage and through the door.

...

Ten minutes earlier, Gulfsyde arrived at Wesley Broome Primary. To Glenn's surprise the directions were accurate, as the school was located near another community—Old Orleans— which had been made vacant since Over de Wall's takeover. There was a great military presence around the outskirts, though the forces didn't dare venture past a certain point. Whether it was out of fear or something else, he didn't know, but it was a solid indicator all the same.

"Yeah, guys, you all know what the plan is, right?" Glenn asked; the others nodded in reply.

"I gine pick out de scouts, while you all sneak in and wipe out the rest." Justin said. It was no different from his roles in the past.

"Yeah, but try to maintain the element of surprise for as long as you can. It don't look like they catch on to we yet." Glenn regarded the defenses around the fortress, where various lookouts were posted at high vantage points. At the ends of balconies, on the top of staircases, rooftops and the like, plus each lookout was armed with semi-automatic rifles and anti-aircraft guns; the kind with armor-piercing rounds that could take down a helicopter if it wished.

"Cool. I gine try not to keep much noise." Justin said, without an earnest tinge in his voice.

"I serious, B. I ain gotta remind you of the stakes—"

"Yeah, yeah, I get you." And with that, Justin leapt to the nearest building block. Dario followed suit, grasping his palm leaf and murmuring,

"I guess I'm off."

Leaving only Glenn and Rasheda on the boundary of the battlefield. He still wasn't sure if she was ready, regardless of how tightly she clenched her sword. "There's still time to turn back, yuh know."

"You mekking sport now?" Rasheda barked.

"No, I just mean… Never mind. Just be careful."

Rasheda sucked her teeth before setting off to the school. Glenn smirked and followed close behind.

It was Justin who made first contact with the enemy, spotting one on an adjacent rooftop after his third hop. He was still unseen, bounding across the buildings with the lightness of a cat (in spite of his stocky size), and although it was against his nature to act so stealthily, he managed the charge with utmost competence. "Shit. I really wanna blow this guy up." Justin grunted, pulling out a stone which he gathered on the run up there, and hurled it at the unsuspecting head.

Brax! The blow had a satisfying crunch, as the target went limp and slid to the ground without a gripe. Not wanting to break his pace, Justin strode along the wall, spotting the next target thirty meters away. Another stone sailed from his grip and in a second the lookout slumped out of sight. This trend continued for seven building blocks, three hundred meters, and nine Over de Wall scouts. The plan was moving efficiently as Glenn and Rasheda sprinted below, watching the red-clad cadavers land in their path.

All right, Justin, yuh gine good. Glenn remarked on the Pel-Ting's skill which he'd come to rely on so very often. But they weren't in the clear yet. Ground forces were still lurking about in pairs or threes, and even if they had no clue they were under attack, the patrols still proved to be a threat. Upon seeing two such foes, Glenn dashed forward, *Now if I could just take out these men quickly before...*

Thunk-Thunk-Thunk.

He plunged a closed pair of scissors into their vital points, killing them instantly. It was like this whenever he encountered an enemy, and in spite of Rasheda sticking at his heels, Glenn would suddenly outrun her and take care of the opponents before she could even assume her stance.

It's like he trying to get rid of them before I get de chance, she thought. It was clear that Glenn didn't intend for her to fight unless absolutely necessary, and he sought to prolong that time for as long as possible.

At least a dozen foes fell on their side, and they still had no clue how much Dario encountered. For the dreadlocked boy didn't follow the same route they did, instead checking inside of rooms for large groups, and dispatching them at once before they could counterattack. After Justin knocked out one scout, he saw a glimpse of that blurring green palm leaf as it dipped into an old form room. Ten red silhouettes were spotted through the windows, but when Dario entered the shapes twisted and wobbled until they fell out of view.

Shite, boy, that man ain easy. It was the first time Justin had seen him fight with his own eyes, but he had to admire the Rasta's ability. He continued his task for five more buildings, catching a few foes off guard as they limed by what used to be a canteen. That was when he heard it: the gunshot that pierced the air. "Shit… We get catch?!"

His first assumption, and the following two shots only solidified this thought. "Crap!" Justin wondered who got caught. Glenn or Dario wouldn't let an enemy stand long enough to fire a shot, so that only left, "Rasheda. Damn, that girl shoulda stand home."

These notions skipped along his mind much like he skipped along the rooftops. The plan had changed. This was not a matter of infiltration anymore but destruction, which was all the better for Justin. Reaching into his bottle case and seeing a tempting group of red shirts…

BOOM!

"Frig!" Glenn hissed, after hearing the explosion and spotting a slim billow of smoke from behind an old water tower. "I tell de man to maintain de element of surprise!" But it was too late, and soon Justin's mistake bore sour fruit as more red shirts hustled out to see what caused the commotion.

Thunk-Thunk-Thunk-Thunk-Thunk.

Five enemies fell in quick succession after meeting Glenn's scissors, and as more drew their weapons, he too followed suit with the old fork and ice pick. Rasheda was enthralled by how brilliant Glenn fought, easily weaving through ten bodies with mortal precision. But he couldn't handle everyone by himself; soon she would have to take part in the assault.

Like clockwork, a group of red shirts noticed Rasheda, turning their barrels towards her with trigger-happy fingers. But Rasheda didn't flinch—not even for a second. In moments, she drew her cutlass and darted to the nearest foe. Within two steps her sword slapped his chest making him reel in pain, then three steps to the left lead to the second foe, whom she chopped right under the arm to disable him, then another five steps back and her blade met the stomach of another opponent, and finally her sword clapped the throats of two more. The blows were precise, devastating, and had they been from any other warrior they would've proved fatal. But this was not for any lack of skill. Glenn paused his assault to glance at Rasheda's skirmish.

She aiming at the most critical spots and striking them wid concise motions.

There were no wasted movements; that was not the way she was trained. To be ever flowing, continuous, that was the key principle behind Aunty Yvette's teachings. Rasheda practiced them well, counterattacking with fluidity whenever a mistake was made. And Glenn noticed something else,

Her blows aren't mortal.

Where a limb should've been lost, or a torso slashed open, there was only a shallow lash from the dull, reverse edge of the blade.

Just so she wouldn't kill, she's fighting like this?

It was such a stirring notion that Glenn ignored the red shirt with a glock at his head.

"What de hell you staring at? You wanna dead?" Rasheda barked, as she slapped the cutlass across the enemy's back.

Snapping out of his daze, Glenn said, "You could chop them heads clean if you was using the right side."

Rasheda sucked her teeth and managed the rest of the fray until Glenn rejoined her. In the distance they heard more frantic gunfire, and if they took a stray glance on the rooftops, they would see Justin scuttling above—throwing various projectiles from his hand.

BANG!

A flash of orange and a wave of smoke signaled his ammunition's potency. "At least Justin mekking good use of them bottles."

The Pel-Ting was the most effective in quelling the enemy. Pinpointing the most crowded areas, like the hall entrances where numerous red shirts gushed out upon hearing those explosions. Like throwing dynamite in a barrel of fish, Justin hurled a Bomber Bottle at each door way, charring dozens upon dozens of Over de Wall soldiers. Eventually the door became too hazardous so they tried the windows upstairs, taking sniping positions and attempting to catch the troublesome Pel-Ting. But that was their mistake, as one skillfully placed bottle cleared everyone from along the corridors.

"It ain mek no sense trying to fight back. Wunna barely trapped inside there like rats…." He flung three more bottles, with a combined force strong enough to wipe out the entire structure, killing everyone inside.

Glenn sensed victory. Everything was more or less going according to plan. But when he watched the bottles sail through the air, he heard a shot and saw the sky ignite in a dazzling display of flames.

…*The hell?* Glenn thought. Justin was appalled as he watched the flaring bubble above.

"That was only one shot, but all three of my bottles get tek down." The smog dissipated, revealing a hazy figure who ambled through the smog. It was a girl, no older than twelve from the looks of it, with a small frame, boyish features and dead eyes. She came armed for slaughter with a belt of bullets across her waist, various straps holstering every kind of gun she could carry, along with the twin .45 caliber semiautomatic pistols in her hands.

"Who de hell is you?" A spray of bullets answered Justin's question.

"Kamilah…" Glenn said. He and Rasheda had entered the courtyard from below, putting them closest to the girl. "Guess you the bodyguard them fellas mentioned."

Kamilah ignored Glenn, loaded her clips, and opened fire. After felling dozens of foes that night, Glenn had learned to read arm posture and muscle movement, in order to preempt shots with a strike of his own. That wasn't the case here. Glenn didn't know if this was a matter of speed or skill, but whenever he countered, Kamilah had already drawn another gun and taken aim.

Bang! Bang!

Glenn dodged the shots, swaying his arm in an attempt to knock the weapon from her grip. Yet when he managed that small feat, Kamilah had a replacement firearm cocked and ready to fire.

Crap! It's like she has four arms! Glenn thought, as he somersaulted away for some room. When his feet touched the ground, Rasheda darted across his side at the opponent. Glenn's stomach wrenched. *"No!"*

Rasheda rushed forth despite his call, confident and reckless. However, before Glenn could intervene, she had sidestepped Kamilah's line of vision, swinging the blade at her exposed neck. This time the sharpened edge wasn't reversed; Rasheda intended to cleave that head right off.

Chink! The blade was caught against the pistol's barrel and calmly parried away, so that it left Rasheda off-balanced. As she stumbled past, Kamilah had drawn another pistol (a compact Mini-Kahr) and aimed directly at Rasheda's eye.

Crap! Rasheda gazed at the barrel, thinking it would be her last image. But before Kamilah could pull the trigger, a palm leaf lashed her across the arm and forced her away.

"Are you okay?" Dario whispered with his back to Rasheda. No one noticed his presence. Not Rasheda. Not Glenn, who was still rooted in place several meters away. Kamilah was the most surprised, though her face showed nothing as she inspected the scratch.

"Fast … and carries a palm leaf. You must be Cutup." She regarded the name like a grocery item, but Dario didn't respond. Kamilah then looked to the rooftop, "And the one with great accuracy and a bottle case on his back … Pickout."

Justin grunted while reaching for another Bomber Bottle.

"That mean is you who captured those idiots … Juckup." She looked at Glenn with the most unimpressed expression.

"I guess you hear 'bout we already."

"Yeah. Wunna belong in friggin comic books, though no one mentioned a girl with a cutlass." Kamilah didn't bat an eye at Rasheda. "Either you new or you just not worth mentioning."

"The name's Headgone, yuh brat. And I gine live up to my name the next time I get close to you!"

"Don't worry. You won't." Kamilah brushed off the threat. "In fact, none of you leaving here alive. I gine end your legend here and now."

Her words were simple but the intent behind them was felt throughout the courtyard. Even Rasheda, who was so confident a few breaths earlier, now found her chest pounding as Kamilah's hands eased towards her holsters. Just what would happen when she drew her weapons? Would they be able to handle it? Would Glenn?"

She glanced over at the boy and saw his poise undisturbed by Kamilah's declaration. In fact, he seemed so indifferent that Rasheda thought he must not had heard it at all. With arms in his pockets, Glenn's repose had almost dispelled the tension. Almost.

It gine be okay. We can handle this. Rasheda reaffirmed. Only seconds had passed, but it seemed much longer before a flying bottle interrupted the standoff.

KA-BOOM!

The blaze showered embers and smoke over the group. Kamilah may've shot the bottle before it detonated, but it was still enough to cloud her vision—a tactic which Gulfsyde sought to exploit. Dario was the first to strike; his palm leaf parting the mist while he swept towards her head on. Glenn followed suit, dashing at her back with the intent of planting an ice pick into her spine. The girl, though formidable, would still be defenseless against a pincer attack. However, when Dario reached Kamilah, she had drawn an M37 shotgun and aimed straight for him, while Glenn was greeted by an assault rifle.

"Frig!"

Speed aside, it was miraculous how Dario dodged such a wide burst, or that Glenn evaded that shower of bullets. But even more astounding was Kamilah's combat ability. By now Rasheda had rejoined the fray, slashing wildly at any available body part, and Justin—who'd run out of bottles—was reduced to throwing stones from afar. Yet against this onslaught, Kamilah had fended off the renowned Gulfsyde effortlessly. It was the skill of gods.

"RAH!" Rasheda roared, as she brought down her sword

so hard that it would've parted the shotgun in two. She wasn't fighting with the same prudence as before. She'd gotten desperate, her resolve cracking in the face of this fearsome opponent.

It was as Glenn feared. Justin had met strong foes before, and Dario had the composure to handle any situation. But Rasheda was different. This was her virgin sortie, and encountering an enemy of this level served only to push her over the edge. *I gotta end this quick before she gets herself killed!*

Glenn had the ability, but there was a bigger threat lurking ahead. Even if he stayed, the other three would have to deal with Mix Drink and that wooden doll. There was no way to shield Rasheda from both....

"I'll stay." The whisper brought Glenn out of his musings, and as he looked up, he saw Dario glare with knowing eyes. "You guys go on ahead. The leader is still around somewhere and we don't have time to waste."

"Don't be stupid!" Justin called after landing next to him. "I know you hard but you can't handle she by youself—"

"Okay." Glenn agreed, but the others couldn't understand why. If all four of them struggled against Kamilah, how could one man do any better? Especially if it wasn't Glenn? Perhaps the one most startled by the decision was Rasheda, who still had the meek form of Dario fresh in her mind.

"You can't, yuh poppit!"

"I'll be fine." Dario's lips curled beneath the dreadlocks. "You guys just worry about finding the leader before he escapes."

"Not happening." Kamilah said after firing her AK-47. "You ain gine lay your filthy hands on Alvin." Her words were just as hostile as her rounds.

If she wasn't trying to slaughter them before, there was an extra effort to do so now. With two assault rifles in hand, Kamilah rained gunfire on the group. That is, until the palm leaf intervened.

"Go now. I'll handle things here." Dario repeated; his tone now harsh and demanding—a complete contrast from his modest tongue.

"Not fuh hell!" Kamilah screeched, but her movements were halted completely.

"Go." Dario's eyes were fixed solely on the startled girl before him. "And Glenn… Please finish this."

This simple request was enough to quell Glenn's doubts. Dario hadn't forgotten the greater goal here; the reason they took on this dangerous mission in the first place—to stop Over de Wall from terrorizing their village. Glenn appreciated that moment of clarity.

"Okay. I will." Glenn nodded, and then jetted towards the nearest exit with Justin and Rasheda in tow. Rasheda still protested this change of events.

"We just can't leave he dey. He gine get kill if we—"

"I trust him." Glenn answered simply. "I trust that he will keep her at bay. The same way he trusts we'll beat this Mix Drink guy." Rasheda was quiet after that. Glenn believed in Dario's ability and Dario believed in theirs. However, none would understand the full extent of the Rasta's strength more than Kamilah, who was still pinned under the palm leaf's pressure.

Shit… I can't move… She struggled under its weight, which shouldn't be so heavy for an ordinary palm leaf. It was only when she looked past Dario's dreadlocks to see the bloodlust lurking within his eyes, that Kamilah recognized the demon before her. Abandoning her guns, she skipped a couple meters away to reexamine her opponent waiting patiently ahead.

"… I was sure that your friends deserted you, but it look like you got some skill."

"No. I'm the one who is surprised. I didn't expect to find a Shotta Boss here." Dario watched Kamilah for a reaction, but she was forever stoic so he continued, "All this time I thought they were just fairy tales, but to meet one in person, let alone in battle."

Shotta Bosses, according to Dario's master, were warriors who had ungodly skill with firearms of any kind. A rarity in the Caribbean since guns were uncommon and expensive, yet there were people out there so versed with guns in combat that one of them was worth at least twenty men. Dario's master had only met one in his lifetime; a man who embodied this myth and proved that these abilities weren't just misguided exaggeration.

"Tell me, do you also know Odane?" This time Kamilah's

face turned pallid.

"No, never heard of him." Kamilah shuddered as his words disturbed her spirit.

Dario pressed on, "But I do remember Odane was accompanied by a little girl once. Could it be…"

At this point his gaze lingered on Kamilah, who was visibly shaken by the topic. In her mind, she saw a disheveled man standing over her with an arm outstretched. She heard his comforting words as the void of abandonment swelled within.

"I gotta be leaving now to tek care of something. But don't worry, my boy here promised to look after you."

A nine-year-old Kamilah bawled. She was alone again. Vulnerable. Scared.

Odane grinned, the scar across his nose contracting with his cheeks. His eyes glassy as he watched Kamilah cry. She'd come so far since he found her. Laughing, crying, speaking… Now was not the time to leave her, but only violence lay in his path. He couldn't expose her to that, anything but that. Regretfully, Odane introduced her to the boy standing nearby. *"Kamilah, this is Alvin—"*

"I tell yuh my name's Mix Drink now, yuh Johnny!" The boy growled. He was untidy, but not in the same way as Odane. His red shirt tail slopped over his belt. His pants were sagging and oversized, and he looked disgruntled. Kamilah didn't like him, and her eyes spilled fresh tears as he approached. Odane knew how to calm her but his pockets were empty. Then Alvin said, *"Anyway, girl, tek these."*

Kamilah hesitated as she saw the sugar daddies. They were good omens. She knew that ever since Odane saved her. Gave her life again. And now that this stranger offered these omens to her, Kamilah doubted if they were still safe. Perhaps this boy had tainted her luck. Perhaps he was the reason Odane was leaving.

"It's okay—he cool." Odane assured. Kamilah didn't believe him.

"Damn right, I cool. I gine rule this island someday, yuh know. Watch and see." Alvin puffed out his chest and pounded it like a gorilla, which made Kamilah smirk. *"I serious. I gine tek over*

de Government and give justice to de people of this country."

Back then, Kamilah didn't understand what he was saying, but she recognized the effect Mix Drink had on Odane. He was inspired by Alvin the hooligan. That was enough. Kamilah accepted his good omen, though the void inside grew larger still. An emptiness that had long since been buried and had only resurfaced at the mention of his name.

"Oh… I didn't mean to upset you." Dario said, cold but sincere.

"I pegged you as the silent type earlier, but you mouth like it don't got nuh owner."

"I speak when I get curious." And that was when Kamilah saw it. Piercing through the bushel of dreadlocks, within those deep brown eyes and amidst that bloodlust, was the most sinister sensation she ever felt. Akin to a starving lion, Dario's expression only spoke of his voracious interest. "And in this case, I'm intrigued about the strength…"

Dario's slender frame vanished and appeared from an angle that totally escaped Kamilah's vision. *Fwish!* The palm leaf brushed her fingertips as she skipped away.

"…of a Shotta Boss."

"Y-You! I thought you stayed to protect your friends. But you just wanted them to leave, nuh?"

"Something like that." Dario uttered while a wave of green slithered forth. Kamilah fired a couple shots to divert its path, but for the most part she was struggling to keep up. "I didn't want anyone to interrupt our duel."

"Duel? You think Over de Wall so noble?" She asked, as a grenade trickled down her pants and skipped along the stone tiles towards Dario. The resulting blast, though flashy, didn't cause any damage as he slid away unscathed—resuming the conversation.

"Shotta Bosses are supposed to be noble. I hoped that you weren't a thug like the rest."

"You very wrong." Kamilah drew more firearms: an MP5 submachine gun and M4 Carbine, purging entire clips on the slithering silhouette. But as the kickback from her weapons shook her frame, and the scorching shells from spent bullets brushed her face, Kamilah felt a sense of dread. *He's fast… Not like before when he was just agile. No. This is a different kind of speed. My eyes can barely keep up, much less my shots.*

It was true Dario's speed had increased, or rather he was never moving at his true pace until now. His dreadlocks and palm fluttering as he zipped by, giving the illusion that he dodged the bullets; but that would be impossible … wouldn't it? Kamilah wanted to believe so, as her finger nearly broke from squeezing the trigger. Then she heard the empty click… *Frig! Out of ammo!*

Dario pounced from twenty meters away, his speed uncanny and most certainly real. Kamilah, realizing that she could never reload in time, tossed aside her rifles and drew the only remaining firearms she had.

Pap-Pap! The two shots stopped Dario right in his tracks as he remarked on the newly drawn weapons.

"Oh? This is interesting. You are going to rely on revolvers—a gun that requires so much effort to use, much less reload. Either you must be blindly confident or completely desperate." Kamilah responded with bullets, firing three at the drifting serpent. However, the most peculiar thing happened when they touched the adjacent walls. Upon piercing the concrete, a black luminescence suffused throughout the structure until it crumbled into powder. "Ah. I see."

Kamilah shared his reaction as she goggled at her firearm. These were Odane's guns: .357 Magnums, Blackhawk models, each with a cylinder of polished sable and barrels that were always cleaned. The only pair she didn't earn. Parting gifts. As a result, she didn't disrespect them by using them in combat. But the situation was desperate, and it was just her luck that the revolvers were so destructive. Good omens.

Cocking back the hammer Kamilah prepared her next shot, but Dario wouldn't allow it—slashing at the girl with his palm. His movements were more aggressive now. Panicked. *I cannot let her fire again.* His swipes reflected his thoughts as they focused on Kamilah's arms. Knowing that revolvers were tedious to use, Dario exploited this by aiming at her wrists every time she reached for the hammer or the barrel. In essence, the Shotta

Boss's divine skills were sealed.

Damn! He's strong … He's way too strong! She squinted through the tempest tormenting her body. She never thought the one left behind would be this formidable; that behind that modest demeanor a malicious demon prowled, waiting for a chance to feast on those worthy. Kamilah didn't want the honor. *I can't let him get to Alvin. I got to stop him here and now, otherwise…*

The very thought of failure struck her harder than any palm leaf could. It was her duty to protect Mix Drink. Kamilah couldn't betray that promise. She couldn't betray Odane's request…

"Please take care of him."

With these words in her mind, Kamilah knew what had to be done. Time was running out as the serpent slithered to her back, eager to deal the finishing blow…

Pap!

The shot resonated throughout the courtyard, followed by an explosion in one of the abandoned classrooms nearby. Dario regarded the structure as it collapsed.

"If I hadn't reacted in time that could've been me…." He then turned towards his opponent who was still backing him. "I still can't believe it, though. Shooting through your shoulder to catch me off guard…"

Dario was enthralled by the stub where her arm should've been. Kamilah didn't wince, but her body betrayed the immense pain with spasms. Dario continued, "To think that you'd go so far, and at such a young age, too."

"…I'm sixteen, yuh idiot…." Kamilah finally spoke, her words stable and clear. "And a demon like you wouldn't understand what it means to protect someone. You, who does fight solely for pleasure and twisted curiosity…"

The statement stung Dario. How could his fascinations be twisted? If anything, violence was engaging, even beautiful. "So, you would throw away an arm for the sake of one man?"

Kamilah didn't respond; that reckless determination was answer enough. Dario understood this resolve well. After all, he'd seen it in his comrades who were off to confront Mix Drink. He had no right to be playing around here, but he was having so much fun…

"I see. Well, I think it's time we put an end to this."

Kamilah gripped her revolver, only one of those enchanted bullets remained in the barrel so this shot would be her last. With heavy breaths, blurring vision and a harsh ache by her mangled shoulder, she watched as the serpent resumed its slither. It would be impossible to dodge. She knew that. There was only one option left if she wanted to defeat Cutup. In an instant, Dario's slender frame distorted into a long winding movement, wriggling his way towards her. She could sense him, but just barely. *He gine flank me from the left…* It was the best course of action since Kamilah had no limb to defend herself.

The serpent writhed closer and closer until the palm appeared right by her side. This was the end. *Bang!* The eruption covered them both, and when the haze cleared it was Kamilah that lay on the ground. Looking down at his fallen foe, Dario said, "You were planning to shoot through your torso in order to kill me, weren't you?"

"…Finish me off."

"I won't."

"The battle is over. Finish me off!" Kamilah cried. How mortal she seemed in this moment. Cutup was her god now.

"That's why I won't finish you. The duel is over and the victor is clear."

"What the hell? Why the fuck won't you kill me?" Her voice cracked under the pain, and shivers came with every word.

"—Because you have your whole life ahead of you. There's no reason for you to die here."

"Ha…" Kamilah gave a wry laugh. "You really are a cruel one, nuh? Telling me to live on in *this* state? You demon…"

"I am sorry you feel that way." Dario couldn't understand this line of thought, but then he couldn't understand her reasons for fighting either. Bemused by these notions, he made his way out of the courtyard, following the trail towards Mix Drink. With any luck, the others would've finished him off already. Or better yet some larger threat would've surfaced, one larger than the fabled Shotta Boss.

The fallen Kamilah gazed at his back; her body searing from

the finishing blow and the loss of her left arm. The wound hemorrhaged as the world turned black. Death approached. And yet instead of meeting it with open arms, Kamilah shunned it. She clung to life.

Sprinting along the deserted compound, Glenn and crew listened for the battle they abandoned. Upon every step an explosion would roar behind them, and with each boom or bang a thought rang in each of their heads:

Maybe we shouldn't have left him behind.

They could only imagine the mayhem going on behind their backs, and Rasheda for one was visibly disturbed by the notion. Without turning to face her, Glenn said, "Don't worry. He'll be fine."

"How you know?"

"Just listen…" And the commotion became even more boisterous. "If he was dead already, there wouldn't have all that racket gine on."

"He right, yuh." Justin affirmed, as he hopped along the above railings. "De man mussy holding he own back there. Don't mind he look soft." Looking behind with secret disappointment, Justin wished he could've stayed in that courtyard. On the one hand, there was that little bitch with the guns, but on the other, there was that chance to see Dario's palm leaf in its full violent glory.

The group was even more disturbed by the hush that lay ahead. Why weren't they being attacked? They hadn't eliminated Over de Wall; some should've escaped to warn Mix Drink, but there wasn't a red shirt in sight. Only abandoned faculty buildings observed them as they passed, their gaze ominous.

"This real odd, though." Justin finally voiced what was on everyone's mind.

"You mean that we ain meet nuhbody yet? Yeah… I feel it strange, too." Glenn reached for two pairs of scissors, while keeping a vigilant eye on the rooftops. "Them mussy feel Kamilah took care of us already."

"Nah, something wrong here." Bullets whistled past him as Justin spoke. The enemy was there, albeit concealed behind louvers with mounted rifles and armor-piercing rounds. "Frig!"

Wasting no time, Justin leapt onto a ledge and flicked several stones in the direction of the shots. He must've landed on target because the gunfire ceased from that particular window, while more sporadic shots erupted from the other areas.

"Justin, you clear a path and we gine bust through!" Glenn shouted from below, but the Pel-ting was already on it. As the frontal assault, Justin vaulted across the walls in an effort to take out the unseen foes. Meanwhile Glenn, with his back towards Rasheda, reached for her hand and said, "Stay close."

Rasheda didn't object, clenching his hand along with her sword and following Glenn's fearless sprint. The mayhem above was nothing like Kamilah's encounter, but for some reason she was twice as terrified. They were approaching the final battle, where the leader of Over de Wall awaited. What kind of person was he? To have someone like Kamilah under his command, Mix Drink had to be just as terrifying.

"We're here." Glenn announced.

Rasheda saw a lofty, grey concrete cube standing before her. It resembled the hall Justin destroyed minutes before, aside from the colorful mural painted on the front wall. A collage of animals, of plants, of fantastical creatures. Rasheda found beauty in the wall, though her admiration ceased when Glenn halted.

Inspecting the glass door, he contemplated using the row of windows above for an alternate entrance, but when the door suddenly blew inward (almost like it was inviting him to come), Glenn decided to oblige. The first things they noticed were the cascading steps leading to the top of the room. Chair-desks lining each stair, the chamber resembled the lecture theatres that Rasheda used at school. In this case, the room helped craft the imaginations of children as they took part in drama class, danced in plays and told stories. Glenn saw that they loved this place; just like outside various paintings were pinned up on the walls—simple masterpieces crafted by the puerile. However, this room, much like the entire school, was no longer enjoyed by its curious students. Defiled by new inhabitants, its walls brushed in their own colors with red smearing every surface in tribute to Over de Wall. And reveling in the profanity was their leader, Mix Drink, who sat at the summit with crossed arms and relaxed cast.

"…I see de roaches manage to sneak into my yard."

"I guess you the leader, then, Mix Drink? Funny how you look exactly like I imagined." It was true as Mix Drink—clad in his black mesh vest, dark-brown cargo pants and aviator sunglasses—resembled the sort of revolutionary that one would see in newspapers. His face was the very definition of scruffy, with tuffs of hair curling across his cheek and chin. Despite his shoddy appearance there was an odd charm about him, the trait that enabled him to command scores.

"So, if wunna manage to get this far, that mean Kamilah…"

"No. We managed to get past her thanks to our friend. They probably still fighting now." Glenn didn't know why he told the enemy this. Maybe it was his mournful tone, or the way Mix Drink dropped the half-burned cigarette from his fingers. "…Though I don't know for how much longer."

"Safe. Well, I could say de same here. 'Cause none uh wunna roaches can step in my house and live. That is a joke!" Mix Drink raised his hand; a signal which was supposed to summon the remaining red shirts to open fire. But after a moment's silence, Mix Drink realized his forces were no longer available and found a stone hurtling towards him instead.

Poof!

The stone burst into dust before it reached an inch of his person. Mix Drink howled, "Joke, I tell yuh!"

"What the rass…" Justin was incredulous. He thought Kamilah had returned but there was no gunshot.

Mix Drink lit another cigarette. "All uh wunna so is de roaches that did opposing we for so long, nuh?"

Justin hopped from the window. It made no sense staying up there since he'd lost the preemptive edge. But he wondered, what exactly thwarted his attack?

"Payment." The answer came in a high-pitched whine, and upon closer scrutiny, Justin saw that Mix Drink was glancing down at the chair beside him.

"It's hungry, isn't it?" Glenn asked, much to everyone's surprise, but Mix Drink ignored him completely. "You should probably hurry up and feed it."

"He ain hungry. He just want another smoke. De lickerish thing… I give he a whole bag ten minutes ago."

"Payment!" The voice piped again. This time Mix Drink wrestled a bag of herbs from his pocket and rested it on the chair, with rings of smoke billowing from the seat moments later.

"How long did you have one of those?" Glenn continued, his voice severe and cautious. It was a different kind of apprehension the others had never seen from him before. "A *Baku,* I mean…"

"…Baku?" Justin repeated it like an infant's first words. But as the tenth smoke ring rose, a little wooden doll hopped through it and landed on the desk.

"What the hell is that?!" Rasheda flinched, as the Baku took another drag from his long cigar. It was a fanciful scene. There was no way a doll should be walking around let alone smoking a blunt, but that is exactly what it was doing. And for someone who beheld many atrocities over the past couple months; this was just like a distorted fairytale.

"Do you have any idea how dangerous that item of yours is?" Glenn asked.

Rasheda's eyes darted from Glenn to the wooden doll, still trying to understand why he knew about this creature. Mix Drink tended to the Baku, whose cigar whittled down to a stub within a minute. "You is a bare pest, yuh lil—"

"I always wondered how Over de Wall got so notorious in such a short time. Conquering other rival gangs and even running out the military. It was because of *that,* wasn't it?" Glenn persisted.

Clinking echoed through the theatre, as Justin rested the bottle case on the ground and propped his foot on it like a stool. "…How you mean?"

"A Baku is a rare item which grants its owner anything he

wants but for something else in return." Glenn explained, while the doll lounged in front of Mix Drink. "I feel in this case you mussy ask for all the artillery you could use, and the payment got to be…" Glenn focused on the long, rolled-up blunt in its hands. "That's why the normal authorities can't touch you, because you got more weaponry than the entire Bimshire Defense Force."

"Heh… Yuh right. I got more guns than any uh them Babylon roaches. And I gine use them to burn down de government just now!" Mix Drink harangued like he was before his red-clad congregation, but Gulfsyde wasn't impressed.

"When I hear 'bout the wooden doll it all mek sense. Of course, it had to be a Baku…."

Rasheda shifted as Glenn spoke. This conversation was too much for her to fathom. She didn't know of obeah magic, about the powers that defied reality and everything that made sense. Glenn had witnessed the Baku's ability once. Not directly, thank goodness, but what he saw of the province ground to ruin under its wrath was enough to stamp fear into his mind. Looking at the creature, he was grateful that Mix Drink lacked the foresight to use it properly. Otherwise, Layer's Gap would've been long gone by now.

"Two years ago," Glenn continued, "a Baku had gone missing and I was sent to retrieve it. My search led me to Layer's Gap, but I ain see nuh signs so I decide to settle here."

Glenn paused, noticing Rasheda's eyes upon him. She was shocked. Scared. As she should be.

"I got comfortable. Things were simpler in Layer's Gap, and I grew to like the people, yuh see…. Then the attacks happened, and I could only think about revenge. *Blood for blood* and what not. I guess some habits die hard." Glenn huffed. "But now the Baku resurface, I know my original mission ain change."

It had never occurred to Rasheda that she barely knew Glenn from down the street. Where did he live before? Did he have a family? Friends? How did he get so good at fighting? …At killing? There was so much she didn't know and now was not the time to ask.

"The fact is, we ain come down here just to stop Over de

Wall. We come here to stop Mix Drink from using that Baku. And if we leave things as they are, then the whole island gine be in trouble. Not just Layer's Gap."

Despite the severity of Glenn's words, Justin wasn't worried. "Man, don't watch nuttin. Once I get to crack some heads, I good." Justin stretched, flicked up the bottle case with his boot, and regarded the Baku. "Besides, I might just cess one for myself."

"Trust me, B, you don't want that." Glenn adjusted his scarf. The stakes had changed; not only were they saving their community, but the entire country as well. The feat towered over Rasheda like the sun above. It seemed impossible, but when she glanced at the other two beside her, Rasheda knew that impossible was nothing foreign to them.

As they ambled toward the enemy, Rasheda forgot these were the same troublemakers that wandered about the neighborhood. Their resolve swept over her like a breeze, intoxicating her, and granting her the courage to hold her sword steadfast. Mix Drink felt it too, since he stopped tending to the Baku.

"Wait… Wunna still in my yard fuh real?"

Mix Drink sucked his teeth, by now either Glenn or Justin would've taken him out, but they didn't. Something filtered into their minds, advising them to take caution. There were just too many anomalies when it came to Bakus; too many possible scenarios and forms of attack, so that it wasn't simply fear that held them but uncertainty. Mix Drink stalked along the stage, visibly roused by his audience.

"You don't see it, nuh? The way they whoring out our country to the highest bidder. The way they hiding behind friendly faces while poor people sign way dem life to profit Babylon. Is all a system put in place to tempt, trick and steal from we. You don't see that shit?"

"And you think what you doing is any better?" Glenn asked. "Killing innocent people who not even involved in this?"

"Is wunna fault for living too carefree! You 'bout the place taking the crap that the government throwing at yuh. Paying you taxes, flaunting you big chain and brand-name clothes, living on champagne mouth and mauby pockets, ignoring the crimes that staring wunna in the face—all of you just as guilty!"

The Baku stretched on the desk chair, taking small drags from his blunt and swaying in an inebriated stupor. It didn't care for what happened in the room, but Glenn never took his eyes off it. His fingers clutching the screwdriver in his pocket, he felt an unsettling energy from the Baku which puffed little halos towards the roof. All they needed was one chance. And Glenn knew Justin thought the same, as the Pel-Ting was silent since the argument began.

"If wunna can't see, I does see, though…. And is time we poor people burn down everything and start fresh!" Insanity was in his words, his eyes, and his very breath. Alvin Hunte was serious, and with Jah's gift he would deliver this holy message unto Bimshire. He turned to the Baku and issued his first order, "You know what I want already."

The Baku looked up at its owner, annoyed by the sudden request. Nevertheless, it was bound by their contract, like a genie to whoever rubbed its lamp. So, with a great huff, the Baku breathed a fog towards the group. This gesture alone sent chills through their veins, but it is what happened next that caused alarm.

The aura of the room had changed as the mist permeated inside, its hue going from a dull grey to a radiant, yet ghastly purple. The Baku's eyes shared the same color with slits opening to form huge dots. Gulfsyde watched as the purple smog saturated the chamber, each particle combining and taking various shapes. Nuts, bolts, screws, springs, barrels, hammers, plates and all sorts of parts were conjured into thin air, instantaneously connecting into larger parts until it formed one massive machine. Much like the anti-tank placements mounted on the rooftops, but considerably larger and more menacing. When the mist had solidified a heavy clunk shook the room, signaling the arrival of another monstrosity.

"Oh rangate… That don't look good at all." Justin said in awe, while Rasheda was hushed by the very conjuring itself.

"Listen! You don't know what you dealing with. You can't sustain that thing. It gine give you what you want now, but one day it gine devour you and this island!" Glenn bellowed over the clamor, twirling the screwdriver within his fingers.

But Justin made the first move, hurling a stone at Mix Drink's skull. But it didn't have the expected effect, bouncing off like a sponge.

"I don't give one rasshole!" Mix Drink spat before taking the reins of the massive Gatling gun. The little doll at his side ceased to glow and returned to smoking its cigar; the violet mist quickly dissipating from the room. *I guess that's the end of our agreement fuh now. You lickerish thing, yuh.*

"What the hell just happened?" Justin asked, but his doubts disappeared as the twin multi-barreled shafts begun to spin.

"We gotta move!" Glenn's voice was drowned by a deafening whir, followed by the booming of heavy bullet fire. The three scattered across the theatre; Rasheda needing Glenn's assistance as she was still spellbound by what just happened. In seconds the ground where they stood was perforated, and fist-sized holes were spreading to the walls.

"Be gone, cockroach! Be gone!" Mix Drink howled, just barely above the crescendo of gunshots. He was the hand of Jah delivering wrath to his disobedient subjects. "Hardears, you wun hear? Own way you gine feel!"

Glenn and the others scrambled for cover, but it was no use. Nothing in that theatre could withstand anti-tank rounds. *Shit! We can't keep running around like this!* His legs burned with fatigue yet he showed no signs of slowing down. Rasheda struggled to keep up, gripping his wrists as clouds of dust exploded at her feet. *That thing don't run out of bullets?*

The machine spat carnage for two minutes at a rate of one hundred rounds per second. It was miraculous that they avoided the constant hail without serious injury, but Glenn thought Mix Drink should've reloaded by now.

The Baku... It's still helping. Glenn surmised. If the doll had the power to create the weapon, it should be manifest that it also had the power to keep it supplied with ammunition. *But if that is the case, we can't touch him.*

Justin didn't agree. Flipping around like a grasshopper, his eyes scoured the monstrous firearm for an opening. He wasn't the most patient, grabbing bits of debris whenever there was a missed shot, and hurtling it at Mix Drink whenever he got the chance. With deadly accuracy, even under these intense circumstances, the rocks spun toward their target. Some were powdered under the stream of gunfire, but the few that veered away from the deluge had forced Mix Drink to evade.

"Oh?!" The epiphany accompanied the ceasefire. *He dodged... Why did he dodge?*

Glenn noticed it too, as he caught his breath. *The Baku mussy stop giving him support!*

This was their chance. As Mix Drink yanked at the trigger, and empty clicks replaced the gunfire, he cursed and spat and kicked the machine.

"If we gine take he out, we gotta do it now!" With eager feet and restless screwdriver Glenn prepared to attack, but something halted his movement. More fearful than fearsome, a tight grip came across his arm, reminding Glenn that he was not alone. *Crap...I almost forgot about Rasheda.*

Rasheda was a shadow of her former self; no longer imbued by reckless courage as she quivered behind Glenn. Each tremble a bitter reminder that she shouldn't be on this battlefield in the first place.

This is crazy. I ain ready fuh nuttin like this. This is crazy!

Every instinct was driving her to run. Somewhere deeper inside, she wanted to curl into a ball and cry like a helpless babe. Glenn understood this fear. He experienced it as a child when he first witnessed obeah magic in combat. And now, as he faced the very embodiment of the Dark Arcs, Glenn struggled to keep his composure. But he knew the task at hand. His fingers enveloping hers like a blanket of valor, Glenn glanced back with dark brown eyes that said: *It's gonna be okay. Just stay close to me.*

And in that chaos Rasheda was reassured. Glenn was satisfied by the result, though his chance was slipping away.

He watched dolefully as Mix Drink struggled to control his weapon. So vulnerable and pathetic. Glenn wanted to introduce a screwdriver to his neck, put him out of his misery. However, Justin, uninhibited by notions of gallantry, hopped toward the enemy with two big rocks in hand. Slinging one after the other like the very same bullets he had avoided, he "picked out" Mix Drink's right shoulder and leg before landing in the group. Cursing and hobbling, Mix Drink scrambled around his contraption.

"Come, nuh, you stinking thing. Fire!" The Baku at his feet snapped from its stupor, coughing a puff of smoke in surprise. As the mist rose and brushed the metallic cylinders of the machine, it flashed purple, causing the barrels to expand and configure into something new—something deadly. With a raucous chortle Mix Drink turned to the Baku, "Heh, 'bout time! Gotta give yuh another bag when I done," then he placed a bloody palm at the reins of the weapon—activating the enhancement.

A high-pitched ring filled the hall, along with the clanking of inner workings and the shining of gathered particles. For a moment the machine captivated Justin, but instinct invaded his legs and propelled him out of the way before the sharp light had passed.

BOOM!

An eruption of dust and stone erased the decorated walls.

"What de rangate?!" Justin hollered as another ball of light flew his way, sweeping the area with more debris. Glenn shielded Rasheda, and said,

"Move! We gotta move. Now!"

Fear manacled her feet, but the urgency in Glenn's voice set Rasheda free. As they shuffled to the road side, Mix Drink craned the gun in their direction.

Damn! Glenn could've escaped, but he wasn't sure about Rasheda. They were defenseless as the barrel spun and the light grew…

Then a silhouette slithered across the rubble; gliding over the debris like a work of art, an illustration of lethal grace. Mix Drink sensed that deadly aura as he switched his focus on the serpent. Explosions detonated in Dario's wake, but the palm leaf still approached—hostile and intent.

"Rass!" Mix Drink spat.

White light blasted at the serpent, forcing it to zip to the right while two rocks came from the left—a gift from a somersaulting Justin. With this simultaneous assault, Mix Drink had his hands full and Glenn used the opportunity to get Rasheda to safety.

"Rasheda… We gine have to move again, okay? Can you manage?" Entranced by the events surrounding her, Rasheda could do no better than a nod. The theatre was no more, with three of its walls blown away along with everything else. Moonlight poured in from above. Fragments of ash, ember and shrapnel wafted against her skin. Nearby she saw what was once mahogany trees and crotons reduced to smoldering stumps and blazing bush. Such destruction. It was just like Layer's Gap… just like her home. "Rasheda!"

"Y-Yeah?"

"Come! We gotta move before the others get tired." Glenn was hurrying her away from the skirmish, trying to get her to safety. Why? Didn't he come here to stop the Baku? Why was he trying to get away? The answer came when she glanced over at the battle and happened to meet Dario's gaze; his hidden face in her direction, careful that she wasn't in the line of fire. They were protecting her. Rasheda was so terrified that she became more of a burden than an ally. And that fact distressed her.

"No." She released Glenn's wrist and fastened the cutlass in her other hand. "I come here to fight."

"Don't be stupid!" Glenn hissed; genuine alarm seasoned his voice. "You ain come here to get kill either!" Rasheda stood resolute; her eyes rekindling conviction. "Look, I know you trying to be brave but…"

Glenn sighed, and watched the screaming cannon and the two zipping around it. Resolve, courage and sheer insanity fueled their steps. But where Glenn saw struggle, Rasheda saw hope. "…Wunna still trying, though."

Dario came to a scraping halt before them. His breaths, faint but sporadic, were the only signs he showed of exhaustion. "This is troublesome." He said, with eyes facing the wooden doll. "What is that?"

"It's a Baku—long story." Glenn answered. "What happen wid Kamilah?"

"She's already taken care of." His methodical tone made their blood run cold, but Glenn was somewhat relieved.

"Cool. One less thing to worry about. I guess it's only this guy, then." They stared at their daunting foe with Justin landing gracefully at their side. Unlike Dario, Justin's coughs were violent and full of phlegm, but his body remained unscathed.

"If I had another bottle atall, dread..." Justin looked back at Glenn, who simply shrugged and shook his head.

"Ain got nuh more, so you gine have to do without."

Justin sucked his teeth, thawing the tension if only by a little. All that stood in their path to salvation was one man and his Baku. Just a little further...

"*You*..." Mix Drink uttered. Dario met his glare, dark eyes stabbing through a veil of dreadlocks. Noting the thrashed palm leaf in his grip, Mix Drink understood the significance of Cutup's presence. "If you're here, then Kamilah..."

The thought of his subordinate losing in battle was usurped only by the thought of losing her altogether. Visibly shaken by the notion, Mix Drink stood on the platform in silence. *Those roaches...* At his feet, the Baku dragged on the last tiny piece of his cigarette until...

"Payment!" The squeak stabbed the air like a haunting siren. "Payment! *Payment!*"

Mix Drink ignored it. He didn't care about its hunger or the consequences of its impatience. With Kamilah gone, this entire world could burn and him along with it. Yes. That was a better plan. Let the chaos boil over. Burn Bimshire like he wanted from ever since. And from the ashes he could start fresh. Start fresh with him on the throne...

Glenn recognized the signs with the certainty of an impending storm. "Guys..."

"Yeah; we know." Justin interrupted, and without a second thought he threw another stone; this time at the Baku and not at Mix Drink. The attack, meant more to annoy than injure, hit the doll with a dull thwack. Mission accomplished. The Baku turned its attention to Justin, while the serpent writhed around the other side with palm leaf poised for destruction.

"Get from 'round me, cockroach." Mix Drink pulled out a shotgun (which was conjured from the smoke around him) and took aim at the serpent. But it was too fast, he wouldn't be able to pull the trigger before it sunk its fangs at his body.

"PAYMENT!" The Baku bawled, and everyone within ten feet of the doll was flung away by the shockwave. Its screams paled against its aura, with purple mist spilling from its mouth, and its wooden frame growing by the second. They were running out of time.

"Shit!" Glenn swore, but he saw another opportunity in the dazed Mix Drink. If there was ever a time to kill the enemy, it was now. Rasheda was the first to attempt this task, rushing towards the fallen gang-leader with rekindled valor. Her sword howled along with her voice as she sought to deal the finishing blow, but Rasheda wouldn't make it in time. Mix Drink had drawn another firearm—a small pistol aimed at her chest. Rasheda drew breath as she saw his flicker of desperation, but she wouldn't stop the arch of her blade. If she had to die, then at least this madman would go down with her.

I'm sorry, Aunty...

Then the air changed. A sharp squall followed by a high buzz as something tore through. It wasn't the Baku, which became strangely silent on the stage. Whatever it was, it swept around Rasheda's body and pierced Mix Drink's heart, moments before her cutlass plunged into his neck.

There was no beauty in Alvin's death. His corpse mangled in the same violent fashion as his campaign. But that was the end of it. The battle was over. They'd finally go home. A tremor ran through Rasheda's body, causing her to drop her sword. *So, this was the weight of taking a life...*

"...You okay?" Glenn rushed to her side.

"Yeah... I... I'm good." Her arm trembled; specks of blood trickled down her skin.

"I guess this is it, then." Dario saddled up to the group, dusting off debris from his pants. "Where did that doll go?" They scoured the area, noting the decimation around the compound. There was no purple mist, no hellish screeches, no Baku. The notion of it vanishing into thin air was unacceptable so everyone raked through the rubble. Except for Justin, who kept a trained eye on Glenn.

I dunno. If it was nearby, we woulda know fuh sure." Glenn said, ignoring the Pel-Ting completely.

"So… it's over?" Rasheda asked. Her stomach quivered and her mind raced. Everything was happening so fast and frantic. But Glenn succored her with his grin, just as he always had.

"Yeah. It's over."

BANG!

The sound shattered any semblance of peace they had secured, surpassing Baku roar or cannon fire. Blood sprayed from Glenn's chest before he crumpled on the floor. It was an instant, stretched and prolonged by the pure horror of it all.

"Glenn…?" Rasheda screams broke through time as Dario and Justin looked over at their fallen comrade—Glenn's expression just as startled as theirs.

"Shit! Who is it?!" Justin combed the area until his eyes landed on the young gunslinger from before. Kamilah's maimed body rested on a tree stump; her one remaining hand still outstretched, her semi-automatic pistol still smoking. *"You!"*

Justin didn't even think, in one swift motion a rock was whipped at Kamilah who stood a good ninety meters away—well within his range. Dario would beat the projectile though, slithering towards Kamilah with more verve and speed than before. His aura frantic, outraged and deadly. However, before the stone or palm leaf could even reach her person, the girl did something unexpected.

Bang! Another gunshot, and another spray of red—this time from the side of Kamilah's skull.

"Glenn…? Glenn? Come on, stop playing around. Get up. Glenn…?" Rasheda shook his body violently, ignoring everyone and everything else.

"Wow… This is how it end… fuh truth?" Glenn had a wry smile, blood burbled from his lips.

"No. No. No. No. Don't close you eyes, yuh poppit! Glenn! *Glenn!*" Rasheda drummed his face so hard that an impression was left on his skin. Still Glenn didn't cringe, as he regarded Rasheda with fading eyes. His tongue grew heavy like the rest of his body. There was so much to say but his lips wouldn't move. Too tired… He was just so tired…

Justin brought his attention back to Glenn, guiding Rasheda out of the way so he can inspect the wound. "Shit…The bullet pierce he lung. I ain got nuttin on me to treat this sorta wound. And I ain much of a doctor neither." His words fell on deaf ears, as Rasheda had already swallowed the bitter outcome. Justin spat again, "Damn lil' bitch…"

Dario stood over Kamilah's corpse with an otherworldly repose. One can only wonder what machinations churned behind that dreadlocked-veiled gaze. Justin then felt a cold grasp over his hands; the final flickers of Glenn's life. For a moment their sights met, expressing everything that was on his mind: the Baku, the Pel-Tings, Rasheda…. A silent accent between the two before the final flame faded…

"Glenn? Glenn?!" Rasheda rattled him, warmth draining from his skin by the second. Justin wasn't the type to shed tears but his face was a portrait of frustration. And Dario was a statue above Kamilah's corpse.

It was too early for him to die. They all knew and yet…

Glenn was gone.

Amidst the wailing chorus, the horrors of the battlefield were monitored by an unknown audience. A man dressed in a tailored grey suit regarded the chaos with much approval.

"Well, it seems this operation was a success. Wouldn't you agree, Superintendent?"

A downtrodden man looked at what remained of Wesley Broome with a mixture of fear and disgust. "You…You animals… You people did all this just to prove a point?"

"Don't go blaming us for your mistakes. If you hadn't withdrawn your contract, we wouldn't have had to enact this demonstration in the first place." Pilgrim replied, while stroking one of the cats on his shoulders.

"…But to go to such lengths! Putting a whole community in the hands of lawless hooligans! You don't got nuh regard for human life?!" Taylor's brow glistened in the hot sun, his nostrils flaring as he quarreled. Still, Pilgrim didn't flinch.

"Yes, it is the people's right to be protected by their government. To rely on the nation's law enforcement in times of need. But in this situation the odds weren't in your favor, wasn't it, Superintendent? You were overpowered in terms of ammunition and force, and thus rendered fully incompetent in your duties. Isn't that right, *Superintendent*?" He mocked the title, which enraged Taylor even more.

"Don't you dare blame this on us! You despicable—"

"So noisy…" The sigh came from the third spectator; a man with long onyx hair that flowed down his delicate, bronze face. He was simply beautiful, almost feminine. However, his poise gave him the charm of a true Bajan youth. "Wunna men ain gotta keep so much noise, yuh know. This lil' guy is trying to sleep."

The other two stared at the wooden doll in his arms, resting soundly like a newborn child. How he managed to retrieve it from that violent scuffle, only he knew, but the creature was pacified with a cigarette in its mouth.

"My apologies, *Conductor*." Pilgrim bowed his head just enough to make the two felines on his shoulder shift in discomfort.

"Man, that's cool, Pilgrim. I tell you, it's Sulemann." He smiled, but Pilgrim hesitated at the gesture. "Anyway, Superintendent, I think you got a pretty good idea what these guys are capable of." At this, Taylor swallowed hard and goggled at the sleeping Baku. "If this is what happen when a bunch of hooligans get one, just picture if it was somebody who had more vision."

Thoughts of this prospect flooded in: terrorism, anarchy, the very fabric of Bimshire's society torn apart. Taylor considered the disorder before him and imagined it on a much grander scale—a possibility so unsettling that it made him squeeze the bridge of his nose. "Okay… Okay. Yes, you have our attention. The Commissioner will contact you about renewing the contract."

The words were bitter on his tongue, but the other two endorsed this statement with simpers and short nods.

"Glad to hear, B. Just sorry it took all of this to remind you again. After all, we wouldn't want Bimshire to get like Jamrock or Trinbago, now would we?"

Taylor looked at the young man again; the beam on Sulemann's face was enough to make his blood boil. Taylor couldn't hold his tongue any longer, even if it was at great risk to his life. "Someday you people will be brought to justice. I just hope I gine be alive to see when it happen..."

Sulemann's grin remained, but Pilgrim regarded the Superintendent with a malefic glare which was imitated by the two cats on his arm. Taylor didn't wait around for a reply, turning on his heel and entering the grey Nissan X-Trail parked several meters away. When he was out of earshot, Pilgrim whispered to one feline—the white one on his right,

"No, you can't kill him yet."

"I dunno. He look like a hardworking fella." It seemed like nothing could spoil Sulemann's mood as he cradled the slumbering Baku. "Oh, by the way!"

He called at the vehicle before it had driven off. "Don't forget the terms of this lil' guy's agreement. He's a greedy fella, so you gine need at least a couple thousand pounds to sustain he for de year."

The tinted window rolled down and Taylor peered over at the Baku. It was the same agreement that bound Mix Drink when the creature was in his possession. *Oh, how low we have fallen to harbor illegal drugs.* "Yes. I remember..."

And that was that. The Nissan swerved down the road, away from the turmoil behind it.

"Do you think those idiots could manage such an item?" Pilgrim asked with an air of contempt.

"They should. Don't think we should expect another Hurricane Janet anytime soon."

The two turned towards the school, which smoldered from the battle and was serenaded by Rasheda's screams. "It's unfortunate that so many potential assets were lost in this demonstration, though. We could've used the Shotta Boss and that boy with the ice pick..."

"They were sacrifices for the bigger goal." Sulemann replied. "Besides, I sure dem got some other people we could use."

To whom he referred Pilgrim could only guess, as the remnants of Gulfsyde stumbled around the battlefield while counting their losses. "True. Anyway, I think I should take my leave now. This atmosphere doesn't suit my palate."

"Fair enough, man. Catch you later."

"Goodbye, Conductor." Pilgrim turned with a bow and strode to the nearby bus stop with a piece of paper in his hands. His cats purred as he met the pole, but they wouldn't be there long as a white light devoured them until they vanished.

Looking onward at his handiwork, a certain memory poured into Sulemann's mind. It was a day much like this one, filled with lawlessness but on a lesser scale.

"Aye! What I tell wunna about marking up my van?!"

Sulemann scolded a small group of hooligans seated in the backseat of his minibus. All decked out in red, the crew consisted of a scruffy boy who wore a vest and scarf around his neck, a girl no more than nine with a scowl that would make any of her elders uncomfortable, and two other louts who contrasted in both size and attitude.

"Man, cool it. We just spreading de word about de crimes against de people!" The scruffy one protested; he was the leader of the group.

"Safe… by putting de name 'Over de Wall' on muh chairs?!" Sulemann asked with rising irritation.

"We is de army of de people! And one day we gine show de Government that dem can't mess wid us anymore!"

"I see." It was a brave declaration; one Sulemann didn't expect to hear from a child. *"So wha is de plan, then? Just mark up people property for attention?"*

"No, 'course not!" The boy snapped. If his skin wasn't so dark it would be flushed with red. *"We would do more if only we had more…"*

"More wha?"

"People. Power…"

"Sight. And what would you do if you had more power?" Sulemann's face teemed with interest as he gazed at the boy. But when he saw the resolve in his eyes, Sulemann knew that the next answer would be an honest one.

"I would burn dis whole country down." A hush filled the van.

Music still blared from the speakers, passengers still chatted away, and the engine still droned as the vehicle moved down the road. Yet there was an absence of sound, so that Sulemann's words were a whisper.

"*You serious 'bout that?*" The boy nodded. "*What's your name?*"

"*People does call me Mix Drink.*"

"*Weird name.*"

"*It's because I like to stir shit up.*"

"*Aight then, Mix Drink, I gine sort you out. Just stay till we done this route and I gine grant you your wish.*"

A promise that would change the course of history. And as Sulemann recalled the expression on their faces, and the result of those words, the smile peeled away from his lips.

Gulfsyde's return was far from triumphant. The battle had taken more than its fair share in exchange for their solace. Homes filled with memories were destroyed, lives of loved ones were extinguished, all of which could never be replaced. There were no smiles on the residents of Layer's Gap. Despondent and exhausted, they matched the grey skies above which showered cold drizzles upon them. However, these didn't feel like showers of blessing, as the villagers had no idea how to return to the normalcy they had before.

Gulfsyde had entered the realm of legends but they didn't feel like heroes. They lost too much. Standing over Glenn's grave, Rasheda, Justin and Dario paid their last respects. Wreaths—made with any flowers that weren't scorched along with other trinkets—were assembled before a crude stone tablet. It was all they could muster under the circumstances, but it was filled with the condolences of the entire village.

"So… wunna really leaving fuh truth?" Justin asked, as

Rasheda rested a single scarlet hibiscus on the grave.

"Yeah. I wanna know more about him. What his life was like. What he was doing before he came. And I can't do dah if I stuck down here." She caressed a picture of Glenn that someone took during happier times. His wild afro blowing in the wind while he skinned his teeth; probably from skylarking. It was Glenn's antics they'd miss the most.

"You sure dah's de only reason? Debt Collection ain de sorta job you does go into if you only want answers."

Rasheda rose as Justin made the comment, keeping her back towards him as she replied. "Don't mind that. And you ain leaving, too?"

"Yeah, but I was never from here to begin with." Justin admitted, though he fought harder than most of the people who did. "You sure you could trust she?"

Justin referred to the old hawker who sold roast corn and barbeque pigtails every evening on the street corners. He knew that wasn't her true profession. "You really can't tek the word of a Practitioner…."

"Well, that don't matter. Betty say it is the quickest way to get info 'bout Glenn, and I believe she."

Justin was tempted to reveal what he knew, but his hunches would only disrespect Glenn's memory. Justin owed him that much. "You barely setting youself up fuh trouble."

"Glenn did trust she enough to be a customer, so I could believe what she says." Rasheda contended.

Justin recalled the Bomber Bottles in Glenn's possession, and how finely crafted they were. But skill aside, he couldn't trust the old hawker as far as he could piss. Just like any other Practitioner. "Yeah, but how much did Glenn have to pay?"

Rasheda couldn't respond. Then Justin asked,

"You gine wid she, too?" Dario was a meter away, but his presence was nonexistent. Beneath the shroud of dreadlocks, Justin saw a nod and heard a muffled,

"Yes."

"Suit wunna selves." Justin sighed, while adjusting the black scarf wrapped around his forehead.

"My business ain got nuttin to do with you!" Rasheda

growled. Dario maintained his silence. "And try and gimme that back. It doesn't belong to you!"

Rasheda pointed at the bandana on Justin's forehead; the same one Glenn wore on their last endeavor at Wesley Broome. Not his dearest possession, but Rasheda believed the drifter had no claim to it. Justin didn't agree. "Nah… Glenn would want me to have this."

"Not fuh hell. Gimme it back." Rasheda bore her fangs, not in jest as she usually did, no; these fangs were meant for her enemies. Hostile and dripping with murderous intent. Justin regarded her without a flinch.

"Come and take it away if you want it so bad."

Rasheda scowled; rage aside, she had enough sense to know Justin was beyond her level. And Dario remained lost in his own musing over Glenn's grave. With these odds against her, Rasheda stood down with gritted teeth.

"Chances are the next time we meet, we gine be enemies." Justin said, in his voice the threat of a Pel-Ting was clear. "But until then, tek care of yuhselves."

"Don't worry 'bout that. If I see you again I gine take away that scarf myself. Even if you head come 'long with it." Justin ignored her, after all Rasheda was just a girl coming to terms with her grief. Still, the road she was about to take will forge Rasheda into a formidable opponent should they meet again.

"Fair enough." Justin fastened the bottle case around his shoulders and strode away.

This farewell summarized his relationship with Layer's Gap. Despite the turmoil Justin shared with the inhabitants, in the end he was still an outsider. The drops from the sky were heavier now, riding the livid draft that slapped him in the back. Justin felt Rasheda's glare as he marched, but he ignored it and kept his eyes on the main road. The shroud was still activated, and the few stray cars were oblivious to the scorched earth they passed. Justin surmised that the Practitioner lacked the tools to deactivate it, and whoever held them had no plans of doing so. He looked at the ticket in his hands and regarded the bus stop flickering in welcome.

This was goodbye for the Children of the Gulf.

The night had an eerie calm about it. There was no wind blowing, no sirens in the background, no crickets chirping in the air. It was like Vauxhall was devoid of activity. Kyle wasn't sure if it was the late hour or Sniper's story, but his mind couldn't regard his environment. There was too much information to process at once—a gang that rivaled the military, magical dolls that conjured weapons out of thin air, a village held hostage in Bimshire, and in the midst of it all was Sniper and his two new adversaries. If it weren't for everything he experienced last year, Kyle would've doubted this outlandish tale—but he knew better. However, Collins was still skeptical,

"So, wait… you mean to say so much people get kill, houses get blow up and thing, and nobody know?"

"Yup." Sniper said while squatting under a street light. "The news mention something about gun shots around dem parts, but no one really knew how cruel it was. But dah's the way they operate anyhow."

"They?" Kyle asked.

"*The Powers that Be.* The Admins. Same ones who does pay Cutup and Headgone." Sniper confirmed.

"This sound mess up to me, though." Collins ran his fingers

through his dreadlocks. "Even if there was a battle like that on the island, you can't expect me to believe that Cutup could outrun bullets."

Sniper was silent for a while before he spoke. "It ain exactly *The Matrix*, but you see his speed for youself, right?"

Collins swallowed hard, recalling the blurry serpent that thrashed his body at the beach. "Yeah. I did."

"I never see Cutup fight all out, but I could tell he get faster since then. And Headgone never had a big-ass sword either."

Kyle considered this point. "So, you mean they've gotten stronger over the decade."

"Most likely." Sniper replied; there was no concern in his words. "I would gotta see for myself. But even back then dem men was strong."

"I see," said Kyle.

"Look, it can't be all bad. I mean, we been busting our asses lately, right?"

"And you feel that gine be enough?" Sniper retorted. "Gulfsyde are Debt Collectors. You know what that means? It's a job where dem gotta claim outstanding debts or kill de people who owe. And in that line uh work you does butt all sorta dangerous people."

Sniper hopped to his feet and stretched. There was no arrogance in his words. Sniper spoke with the experience of twenty-five years as a Pel-Ting.

"Trust that whatever you see in Bewitched Gully ain got nothing on these men."

"So, what we supposed to do? Just sit back and let them kill us?" Collins rolled his eyes.

"Nah. I just telling you to go home, don't get involved, and leave these men to me."

"I can't agree with that." Kyle's statement caught the others by surprise. "We're their targets. If Gulfsyde takes their work as seriously as you say, then there's no way they'll back off 'cause of you."

"Yeah, I agree fuh sure." Collins chimed.

"Damn! What sorta debt do you guys owe anyway?" Sniper asked.

"How you mean?"

"Normally de Admin don't send Debt Collection unless it's something serious. And these men don't fuck around…" Sniper trailed off with the thought, remembering past orders from past bosses. Truly a shitty line of work. "Don't matter. I gine got them sort out before they get to you."

"Again, I can't do that." Kyle said, his tone unwavering. "I cannot forgive them for targeting me and my family."

A chill swept through the area. Collins might've mistaken it for the night breeze, but Sniper recognized the sudden hostility. It was similar to Glenn on the day Layer's Gap was attacked. The canewielder was willing to face the devil himself should he come knocking at his door.

"Suit youself." Sniper sucked his teeth. "But when you see Cutup or Headgone again, you better has run."

Neither Kyle or Collins responded, both in silent assent on how to handle their predicament. Sniper didn't say anything else on the matter. Strapping the bottle case across his shoulders, he made his way down the gap. A few steps later, he bounded onto a light pole before sprinting along the above power lines.

The ink in the sky dissolved into a milky orange, and the birds began their morning song. Dawn had crept up on them in the midst of Sniper's tale, and with it the residents of Vauxhall stirred. Garbage trucks started their route around homes, and the most dedicated workers shuffled to catch the first bus. One such person had arrived at the bus stop only to find two suspicious strangers loitering at this early hour. Kyle and Collins didn't pay him any attention, their minds too busy mulling over what they just heard. The Rasta broke the silence first,

"So, what we gine do now, B?"

"What you mean?" Kyle didn't face Collins, but kept his eyes straight looking at nothing in particular. "I'll continue as before, preparing for their next attack. I think you should do the same."

"Guess we don't have much choice. You think that gine be enough, though?"

It was an excellent question; one that Kyle had no answer for. "I don't know, but we'll find out eventually."

That was all he said on the matter, as a pair of headlights and a neon sign rolled in their direction. When they stopped the first bus, Kyle and Collins remembered the girls they left behind.

Shit … Nadia gine gimme an earful later on. Collins let out a sigh, but Kyle mused for the remainder of the trip.

The thirty-minute drive to town had passed within seconds. Kyle didn't even notice the dozen passengers that were in the bus before, so when they all made their exit he was caught by surprise.

"Yo, big man, you all right?" Collins asked tentatively.

"I'm okay."

"Safe… well I guess I better go back to Pops. See if I could learn something fresh."

"Yeah, sounds good. Stay on guard." Then they parted ways, with the Rasta pulling out his phone as he strode towards a parked ZR van, while Kyle continued to the other side of town.

He didn't heed the world around him. The dreary downtown buildings, the early morning parishioners on their way to church, the drone of transport-board buses—everything was just an empty blur until he arrived at home. As Kyle walked down Molasses Drive, he ignored the curious eyes peeking through the windows. Not caring for the scandal festering in their minds.

Upon cracking open the front door, he found Mr. Beckles sitting at the dining table with his usual cup of bayleaf tea. It was past seven o'clock, but his master was already in high spirits, beaming at Kyle as he took off his shoes.

"Wow! Looks like you had quite de night."

"Yeah." Kyle replied, marching past the kitchen cabinets, through the narrow hallway and into his little brother's bedroom. Damien was fast asleep, oblivious to the door creaking or the person peering behind it. Kyle stared at the boy in silence, taking in this rare moment of peace. A myriad of books, games and posters littered the divan so that Damien was on the edge with one leg dangling above the floor. It couldn't have been comfortable and yet he slept so soundly. Kyle felt guilty for waking him, but he had to. There was something the boy had to know.

"H-Hey…" Damien groaned as he stirred. It took Kyle a couple more shakes to fully rouse him. "What the hell, man?"

"Get up. I need to talk to you."

Ignoring the urgency in Kyle's voice, Damien pulled the sheet over his head only to have it tossed aside by his brother. "It's Sunday! Do you have any idea how valuable weekend morning sleep is?!"

"This is more important." Kyle gripped the boy by the shoulders."You remember what I always tell you, right?"

How could Damien forget? It was drilled into his head countless times. "Avoid strangers. If I hear strange noises or music—run. If I ever feel like I'm being watched or followed —run. If someone threatens me in anyway—do not fight, run and call you or Mr. Beckles."

Kyle noticed a hint of derision in his voice but he was satisfied. "I just want you to be careful."

"I am—"

"No." There's no way he could be. He knew nothing. Nothing about the horrors of the past or the ones that lay ahead. "Look, there are certain things … dangers that you should avoid."

"What's going on, Kyle?" Damien's question snapped him into focus. Was he panicking so much that he could no longer hide it from the boy? Should he still be hiding anyway? Damien ought to know what was happening. He ought to know what lurked beneath the shadows.

"Nothing's going on." But the words couldn't roll off Kyle's tongue.

"Nah. I think something is… 'cause you acting real weird." the boy declared. Damien grew accustomed to his brother's quirks over the years, but this is the first he'd seen Kyle so shaken. Kyle himself couldn't understand why he was so anxious after Sniper's tale. The enemy was just human … right?

"I am, aren't I?" Damien watched his brother force a grin, but there was no comfort behind it. Something was wrong. He knew that much, and the notion made his mind swim.

"Yeah, you are. You always act weird and I want to know why."

Kyle locked eyes with the boy, matching his tired, anxious

pupils against the curious ones of his brother. He couldn't do it. He couldn't drag Damien's soul into this world of violence, even if not doing so was putting the child's life at risk. Kyle shook his head and conjured a more convincing smile.

"Everything's okay—I just was worried about all the robberies gine on lately. You don't watch the news?"

"No." Damien said with a bit of disgust. It seemed that Kyle's distraction worked, if only temporarily.

"Well, you should, and stop spending all you time playing dem video games."

"Fine, whatever…" Damien ignored the reproach and pulled the blanket over his head. "I gine back to sleep."

Kyle thought he heard a muffled "Johnny" from under the pillow. *I guess I deserved that.*

He thought before taking his leave. Perhaps he was overreacting? After all, Kyle had more information about his enemy than before. He knew their face, their history, and even witnessed their fighting style without having to face them.

Upon reaching the hallway, he saw Mr. Beckles leaning on the wall while sipping from his porcelain cup. Kyle didn't regard his presence though, only wordless steps followed as he walked to the front house. "I guess you're ready to resume?"

Kyle halted at the question, and replied without turning, "Yeah, let's continue."

"Heh! Lovely." Mr. Beckles smirked before downing his tea and securing his bamboo stick.

Hours before the sun had taken its dominion over the sky, two individuals stood in a deserted cemetery. It was an odd scene at this time of the night, but the only passers-by were the centipedes scuttling along the damp soil. One of them was a young woman; tall and shapely despite her tattered jeans and baggy shirt. She stood over one grave with a vase fashioned out of a sawed-off plastic bottle, and inside it, a meek arrangement of white frangipani which seemed oddly luminescent in the darkness of the night.

The other was a man in a white dashiki with dreadlocks flowing down his back and a long red scarf wrapped around his neck. He had nothing in hand, except for a bandaged item which didn't have any reverence about it.

"It's been a while, hasn't it?" Dario asked, as Rasheda rested a flower on the nameless tombstone. "At least it's in the same condition that we left it in."

"Yeah." Rasheda growled wearily. She didn't know when she fell in love with Glenn, or how, for that matter. But the moment he disappeared from this world; it became a place she didn't want to be in. She wanted to run away at first, but her deprival forced her onto a different path. A dangerous road where Glenn's memory moved in whispers. And since that time, they hadn't visited Glenn's grave, but the regret and sorrow were still heavy. The day when Glenn's life was stolen was still fresh in their minds.

"He was something else, wasn't he?" Dario broke the silence first. "A man capable of so much, even at our tender ages back then."

"Yeah, he was." Dario thought he saw a smile on Rasheda's lips, but it disappeared just as fast as it surfaced. "—Even if he was a brat."

Dario had nothing else to add. Though Glenn's fearsome skill often tantalized his appetite.

"We still ain find nuttin, though." Rasheda admitted bitterly.

"No, we haven't." Upon the Practitioner's advice, the two enlisted in Debt Collection. But instead of finding clues about Glenn, they mounted countless dead bodies as per the demands of their new profession. "It's really odd that no one knows his face, even in our circles."

"I feel dem lying; I mean, not even a name they know?" The fervor in her voice was beginning to show, and Rasheda's beauty contorted into a spiteful scowl.

"It's unlikely." Dario said. Rasheda turned so fast that she almost disturbed the tombstone. "Glenn was a meticulous man. Chances are he left wherever it is he came from with the intention of not being found. If that's the case, then…"

"So, you want me to give up, nuh?"

"That may be best."

"Puh—figured you would suggest dah."

"What do you mean?"

"You ain cover Glenn ten years back, so I ain expect any difference now." Her words tore at Dario with malice.

"I see. So, you do blame me for Glenn's death, after all."

Rasheda turned her attention back to Glenn's grave.

"I cannot blame you for harboring spite towards me. If I had killed Kamilah back then…" Dario lingered on that decision; where he selfishly spared the girl in hopes that she may survive and grow stronger should they meet again. "Glenn would still be alive."

Rasheda remained silent.

"However, I'm sure that Glenn wouldn't want you to spend the rest of your life chasing after his memory."

"What the fuck do you know about Glenn?" Rasheda's glare made his heart leap. "Don't act like you know anything. You barely even left yuh house."

There had been many changes over the past decade, but Rasheda's personality was the biggest. Her outbursts always had a good nature behind them but now they were cold and resentful; especially towards Dario, whom she only dealt with during assignments. It was something Dario had to accept. And then there was that sword…

"You know that I'm right." Rasheda sucked her teeth but Dario ignored it. "And even if you continue to resent me, I shall continue to support you."

The two stood in silence over the tombstone. Above them, the darkness was fading like someone had poured milk into God's cup of coffee. And at their backs the resident wildlife was beginning to stir. It was a clear indication that,

"Dawn is approaching. We better head off soon."

Rasheda didn't acknowledge the comment, her mind focused on the grave before her.

"Our target should arrive within the next couple hours, so

we should be there to give him the proper—"

"I know, nuh!" Rasheda barked. She had never shirked her assignments and she wasn't about to start now. Taking a few more moments to pay her respects, Rasheda secured her offering of frangipani along with the giant chained-up sword resting beside her. *I won't give up, Glenn.*

Dario could only observe as Rasheda strolled towards the bus stop. He sensed the fatigue in her steps. A consequence of her thirst for blood. And what a thirst it was, he imagined, for a woman to wield such a weapon. The sword yearned for her like a beast would fresh meat, sniffing and slurping at her back. It was only a matter of time before it consumed her: blade and business alike. Dario was determined not to let that happen.

"This will be the last." He whispered, before following his partner towards the bus stop.

The morning had been a grueling one, but Kyle didn't expect anything less from his master's sparring sessions. Decorated with bruises from head to toe, he limped through the front house, past the mahogany furniture, cabinets and dining room table, and into the bathroom on the opposite end of the corridor. Kyle struggled the entire way, collapsing on the toilet seat upon arrival. Still, despite his bad state, he wore a broad smirk on his face. "The old man's a monster."

Kyle's muscles burned as he stepped into the shower and ran cold water over his skin. Each ache a potent reminder of every blunder and miscalculation. Mr. Beckles was a pitiless opponent, inflicting more scars than Kyle had bargained for. Nursing one wound around his abdomen, Kyle recalled the error that led to it.

It's like going against a shadow. Even when I think I have him in sight, his body really isn't there. Kyle was exhilarated by the gulf in their abilities. "Damn old man ..."

He could do this. If he could keep this up and survive, he would get stronger for sure. And so, Kyle continued this reckless training regime for the next couple days, fraying his body with the sincere belief that he was improving. His onlookers weren't so confident. Especially Mr. Beckles, who was concerned about the damage he inflicted on his dear student.

"You sure you wanna keep this up?" He asked, after a nasty blow to the stomach made Kyle belch blood.

"Y-Yeah..." Kyle squelched while reeling in the dirt. "Just keep going..."

Mr. Beckles admired the idea. People are forced to adapt when placed in adverse conditions. The same is deftly true for the human body. Chances are Kyle would become stronger, but there was always the risk of dying first. "I know what you trying to do but—"

Mr. Beckles stopped as Kyle stumbled onto his feet. Oh, how pitiful his ward looked, indeed. Kyle resumed his stance, quivering under the pressure of his wounds but his resolve very much intact.

"Guess it ain make much sense trying to change you mind. You were always a stubborn boy." Mr. Beckles then strode towards the cellar underneath the house, where training equipment was usually kept. He emerged several minutes later with a glass bottle in hand. "Here, drink this."

"Um?" Kyle didn't trust any beverage that was stored in a cellar, and the milky color didn't resemble wine.

"Just drink it, you'll feel better."

Kyle wanted to hurl the moment he took the sip. The concoction had a familiar rancidness, like old horse piss or bile. "This is..."

From the horrible flavor to the warmth that filled his body, it had to be the same brew—the one that Collins gave him that night in Bewitched Gully. Mr. Beckles confirmed, "It's Noni-Apple juice. Don't mind the taste; you'll be fine in a jiffy."

The old man didn't lie. As Kyle reminisced, a balmy sensation touched his nerves and he was able to stand tall again. "Where ... How did you get this?"

"Got it from a friend."

"A friend?" Kyle wondered what sort of friends had magical potions in their possession. Then again, this wasn't the first time his master offered strange remedies, like that Cayenne pepper to treat wounds. "Why do you know about this stuff?"

"How you meanin?" The medicines, the errands, his prowess with Stick-licking; no matter how Kyle looked at it, Mr. Beckles wasn't a normal person.

"Who are you?" The question was simple but the answer was not. Kyle could tell from the way his face stiffened before relaxing into a low sigh.

"You're not ready to know that yet."

"Why not?" Kyle persisted. "You took care of us after Mom died, and I'm thankful for that, but there's still a lot I don't know about you."

It was true that prior to Veronica Harding's death, Mr. Beckles had a strained relationship with her children. Though Damien was too young to know any better, back then Kyle didn't—or rather—wouldn't accept this stranger as their guardian even if his mother wished it. Still, the boy understood Mr. Beckles's strength. It was clear on the night when his mother died and the bright lights knocked on their roof.

"What do you want to know?"

"Are you a Practitioner?" The question spilled from his tongue.

"Oh, not me. I ain got the skills for that line of work, boah." Mr. Beckles snorted.

"Then how did you get so strong?"

"I would call myself nuff things, but strong is not one uh them." Kyle wouldn't believe it. The memory of Mr. Beckles marching towards the chaos outside—when green booms poured through the window and Kyle hid next to Damien's crib—was still fresh in his mind.

"I don't know why you are hiding, but I really need to know." Mr. Beckles heard the alarm in his voice. Kyle wasn't the same composed child that he reared over the years. "The things I have to face … And what's coming next…"

Panic. The kind that belonged to the little boy who just lost his mother, and cowered beneath the sheets as monsters scurried outside. Mr. Beckles spent the last decade molding Kyle Harding into someone who could handle any threat. But in this moment, he wondered if he succeeded.

"I…"

A faint patter interrupted the conversation, and as the two turned Damien's leg disappeared through the back door. Lord knows how much the boy overheard.

"Kyle. Your mother left alotta things in place to protect you. This house. Me. You're safe here for de time being—both of you—and I know you always rushing de brush, but recklessness ain de same thing as strength."

Kyle nodded. The days passed without any further training sessions, and Kyle accepted that he could do nothing more to prepare. At least, not physically. His mind wasn't mature enough, nor his resolve. He returned home with this notion one evening, eager to sprawl on his bed and clear his head. However…

"Hello, Kyle."

A girl adorned in a blue empire-waist dress stood before his verandah. She was beautiful, with caramel skin and a delicate physique. And even though she regarded him with warm, emerald eyes and a promising smile, Kyle gripped his cane as if she were an enemy.

"Lianne." Enemy. Kyle accepted her new role in his life from the time she ushered him into Bewitched Gully. "What do you want?"

Lianne grinned again, this time a little less confident than before. "I guess a lot has changed in a year, nuh? I never thought you would look at me with such aggressive eyes."

Kyle didn't hear a word she said. His mind was too busy wondering how to get this dangerous person away from the house! He remembered Collins's story about Content; where Lianne summoned a Baku armed with a giant coucou stick.

"Don't worry. I'm not here on business." Lianne assured him. "But if it really bothers you, we could go further up the gap?"

It wouldn't be enough. Bakus could easily ravage entire communities, but any distance away from the house—away from Damien—was fine with Kyle. Without a word, he gestured toward the street where Lianne was expected to take the lead.

Kyle didn't trust his back to her. Lianne pretended not to notice.

"Why are you here?"

"What do you mean? I haven't seen you in a year. Just wanted to say Hi and—"

"Cut the crap." Lianne felt the chill in his voice. Kyle continued, "Did Gra—*Ms. Pringle* send you?"

"No. She isn't working with us anymore."

"Is she dead?"

"…Yes."

"Did you kill her?"

"Ms. Pringle's license expired, so she's no longer working under us." Lianne said. By now, they reached the top of the hill, and the said witch's house was in full view … or what remained of it. A corroded mass of bricks with a net of lianas draping over it would be a better description. For it no longer resembled a home, and as far as the residents of Molasses Drive were concerned, it never was.

"So, is that what you plan to do? Are you here to kill me, too?" Kyle changed his stance, sugarcane pointed towards her with menacing intent.

Lianne was not fazed. Surprised, yes, but not threatened. "No. Like I said, I'm not here on business. I just came to see you. You know, after everything…"

"I see." Kyle's bearing did not change. "I seriously doubt that you came here just to lime. So say what you've come to say and leave."

"Okay." Lianne noted the caution as he spoke. Kyle was afraid, as he should be. Still, it was unfortunate that their relationship boiled down to this. "I came to give you a warning."

"A warning?" Kyle repeated. From Lianne's point of view, he looked like a cornered animal. Battered and apprehensive, but with enough desperation to fight off his predator.

"Looks like you've been training hard recently." Kyle didn't respond. "Your body doesn't seem to be in much of a fighting shape."

"Don't worry about that."

"I mean, it's all well and good to make sure you at your strongest, but strength alone isn't gonna bring you victory. I suppose you've already realized that." There was no derision behind her words, nor any sneer in her emerald eyes.

"So that is what you come to do? Intimidate me?"

"No. I came here as your friend. As hard as you find it to believe."

"You're right, I don't believe it."

"Fair enough. I guess I deserve that." There was a hint of remorse in her voice, just a taste, but that was enough for Kyle to feed on.

"Tell me something. Why did you wait till Bewitched Gully? I mean, you knew me for a good while—you had plenty opportunity, so why then?"

Wow. I really didn't expect you to ask me that. Was what Lianne's face said, but she didn't dawdle in her response. "Because you weren't of any interest then."

"Interest? What do you mean by interest?" Kyle thought of Ms. Pringle when he heard the term. He didn't know why. *Does this have to do with me being an Inheritor?*

"I can't get into it now, Kyle."

"Why not? You're so eager to kill me; you could at least give me a proper reason." His tone showed no anger, only indifference, and that wounded Lianne even more.

"This is bigger than you." She began. Then…

"Wow."

Lianne didn't recognize the soft-spoken voice, but judging from the horrified look on his face it appeared that Kyle did.

"Damien. What are you doing here?!"

"How you mean?" The boy ran a finger through the shrub on his head. "De bus just come from town."

"Oh." Kyle cursed himself for not checking the time.

"Well, who do we have here?" Lianne said with innocent interest. Damien had similar features to Kyle, with the only exception being the eyes which were dark brown instead of black. "How you doing, little guy?"

"I'm cool." Damien remembered her, from the curves printing through her dress to the hem dancing about her thighs. "Are you guys on another date?"

Lianne giggled at his candor. He was the total opposite of

his older brother. "Um … not exactly. I just came to visit."

Kyle partitioned the two by striding in front. Damien protested from his back, but Kyle quickly silenced him with an outstretched arm and a solemn command. "Go home, Damien."

"Huh? Why do I—"

"Go home."

Damien reluctantly obeyed. He would've debated this for a few minutes, throwing in a tantrum or two to embarrass Kyle. But he didn't, or more accurately he couldn't, for the command wasn't from someone he recognized. No. This cold being wasn't his brother; it wasn't Kyle.

"Um. Nice seeing you again, Damien!" Lianne bellowed after him, perfectly aware of the needles Kyle was staring into her. "Don't you think that was a bit harsh?"

"That's the last time you will talk to my brother." Kyle whispered. "Come near our house again and I'll kill you."

"I see." Lianne knew he meant every word. "Fair enough."

Time stopped as they exchanged gazes, like they were both absorbing each other's image for one last time. It was in this moment Kyle noticed the subtle changes in Lianne's features. She was wearing her hair out now, much like that night at De Horseshoe last year. She also wore more jewelry, though nothing as flashy as the silver bracelet on her wrist. Kyle recalled the azure light that it spilled at Bewitched Gully, and the Steel Donkey-drawn carriage that was brought forth….

It was this same glow that flickered around the area now. Nothing extravagant, but it was enough to distract passing vehicles which screeched around the street in a moment of confusion. It was in this moment that Lianne disappeared. "Goodbye, Kyle."

That farewell lingered no longer than the scent of burning rubber and exhaust, but it would stick in Kyle's mind.

Home was never a comfortable place for Damien Harding. Sure, the boy spent most of his free time locked in the bedroom with his books and video games, but over the past year even that wasn't enough to ease him. Nothing about the Harding household had changed physically. His bedroom was still polluted with various cases, posters and comics, and his divan still had a lump on the left side where he slept. The hallway, the bathroom, the living room, kitchen—everything was preserved, aside from the white linen drapes which Mr. Beckles thought would spruce up the place. And yet the Harding household was different…

Damien glanced through the open louvers and remembered the cause of his discomfort. Someone was killed in his backyard. There was no blood, body or any paramedics at the scene, but Damien was sure of what he saw. This wasn't the first time. He knew of the night when his mother passed away on the kitchen floor. But that wasn't as gruesome as this other death.

Damien could still hear the grunts and clashes resonating from the backyard. It was the first time he'd seen his brother *really* fight. Not like the controlled sparring sessions that Mr. Beckles held on evenings, but a chaotic brawl where his life was on the line. It was from this experience that Damien lost the comfort of his own home, merely passing through to bathe, eat and show his face. He was forced to find refuge at school, joining various clubs and sports teams, much to everyone's surprise. He also took after-school lessons for all of his subjects, which the teachers felt unnecessary as Damien was a straight-A student.

"Chemistry lessons, again?" drawled Mr. Beckles from the other line.

"Yeah. End of term exams coming up, so the teacher want us ready." Damien said, though he couldn't care less about grades.

"I see. Well, I suppose dah's okay, but you been slacking off on your training lately."

"I'll be fine." Damien groaned. "Besides, you gine be busy with Kyle anyway, so I could be doing something productive in the meantime."

Mr. Beckles was bemused by his logic, but he agreed. "All right. Well, I gine tell you brother— you know how he does worry."

"Yeah, yeah, I know. Anyway, class starting. I gine hear you in a bit. Later."

Damien pocketed the phone and sat on a nearby step. A group of students were ambling upstairs where class was about to begin. That's how it was recently; Damien calling home about some after-school event which he didn't plan to attend.

Bailey frowned at him from the top floor.

"You want something?" Damien asked.

"Nope. Nothing at all." Bailey replied.

Damien regarded the boy for a moment. Bailey was the only person at school he tolerated. He knew how to mind his own business and keep to himself, except for now. "Cool."

"Oh, by the way, you want any of these notes from class?" Bailey fastened the large backpack over his shoulder. Bespectacled and tidy, the other students often called him a nerd or geek. This was true, but not in the degrading sense. Bailey was of a different class of society. Not bougie. Not wealthy. But still of a superior ilk. It was that *something* that Damien saw when they became friends.

"Nah, I good—gine probably just cool out here for a while before I head home."

"I see." Bailey tipped his spectacles; an act which annoyed Damien a little.

"Wha happen?"

"Nothing. It's just you are a peculiar kid, Damien Harding." A comment Damien did not expect to hear from a fellow misfit. "One minute you're groaning about how much you hate it here, and the next, you're making excuses to stay late."

"Yeah, I guess. What's your point?"

"No point—just an observation." Bailey shrugged.

"Anyway, I gine kill some time. Enjoy the extra lessons."

Damien rose from the step; he was weary of the conversation.

"Same to you."

Damien never liked scolding, not even from his brother, but he understood Bailey's point. He *was* acting strange. And as Damien ambled past deserted corridors and empty classrooms, he recalled the truth he discovered in his backyard. Magic exists. Perhaps it was the fantasies of the twelve-year-old who enjoyed video games and movies, but there was no other description for what he saw that night.

"There's no mistake. His hand had definitely gone through Kyle." The image of his brother crumpling over the intruder appeared in Damien's mind, along with the haunting cerulean that touched the night.

That battle defied anything he learnt from Mr. Beckles. Someone broke blades with his bare hands, passed his arm through solid objects, and distorted the bonds between them entirely. This wasn't real life, it was a comic book.

"I can't fail."

"I'll have your heart."

"I will clear my debt!"

These were the words of the madman who tried to kill his brother. But what did they mean? Was it just the demented rant of a lunatic, or was it something more? The events of that night would've shaken anyone's beliefs, much less a child's. And to make matters worse, three shadows dropped from the sky and danced to ethereal flute music.

If I hear strange noises or music—run.

A haunting masquerade; that was the best way to describe that night, and as Damien reminisced, the streaks of yellow that came from the shadows' eyes made his blood run cold.

Activities slowed down as the evening matured, with playing fields and courts steadily losing their patrons. It was a missed opportunity to kill some time, though Damien would've ignored the games anyway. The watchmen started to patrol the grounds, looking for any stragglers who refused to go home. Lawlessness prevailed, as people were hidden in the nooks and crannies of the compound. A couple of seniors were cuddled under the stairwell by the science department. Head in neck. Arms fondling. By the woodwork shops, a group of students gathered before a nearby wall with spray cans in hand.

"Okay. So magic real … but what Kyle got to do with it?" Damien recalled the conversations he overheard in the house. Where terms like *Shadow Darts, Practitioners,* and *Debt* were dropped with a grave tongue. But what did it all mean? The question rattled in his head as he stopped by the water fountain.

The P.E. Department was the last active area on school grounds due to the practice sessions that took place afterhours. But at this time the offices and gyms were locked so that it resembled a dungeon.

"And he's been acting so strange, too." The phrase bounced across the corridor walls as Damien strolled towards the fields.

"Waiiiit! Look who just pass through, men!" Damien continued his stride, but the guffaws got his attention. "Wha gine on, Khus Khus?"

Damien cringed at the name; the large tuft of hair on his head resembled Khus Khus grass. They thought it was clever.

"You looking de wrong place for de barber, Khus Khus. He ain back hey." The four chortled in unison. Vandals. The kind that preyed on the meek for their own amusement. Damien was unimpressed.

"No thanks. I don't wanna go to nobody you went to. I don't deal with animal grooming." They were stunned silent, aside for a few snorts spilling from the lot. Damien watched as their leader—who was a boar of a boy—trudged forward with fury in his eyes.

"The fuck you say?" His nostrils flared, and a musty scent brushed Damien when he spoke. "Say it again, if you's a man."

Damien had nothing to prove. His mind was elsewhere, away from the livestock, in his backyard, with the lunatic, the three shadows and magic. Damien walked away, but the boar made the mistake of clutching his collar.

Whack!

Damien redirected the paw with a flick and glared calmly at the group.

"You feel you bad 'cause you Mother does do Obeah?" The bully crooned much to the herd's delight. Rage crystallized inside Damien.

"… I don't really want to hurt wunna men, right? But if you lay another hand on me I gine break it, along with every other bone in your body." He spotted a T-Square several feet away; discarded hours ago by some careless student. It wasn't the weapon he was trained to use, but for now, it was enough.

"Oh, fuh real?" The pig grunted, but his friends found no humor in the threat. Unlike their leader, they were smart enough to sense the hostility pouring from Damien's small frame. Like a rabid dog in a dark alley. The pig persisted, "Dah's how it is? You feel you bad? You feel you bad, Khus Khus?"

He reeled his fist backward to bash this whelp's face in. Damien didn't flinch, his brown eyes appraising the pig. Then silence. An absence of sound. Next, a sharp rattle punctuated the hush, in a way that propelled the stump forward.

WHAM!

The impact of flesh resounded in the air, but when the pig gazed upon his target, he was stunned at what he beheld. His hand hadn't just struck Damien's face, it impaled it; with his knuckles protruding through the boy's afro in the most obscene fashion.

Oh rasshole! Wha just happen? was the phrase on everyone's mind. Notions of murder, police, and life at Glendairy prison, floated menacingly in their heads. That is, until Damien started moving.

"Wait … that's all you got fuh real?" the boy with the skewered skull asked. "I thought you was stronger than that."

The pig squealed, trying his best to pull his arm free, but it wouldn't budge. Damien then grinned, like a spider that had ensnared an innocent fly, and seized the stump within a tight grasp.

"Argh!" The pig lurched as those nails gripped into his skin, and the being that he thought he could overpower began to cackle. It was a godforsaken sound. One that buckled their knees, while their conscience cursed them for standing still.

Damien was thunderstruck at what transpired before his eyes. It wasn't every day that you witness your own death. He didn't exactly die, though. It wasn't even him at all. And as

Damien gazed at his disfigured doppelganger, he could only muster one explanation.

"An illusion?"

"You guess that one right, yuh." The reply popped from his left, much like the person who gave it. Following his instincts Damien hopped several steps away, and to his surprise a young, bronze-skinned man with long onyx hair appeared. Damien recognized the minivan conductor who worked along his school route—Sulemann.

"*You.*"

Sulemann beamed like a child who just won hide and seek. "Oops! You might wanna watch yuh step there."

But Damien didn't heed his advice, backing away for good measure until his foot touched something small and flat. A single domino was under his heel, and what happened next would forever be etched in his memory.

The illusion unraveled, falling apart like a puzzle unmade piece by piece. And sure enough, the horror that the vandals lived for the past ten minutes had crumbled away, leaving behind a bewildered Damien and an amused stranger.

"M-M-M-M-My man?! What the rass just happen?!" one of them stammered. His face seemed shades lighter as he regarded the duo.

"De man is a duppy, and he Mudda is a witch! Wha you expect!? Wha you expect!?" Another one pointed at Damien with a trembling finger. But none was as scared as the pig, who remained at a loss for words while goggling his hand and the boy he thought he killed.

"I leffin from 'bout here. Wunna could stand and get you heart eat out, boah!" They all scattered. No doubt, there will be myths about this incident for years to come, and this time they would be true.

"Cha. I was hoping we could get away before the Mirror drop." Sulemann ran his fingers through his black fleece. "Ah well, what's done is done."

"What the hell was that?" Damien secured more distance for himself, but Sulemann was still lost in his own notions.

"I could always wipe their memories… Nah. Too much hassle … Hmm?” Sulemann noticed Damien, who brandished a T-Square like a fencer would a sword. “Woah, big man, where you gine with that?”

“Who are you?”

“Cha. This is how you does treat somebody that bail you out fuh truth?”

“I could’ve handled it.”

“I ain doubt you, boy.” Sulemann chuckled, while raising his hands in defense. “But I ain trying to fight yuh, so could you put that thing down?”

Damien didn’t budge.

“Okay. Fine then. Whatever mek yuh comfortable. Anyway, you mind passing that over to me?” Sulemann pointed to the card at Damien’s feet.

“Why?”

“ ‘Cause it’s expensive and I don’t wanna go through the hassle of forging another one.”

What exactly did he mean by *forge*? Damien wondered, but a more pressing question came off his tongue.

“Was that magic?”

“Kinda like that. Now would you mind?”

With some hesitation, Damien kicked the domino towards him, vigilant that the man didn’t move suspiciously. “So, what do you want? Why did you help me?”

“Damn. You is a curious fella, nuh?” Sulemann inspected the card for any scratches, and when he was satisfied, he said, “Because it look like it was ‘bout to get messy.”

“It wasn’t your business, though.”

“I know, but I’m a malicious person.” A grin punctuated the statement. At that moment Damien believed he meant *malicious* in every sense of the word. “Anyway, I gotta roll, got some business to take care of.”

“But you didn’t answer my question.” Damien protested. His answers were slipping away and he couldn’t have that, not when they were this close.

“If you really wanna know wha gine on, we will end up meeting again.”

“Wha sorta BS is that?” Damien was desperate. He didn’t

know why.

"Don't worry, you gine see me." Sulemann strode away. "I know because we got the same eyes."

Enigmatic words from an enigmatic man, and as Damien observed the conductor's departure, a white light enveloped him until he vanished.

"What a weirdo." Damien grumbled, though Sulemann had sparked his interest. Against his better judgment, as there was a certain malevolence in the man.

I have to know wha gine on with Kyle.

Damien convinced himself as he walked to the front of the school. The sky looked like rebellion, with fires in the clouds as they battled the fading sunlight. The road was devoid of traffic, and it would be another thirty minutes before the next van came. Damien would get an earful when he got home but that was the least of his concerns. Leaning against the bus stop, his thoughts were solely on the events at hand and Sulemann's invitation.

It was a long day for Seifert Brathwaite. From the wee hours of the morning, he was busy toiling in the fields as his trade required. You see, Seifert was a worker for hire. A mundane profession in these times, but it paid the bills and Seifert wasn't above menial labor. He took pride in his work, smiling from ear to ear as he sauntered down the hill of Cane Vale. His clothes barely showed their original colors, with brown splotches covering a cream shirt and grey trousers, both of which were faded from years of washing and drying out in the sun. His skin was ashy and callous from hours of digging up in the fields.

It was no wonder people ignored him as he passed, but Seifert didn't mind. He never paid much attention to people anyway. Cars whizzed by every couple minutes, and the drivers hardly spared a glance. The reason for this was simple; he was a sparrow. Homeless. Technically, he lived inside a cave which many would frown upon in Bimshire. But Seifert was comfortable with his place, working hard, keeping to himself, and enjoying life in its simplest forms.

Then something disturbed this peace.

A youngster had approached him one day while he was running his routine errands.

"Wait! Are you a Canecutter?"

"Are you… like me?"

Seifert remembered the Rasta's eyes; they belonged to someone who had lost his way in the world. He supposed he was compelled to train Damian Collins, though Seifert never thought that would happen again in his lifetime.

"Welp. I hope de young fella gine be ready." Seifert sighed. Collins grew resilient as time passed, finishing his drills without collapsing and only having a few scars on his skin. He had improved but Seifert wasn't satisfied. "I already teach him all he need to know."

The sky became murkier by the minute with a chilly draft brushing his skin. Seifert didn't cringe; instead, he buttoned his collar and quickened his step. "De rain setting up. That boy mussy slacking off, yuh."

Seifert didn't believe it. If Collins hadn't broken under his regimen yet, he was never going to break.

Despite the dismal weather, the scenery from Cane Vale was breathtaking. From where Seifert stood he saw the rooftops of nearby houses, the bustling traffic and activity of Oistins, and even further beyond was the ocean whose rich aquamarine blackened as cloud cover increased. Seifert witnessed this view at least once a week since he often had jobs in the area, and every time he forfeited a few minutes to take it all in. But today was different. He didn't even glance to his side when he passed by,

"I could only hope that he learn well."

Seifert's concern for Collins was beyond him. After years of seclusion, he grew accustomed to caring only for himself, but for some reason Collins reminded him of someone.

"…Then again, if he related to those two, I shun' have nuh

doubts."

Seifert slipped into his thoughts until he reached the bus stop. There was a flicker of purple but he didn't pull out any paper. Instead, the old parrow rested on the black-and-white pole, fishing quarters from his pockets.

That was when he saw them; the two individuals waiting on the opposite side of the road. They were a conspicuous bunch: a young woman with a fierce scowl, and a young man with a red scarf around his neck and long thick dreadlocks on his head.

…*These youngsters nowadays does wear some get ups.* Seifert's first thought, but something else arrested him. They both held malice so dense that it thickened the air. Stagnant and chilling.

"Good afternoon, sir." The Rasta greeted him first. Seifert thought he was the complete opposite of Collins—cold and reticent.

"Afternoon, sonny." Seifert also noticed the woman wasn't paying any attention.

"We might have to wait a little while before the bus arrives. Nothing came up from town, and I doubt anything down the road, either." The Rasta's tongue was polite, but there was only darkness in his eyes.

"That okay. I feel I gine catch one from down de hill." Seifert tipped the brim of his fedora in gratitude. "By the way, I kinda low on change. You mind lending me two dollars so I could get in town?"

"Stupse." The woman sucked her teeth. Apparently, she didn't take well to begging, but then the average Bajan felt the same way.

"Sure. I have an extra two dollars to spare." The Rasta handed him a crumpled blue bill. "Here you go."

"Thank yuh, hear?" Seifert grinned as he made his approach. He wasn't above handouts. Whether it was a pinch of salt or spare change, it was expected to help thy neighbor should the need arise. But there was a reason Seifert beseeched this couple, and it became clear when he extended a hand.

The Rasta was the first to realize as Seifert caught his arm.

His grip was strong. That skeletal limb like a vice: sturdy and powerful. Then the hoe's blade thundered down at his skull…

Clank!

The weapon scarred concrete, while the two shifted to Seifert's side. He was the Cheshire cat among cornered mice. "Ah shoot, I miss… or better yet, you dodged."

"When did you notice?" The Rasta inspected his torn sleeve.

"Who could miss de scent of blood pouring from wunna?" Seifert dusted the bits of gravel off his hoe before propping it on his shoulder. "It would mek de dead restless in dem grave."

"As expected from Seifert Brathwaite, or should I say, *Father Hoe?*" The Rasta chuckled, but Seifert didn't bat an eye.

"Oh, so you know about that, huh?"

"Father Hoe; one of the legends from the Parish War. A demon warrior who decimated any enemy that came into his path. An integral member of the Opposition who contributed to the stalemate that lasted years. And also, one of the last—"

"I sure you didn't come here to gimme a history lesson." Seifert interrupted. The Rasta probed him for a reaction but he found none.

"Aight then, wunna wasting time!" A loud clunk diverted their eyes. The young girl had dropped something heavy onto the ground. "We could hurry up and kill this man or wha?"

"I guess since we're done with the pleasantries…." As he spoke the Rasta pulled out a long pole swathed in thick, white bandages. While the girl drew what looked like a massive cutlass bounded in chains, until a red flash revealed something far more sinister. It made Seifert's hair stand on end.

"I see. So *that* was where that bloodlust come from." His expression was severe but his body relaxed. "That I would find one of Coalpot's works in a place like this. Can't remember de last time I see a Greedy Weapon, boy."

The girl didn't answer but simply pounded the ground, as her partner disappeared from her side. A silent movement, scuttling several meters in the blink of an eye until the Rasta was upon Seifert. "And you is a quick one, young fella."

Whack!

Seifert sidestepped the strike, and parried the follow-up so that a palm leaf was revealed under those bandages. A palm leaf with bristles as black as charcoal.

"Fast movements and a palm leaf—just like Sweeping Mongoose." Seifert muttered while the two resumed their stances. They were an intriguing pair, with each being a token from decades past. "Tell me your names."

"Why de hell we should tell you dah?" the girl barked.

"Now now. The legend himself has acknowledged us. We could at least be polite." The Rasta admonished her before replying. "Dario is my name, but my enemies refer to me as *Cutup.*"

"Tch. *Headgone...*" Rasheda growled.

"Cutup and Headgone." Seifert straightened his fedora. "Lemme tell yuh, there's a chance wunna might not survive this. Tek care."

"We won't know for sure unless we proceed, Father Hoe." Dario strode forward, vanishing on the second step and emerging at his target's right side (where the hat had slightly covered Seifert's eye).

Shink! The slash, even though well placed, was easily parried with the tip of the hoe, halting the palm leaf's path. *Attacking a temporary blind spot before I could react—a good plan but naïve.*

Seifert's thoughts were cut off by the giant blade over his head...

BOOM!

An eruption of debris showed the attack's potency, and as Seifert shifted away he noted the massive cleft left on the street. Headgone glared at him in disgust, but it was nothing compared to the malice at Seifert's back. "Ooops!"

Again, the hoe was there to intercept, guiding the sharpened bristles away from Seifert's body while he hopped to safety. Seifert: the nimble parrow who danced around his foes. "You youngsters are pretty coordinated. Each attack leads me to a blind spot where de other would got a preemptive strike. That level uh teamwork... you mussy know each other a long time. Married?"

Rasheda skinned up her face. "*No.*"

"Ah. That's a shame. Wunna look good together."

"You're being too kind, Father Hoe." Dario said, before the girl lost her temper. "You live up to the name well, defending with such a flimsy weapon. But I think you are still underestimating us."

"How yuh mean?" Seifert couldn't fool Cutup's hunger. He was holding back, careful not to retaliate with any attacks of his own.

"I am well aware of your abilities, Seifert Brathwaite. Despite the weapon you choose to wield."

"Is that so?" Seifert scratched his neck without batting an eye. "And what exactly is wrong with my weapon?"

"It's a strong tool in your hands to be sure, but it isn't enough to defeat us."

Rasheda heard something foreign in Dario's tone: arrogance. A sentiment he never cared for in the past. Was the presence of this legend fueling his reckless curiosity? *Whatever. Just finish the job, that's all that matters.*

"Really?" Seifert smirked, and in one breath his scrawny frame stepped right next to Cutup. "And here I was thinking that I gine tek it easy 'pon wunna young folks."

It was for an instant that Dario lost track of Seifert, and in that time the old man had closed such a distance. Frightening. Truly a frightening sensation, meeting an opponent who was this strong. *This worthy.*

"Cool it, youngster. It ain time for you to die yet." His prey was taunting him. *Absurd.* Dario's composure crumbled away as his palm leaf was poised to strike. Then the sky salivated…

BRAX! Another eruption parted the two and from the cloud Rasheda stood with her blade in hand. "Aye, Dario, yuh laggin!"

Dario didn't respond, slithering towards Seifert in silence. Seifert also noticed the aggression fueling that palm leaf. No matter. He only needed a few adjustments to adapt.

Then the serpent vanished, if only for a heartbeat, and when Seifert caught his bearings, he heard the clicking of a cash register.

Ka-ching! The sound came from his right, and with it, he felt the air burn and bleed scarlet.

The explosion hurtled Seifert over the embankment and onto the houses below. Landing on a galvanized rooftop, he regarded the previous attack and the weapon it came from. *Close. Too close. I shoulda expect dah from one of Coalpot's works.*

A gaping fissure was left between the pair looking down from the road above. Headgone's blade radiating a rich, ruby light. *That destructive power ain nuh joke…*

Seifert inspected his hoe, realizing that the square, flat-blade had been mangled. Dario remarked, "Again, your skill is not embellished at all. To counter a strike from Headgone's released blade with a mere garden tool. Truly remarkable, Father Hoe."

"Thank yuh."

"But if you continue like this…" Dario disappeared again, emerging before Seifert with blurring black. "You will be the one to die!"

Even with the mutilated weapon, Seifert parried the lashes with deft skill. The problem was balance. Like a serpent would a scurrying chick, Dario hunted his prey across the rooftops. And when Seifert created some space, a flash of scarlet came from the heavens.

BOOM!

By now homeowners peeped outside to see what commotion lay above. Their faces agape as they witnessed three strangers hopping with explosions at their heel. A film shoot, obviously, though such things never happened in Bimshire.

Seifert was sandwiched between the two assassins, each one encircling him like a pair of lions to a wildebeest. The glorious hunt! Dario spoke with a satisfied gleam peeking over his scarf. "It appears your weapon has failed you, Mr. Brathwaite. But we both know that isn't a problem."

"Heh. Seems like yuh right."

"Now will you show them to me, Father Hoe? Those Canecutter techniques that helped you etch your name on history's page."

Yes. Step into the light.

Seifert didn't want to accept the invitation, but he had no choice. The crowd of bystanders grew by the second, a perfect meal for Headgone's Greedy Weapon. Time was running out.

"Tell me. When you attacked my student earlier, it was me you were after, wasn't it?"

"Does it really matter?" Cutup replied.

"I guess not, nuh?" Seifert made his decision, caressing the shattered hoe until he reached a certain nook near the center of the handle. He applied pressure; there was a click, followed by a gushing white light. *Can't believe I ended up breaking this seal again.*

Something else was broken. As the pieces of wood transfigured into two brilliant blades of silver, Seifert recalled a promise from long ago.

The era of the Canecutters is over. As long as there is peace, I will never wield these blades again.

But was there peace? Even as he stood before these products of the past, Seifert believed in the current Bimshire. Things were a far cry from the madness that wrought the island back then. But now, as the lives of innocents were in peril, Seifert couldn't abide by his pledge.

There's nothing more I can teach him. He has all the tools he needs. Seifert could only trust in Damian Collins. After all, the youth are the future of Bimshire.

"This is more like it." Cutup approved. "Now you look like a swordsman."

Seifert adopted his stance, right arm crossed over his left with a majestic cutlass held in each. He came from a story book; a fabled warrior whose mystery was only surpassed by his skill. Dario ogled the sight.

"I sorry, youngsters, but wunna ain gine survive this fight." Seifert said.

Then the three rushed forth.

Damian Collins was confused. After Sheraton he was between minds whether to continue training as before, or if to follow Sniper's advice and go into hiding until everything blew over. The second choice made him chuckle. When did he become such a coward? Even in the chaos of last year, Collins wasn't this afraid. But now the enemy breathed down his neck. At least, that is what his mind told him. Every unfamiliar face was scanned with trepidation. His fingers quick to draw a blade should a passerby be more than a tourist, a child or an old woman. Perhaps this was Kyle Harding's life, where one walked with a bulls-eye on his back for the rest of his days.

As usual Collins's stomach sank when he approached the bus stop. His cutlass restless as the vehicle trudged on. "Wha really gine on with me atall?"

This tension was foreign to Collins. It was the kind that hardened resolve and eroded comfort, in a way that explained Kyle Harding. During that week Collins consumed himself with training, callusing his body with bruises and scrapes. He wasn't exhausted, due to the tamarind ball he forced down after every session, and today Collins thumbed the sour morsel before reaching for his phone.

"Nadia again." Collins guessed as his pants' leg vibrated. Sheraton had unhinged his girlfriend even more than Collins himself.

Who were those people? Did you get out okay? Are you hurt?

Doubtful looks replaced concerned eyes, and there were twice as many calls or text messages. He answered to let Nadia hear his voice, repeated the errands he had today, and said his farewells. A wasted effort. There was no way to quell her fear, for the enemy was ever present. Ever threatening.

This thought rattled in his mind when he disembarked, and that was when Collins felt it. Something was wrong. Inching towards the secluded entrance of the beach, Collins caressed his blade's hilt.

An invisible chain had fastened his legs as he took each step. Was he really that afraid of Gulfsyde? Even after everything he witnessed last year? Brushing away the foliage he crept ever closer to the sheltered shore, inspecting anything his eyes could see and everything they could not. There was something here; something grave and dangerous, perchance. It was only when the sand clumped between his toes that Collins noticed the source of his discomfort.

"This is private property. Trespassers are not allowed." A cold voice greeted Collins, and before him was a peculiar trio sitting in the sand. Clad in wide-brimmed straw hats with a single cloth hanging over each face, they regarded him like a dog would an intruder.

"Wha de hell you talkin 'bout?" Collins pushed through his initial apprehension. "I've been coming to this beach for weeks and I ain see wunna yet. Who wunna is? Part Pops?"

"Oh? Is that a friend of Seifert?" A courteous drawl came from beyond them, from Father Hoe's grotto, and yet the question sounded like a whisper in his ear.

"You mean the old man?" Collins, feeling a bit more assured, strode forward as he asked the question. And when he got within five meters the trio rose to their feet; a simple, innocuous act which paralyzed Collins. "...What do you want?"

They were silent statues standing in the sun. Intimidating idols with skin of solid rock and coffee. It was suicidal to take another step, so Collins retained his position and rested a hand on his pocket. The polite rasp chimed in again,

"Please calm down, dear. We wouldn't want any more unfortunate events this morning." A podgy old woman wandered across the sand. Like the three idols, she wore a straw hat except there was nothing blocking her face. Her rumpled, coffee skin barely visible under the brim, the lady's stern expression was aimed right at Collins. "So, you were a friend of Seifert? What's your name, young man?"

"Collins ... Damian Collins." He said reluctantly.

She appraised Collins some more and recognized the hilt of his namesake. "A cutlass... So you are a Canecutter, too?"

"Yeah, I am."

"I see. Well, young man, I sorry to tell yuh this but Seifert ... Father Hoe has passed away." Like stones cast against a wall, her words met Collins's ears.

"What?" Just yesterday Father Hoe scolded him for slacking off his drills, and fed him sour tamarinds to quell his injuries. How could he be dead? "You kixxing, right?"

It had to be a joke; the cruelest, most bitter joke that a strange old woman could conjure. But there was no mischief in her words. In fact, Collins heard a bitter melancholy as she gave her declaration again. "I would never joke about death, young man."

She then reached into her bag and pulled out a fedora—Father Hoe's fedora—but with splotches of red all over the grey brim. "...How did he die?"

"Stroke. He's been working too hard these days, and yuh know the sun hasn't been very—"

"Bullshit." Collins said. "I see Pops run up and down this beach for a whole day without breaking a sweat, so I know that ain how he dead."

Her eyebrows were raised as she scrutinized Collins. Lying was futile.

"There was a conflict up Cane Vale this morning." She began like she was reading a weather report. "Father Hoe was confronted by two individuals—assassins, most likely. In an act of self-defense, he engaged them in battle, but he was eventually overpowered."

"Overpowered? Are you kidding me?" Collins couldn't see it. Once upon a time Father Hoe dispatched a group of assassins with ease, far less two. "Wait a minute. Did any of these guys have a palm leaf?"

It couldn't be them. Impossible. The old woman took too long to respond, like she was balancing the truth or more lies on a mental scale. "I believe so, yes. Have you seen them before?"

"Yeah." Collins faced the notion of his master falling before the very enemy he prepared for. An impossible notion. A notion he couldn't accept. "A couple times..."

"They were spotted on the scene, so I would reckon they were somehow involved." She continued. "The damage to the surrounding area matched their weapons as well, but one can't be too sure."

"And you just stood there?!" Collins didn't know where the outburst came from. "He ain you friend?"

"Now, son, de situation wasn't so straightforward—"

"Bullshit!" Dreadlocks and arms flailed and the trio stepped forward, to which she gestured them to halt. "You friend just died and you did nuttin!?"

She mopped her brow with a washcloth before speaking.

"I don't know what you think this is, young man, but we don't operate that way. This isn't the Wild West where you go 'bout the place killing every Tom, Dick and Harry."

"That's what they did with Pops." Collins retorted; all the rage evaporated from his voice.

"Yes... but they operated within the bounds of the law."

"What law you talking 'bout? What kinda law does let you get away with killing a man in cold blood?"

"Theirs."

Collins had no idea what this meant, nor did he care. He was exhausted. Broken. His knees almost buckled as the reality settled within.

"Mother Sally. Please do not forget your appointment at ten o'clock." The trio announced in unison.

"Oh yes, it's that sorta time, fuh truth." Mother Sally replied, sighing as she adjusted her hat. "No one is sorrier than me that this happened, young man. Seifert ... Father Hoe was a dear friend to me."

Collins wanted to interject again, but she continued,

"But there's nothing to be done about the matter now. He's gone. The one saving grace is that we managed to retrieve the body and was able to conduct a proper burial. You're welcomed to visit his grave if you like."

"… Where is it?"

"The interment took place in front of his home as he wished. Though I urge you to tek care when you go 'cross there. His grave is now a sacred place." Collins ignored the way she lingered on the last two words and began his trek past them. By now the trio had surrounded Mother Sally in a sort of defensive formation, disregarding Collins completely. "Goodbye now. Hopefully we meet again, God willing."

I hope not. Collins wished to himself. He heard a *poof* behind his back, and didn't bother to look because they were already gone.

The beach was still from that moment onward; even the waves seemed to be in mourning. Collins disregarded the hot sand in between his toes as he walked towards the burial place. His steps wobbling as he approached. The grave was surprisingly bland. No reefs, no flowers, and a solitary stick for a makeshift tombstone. It wasn't worthy of a true master, let alone a dear friend. "This is all she do fuh truth?"

Collins got within a foot of the grave before halting. For some reason he didn't want to get any closer. Perhaps it was out of respect, or that it mirrored the grave he made for his parents— either way he kept his position.

"…"

The crypt lost Collins for an hour. Too many things crossed his mind, horrific things. *Why did they come after you? Was this my fault? How could you lose against them?* "…I'm sorry."

Collins bowed before he left. The path to the entrance was clear; one couldn't even tell that a group of people stood there moments ago as the sand was undisturbed. However, Collins noticed something different from when he passed before. Propped at the base of a palm tree was a blade much like the one Collins had at his waist. A cutlass whose edge caught the rays of the overhead sun. It was lighter than his, and the blade itself had a simple design—akin to a machete.

"*Hmm. you gine need a sword just now.*"

"*How you mean? I already got a sword, Pops.*" Collins replied.

"*No, yuh poppit! I mean another sword to go wid de one you got already.*"

The conversation was still fresh in his mind despite being a week old. Too much was stolen from him. There was still so much he had to learn.

His pocket trembled wildly—Nadia again. "Hey … Yeah … Listen … Can I see you later? Yeah … Tonight. Okay…"

Collins slid a finger over the screen and resumed his stride towards the end of the bay. Disorder stewing in his mind; revenge simmering in his heart.

Linseed Beckles cherished days like this one. Damien had left earlier than usual for school, which seemed to be the case as of late. The boy no longer needed any prodding to get out of bed, much to his brother's approval. And on the days Kyle wasn't sparring, he was holed up in his room or away from the house altogether—in equal bouts of rest and mental preparation.

Linseed appreciated the free time, and with no other errands to run the old soul would finally enjoy something he considered a rarity: a good rest. Very seldom would Linseed sleep in the Harding household, despite having a room reserved for such moments.

He believed the boys deserved a little privacy now and then, especially now that Kyle was a capable young man. Cracking open the door to his chambers, he noted how preserved the divan looked next to the empty dressing table; with the afternoon sun creeping through a single window, the room had sufficient air and lighting for the old man. Actually, *sufficient* is the word

Linseed would use to describe the entire room, as it had all he felt was needed to rest. Lying down against the pillow, Linseed remembered the last time he slept in this bed. It was only a year ago that Dorian Nelson attacked this house; a Heart Man who targeted Kyle in the wee hours of the morning. Fortunately, Linseed didn't have to intervene as his student handled the situation, but he still felt the need to stick around just in case other parties wanted to join in that night.

Images of a sneering old woman and a young fifer skipped in Linseed's mind. With flashes of blue and yellow brushing the dark, still night, and the sound of clashes serenading his ear, the old man drifted off to sleep. That is, until he felt a ringing in his ear,

Linseed!

The call snapped him from slumber, and as Linseed's eyes darted about the room he realized that it was soon nightfall. Feeling his way around the dim chamber, he climbed from his bed and fished for his flat cap. Linseed slept for hours as the house was covered in darkness, save for Damien's room which had a golden hue seeping from inside. The boy came home and hadn't left his room since, but just to be sure Linseed rapped on the door.

"Damien, you good?"

"Mmm–Hmm."

Linseed cracked open the door and saw Damien face down in his books, completely oblivious to his surroundings.

De boy wun even look around in case somebody brek into de house. Linseed thought, but he knew such a thing was impossible. Veronica Harding had taken steps to protect the household when she was still alive, and even if by some rare circumstance her defenses were bypassed, Linseed himself would be there. No wonder the boy seemed so carefree, though the same couldn't be said for his older brother.

Kyle shuffled into the house looking restless as ever. His eyes were drained, his movements sluggish, and his voice exhausted as he greeted Linseed. "Hey."

"Evenin', Kyle. Rough day, nuh?" Kyle shook his head while trudging past, stopping to peek in at Damien's room before disappearing into his own. The ringing resumed.

Linseed.

"All right. All right, I comin…." He muttered, whoever had beckoned him was growing impatient. "Hey, Kyle, I heading off for the day. You gine be good?"

"Yeah, you go 'long."

Linseed tried to ignore the weariness in his voice.

Hmm. I gine have a chat with him when I come back. He thought before setting off.

Linseed was still adjusting to his walks up Molasses Drive. With Rachel Pringle gone, he no longer had to worry about any traps she hid in his wake. No more plum-shaped mines or man-eating cracks in the ground. The road was completely clear, allowing him to reach the top of the hill with more ease than before. Better yet, Linseed need not be concerned with these hazards endangering other people, especially Kyle or Damien. Regarding the disheveled mass of lianas where that peach chattel house used to be, Linseed didn't miss Ms. Pringle one bit.

He sighed upon reaching the bus stop. Linseed could've saved an hour's trip if he really wanted to, but that would create a whole host of problems. If only things were different. The notion crossed his mind as seldom as he used the Transit, and after ten minutes the whirring of the bus's old engine caught his ears. It was a short trip, though with a second bus to catch Linseed wished for something more instantaneous. He didn't care for the dancehall music blaring from the speakers either, but it was better than the static in his ears.

His destination was a bit strange. Dropping a two-dollar bill into the conductor's palm, he sauntered from the bus stop towards the edge of the roundabout. Warrens was the location; a place that had seen plenty misfortune over the past year despite its welcoming appearance. Many quaint concrete buildings lined the streets when he passed, each one housing some respectable business. The most outstanding of these structures stood on Linseed's right; with a white dome housing expensive cars through the glass, Bimshire Shipping and Trading towered like a beacon throughout Warrens. And to its right were much less extravagant buildings, where a furniture retail store and a restaurant resided. Linseed regarded the latter, which was full with the evening crowd, and felt his stomach growl.

"Crap. I forgot to eat something before I left de house." The sweet aroma of rotisserie chicken teased his palate, while he looked at the yellow-and-red neon of Chicken Barn. Linseed was tempted to stop but the static had returned; this time with a louder hiss and an urgent tone. "Geez."

Several cars buzzed past as he continued his trek, and it was quite the task crossing the highway without getting knocked down. Skipping across the road to the protest of startled drivers, Linseed made his way down the belt looking as aimless as ever. However, his destination became clear when an old hawker, sitting patiently next to a burning coal pot, waved at him.

"Finally! I was beginning to think you didn't get my Call."

"Oh, I get it all right…." Linseed rubbed his ear expecting blood to be on his fingertip, but there was none. "Is everything okay, Betty?"

Betty fished a blackened corncob from the pot, placed it in a husk, and handed it to an appreciative Mr. Beckles. He was about to sink his teeth into the morsel when she said, "Seifert is dead."

That statement sucked the flavor from the bite he just took, and Linseed simply glanced at her. "Are you serious? Father Hoe—*the Last Blade?*"

Betty nodded solemnly. She'd never forgotten that Seifert Brathwaite was one of Bimshire's living legends, but as a dear friend, she never once considered using that title when referring to him. It was the same for Linseed Beckles.

"How?"

"There was a skirmish at Cane Vale this morning involving Seifert and two others. He was ambushed … at least, that's what they say in de news." Betty didn't mean the evening news that was broadcasted every night at seven o'clock. No. She meant another type of media which only a small portion of Bimshire's populace was privy to. Fetching a newspaper from the stool she was sitting on, Betty pulled out one page which seemed blank to the average eye until she tapped the sheet and words started to appear.

THE LAST BLADE FOUND DEAD headlined the page with a small blurb detailing what Betty described earlier. Still not registering this information, Linseed asked, "Ambushed? Father Hoe doesn't get *ambushed*."

No, sir. Not Father Hoe. The Parish War had ample time to prove that. Even with numerous enemies, unfavorable terrain and clever magic, the task of taking down Father Hoe was next to impossible. Linseed witnessed this himself.

"Who did it? Did they say?"

"Nothing was released officially, but I hear it involve Debt Collection."

"Debt Collection?" Linseed's eyebrows nearly popped through the brim of his cap. "You telling me the greatest Canecutter in Bimshire get tek out by a bunch of Debt Collectors?"

Betty understood why Linseed smiled wryly at the notion. It was nonsensical when you said it aloud. "…Do you think de Admin's involved?"

"Seifert was still dem enemy, regardless of what peace agreements get draft."

"Yes … but it can't be that simple. Seifert, like all other surviving members of de Opposition, was granted amnesty from dem actions during de Parish War in exchange for peace. Dem can't just kill he so."

"Why not?" Linseed bit into the cob, mostly out of courtesy than hunger. "If they really want he dead, they could always find some loophole to justify his assassination. It was only a matter of time before it happened anyway."

"You really think so?" Betty noticed his forlorn expression. "…You think someday they'd come after you?"

"Like I said, it's only a matter of time." He nibbled on the cob once more as the pot crackled beside him. Orange embers danced underneath while the flame struggled against the night breeze. Betty didn't try to maintain it, nor were there many corncobs on the grill. She wasn't in an area that guaranteed customers, unless the hawker was selling her more peculiar wares. That was when Linseed got an idea. "Did he buy anything from you recently?"

"…Yes. Seifert does buy from me once in a while. Not as

often as you, but off and on…" Betty rubbed her palms into her skirt and fed a handful of coal into the flames. "What you thinkin?"

"That maybe he broke some hidden clause in de agreement. Like dem find some technicality to catch he on." Linseed finished his cob while Betty mused over his words.

"Well… He used to buy some Manna Tamarinds from me, but I can't think of anything else right now."

"I see." Linseed gazed at the white streaks passing along the road, following one particular pair towards the gas station nearby. He recalled that incident last year, when a gas attendant's body was found several blocks away. Dorian Nelson stole her heart, too. "This place has seen its fair share of adversity, nuh?"

"Hmm?"

"I mean wid de girl dem find down de road, and that accident that happen couple weeks back." So much tragedy had befallen Warrens that it could've been a valuable resource for the Dark Arcs. Linseed knew little about obeah magic, but it was not rare to see Practitioners setting up shop near crash sites or murder scenes. Depending on the level of misfortune, they would stay in the area for months, even years. Betty must be doing the same.

"To me, it's not any worse than de ole days. At least we ain losing anybody that regular." Linseed caught the shadows behind her, stretching under the hue of overhanging street lights like an intricate spider's web. "My weapons are involved, you know…"

"*Lickerish Arms*? You sure?"

"A good artisan always knows the destiny of his works." Betty recited while the web stretched across the night. Linseed was captivated by it. "At least one of my pieces in de island. I recognize dem from a couple years ago."

"So dem connected to Debt Collection, you think?"

"Might be. All I know is my pieces grew significantly in malice since then." Betty gasped. "You don't—"

"I don't think anyone in Debt Collection could tek out Father Hoe, to be honest. But if you Greedy Weapons involved…" Linseed removed his flat cap and scratched the grey mat on his head. "Man, I don't know, hear?"

"It's okay, Linseed. What's done is done." Betty's tone betrayed her words, and she averted his gaze as she tended the pot. "I guess this is the end of de Canecutters, then."

"Not nearly. One of Kyle's friends look like one, too. I don't know how he slipped through de cracks, but I point him in de right direction."

"Fuh truth?! So, you mean Seifert had an apprentice?" Endless theories scrolled through her mind, but Betty didn't neglect her pot, much to Linseed's surprise.

"Like you say: this ain as straightforward as I thought. But if de boy did find Father Hoe…" The spider web retreated into Betty's shadow. She'd finished harvesting for the day.

"De news had me so good that I ain even ask for de boys. How dem doing?"

"Dem good. Kyle overworking himself lately, but Damien seems fine." Betty noted the waver in his voice. "He may be facing some tough opponents soon, though."

"Oh dear. I just hope it ain got nuttin to do with my weapons." Betty was sincere in her wish; she knew what carnage her creations had wrought in the past. However, Linseed expressed another concern,

"By the way, do you have any news about Sulemann?"

"The Conductor?"

"Yes. I hear he was spotted in de island recently."

"He was. But I ain hear nuttin else since then. You know well enough that if The Conductor don't want to be found, nobody gine find he." Mr. Beckles grunted in agreement.

"Just keep me posted."

"You know I will. So de Admin really—"

"I just tell yuh I ain know." Betty knew she was a broken record, but she understood his frustration. Linseed liked to have all the pieces of the puzzle, especially when the puzzle was this dangerous. "But don't count out Sulemann from this. I certain he can't be up to anything good."

Betty nodded in agreement, yanking one more cob from the crackling coals while conjuring a bottle and two glasses from the shadows. "Here."

The sweet fragrance tickled Linseed's nostrils. "Mauby and

falernum? Betty, I don't drink alcohol, yuh forget?"

"But it's only a capful fuh flavor, Linseed—it can't kill yuh."

He grumbled as she poured some of the mixture for herself.

"Oh, all right. But only fuh Seifert." The two clinked glasses and took long swigs. The alcohol was enough to ignite Linseed's stomach but not dull his wits.

"So, what happens now?"

"Nuttin else to do but wait, I guess." He inspected the glass and looked morosely at the contents. Betty added another cupful without forcing him to ask. "I more worried about Kyle, to be honest."

"Well, those boys were brought up by the great *Bruggadown*. You should have some more faith in them."

"Fair enough. But if he was to come up against a *Coalpot* original…" Betty was aghast at the thought. "Ah well. You probably right, I worry too much."

"Linseed… If anything was to happen to them because of something I made… I couldn't—"

"No no, I sure that ain gine happen anyway." His words were for Betty's sake, but the truth is, Linseed was troubled by these series of events. His old comrade dead. Debt Collectors. Lickerish Arms. And at the heart of it all: The Conductor.

Things were about to change. Linseed couldn't say how, but he felt as sure as the sweet taste of falernum on his tongue.

Nadia had never been happier to see a bed in her life. Rousing from the wee hours of the morning, hustling to school, slaving at work, dealing with tedious people and failing to keep her calm during the commute back home, it was clear that this was the hardest day in recent memory. Kicking off her heels, she plopped herself onto the divan face first.

"Finally…"

Sighing from under a pillow, Nadia noticed that her bed was still unmade from this morning. It stood out in an otherwise organized room which was coded in pink, purple and white—her favorite colors. The evening sun poured through the windows, casting its light upon the cabinet by her bedside. Scattered across the mahogany were phials of perfumes, creams, powders and brushes, which trembled as a phone vibrated nearby. Nadia ignored it, until the fifth buzz became a nuisance.

"Who is this now, nuh?" Nadia groaned while reaching for the phone. The obscenities were hot on her tongue; but her mood softened when she saw Damian's name on the screen. It was the longest relationship she ever had, spanning three years. Normally one to prefer flings, Nadia fell for Collins when he became more than a pretty face. Funny, caring, attentive, his qualities read like a grocery list, but Nadia soon discovered that everything wasn't gold. Collins had secrets. Nadia assumed he cheated with one of the leggings that swarmed him every day, but after Sheraton she knew different. Collins held something darker—more severe.

"…" Nadia stared blankly at the phone, which had stopped ringing so she had to call him back. "Hello? Damian?"

"Hey." His husky voice spilled from the receiver. Nadia almost didn't recognize it.

The conversation was brief. Nadia noted the distress in his tone. He was distracted. No. *Empty.* Something had sucked the life out of her boyfriend's words. "I wonder what's wrong…"

Collins wanted to meet that evening. He'd say nothing more until then. Though Nadia got a grim notion that it involved the two weirdos from Sheraton.

Hours dissolved into nightfall, and in that time Nadia couldn't rest. She showered, rustled up an outfit, and did something with the bob-cut on her head. She regarded her reflection with slight disapproval, when the phone vibrated again.

"Must be Damian." His name flashed across the screen. It was a mad rush to the door to greet Collins instead of her parents, or worst yet, her pet terriers.

"You expecting somebody, Nadia?" Her mother asked from the kitchen. Nadia rolled her eyes; drama was the last thing she needed right now. So, with sandals in hand, Nadia eased outside with only a vague farewell. The terriers barked at her ankle the moment they spotted her.

"Yeah, mom, I gone."

Collins stood in her driveway with a bewildered look on his face. He wasn't too dressed up, wearing a blue Evolve T-shirt, a pair of cargo shorts and canvas sneakers. "Hey…"

"Hurry up and get in, nuh!" Nadia barked while swinging the ignition of her Runnex. Collins noticed the window drapes shifting as they pulled into the street.

"Trying to get 'way from the folks, huh?"

"…I ain in the mood for nuh stress." Nadia sighed. She craved the sleep that was promised to her this evening.

"Want me to drive?"

"Yes please." Stopping the car as they cleared the corner, Nadia remembered how often Collins had taken the wheel—both literally and figuratively. He always knew when she needed comfort. She didn't even have to ask.

But Collins was somewhere else tonight; a place where a bus stop was frightening enough to set his jaw. Nadia asked, "You okay?"

Collins nodded over the engine. Its hum stifled by the bass-heavy beats of some pop song on the radio. "Hey, you still got dem CDs I lend you a while back?"

"Yeah, I should still got them," Nadia retrieved two CDs from the glove compartment; one of which filled the car with Bob Marley.

"Thanks." Collins grinned. It was eight o'clock on a Saturday night yet the road was empty. As they zipped along the west-coast roads of St. James, Nadia didn't even see a headlight from any passing vehicles. It was strange, but not as strange as Collins's behavior. "I lost someone today."

"Huh?" The words were a whisper over the guitar solo, but Collins repeated.

"My … Grandfather passed away today."

"Oh no…" Nadia's stomach sank with the remorse that gripped her. "I'm so sorry."

"It's cool. We weren't that close." Suddenly Nadia saw the

cracks in his cheerful façade now that she was paying attention.

"You weren't?"

"To be honest, we only met a couple weeks back." The laugh was a hollow one. Had they grown so close in only a few weeks? "But… He was a good man."

"I'm sure he was." Discomfort cloyed at Nadia's throat, fastening her tongue. It was the first time this happened around him. "How your folks taking it?"

"I don't have any folks."

It didn't register at first, what he meant by that statement, but then Nadia considered if she ever met Collins's parents or if he ever mentioned them at all.

"My parents died when I was younger." He confirmed the horrifying epiphany.

"…I'm such a poppit."

"Nah, it's okay. I never tell you 'bout them so you wouldn't had known." Collins reassured her. "It was a car accident. They were walking alongside the road when a driver got distracted—he was on the phone or something, they say—and ran off the road. The car was moving too fast for them to react and…"

Rubbish. Absolute rubbish. His parents were *Canecutters*; of course, they were able to react. This detail always jangled in his mind, like some unknown, broken part in an otherwise fine-tuned machine. It drove him down this path, where magic and violence paved each step. Nadia assumed his silence was a result of the subject.

"I'm really sorry. I shouldn't have brought it up."

"Well, at least they didn't go like Pops did." Collins gave a wry smile. He wasn't so sure.

"How did your Granddad die?"

"Stroke." Collins thought it rolled off the tongue better than assassination. "He was the sort of guy who liked to spend all day in the sun, even for his age. Guess it finally got to him…."

As he recited the same twaddle that Mother Sally tried to sell him earlier, Collins couldn't help but feel repulsed. It was for the best. Nadia wasn't ready to enter his world—not now—maybe not ever. Her eyes bored into him, to the point where Collins nearly drifted off the road. Panicked horns smothered the music.

"We should probably stop somewhere and talk." Nadia suggested.

"Yeah, you're right."

Time escaped them as they talked, and before she knew it, they were on the outskirts of St. Peter. The golden lights from grandiose west-coast hotels were replaced with white hues from charming abodes. The beach was no longer hidden by private properties and guest houses. Nadia gazed at the expanse of black, while the opening lyrics of *Exodus* oozed from the speakers. It was a relaxing atmosphere they couldn't indulge in. Collins especially, who remembered the chaos that rent the north of the island last year; where Bakus animated bicycles and clothespins to do their nasty bidding.

"So, where we gine?" Nadia asked.

Collins didn't know. He was just driving for driving's sake. Using the music, the engine's hum and blurring night to dull his thoughts. Upon reaching the Speightstown stoplights, he turned right and drove up the hill to Mile and a Quarter. "Feel we should head up Farley Hill?"

"At this time?!" Nadia glanced at the growing darkness around her and wished for someplace more illuminated. "I guess we could go...."

"Cool." Farley Hill wasn't far, and at the speed the Runnex was cruising they would reach within ten minutes. In that time Nadia wrapped her mind around Collins's childhood.

"So, you grew up alone?"

"Yup."

"But—How does that?" Nadia scrambled for words. "What about school? Nobody ain ask you nuh questions? Teachers?"

"I had Ms. Marshall sort me out at times like that." Collins described his living arrangement throughout the years. Ms. Marshall, a close family friend, would often check in on little Collins to see how he was doing. There was no mention of other family members, or social workers, or foster care. Still Ms. Marshall was there, doing laundry, preparing meals, and helping around the house. She was a guardian for the orphan Collins, except he didn't want a guardian, he wanted his parents.

"I can take care of myself."

Collins remembered saying those words. Remembered Ms. Marshall's bemused expression. Remembered not caring if they hurt her or not. For his hurt was all that mattered.

"Wow … I can't believe what I hearing." Nadia said.

Farley Hill National Park was one of the most renowned places in Bimshire. For years it was the venue of family picnics, church excursions, and the odd concert during the Crop Over season. A natural vista of exotic trees, vibrant thickets of gold, purple and green, and the remnants of classic architecture. The night concealed all of this. Only darkness extended beyond the window pane when Nadia stared outside.

"I can't believe I never noticed." Nadia questioned their entire relationship. How much was he hiding from her? Did she really know him at all? Nadia often visited Collins's house, and in all those visits she never saw or asked about his parents. Too focused on getting some, or spending quality time. Only thinking of herself—*always* thinking of herself. *How could I be so selfish?*

The sky began to shed tears, each drop crashing into the hood of the Runnex. Bob Marley was drowned by the surrounding pitter-patter, but his music fell on deaf ears at this point. Collins continued,

"He didn't deserve it, yuh know." Nadia turned to him in silence. "To die like that, I mean. Pops was a good man; he didn't deserve to die like a dog. And it is my fault."

"From a stroke? But how that get you fault?" Nadia asked. Collins was shuddering, his hazel eyes lost in the abyss.

If I never met him—if I never asked him to train me—Gulfsyde wouldn't have found him. They would've focused on me and Kyle. He would still be sitting on the beach, eating snack boxes and shitty tamarinds. Collins looked at Nadia, and his chest hammered with the notion. Was he doing the same thing? Was he inviting death to her door, too? "I push he too hard, I mean. Used to cause he stress all the time—you know how I is."

"I understand." Nadia replied.

"I don't think you do." His words had stung her just like Ms. Marshall. Collins didn't want that. "I mean you been with your folks all your life, right? Lived together, heard old family stories, met relatives—even the ones you don't like very much."

Collins laughed, and Nadia observed him carefully.

"But me now… I only had my parents. I ainno a thing about my other family. It's like a whole chapter full uh blank pages from a book I can't find. Yuh know?"

"Yeah, I know." Nadia rubbed his hand. Her fingers tender and warm over his skin. Collins hadn't noticed her this evening. She was there, but he wasn't relishing in her like usual. She wore a sleeveless Chambray shirt and a pair of khaki capris. Her hair was a little rustled but Nadia had never looked more beautiful.

"Sorry. Bet this wasn't your idea of a date tonight, nuh?"

"Nah it's cool, I miss hanging out like this." Collins raised his eyebrows, and then they giggled. "Plus, you had a lot to get off your chest."

"True. I could tell yuh which chest I wanna get 'pon now." Collins beamed, and Nadia sucked her teeth. Thankfully her boyfriend had returned.

"Perv!"

"Only where you concerned, hun."

Without another word Collins leaned towards her; the motion so sudden Nadia gasped in surprise. She was soft, really soft. How long had it been since he held her? Collins wondered as he inhaled her cinnamon scent, the fragrance now novel to his palate. "Thanks…"

"For what?" Nadia asked from under his embrace.

"…Being here."

Collins stirred a few hours later. He had no idea when he fell asleep, but it was clear how as Collins regarded the naked beauty lying on his chest.

"O-Oww!" He winced while Nadia shifted on her makeshift bed. For a second, Collins wished she had been in the other passenger seat, but she seemed so peaceful in slumber that he ignored any discomfort.

Then Collins felt it: a chill so bitter that it undermined the warmth of Nadia's body. It wasn't the wind. The windows were up, and the air was saturated with cinnamon and sweat. Peering through the pane Collins only saw fog and black, but there was no mistaking it. *Something is here...*

"Hmm?" Nadia stirred in his lap. He had to get her away as quickly as possible. But nothing happened when he swung the ignition. Only silence.

"What the hell gine on?" Collins muttered while eyeing his phone; the screen was white and he couldn't call out. *Damn...*

Collins felt the voracious gaze of his unseen predator. Like a rabbit aware that his death lay beyond the black. His options were few: no communication, no transport, no escape. It had to be Gulfsyde...

Collins reached for the blades lying dormant at his feet. There was no doubt that he would need them tonight, and like an invitation the door eased open on its own volition. "So that's how it is, nuh?"

Collins accepted, securing his blade and clothes while easing out of the Runnex. He took a fleeting glance at Nadia before locking the door. It wasn't much, and Collins could only hope she was secure while he was away.

Fuck... Collins began his trek through the night. A bitter draft nipped his skin as he strode, and as he glanced at the sky there wasn't a star to be seen. Only masses of grey amidst the ink. His footsteps heavy from the damp soil clinging beneath, Collins urged forward until the Runnex was no longer in view.

Where are you? Collins wondered as he traversed those hostile shadows. Above him, the wiry canopies of North Island Opines watched closely. Perhaps the enemy lurked up there? He regarded the feather-like branches, but that enmity that lured Collins from his car couldn't be found anywhere near. No. His adversary was further beyond, past the old wooden benches, the Casuarinas and the Traveler's Palms. Not a street light was on, and what would normally be a nice scenic walk to the top of the hill, was now a dreadful march into the unknown. "Come out, you bastard."

Behind him the Runnex was swallowed by the darkness. It was just as well—the further they were from Nadia the better. Nevertheless, with each step Collins grew uneasy as he scoured every trunk, shrub and branch for his opponent until finally he came upon a towering structure. No longer complete, the building stood before him like a mansion would a pauper—elegant yet imposing. Farley Hill Great House was once home to the wealthy elite of Bimshire; among its guests were royalty from the Mother Country in colonial times. An edifice of extravagance, the house provided many days of entertainment for its guests. Word of the parties and picnics were rumored amid the bourgeoisie, not only of the island but of the entire region. However, after the owners passed, the mansion ran to ruin due to the rising cost of its upkeep. Generations later, the Great House was reduced to walls of weathered stone, pillaged by man and nature alike. Still, this structure was never desecrated, and as Collins sauntered into its abandoned halls, he felt just a hint of the history there.

"He's here." The hostility touched him and sprouted gooseflesh. Collins drew his blade, combing each wall for the slightest presence. He could only imagine the characters that passed through these vestibules. They probably wined and dined like no one else in Bimshire—engaging in frivolous chats about fashion or politics. But tonight, there were no such festivities; something much more dreadful awaited the mansion's guest. The moon surfaced through the ink sky, shining its light upon the roofless abode and onto the figure before Collins.

It was Dario.

"Ah, Canecutter, I see you finally made it." He was seated on a pillar of concrete.

"…How did you find me?"

Dario held up a lock of hair which Collins recognized as his own.

"Did you think you could hide from us, Damian Collins?" There was no malice in his voice, just cold, calculating affirmation. "From the beginning, you and the Harding boy were always well within our reach."

"Wow. Yuh know for an assassin you kinda suck at your

job." Collins ambled forward, ignoring the quiver in his legs. *When did he get a piece of my hair? Was it from back at the beach or was it before?* These questions made his mind stir but Dario had one of his own.

"How do you mean?"

"You had ample time to kill me when I was walking up here, but you 'bout de place liming." He had to buy time. Despite the open ruins, Collins knew that he couldn't escape Cutup. Not with that speed.

"True. I do see your point." Dario fastened the red scarf around his neck against the heavy breeze. "If I wanted to, I could've killed you long before you arrived at this place. But what fun would there be in that?"

"Fun? Is this some kinda game to you?"

"No, not at all. I'll have you know that I take my line of work very seriously." Dario stood, perhaps a little offended by his target's allegation. "It's just that after killing so many people on a regular basis, the task has lost its appeal. Nowadays, most don't even resist in their last moments. It's as if they didn't value their lives enough to fight back."

"I see." Collins mused. "Is that why you went after Pops? To see him fight back?"

"No. Seifert Brathwaite was a different case."

Seifert Brathwaite. Collins never knew Father Hoe's real name. He supposed it was one of the many things he didn't know. "So, if he was a different case, why you had to attack de man? He ain got nothing to do with me or Kyle Harding."

"Hmm. That may be true, but I'm afraid Father Hoe's battle was a bit indulgent on my part." His words were authentic but they still infuriated Collins. "You see I was curious."

"Curious?"

"Yes. Can you blame me, though?" Dario outstretched his arms and bowed his head, as if before an invisible altar. "He was *the* Father Hoe, after all. A living legend from the Parish War. Who wouldn't want to fight him?"

"The Parish War?" Collins lingered on the term. As far as he knew there haven't been any wars in Bimshire, or the Caribbean for that matter.

"Surely you have felt the same at some point, right? You have the blood of a warrior flowing through your veins." Dario was deranged, that much was clear, yet there was a time when Collins could relate to that twisted passion. A time when the sight of a Stick-licker practicing in the school yard made him draw his blade. He was *curious* about Kyle Harding, too.

"*Man. If I was to find one right now, those warriors I mean, I'd challenge one to a duel on the spot!*"

I actually said something like that, nuh? Collins thought in secret shame.

"You don't understand either. A pity. You are just like her." Dario shook his head while memories of the Gulf returned to him. Collins had the exact portrait of contempt that Kamilah wore back then. The kind that stirred Dario's hunger more. Still, it was Collins who drew his weapon first, assuming his stance with the blade facing in front. "Oh? Have I offended you?"

"Nah. I just get tired uh waiting for you to kill me. So I decide to put up a fight before I go—yuh know, kicking and screaming and what not."

"Interesting." Dario's cheeks rose over his scarf. "Just like Mr. Brathwaite—he, too, chose to skip the pleasantries."

Collins didn't see when he hopped off the beam, landed on the ground and dashed twenty meters to reach him, yet there Dario was with weapon outstretched, ready to take his head.

Clang! Somehow the cutlass was there to parry it, giving Collins enough time to distance himself from the enemy.

"Congratulations. You've passed the first test." Dario brushed the hem of his robes. "The fact you've managed to block that strike means you have improved."

"Thanks." Collins replied hollowly. His arm still trembled.

With a flick of his wrist, the bandages around Dario's weapon unraveled to show the black palm leaf. Its bristles and stalk stained like the night above.

"The hell?" It wasn't from any tree in Bimshire, and as Dario dragged it across the stones below, Collins's suspicions were confirmed.

"Oh? Has my weapon caught your interest, Canecutter?" Collins dared not respond. "It's nothing really; I just managed to get my palm leaf enhanced. I'm not sure what the procedure was exactly, but I've been assured that it's more durable. As you can see…" Dario scraped a nearby wall and a chunk of concrete was shaved off easily.

Damn… As if a normal one wasn't bad enough. Collins fortified his stance, despite the chill strumming his nerves.

"Good expression. You didn't even cringe at the sight of my weapon—very good." There was no emotion behind the accolade but Dario was sincere. "Get ready."

Dario vanished once more, appearing this time to Collins's right with palm leaf overhead. Like a provoked viper, it bit into his blade with so much force that Collins skipped backwards. *Shit!*

Each strike was swift and precise, as Dario aimed the palm leaf at conflicting areas of the body. From the head to the toes, to the arms and the waist, his mixups caused Collins to scramble in defending them. "What's the matter, Canecutter? Where is that conviction you had mere seconds before?"

In the face of this onslaught Collins had no options. Each swipe was so potent that his arm flew with every parry he made. It was a struggle to even hold his sword. But he held on, hopping away to study his situation.

There's no way I can keep this up. I gotta attack somehow, but that weapon … It has too much reach.

The black palm leaf stretched seven feet away from Dario's body, and from the way he wielded it, the weapon was light and flexible. Dario moved forward, a snake in the dark, slithering towards Collins who barely deflected the blade while sliding to his side. This time Dario saw a glint of silver nipping at his neck.

"Oh ho." Dario said; his throat unscathed from the counterattack. His prey had assumed a different stance than before. One that was very familiar to the assassin. "You really are his apprentice."

By now Collins had drawn his second cutlass so that he wielded two swords. The first blade was held in his dominant right arm with the cutting edge pointed outwards, while the second blade was held in his left with the defensive edge before his face. In short, the swords created a ying-yang formation of defense and offense which had been passed down from generation to generation of Canecutters—a stance which was last adopted by the late Seifert Brathwaite.

"*The Dual Machete Style* ... I am pleased to see it again." Collins didn't respond, but hardened his grip around the blades' hilts. "Now show me if you are up to par, Damian Collins."

Several droplets of water drizzled from above while the wind churned throughout the ruins: a perfect arena. Dario disappeared, writing through the downpour with bloodlust fueling his gait. Yet when he emerged to Collins's left, the fresh blade was there to meet him. *Skreee!* The screams of metal against leaf echoed as they exchanged slashes. At first things were looking up for Collins. With his new fighting style came advantages, as he was granted an extra second with which he could use to counterattack.

That is, if Dario allowed it.

The assassin had quickly adapted to the new stance, brushing aside every repost with vigor and fluidity. The difference in ability was clear.

"Shit!" Collins groaned, as sharpened bristles grazed his leg after one well-placed parry. A flurry of black danced about his body, forcing him to sacrifice his blades to the barrage in order to save his flesh. *I can't keep up!*

"Tsk…" Dario gave another thrust which sent Collins scrambling to regain his balance. "You execute the technique well but… It's not the same. You're not *him*."

Collins didn't respond.

"Something is lacking." Dario patted his robes, but Collins dared not move another step. "And I even refrained from using objects that were advantageous to me."

For a second, Dario gazed onto the horizon before returning to his prey. Then in a placid tone he asked, "Tell me, have you ever killed someone before?"

The bemusement on Collins's face was an adequate response.

"I think I understand what is missing from your blade, Damian Collins: *violence*." At that, the serpent pounced again, shaving the two cutlasses with its bite. Sparks and blood swirled among raindrops, and Dario offered no reprieve. "There is no vigor behind your sword. No *intent*. That is the fundamental difference."

His mind drifted off to past battles, against the Shotta Boss and Father Hoe. *Oh, what malice surrounded them!* His musing would be interrupted by two sharpened edges, which Dario calmly swatted away. Cracking a defiant grin, Collins skipped backwards and resumed his stance.

"Oh, fuh real? Then how 'bout you offer up your neck and let's see how that works out?"

"Your courage is commendable, but the sword does not lie." Dario tugged his scarf. His eyes piercing over the scarlet around his neck. "Every action you take is driven by panic. When you defend, your blade scrambles to protect you from harm. When you attack, your blade scrambles to harm your opponent. Put simply, your style is reactionary. Afraid."

Clang!

"You talk too much." Collins planted his cutlass into the black palm leaf. Dario resumed his point.

"It is clear that you are not accustomed to this environment. Where death lurks around every corner, and brutality is a natural part of the day. For you, violence is just a course of action which you are forced to take, but for me, violence is a way of life."

The serpent demonstrated by lashing its fangs at Collins again; however, its bite was more ferocious than before as Collins felt his blades curling under the pressure of that palm leaf. The pouring rain did nothing to quell the burn in his limbs, and he struggled under the weight of blood loss. This was a losing battle. "Still… I can't afford to die here."

Collins huffed to himself while the enemy marched forth, dragging his weapon against the flooded concrete. "In the end you will lose, not because of my superior skills, strength or speed. Oh no. You will lose because you lack resolve."

It wasn't a lie. Cutup was far beyond his level, and no amount of training could sway his fate. Still, Collins clung to his swords as if they were his very breath. If anything, resolve was the only thing he had left. Then Collins remembered Father Hoe. The parrow had left behind another memento besides his new machete. And as Collins fished a small inhaler from his pocket, he recalled his last conversation with his master.

"Welp. I think dah's de end uh that. I ain got nuttin more to teach yuh."

"Seriously? That's it?" Collins asked. After several grueling weeks with the parrow, Collins felt no different.

"Yeaz, nuh! Wait. You trying to tell me that you ain understand nuttin from my lessons?" Father Hoe sucked his teeth.

"I mean, to be honest, we ain do anything different from what I normally do. Aside from dem heavy-ass weights…" Collins muttered while looking at his calloused ankles.

"You ain gine realize it now, but trust me when I say you done."

"Pops… If you need more snackboxes I could always sort you out, yuh know?" Father Hoe howled while tossing him an object from under his hat. *"What's this?"*

"It's Sinse herbs mixed with some horehound extract. Just inhale some of that when you get in a dangerous situation."

"Am. I don't really do drugs, Pops. Looks can be deceiving, yuh know." Collins rolled his eyes, but Father Hoe had a stern expression.

"Back in de day, there was a theory that select Canecutters had a certain reaction whenever they inhaled the smoke from Sinse herbs. I never took it seriously until I saw it for myself. She was a delightful girl, too…"

Father Hoe drifted to a more violent time when he stumbled onto this young couple. They were a charitable pair, even in the midst of that carnage, and Father Hoe couldn't understand how for the life of him they managed to be so kind. It was the girl who revealed the effects of that drug after she was forced to use it in battle.

"Listen. I know you mussy hear how dangerous Sinse is, but this particular strain is even more potent. Use it only when you at the end of your rope. And even then, please give it proper consideration."

Father Hoe's warning drowned out the downpour as Collins examined the inhaler in his hand. What would happen when he smoked these herbs? Was it worth the risk? As Dario strode forward in a deadly march, Collins believed that this was an "end-of-your-rope" situation.

"Sorry, Pops, I don't really got nuh choice…."

He raised the mouthpiece to his lips; apparently there was some mechanism in the inhaler that burned the dried leaves inside. The sour white mist spewed down the back of his throat like fire. Collins had never smoked before so the coughing was expected, but he didn't anticipate the ringing in his ears, the trembling in his fingers or the blurring of his vision. The world had turned black and white. And all light was sucked away from anything that didn't move.

"What the hell is this?" Collins hacked, while glowing droplets fell from above in slow motion. The sound was absent as well, except for the thunderous pounding of his heart. Regret filled his mind while he struggled to hold his blades. Then he noticed something else within the darkness: a great serpent, with scales like the moon, writhed towards him at a menacing pace.

Nothing had changed. He had poisoned himself for nothing; that was what Collins thought as the sharpened palm leaf plunged at his face. But this was different. Now the weapon was suspended in midair for eons. Like the rainfall, Dario's movements had slowed down but Collins had not. With a mixture of confusion and relief, he raised the dull end of his machete, guiding it away from his body. The parry sent Dario askew, and the assassin quickly backed away to examine this new development.

"This is…" His nose peaked over the drenched red scarf. "Sinse…?"

Dario was incredulous, and for the first time Collins felt he had an advantage in this battle. Caution seasoned Dario's approach as he scrutinized his prey. Testing Collins's abilities, Dario aimed his leaf towards the most awkward spots on his body. Nevertheless, every time his ankle, torso or kneecap was targeted, a blade was there to protect it; easily providing not only shelter for Collins but a vanguard as well, with movements as fluid as the water around them. Dario noticed the change in his quarry's motions as he gazed at the flickering white pupils glaring back at him. Collins had the eyes of a Loa, with two stars penetrating the black. Alert and aware.

I can see. Collins thought, as he marveled at the black-and-white world. The streaks of light piercing through the ink were more beautiful than threatening. The serpent's shroud had lifted, revealing a sprinting Dario whose scarf billowed behind him and whose palm leaf dragged on the ground. Collins was impressed by the brilliant white footsteps which glided over the slippery tiles below. He never noticed it before, but everything was in his perception now. *I can see!*

There was panic behind the palm leaf as it was guided away from its intended targets. Frustration and thrill seasoned every slash, and Dario pursued his prey with earnest fervor. Collins hopped to safety, but his body failed him when he tried to counterattack.

"Shit…" His legs, like the enchanted sandals he wore during training, were too heavy to lift. A quiver ran through his bones, forcing him to drop his swords, and his gullet felt like someone had stuffed Bomber Bottles inside.

"It appears that drug has finally taken its toll." Dario relaxed his stance. "I don't know what you expected to happen by using Sinse, but I commend you for taking the risk."

Heavy blocks of ice bombarded Collins's skin, and the world of black and white had turned milky grey. Now on his knees, Collins was shackled to the ground as he glared at his aggressor. A rumble filled his chest and a squeal filled his ears, that glorious world of clarity was nothing but chaos. "S-Shit…"

"To go this far in your pursuit of victory … I have underestimated your resolve, and for that I apologize." There was genuine approval in his tone as Dario bounded onto another stone pillar several meters away. "Let me at least give you the dignity of death under my fullest effort."

Dario spoke gibberish as far as Collins knew, for words and all manner of sound were noise to him. Color had flooded the world now, mostly purple, in infinitesimal shades.

Guess it's over, huh…?

Collins's final thought, before the two-headed serpent writhed towards him with open jaws.

Nadia stirred with a bit of distress. She'd never slept in a car seat before, and from the ache in her neck she would never attempt to again. Aside from this and the stifling heat, what roused Nadia from her slumber was the absence of her boyfriend.

"Damian?" She searched groggily, but it was only when her vision cleared that she became worried. "Damian?"

The Runnex was under siege from the weather as torrents poured down foggy window panes; obviously her boyfriend hadn't gone for a stroll. So where was he? Nadia reached for her phone and was greeted by a white screen when she tried to call out. Panic settled in the pit of her stomach while she scrambled for her clothes. Surely Collins would not have brought her into the wilderness just to abandon her after a bit of frolic, right? Nadia discarded the thought and stepped out of the vehicle, the frigid droplets on her legs a stark contrast from the warmth inside.

Shadows devoured what she remembered of Farley Hill, making it foreign. Nadia's stomach lurched whenever she approached a tree or a nearby bush; however, the urge to find shelter and her missing boyfriend far exceeded her fear. Abandoning her connection she used the phone as a flashlight, casting its white hue as far as she could manage.

"Damian? Damian?!" Her cries drowned by the deluge, she stumbled around the black like an abandoned pup. Abandoned; that was what Nadia's lover did to her. A great weight had landed on her chest, but the notion was quelled when she heard a noise in the distance.

Clang! The clashing penetrated the staccato around her. Nadia could not ignore it. With knots in her stomach, she approached the towering ruins from which the sound came. Recognizing the mansion from earlier visits, she eased forward, though any familiarity dissipated with the next series of howls.

What de hell? She dared not ask aloud, edging closer down

the aisle. By now the scraping of metal was punctuated by roars and bangs, and every instinct in Nadia's mind advised her to retreat. The next scream would compel her to move; it was pained, terrified and known.

"Damian…?" She whispered to herself. Never before had Nadia heard such anguish in her lover's voice. Driven by concern, she rounded the corner to find two individuals facing each other in the rain. Parallel to her was Collins, on bended knee with cutlass in hand and streaks of red over his body. His locks hung haphazard over his face. Before Collins was a stranger who stood upright with a scarlet scarf around his neck, locks flowing down his back and a palm leaf in his grasp. If it wasn't for the horror of the scene, Nadia would assume it was from a TV show.

Then a flash of purple blinded her, another squelch filled her ears, and when her senses returned she saw Collins sprawled on the flooded concrete. "*No!*"

Nadia couldn't explain the sudden valor in her steps, but she was desperate to save Collins—even if she didn't know how. In a panic, she picked up a nearby stone and threw it as she yelled. Dario swatted it away without even acknowledging her. Desperation consumed her body, and Nadia flung herself over Collins as if to shield him from the assassin's wrath.

"You disrespect him, you know." A cold voice came from beneath the scarf. "Protecting him like a helpless child, instead of letting him receive the warrior's death he deserves."

What are you talking about?! Terror arrested Nadia's tongue.

"His heritage is unknown to you, isn't it?" Dario confirmed from her expression and then raised his palm leaf. "Stand aside."

"N-No!" Nadia bleated. The Devil gazed from on high, pressing her to the earth.

"Then you will also bear the warrior's burden."

Nadia couldn't move. Her body manacled by fear as the killer brandished his weapon. She was going to die here; butchered in the wilderness while embracing her battered lover in the rain. It wouldn't be romantic either like in the tragic tales of old—only cold-blooded murder. Nadia then felt a stir by her arm; it was Collins who was struggling to get upright. For a moment, she imagined her boyfriend rising up to save his damsel in distress, but she knew he could never save anyone with those injuries.

"Do you want to save him?" Nadia didn't reply to the question at first, too shocked to believe it was being asked in the first place. Dario asked again. "Do you want to save Damian Collins?"

She nodded, not knowing what to make of the offer. Was this some sadistic way of toying with his victims? Collins coughed up blood on her side. She couldn't afford to hesitate when Dario handed her a tiny slip of paper.

"There is a bus stop located one hundred and eighty-five meters away from where we are standing. If you wish for Mr. Collins to live, you will carry him there along with this ticket. Visualize the place you want to go and say it aloud. Make haste. His injuries are severe and he doesn't have much longer."

In the time it took to recite these instructions in her head, Dario had disappeared. Nadia felt a wave of relief, until a cough from Collins reminded her of the situation. "Oh shit! Oh Shit!"

"Nadia...?" Her lover whispered with strained breaths.

"Shh... Don't try to talk. Save your strength." Nadia tried not to tremble, but from the reassuring hand on her shoulder it was clear that Collins noticed. "We have to get to the bus stop. That's what he said."

Collins nodded, giving a few hacks in confirmation. The downpour had abated but it still added to their discomfort, Collins especially felt a dull throbbing with every drop.

"Okay. Here we go." Nadia grunted under his weight. One hundred and eighty-five meters seemed like an impossible distance, and Collins's blood flowed down her arm. They were out of time.

Collins winced with each step, but he saw the strain he was putting Nadia under. A pang of regret filled him as the world became ink. "S... S..."

"Stay with me!" Nadia bellowed, hurrying her steps with an extra huff, but it was too late. There was absolutely no way she could make it to that bus stop. And what would happen if she did anyway? If a bus had arrived it couldn't get to Queen Elizabeth Hospital fast enough, even if it flew. A flicker of white kindled in her palm: the piece of paper.

Nadia slowed her steps. Was this supposed to happen? She saw a similar glow near the entrance of the pathway—where the bus stop was—Dario's parting instructions echoed in her mind.

"*Visualize the place. Say it out loud.*"

Croaking under the light, Nadia glanced at Collins who had already passed out. "Hospital! Take me to QEH! Queen Elizabeth Hospital!"

Her arm vibrated, there was another flash, and then a rich white melted the darkness around them. Before Nadia's heart could properly skip a beat, her body was afloat, zipping past bushes and trees with the force of a cannon shot. Air ripped through her lungs as she flew, and Nadia squeezed Collins's arm the tightest she could in fear that he would disappear from her. Bending and twisting in ways that weren't humanly possible, Nadia slipped through the bus stop and slammed hard on dry concrete. In front of her, rows of ambulances were parked and a looming blue building towered above.

"Holy... Shi... We." Nadia blinked at the flashing sirens and passing headlights. The air was cold and dry, a stark contrast from the downpour seconds ago. Collins coughed, snapping Nadia from her daze, and she scrambled for the nearest person she could find. The three attendants in the lobby greeted her with horrified expressions. "Please! Someone help him!"

Collins was inert now, with clothes drenched in blood and water as he flopped in her arms. Nadia could feel a faint rise in his chest, but she didn't have the prudence of a doctor. "Damian!? Babe!? Stay with me!"

Frantic hands secured her lover's body and placed him on the gurney while she watched. Powerless, anxious and confused. Even after the miracle she just experienced, Nadia prayed for another one to come her way.

THE PRICE TO PAY

Kyle had not settled in days. Lianne had sparked an extra vigilance in him. The windows remained closed at all times, with heavy drapes covering the panes from watchful eyes. Kyle would've opted to board them up with plywood if Mr. Beckles hadn't protested against it.

"Wait, wha get into you?"

Kyle no longer felt secure leaving the house unattended. The only exception came whenever his brother left for school.

"I can manage on my own." Damien groaned, while fending off Kyle's attempts to escort him. The boy had to rouse at the crack of dawn just to leave the house unnoticed.

"You acting like yuh mother." Mr. Beckles remarked one morning. There was no reproach behind the statement but Kyle still took offense.

"Maybe she had good reason for doing so."

"That is true." Mr. Beckles grunted and downed the rest of his bay leaf tea.

Kyle watched him, *really* watched him. Mr. Beckles was a strong man—that much Kyle knew— but that was only in the arena of martial arts. He never displayed any magic tricks, no rabbits out of the hat or tied handkerchiefs from his ears, and yet Kyle knew Mr. Beckles was strong. Then Lianne's warning plagued his mind. In the end, maybe martial arts were ineffective against obeah magic….

"Question. Are there people stronger than you?"

"There's always someone stronger." Mr. Beckles chuckled, though Kyle found this hard to imagine in spite of all he's seen.

"So, what happened when you met an opponent you knew you couldn't beat?"

"When you find an enemy that you know you can't beat, the best course of action is to retreat." His master recited the words like a nursery rhyme; one that was often drilled into him as an apprentice and then passed on to his own apprentices. "Of course, dem gine always be a situation where you can't afford to run away and you ain got a choice but to fight."

"What happens then?"

"You do what you have to in order to survive." Mr. Beckles said. There was no grandeur in his words, just cold, simple truth. And suddenly Kyle was reminded of Lianne's appeal in Bewitched Gully.

Survive.

Kyle mused for the next hour. The days since Gulfsyde appeared at Sheraton had seemed like ages, and the only other agent of the Dark Arcs was Lianne, who seemed to have postponed her head hunt for now. Kyle had abandoned the media. Any weirdness was cleverly kept under wraps, much like the Baku attack at Content last year. Yet when he saw a copy of the *Daily Nation* on the table, he couldn't resist the urge to scour through for relevant news. Kyle found nothing. Save for an interesting story about a landslide at Cane Vale earlier in the week.

Kyle would turn to Damian Collins next. Perhaps he had learned something new in that time, or at least offered some cheerful distraction. Kyle sifted through his cell phone which vibrated in his palm shortly after.

CHARLENE.

A name Kyle had not expected to see on the screen, as it was the first time it appeared after he recorded the number a year ago. His stomach lurched while he listened to the raspy voice.

"Hey, Kyle … are you there?"

"Yeah, Charlene, I'm here." Kyle noted her alarm, which was different from her usual upbeat self. "What's up?"

"I'm at the hospital." Charlene started, and as she spoke his stomach sank further into doldrums of distress. "It's Damian… It's pretty bad. Just come."

Kyle didn't ask any more questions; his worst fears were already confirmed. *Gulfsyde.* Pictures of an ambushed Collins, easily slain by his superior foes, had surfaced in his mind: bloody, mangled and lifeless. But Collins was in the hospital so he must have survived—just barely.

Without mentioning a word to Mr. Beckles, Kyle slipped out the house with cane in hand. He wished he knew how to activate the bus stop. And to make matters worse, the bus was running late, forcing his concerns to marinate for an extra half-hour. Queen Elizabeth Hospital was an ominous building for those who approached it, with an arrangement of multiple five-story blocks at various stages of dilapidation. Kyle had never entered before, so he followed a passing ambulance until it parked in front of a blue building, which turned out to be the main lobby.

"Ward twelve…" Kyle recited the room number from Charlene's call. With the scent of Dettol tickling his nose, he walked the crowded hallways where distracted staff scurried past without even glancing at Kyle or his cane. The celeste-painted walls were bare, save for the occasional anatomy chart or poster advertising medical care. His aimless stride led to several departments he had no business in: *Radiology, Postnatal, Cancer Research* were some of the names Kyle stumbled across before he tried the stairs. With each floor Kyle grew more uncomfortable. Groups of concerned relatives spilled along the corridors where he passed. Each face anxious as they waited for visiting hours to be announced, or some word back from the nurses in charge of care for their loved ones.

"Ward ten…Eleven…"

"There you are." Charlene greeted him with a little less charm than he was accustomed. "Took you long enough to get here."

"Sorry. Bus. How is he?"

"It's pretty bad. He's still unconscious and the doctors are keeping an eye on him." Kyle followed Charlene into the ward. "Come."

The room was deserted, save for a lone hospital bed which was surrounded by various life-preserving apparatus. Tubes, ventilators, IV drips and the like were propagating into an intricate web with the bed as the center, and on it a swathed body lay. Collins was unrecognizable under the bandages, except for the few dreadlocks that peeked out between them. Collapsed at his side was a female body that Kyle identified as Nadia. She didn't budge; her head buried deep within her arms.

"Multiple lacerations around his body, blunt-force trauma, massive blood loss, minor lung damage and cardiac failure, that's about as much as I could get out of the doctor." Charlene's recital sent a chill down Kyle's neck. "It's a miracle he survived long enough to get here."

"What happened?" Kyle already knew. Charlene shook her head. Apparently, Nadia hadn't told her anything, and as her face remained at Collins's bedside, it was clear Nadia wasn't planning to either.

"Nadia, sweetie…" Charlene cooed. But Kyle was impatient; the urgency overwhelmed any sympathies he had.

"Were you attacked by the man with a palm leaf?"

There was silence; Charlene shot him daggers with her eyes before Nadia eventually stirred. It was the first time Kyle saw her without any makeup. Her face was puffy, with dried tears caked along her cheeks. Her hair disheveled with strands barely covering her eyes, which formed a gaze intent on stabbing him.

"It was him, wasn't it?"

"Kyle…" Charlene tried to mediate but a hollow voice intervened.

"We were just hanging out … talking and hugging, you know?" Nadia was struggling under choked breaths. "Next thing Damian's on the floor… There's blood everywhere … and then … *that guy* starts walking over…"

Nadia shivered. Charlene chimed in again.

"It's okay, sweetie, you don't have to—"

"Why would he go after Damian?" Nadia asked Kyle with a

sudden sobriety. "We didn't do anything to him, so why would that guy come after us?" There was no reply, leaving Nadia to decipher the horrors for herself. She recalled the billowing red scarf, those long dreadlocks and piercing eyes. "Wait. He was there too, wasn't he? At Sheraton?"

Kyle swallowed hard. He knew what question would come next.

"Do you know him?"

"No." Kyle lied. The two girls didn't believe him. "Not really. Did the police come for a statement or go after the guy?"

"I don't think they'll be much help here, Kyle." Charlene added with a wry smile, and for a moment Kyle wondered how much she knew.

"I guess you're right." The tension thickened with every minute, and Kyle found himself unable to meet anyone's eyes, focusing instead on the mummy who lay silent on the hospital bed. Guilt engulfed him. It was his fault. The thought cycled in his mind much like the beeps from the ventilator. Collins should've never been involved. None of this concerned him. As muffled sobs filled the room, Kyle regarded the damage caused by his reliance on the Rasta. This bloody path was his alone to tread. "I'm sorry."

"...Kyle?" He was in the corridor before Charlene got to her feet. "What are you going to do?"

"I..." Kyle hesitated. He wasn't sure if this person knew of his violent lifestyle, nor did he care. "I'm going to find them."

"...And what's going to happen then?" Charlene prodded. "Are you going to kill them? ...Do you think you can?"

Kyle met her eyes—brown, apprehensive eyes—but he did not avert his own. "No. Listen, I didn't mean for—"

"Just be careful, okay?"

"Yeah."

Charlene gave a polite nod before returning to the ward. Kyle trailed her with his eyes, until his sight lingered on nothing in particular. He tried to imagine how the battle would've gone. How long did Collins last? Was it quick and painless or did he struggle? Were these weeks of training any benefit to him, or did they offer nothing to ensure his survival? Rage usurped curiosity, just as quickly as antiseptic filled his nose. Kyle never noticed how much he depended on Collins. He assumed Collins would be at his side in the final foray, fighting the enemy with the fresh techniques they trained so hard to obtain. But things were different now. Collins was engaged in a greater battle. And instead of being afraid to face Gulfsyde alone, fury distended in Kyle's heart.

"Shit!" Kyle huffed. Before he knew it, Kyle was back at the hospital entrance, where two nurses goggled at him before resuming their busy routes. Sirens howled as an ambulance left the garage, probably off to save some poor soul on the verge of death, much like Collins. Kyle's anger had solidified into something cold and hazardous. Only vengeance was on his mind now. They had to pay. And as the bustle increased around him, Kyle thought he had an idea where they were.

Damien Harding was disturbed ever since that encounter at school. This was his second exposure to obeah magic, and he couldn't deny the experience no matter how hard he tried. His leg touched a comic book perched at the foot of his bed; its contents more plausible than reality.

"Magic, huh?"

Common sense told him otherwise. And so, a great melee occurred in his mind, one that continued when he escaped the house and went well into his time at school. Damien found the campus even more hostile, as news of his bizarre attack spread throughout the student body. The lies from those bullies were echoed in whispers.

"I hear that Harding fella call duppies 'pon de men."

"Yeah, right! Wunna always picking 'pon the boy. He never do you nuttin."

"Nah, they say it serious. They witness it for themselves. One of the men don't even want to come school nuhmore, B. Say he too bewitched

to even leff home!"

Damien ignored them and went about his business; the noise from his internal battle drowning out any malicious rumors. He found himself in the area where he saw Sulemann last. A game of road tennis came to an abrupt end on Damien's approach—they too had been an audience to the gossip. As expected, the PE Department had no signs of the illusion. It was magic, after all.

"There has to be something else." Damien recalled the falling domino, and knew only Sulemann had his answers. The problem was finding him. For days Damien had stalked the van stand in town where his normal route vehicles were stationed. But no Sulemann; only frustrated PSV operators who were upset that Damien wasn't a paying passenger. Today his expectation was no different. Alone in the backseat, which students had scorned because he was already there, Damien accepted that he would never see the conductor again. Yet there he was, resting on the engine with languid flair.

"Yo, big man." The greeting was unheard by anyone else in the vehicle, stabbing the ocean of music and babble and reaching his ears. Damien was no stranger to this phenomenon, and now with the knowledge of Sulemann's abilities he accepted the sensation. "Long time no see."

"Is this another form of magic?"

"Something like that." Sulemann gave a sheepish wave. "Kinda straight to the point, nuh?"

"I don't have a choice." Damien replied bluntly. "There's no telling when next you gine disappear, and there is too much that I want to know."

"Oh, fuh real?" Sulemann leaned forward. His face teemed with the excitement only an artist eager to show his latest work could understand. "So, what is it you want to know?"

Damien glanced around him; all was silent now saving their voices. The world was shrouded in grey, as passengers went about their conversations, unaware of the discourse between the two. Thus, his first question was, "Other than illusion and the control of sound, what else can you do?"

Sulemann reached into his pocket and tossed another domino onto the floor, just like in the school courtyard. "A fair amount, actually."

Damien watched as the world dissolved: the passengers, the seats, even the floor melted into white, and he had to stand up before losing balance completely. When Damien secured himself, the interior had disappeared and beneath his feet was concrete. "…Translocation, too?"

"That's another one, yeah." Sulemann had joined him on the street opposite the Queen Elizabeth Hospital. As far as Damien knew, this was a full parish from where they were seconds ago. "You don't seem too surprised."

It was the fourth magical experience. Damien had not lost count. "Oh, I am…"

Damien held a cautious grasp over the stick peeking out of his backpack. Due to recent events, he thought it best to have a weapon at hand, at the risk of drawing attention like his brother. Sulemann didn't seem to notice this, as he led the way across the street and through the emergency entrance of the building. It was here that Damien saw something even stranger. The lobby was full of the ailing and injured, anxiously waiting for the front-desk nurse to announce their turn for treatment. Saturated with despair and disinfectant, Damien felt discomfort as he strode through. However, no one seemed to notice him. It wasn't that pain distracted the patients, no, they didn't see Damien or Sulemann. It was like the two weren't there.

The same trick from the minivan… Cloaking? Magic trick number five. Or was it still number four…? "What are we doing here exactly?"

"I gotta visit an old acquaintance. Yuh see, I got so caught up wid business that I kinda lost track of time and let things get a little outta hand." There was genuine exhaustion in Sulemann's voice as they strolled up the stairs.

It was a surreal experience for Damien, notwithstanding the enchantment around them; he had never set foot in a hospital before. The concerned faces of staff and visitor alike were different from the daily contempt he was accustomed, and one in particular made him stop in his tracks. Rage. That was the best way to describe it: pure, unfettered rage. It was the kind that made your features twist and contort into something monstrous. Something dangerous. This one had a darkness in his eyes that made Damien grip his weapon even tighter, though the chill in his bones prevented him from drawing it. His brother had never looked so menacing.

"Is something wrong?" Sulemann asked.

"It's nothing."

"Really? It's perfectly normal to be afraid of spells you now experiencing—"

"I'm fine. Please continue." Damien watched his brother stalk down the stairs, wondering what had happened to make him like that. The answer came when Damien followed Sulemann into the hospital room. There were three people inside. Two ladies, who had seemed vaguely familiar but Damien couldn't figure out why, and the third person who was lying in bed, fully swathed in bandages. Damien had to get closer to identify the patient, and it was only when he saw the trident pendant by the bed that he realized... "Collins!?"

But Collins couldn't hear him. No one else in the room could except for Sulemann, who was shaking his head. "They can't hear you either, I'm afraid. The spell blocks out our features; anything from our looks, voices, or even scents are kept hidden as if we weren't even here. At least from their perspective."

"What happened to him?" Damien asked, after soaking in the image of the disfigured body before him.

"He ran into some trouble and bit off more than he could chew." Sulemann said. Damien recalled the visits Collins made to their house, and the conversations he overheard between Collins and Kyle. This was the reason Kyle trained so hard. The enemy had to be strong. Stronger than the Heart Man who invaded their home.

"Can you help him? Is there anything you can do?"

Sulemann didn't balk under the urgency in his voice, walking towards the bedside with a relaxed step. "Well, that's why I here in the first place. It too early for him to die just yet."

Sulemann then pulled out another domino and rested it upon Collins's chest, where it disappeared moments later. The two girls didn't react to their presence at all; the one with cornrows was still comforting the short-haired one, who had her head buried in her hands the entire time. When Sulemann backed away from Collins and returned to Damien's side, the girls still did not notice.

"Okay, that should be good."

"...Is that it?" Damien had expected something flashy and instantaneous.

"Yeah. We should probably give him some time to heal, but everything covered already." Damien couldn't understand how, but he didn't question anymore. Following Sulemann through another miracle of magic, he took one final glance at the persons in the room.

"What happens now?"

"Well, that depends on him. He seems like a strong fella though, so you shouldn't be too worried."

"So, we just wait?" Sulemann nodded in response.

"Not here. I got some other matters that need my attention." That announcement was enough to snap Damien back to his senses.

"What about my answers?"

"What about your questions?" Sulemann scratched his head much to Damien's frustration. Where to start? There was too much he wanted to know.

"Are there any more people like you out there? You know ... *wizards*?"

Sulemann snickered at the notion. "We ain really wizards, yuh know. This isn't the *Hobbit* or some fantasy movie. People in my line of work usually call themselves Practitioners and dem got quite a few."

"Practitioners..." Damien repeated the word. Did Kyle ever mention it before? Then he wondered what these Practitioners were like. Did they mirror the man before him or the murderer with the glowing arm in his backyard? "Are all of you dangerous?"

"I'd say most of us are, but only if you owe us." Sulemann snorted as they approached the exit, where scores of passersby were still oblivious to their presence. Desperate screams from the Heart Man entered Damien's mind, and suddenly he lingered on the word, *debt.*

Is that why they are after my brother? Damien wanted to ask, but Sulemann didn't seem to know anything about it despite his expertise. He noted how Sulemann ignored Kyle when he passed. "Are you a friend of Collins?"

"Not exactly."

"Then why save him?"

"I have my reasons; though one of them was to kinda show off some more." Sulemann's vanity was sincere, and though thrilled by the demonstration, Damien had the sudden urge to clock him in the back. "Did it work?"

"No." Damien lied. "Not exactly."

"Touchè. I like dah wun!" Sulemann's last words before vanishing into thin air. Damien only noticed after a blink, but by no means did he believe the conductor was gone.

"Wait! I want to learn!" Damien shouted, and people turned in alarm as this screaming boy appeared out of nowhere. "You hear me!? I want to know more!"

Passersby pointed and whispered amongst themselves but Damien didn't care, the outrage was too much to quell his tongue. In his tantrum, Damien didn't notice the buzzing in his pocket, and it was only after the fifth buzz that he bothered to check his phone.

Kyle—5 missed calls.

Damien swallowed hard as the words flashed across the screen. His brother's devilish form still potent in his memory. "Hey…"

Layer's Gap was truly a shadow of its former self. The chattel houses were ramshackle, with peeling wooden boards and nets of lianas covering the roofs. It was a wonder anyone still lived inside them, though Kyle noticed the movement of window blinds when he passed. If any residents remained in Layer's Gap, they didn't risk leaving their homes. As he ventured down the deserted streets, Kyle saw piles of discarded trash bags balanced unsteadily by a nearby light pole; a feast for rats and stray dogs alike. It was clear that garbage men skipped this area on their daily routine, and the pillars of smoke told how the villagers disposed of their waste.

"This place really is forgotten." Kyle remarked on the wooden sign above his head which hung askew from its post. The black letters faded amongst the white. It was worse than Sniper described, as the signature of war was still clearly marked on this village. Discarded trays and tables, from past vendors plying their trade, were scattered on sidewalks. Potholes—no more like craters—littered the very road he walked, and the pastures and gardens were thoroughly ravaged. Truly a forsaken place; it was the perfect hiding ground for a criminal.

As Kyle regarded an empty playground he remembered Damien, who should've arrived home by now where it was safe.

"You took very long to answer the phone. Where are you?" Kyle asked after several missed calls.

"I now get into town. Should be reaching home soon." Damien recited, much like he did whenever Kyle called. His voice was a little frigid over the receiver, but other than that he seemed fine.

"Oh, good—was just checking up on you."

"...Are you okay?"

"What do you mean?" The question came out of nowhere, but even more worrisome was the boy's concern. There was a pause and then Damien said,

"Never mind."

"You sure?"

"Yeah, I'm good. Don't worry about it." Damien abandoned his inquiry. It was clear that his brother wasn't an easy defendant like Sulemann. "Anyway, hear you later."

"Cool. Just be careful, okay?"

"I will." The conversation was far too awkward for Kyle's liking, then again most of them often were. No matter. Damien was safe, and soon Kyle was able to pocket his reservations and focus on the mission ahead.

Slowly, the remnants of the community were giving away

to woods and debris. These were the homes that were hit the hardest, as the perimeters were least protected from Over de Wall's attacks. One home had a gaping hole through the front door, leaving the kitchen and bedroom at the mercy of the elements. Kyle imagined the horror of having his own home blasted open by invaders, but then he was reminded of the night his mother passed—the rumbling of his rooftop, the flashing lights through the window....

"Get it together, Kyle." He admonished himself, now was not the time for fear. Gripping his cane as he urged forward, Kyle resembled a common thief who took great care to mask his presence. For there was something that lurked just beyond his approach; it wasn't any villager who was brave enough to venture outside. No. This being was far more dangerous. Its aura: more beast than man.

The enemy was close. Kyle felt him through the bushes, and upon crossing the last bramble he saw them. A vast field filled with heaps of dirt—graves, it seemed—was created on the outskirts of the village. Though these mounds were dug with care they weren't maintained, as tombstones of rock and wood became weathered throughout time, and weeds replaced flowers for ornaments. Even the dead were forgotten, Kyle thought, but he recalled his mother's burial place in his backyard. A place rarely visited but still respected. There was a figure in the middle of this cemetery, like a scarecrow of sorts, save for the massive sword on its back.

Rasheda gazed upon Glenn's tombstone with weary eyes. She'd lost count of the hours spent before the grave, though her exhaustion wasn't from standing too long. Rasheda replaced the white frangipani that had withered in its crude vase.

"Why weren't you honest with me, nuh?" The question on her mind for the past ten years.

"That's why I never liked you, yuh know? You were never honest with me. Could never answer a question straight. Always had a plaster fuh every sore and always skinning you teeth."

At this Rasheda sucked her own, while rubbing her fingers through the plaits on her head. "You used to piss me off so much. I could never tek you seriously, with you nappy head and stupid jokes…. Still, everyone really looked up to you, nuh? Aunty Yvette. Ms. Betty. Even Dario—they all looked up to you… I guess that's why I fell…"

Memories trickled in, and Rasheda found herself giggling at them like a corny scene from *Days of our Lives*. Perhaps even the seasoned assassin believed in romance once upon a time. *"Fuck!"*

"Such a friggin idiot… You shoulda tell us everything from the start. The Baku. The business. Where you were from—*everything!* That way I wouldn't be stuck doing this… *shit!*" Rasheda glowered at her weapon; its massive hilt barely covered by her fingers. The sword was more of a burden than an asset, though in her line of work it became an efficient tool for murder. Her lips twisted in disgust as she counted the lives stolen by that blade. And the freshest morsel would appear before her to be devoured.

Like a shadow, Kyle Harding waited behind the assassin; his cane ready to take advantage of this preemptive strike. But he didn't budge. Some unknown force had rooted him to the spot and whispered caution into his ears.

"How you manage to find me?" Rasheda spoke without turning. "Wait. It was that backstabbing bastard, wasn't it?"

Rasheda meant Sniper. Kyle confirmed nothing.

"Frig it! That don't matter. At least I ain have to go through the hassle of finding yuh." With that, Rasheda picked up her cutlass and rested the oversized blade on her shoulder. How she didn't crumble under the sheer weight was beyond Kyle, but that was one of the many mysteries surrounding her weapon. It was voracious. Kyle had never felt anything like it, not even from the Heart Man or Jamba. It had a hunger that surpassed any living beast in Bimshire, though it didn't appear to absolve its wielder.

"Where's your partner?" Kyle asked after creating some distance.

"Fuck should I know? He mussy dead and gone 'long already."

Cutup hadn't returned after defeating Collins, at least not yet. Kyle had to act now. It was impossible to fight both simultaneously, that much he knew. Rasheda observed his face as it hardened and grew cold. A silent calamity.

"And wha 'bout you? I don't see your Rasta with you either, unless he mussy get deal with already."

Again, Kyle didn't answer, his eyes black with hostility.

"Wait, why you staring at me so fuh? Um like it so in truth…." Rasheda marched towards her prey, sending Kyle to step back in kind, stance adopted with cane pushed forward. "Oh, I see. That is what you here for, nuh? To get revenge on your friend? All right…"

Rasheda swung her great blade to create a stance of her own. Kyle noted that she didn't strain while wielding the weapon, but then Rasheda showed no effort in the battle with Sniper either. And her weapon—that preposterously large sword bound in chains—worried Kyle as well. For if his cane nurtured him with its presence, that sword seemed to torture her with its own. This woman was not to be underestimated.

"Come forward if you bad, then." Rasheda barked and Kyle dashed forth in earnest. *Clang!* It felt like he struck a brick wall with a stick, and the resistance went through his arms, sending his body askew. "Cute."

Indifferent to the blow, Rasheda retaliated with a slash to the torso, which Kyle barely rebuffed at the latest second. But the cane didn't offer the solid guard he was accustomed, recoiling instead as he was knocked several meters away. *So heavy!*

It was the heaviest strike Kyle had ever faced, and after blocking some more, he was convinced that it rivaled Jamba's concrete slab. But how could that be? Rasheda was just a human girl…. Kyle tried to devise a counterattack. He contrived so many scenarios after watching her at Sheraton, but it was entirely different experiencing those thrusts firsthand. *Must close the distance … But how?*

Kyle shifted around Rasheda. She too was interested in her opponent's weapon, albeit with more chagrin. *Frig. I know I getting proper hits on him, so why it ain breaking?* She considered how easily Father Hoe deflected her attacks with just his flimsy namesake, but that was a matter of skill; skill which she knew was far beyond her current prey. *Why?!*

Rasheda heaved the blade over her head and brought it down like a guillotine passing judgment. Still the cane did not yield, and Kyle managed to block all three chops while staying unscathed.

"Ragh!"

A scream and an eruption on his heel, Kyle clambered away while soaking in the present information. *Six. No. Seven feet in length. One-and-a-half feet in width. The blade itself is six inches thick, and judging from the force it has to weigh at least two hundred pounds.* She would need some menacing upper-body strength to even wield it efficiently. But efficient Rasheda was.

In the Caribbean, there was a huge difference between a person using a cutlass and a person who *wields* a cutlass—in this case a Canecutter—and it was clear that Rasheda was the latter. There was nothing maladroit in the placement of its edge. Her precision was comparable to that of Damian Collins. And yet Rasheda didn't have a weightlifter's physique, so how was she able to wield it? Kyle examined the enveloping chains around the blade. Magic had to be involved, but how much was the question.

"You little shit!" Rasheda growled with a pirouette of her sword. Kyle was measuring every attack she made; she knew it and she was irritated by it, as always whenever she met difficult marks. Thus, Rasheda swiped and swiped, each time with escalated fervor, but Kyle kept slipping through and soon he would be within range of dealing damage. Rasheda could not allow that.

Just a little closer… Kyle was cautious. He wouldn't have long once he breached her defense, and when he did the blow had to be exact and lethal. Still, he was hesitant…

Just a lil further… Rasheda recorded measurements of her own; seeking the optimal spot away from Glenn's grave and closest to the distant bus stop. Kyle didn't notice though, his attention focused on that blurring metal.

"There!" The angle was perfect. One precise stab to her diaphragm was all Kyle needed to win. But Rasheda had seen through his ambition, releasing one hand mid swing, and spinning her body around the hilt when the blade had pierced the ground. The result was a swift kick to the chest which made Kyle reel upon impact.

"Weak. That's how you come fuh truth?" Rasheda brandished her weapon. She was far enough now, she thought. No more games. "Amplifier activate: *Anjèd San.*"

Kyle was bemused as he steadied himself. First there was a strange reaction in the air, akin to an electrical current which made his hair stand on end. Then the air screamed despite the absence of wind; a stillness that, in spite of everything, seemed eerie and abnormal. Perhaps the most notable change was the purple hue which Kyle found very familiar.

"Amplifier?" The word echoed in his mind.

"*Yes, Amplifiers—that's what we call them among our lot.*" Lianne explained, but even back then Kyle was confused. As far as he knew, bus stops were only transportation devices. Lianne continued, "*I'm sure you have used them before. I mean, how else did you escape Bewitched Gully?*"

Kyle glared at her without a response.

"*Generally, these are often utilized for that purpose. Once you have a ticket, you can be transported to any area throughout the island as long as there is a connecting Amplifier at your destination. Think of it as a subway system … sort of.*" Lianne ran her fingers through the cloud on her head. She never had the knack for explaining things, or the patience. "*However, the more… 'specialized' Practitioners use Amplifiers for their original intent: as a device which boosts the performance of any obeah magic within a specific radius. Usually around one hundred to one hundred and ninety meters—I can't remember—these hotspots amplify magic exponentially depending how close you are to the access point. Kinda like Wi-Fi or an antenna.*"

Kyle scoured the cemetery until he saw the glowing bus stop through some brushes in the distance. The epicenter of this volatile tremor; he remarked on the post with both horror and wonder.

"*I'm guessing that cane of yours might be associated with obeah in some way. So this information should be beneficial, assuming you know how to activate it…*"

"*…Activate it?*" Kyle recalled the way bus stops flickered whenever he passed. "*How do I do that?*"

"*I'm not really sure.*" Lianne answered truthfully. "*To be honest, my abilities don't work the same way as others.*"

"Why are you telling me this?"

"Because you'll need this if you want to endure what's coming next. No amount of training will compensate for not knowing how combat works in our world."

"Yes, but isn't that the point? Aren't you guys after my life? If so, then why help me?" Lianne was silent on the matter. Her emerald eyes met his sable eyes with a firm gaze.

"You must survive."

That task became harder with each passing second. The air screamed. The ground flushed. All to signal the amplification, and through the noise Kyle bore witness to a frightening transformation. Rasheda's sword—*Anjèd San*—had broken free from its chains. A form of seal apparently, as the links became light and the blade rapidly grew in size. The design was different too; resembling a pseudo cash register with dials, buttons, and other minute mechanisms littering the face of the blade, along with something alive. An eye of sorts; one that danced around at angles before focusing on the next meal before it.

"So, this is the true form of her sword…" Kyle breathed. As he bathed in this vile atmosphere, Rasheda barked,

"How you expect to kill me, when you don't even know how to fight?!"

Anjèd San, which translates to *Blood Eater* in creole, lived up to its name through the countless corpses tendered throughout her career. But that wasn't the only thing special about the blade, something Kyle would soon discover. In spite of its new appearance, he surmised that *Anjèd San* was just a sword. He only had to discern its new abilities in order to conquer it.

Ka-ching…

The blast tore through the earth, the air, and everything in between. Kyle felt it as he dove to safety. *The hell was that?!*

Rasheda didn't give him any time to recover, dragging *Anjèd San's* teeth through the earth as she marched. *Ka-ching!* It took every muscle in his body to twist out of harm's way. The scarlet light blinding as Kyle scampered for solid ground. *She's gotten desperate. She has the advantage, so why is she desperate?*

Indeed, Rasheda showed panic in her swipes but she had her reasons. Amidst the boom from her last attack, she heard the words of the hawker who sold her the weapon. It was the eve before her departure from Layer's Gap, and into the unknown world where Glenn once belonged. Rasheda visited Betty, whom she suspected to be more than the average street vendor.

"*I knew you would come to me some time.*" Betty said, while stirring the ears of corn in her pot.

"*You're the one who gave Justin those exploding bottles, nuh? Don't lie. I just see him leave here, and I know he don't eat no corn.*" Betty's laughter only made Rasheda more frustrated.

"*I suppose you didn't come here looking for any either, child. Perhaps you want a little something for your trip?*"

Rasheda's face hardened; this was her first dealing with an obeah woman, and she didn't know how the process actually worked.

"*I want something powerful. Something that would help me find answers about Glenn.*"

"*I see. Well, I dunno if I could give you the answers you need, child. Glenn was a very private man, despite his gentleness. But if it's something powerful you want, well…*"

Then something happened that Rasheda couldn't quite explain. The stall they were at, no, the entire street was covered in darkness, as if a light switch went off in the sky for a moment. Then the shadows converged over the coal pot, and a hilt emerged from the embers which Betty grabbed delicately.

"*This is called Anjèd San—one of my Lickerish Arms that I forge recently. You see, it was built on a system that uses a very archaic form of currency from generations ago called Blood Money. Like the name suggests, it is human blood which is converted into bills for the blade's consumption. In exchange, the wielder will have explosive damage at their disposal—once they withdraw those funds from the account, of course.*"

"*How much?*" Rasheda's heart leapt as she marveled at the sword and its inner workings. It was exactly what she needed for monsters like Kamilah or that Baku. Even if the sword was a monster as well.

"*I find this is a sensitive position. You see, I feel good that another one of my works has found someone brave enough to wield it. But at the same time, I'm afraid that this bravery gine only destroy you in the long run.*" Betty looked at Rasheda. Her eyes glassy and remorseful. Her smile proud. Then she continued, *"Anjèd San is always in deficit. It gine always need feeding with Blood Money to balance the account in the blade. You understand what this means? In essence, you must constantly slaughter in order to wield Anjèd San; otherwise, it is your blood that gine be devoured. It's a very expensive article, you prepared?"*

"I am."

"This path you about to take gine break Yvette heart, you know that, right?" Betty gave a final warning, but her patron's mind was made up.

"I know." Rasheda followed these instructions throughout her career as a Debt Collector, and in time she grew accustomed to the transaction of which her blade was bound. With that in mind, she monitored the digits which hovered over the face of her sword. *The average human body got like ten pints of blood, with each pint equaling one Blood Dollar. Twenty bucks. That's the balance I have left. Fuck.*

This job had cost more than Rasheda expected, especially after the battle with Father Hoe. Time was running out. As the balance steadily declined, she sent a wild slash of crimson at her target.

Damn… Kyle leapt over the resulting fissure and tumbled away to safety. His limbs were on fire, assailed by flying debris, exhausted muscles and the stress from training; it became more difficult to maintain this elusion. Still, he had no choice. Rasheda allowed no counterattacks, and Kyle failed to analyze the weapon. *The distance from those blasts is so unpredictable. I can't get a proper bearing on them.*

Another scarlet flash plummeted towards him. The jaws of *Anjèd San* belonged to Limba himself. *Ka-ching!*

If I can't read the weapon, I gine have to focus on its wielder.

And at that moment Rasheda looked flustered. Her face glistened with sweat. Her shoulder's slouched to show fatigue, and more importantly, Kyle saw branches protruding through her skin. Veins. *Her blood flow… That weapon bothers her blood flow.*

Shit… Rasheda's grip weakened around the hilt; the balance of Blood Money was nearing zero. Nevertheless, she followed through with her next slash and took another withdrawal from the account. Kyle had no energy to evade, his legs like magnets upon the earth. It was with absolute desperation that he raised his sugarcane…

Clank!

His body tumbled away like a pebble over water, but it was still intact, save for some gashes on his knees and scrapes on his elbows. The graver wound was on his sugarcane, where a single crack had formed in the middle. Broken. Just like its wielder. It protected him for so long, and helped him through so many ordeals, that when Kyle saw the scar on his weapon his stomach churned.

Rasheda was equally shocked that her quarry wasn't mangled into pieces. She had guessed long ago that that cane wasn't normal, but to endure *Anjèd San* … "No wonder you survive Bewitched Gully." Her tone had a hint of respect, which was stifled by the ringing of that cash register. "But for right now you got to *dead!*"

Kyle resumed his stance, disregarding the anxiety as he pushed the sugarcane forth. His feet quivered. His body numbed. And Kyle could only wait as those voracious jaws descended upon him—his sugarcane like a pick between its teeth. *Snap!* The sound echoed within his bones, as the sugarcane dismantled in his grasp. The agony bursting through his chest, through his soul.

This was the end.

The world had ended for Kyle Harding. At least, that was his assumption when he opened his eyes and found himself somewhere other than Layer's Gap. If this was supposed to be heaven then God must have a sense of humor; placing him in an abandoned canefield surrounded by towering stalks. The same kind that failed him seconds before. The skies above were in mourning, with grey clouds weeping raindrops while he traversed the field. Pain evaporated from his body, and he felt he could run a hundred miles.

"Where am I?" Kyle asked, as he sprinted for what seemed like hours. Neither Headgone nor *Anjèd San* was anywhere to be seen. Still, Kyle couldn't afford to relax, scouring the forest of green around him. "Was I transported here?"

There were no bus stops around, and when his sprint had slowed to a stroll Kyle made another discovery. A young woman clad in white stood before him. Her beauty transcended the rain like a beacon guiding lost souls home. "Mom…?"

Veronica Harding beamed and her aura diffused all the misery in the air. Kyle's eyes had stung with tears as he rushed toward this ghost. She could only be described as that; for he knew his mother had long passed away on the kitchen floor. Kyle soaked in every feature that had dimmed in his memory throughout the years. Her thick black hair was neatly tied in one, and her flush cheeks and auburn eyes had welcomed his approach.

"I guess I'm dead, huh?" Kyle touched her hand. She was warm and smelled of chamomile. "I've failed…"

"Not exactly." Ms. Harding spoke, and her voice matched that of the woman who raised him. "You're actually still alive, Kyle, at least for the moment."

"Where are we?" If the Dark Arcs had introduced him to many forms of magic, Kyle never imagined resurrection was one of them.

"We are inside your psyche. It's complicated. And as much as I'd like to get into the details, I'm afraid time isn't on our side." Suddenly the fantasy unraveled around him, and Kyle recalled the numerous ordeals that brought him to this point.

"Figures you wouldn't give me a straight answer."

"Okay. I deserve that. By now you mussy hear some things about me, and I can only imagine you have a lot of questions."

"You have no idea what we had to go through. *None.*" Kyle was shocked at how cold his words sounded. He couldn't stop the knives from rolling off his tongue. "Not being able to sleep at night because of what lurked in the shadows. Then when that *thing* come after me… They came to our house, Mom. *Our own backyard*. They could've gotten to Damien. I—"

Disjointed and scattered, his phrases came out without any fetter, so much Veronica Harding grew even more concerned for her son. Guilt etched her face as she frowned at him, "Do you blame me?"

"Yes! If it weren't for you—If you didn't get involved in this Dark Arcs nonsense —we wouldn't be stuck paying *your* debt." Kyle was being petulant but he didn't care. He had to get it out. She had to know how much trouble she caused. Veronica Harding said nothing; even in death she still held bitter regrets. Kyle reluctantly met her gaze and saw a history behind it. One that he knew she wanted to relinquish, but chose not to out of urgency and shame.

"I'm sorry." She spoke to her son as the adult standing before her now. "There is no excuse for what I've done, or for any of the hardships I left behind. I wish I could take everything back, but I'm afraid there's no spell or potion for erasing the past. One day—if we ever get to this place again—I'll be able to explain everything. But for right now, all I can do is apologize and hope that you'll forgive me."

"I... I don't think I can protect him, Mom." Kyle admitted. Fear entangled his body, just like that night when he was huddled next to Damien's crib. "No matter how much I trained, it wasn't enough in the end."

"I know, Kyle. I've seen you trying your best. I was there when you took your first stance. I was there when you blocked your first strike. I was there when you met your first opponent and when you survived it all, I was there." She rested her palm on his face, so that her fingers lathered his cheek with reassurance. "I'm even here with you now to help you through this battle."

"What?" The canefield shattered around Kyle, leaving him in a world of white once more.

"Trust me as you always do." Then Kyle felt it again: that suffocating aura from the active Amplifier. He had returned to Layer's Gap; where a field of tombstones besieged him, and the ground was perforated from failed attempts on his life. His body surrendered to agony. His limbs grew heavy once more, and as he looked up, the ravenous jaws of *Anjèd San* were open and ready to consume him.

However, something stopped its bite…

Bram!

Above his head, Kyle saw a piece of wood no more than an inch long floating in midair. Its skin was a brilliant green, but with symbols he did not recognize etched onto the surface. Meager in size, the piece accomplished the impossible task of stopping that massive blade, and none were more surprised than Rasheda.

"De hell?" She spat in disbelief before striking at her prey again, but *Anjèd San* would not break this guard. For Kyle noticed that other pieces of wood were encircling his body and interrupting every slash from that sword. Upon closer inspection, he realized that each piece belonged to his shattered sugarcane, which he thought had died moments ago.

"*Segmentation.*" Veronica Harding whispered in his ears. "*This cane has the ability to divide into multiple segments or 'cuttings' to do as you will.*"

Kyle tested this theory, willing each cutting towards his vulnerable spots so that his body was left unscathed. They even sheltered him from the scarlet.

"Gaddamnit!" Rasheda swore over desperate swipes at her target. Even amongst the spectacles that occurred in her career, she never witnessed anything that outright resisted *Anjèd San's* bite. Rasheda watched as Kyle Harding became a predator himself, with the pieces of wood collecting in the form of his revived sugarcane. Only this time it was as tall as his body.

"It's longer now … How comes?" Kyle asked no one in particular, but a soothing reply entered his ears alone.

"*This weapon—like its wielder—has grown in ways you have yet to comprehend, Kyle. I'm hoping you will adapt in time.*"

"Fair enough." Kyle confirmed as *Anjèd San* stabbed at him. Before that attack would've knocked him several meters away, but now his feet were planted firmly onto the ground. Blocking each strike was easy, as the sugarcane absorbed the impact from *Anjèd San's* jaws. Rasheda panicked. The digits on her blade were dwindling rapidly.

Only six dollars left. If I ain careful this thing gine turn on me.

Caution fueled her offense now, but this only encouraged Kyle more as he rammed the blade's eye and sent Rasheda reeling backwards. She didn't like this position. The job was shitty enough as it is, and she'd be damned if she was cornered by her mark. "*Offa me!*"

Kyle was in midstride when it came. He didn't panic, instead raising his guard with utmost finesse so that the cane separated again. What was one had become two. Now with momentum on his side, Kyle sidestepped *Anjèd San* and exploited every critical point. Ribs, stomach, leg, shoulder—a lethal combination that ended with one nasty blow to the jugular, and as Kyle made his intent clear, Rasheda realized there was no escape.

Is this it? I gine die here? In a place like this? By this poppit?! The sheer horror of this notion was only surpassed by her disgust. Her throat burned from the upsurge of bile and blood. Her chest pulsated and her eyes watered. This was the advent of her demise but she was not prepared to greet it. Not yet. *I can't die here. Not now! I ain find out nuttin yet! There's still too much that I don't know…*

Rasheda slashed wildly at the cutting barrage, but the inevitability of death couldn't be denied. *Glenn, help me.*

Then Kyle felt the dull thunk of cane impaling flesh; a sensation alien to him as he never killed before. The gouging of meat, the savagery of it, made him wretch. Kyle was only too glad to be done with this duel. But when he looked up it wasn't Headgone that he impaled, but someone else. Someone dangerous.

Who is that? Kyle thought it was Cutup, he was wrong. Cutup had a semblance of humanity behind his bloodlust, but this being was not human. He had the frame of a man; a short, slender one with an afro that surpassed Damien's and a black bandana over his face. But his aura was not of this world; much like the Shaggy Bears, Jamba or *Anjèd San* were not of this world. They were all arbiters of obeah and the Dark Arcs. Kyle backed away with two cane pieces in hand, but Rasheda didn't share his anxiety.

"…Glenn?"

"Glenn?" Kyle looked at him closely; he was exact to Sniper's tale. *Impossible. Isn't he supposed to be dead?* Kyle recalled his mother and dismissed the notion. Rasheda, thunderstruck, reached out to the figure with trembling hands.

"You… You came fuh truth? You really come to save me?" In that moment Rasheda softened, resembling a giddy school girl instead of a seasoned killer. She dropped *Anjèd San* and embraced the being. Abandoning all reason for pure joy.

Until an agony punctured her chest and she saw blood—her own blood—spraying in the air. "What?" Her last word as she collapsed on the ground at Glenn's feet.

BUS
STOP

Things were busy at the Queen Elizabeth Hospital after Damien Harding left. His outburst had caused such a stir that it spread throughout the compound via trivial gossip and grand rumors. It was amidst this banter that the pair made their entrance. One: an unkempt middle-aged man with a faded dungaree shirt spilling over his guts. The other: a bespectacled boy who belonged in a student manual with his pristine khaki uniform. An odd pairing, to be sure, if anyone observed them; but that wasn't the case here as the passersby didn't even glance in their direction.

"I hope we ain too late." The middle-aged man said; his balding head beaded with sweat. "You think we gine make it in time, Bailey?"

"I hope so, Barrow." While they walked, two marbles orbited them like satellites to a planet; another ornament to this awkward spectacle. Passerby would veer away from each marble as the two approached. Bailey tended the nearest one as he spoke, "Mother Sally will not be pleased if he passes away."

"How come this guy so important now?" Barrow huffed as he climbed the staircase. He wasn't the biggest fan of climbing or stairs.

"Now that Seifert Brathwaite is dead, Damian Collins is probably the last true Canecutter in Bimshire. Perhaps even the Caribbean." There was a systematic flavor to Bailey's tone. "Also, he is a direct apprentice to Mr. Brathwaite, which makes him even more valuable."

"More valuable than de Harding boy, you think?"

"I think so." Bailey convinced himself, even though he didn't agree with Mother Sally's decision. After monitoring Damien Harding for over a year, he became very interested in his mark. There was a connection between them, he thought; one of intelligence, as if cut from the same cloth. Of course, friendship never intervened with business, but Bailey wasn't too keen to babysit Collins either. "It was our duty to guard him in case of attack and we failed in that task, so it's up to us to rectify it."

"I guess. But how we was supposed to know they were tracing him? I mean, if they had that kinda spell ever since, why dem wait till now to make a move?" Barrow sidestepped an orderly who was finding it difficult to bypass a wall of air.

"I don't know. Usually, the Modus Operandi of Debt Collection is to receive outstanding fees or to punish defaulters, but this doesn't fit."

"Maybe the Conductor's involved again."

"Possibly. Though his interest in Damien Harding is far more notable." Barrow detected bias in his voice but he didn't remark on it. "No use crying over spilt milk anyway. The most we can do is amend our mistake."

Visiting hours were over, and the relatives had been ushered away from the wards so that their loved ones could recuperate. Still, Bailey maintained the enchantment, taking special care to examine the visitors in case an enemy was among them. Barrow fidgeted with his collar, which was heavy on his neck with sweat, and the scent of Dettol was making him gag.

"Can we please make this quick?"

"Oh, stop it! The scent isn't that bad."

"You only saying so 'cause you always douse way with Olbas oil and you used to it."

Bailey shot him darts before stopping at Ward 12, where

Collins was said to be resting. With a tap, he sent one of the marbles through the half-opened door, and after a minute it returned with a message only he could decipher. "Okay, we have a problem. There appears to be a visitor still in this ward. Not sure why, but we can't enter if she's still there."

"We can't just walk in? It's not like she could see we anyway."

"No, we can't." There were limitations to Bailey's marbles and the incantations they cast. Some so strict that it was difficult to maintain multiple high-level spells simultaneously. This fact was carefully locked in his mental vault, and Bailey wasn't planning to open it. Not even for a colleague. "In any case, I will need you to go in there and distract her."

"Wait, why me?"

"You were so eager to enter just now; I took it as a volunteer request." Barrow grumbled, while the boy dropped his shroud of concealment and directed another marble around his partner. In mere seconds, the balding, greasy middle-aged man was transfigured into a brown-skinned nurse with alluring features. "Much better. You may proceed."

"You couldn't at least keep me as a man?" Barrow hissed as he slinked into the room. Nadia ignored his entrance. With her face still buried in her lap so that she resembled an armadillo. It took a couple beckons from Nurse Barrow to finally rouse her from her stupor. "Am. Excuse me, miss? I'm afraid we have to clear this ward to tend to the patient. Do you mind stepping outside, please?"

"…Is there any change in his condition?" Nadia asked without looking up.

"That's… what we are trying to examine now, Ma'am. Now if you please—"

"Please, if you can do anything to help. I… I can't lose him!" Her eyes were puffy and red, like she had spent an eternity sobbing. Barrow regretted ever rousing her. He never knew how to handle people in mourning; especially women.

"Don't worry, Ma'am. We're doing everything we can to help your friend."

Normally Nadia would've shrugged off the hollow promises from hospital staff, but for some reason the twinkle in this nurse's eye reassured her. Cherishing this inkling of hope, she complied with Barrow's request and vacated the room. Part of her wished Charlene was still there to charm her way around this, but unfortunately, she was in the cafeteria at this time.

"I guess I could get some coffee…"

"Thank you. We won't be long." Nadia didn't notice Bailey when she passed, and to the boy it was as if she were the one invisible. Barrow groaned when he sensed his partner had entered.

"Nicely done. You almost convinced me." Bailey said.

"Well, it ain like I lie. Anyhow, you could hurry up and change me back to normal?"

"No." Bailey replied, as he sent another marble towards the mummy on the bed. As it revolved around Collins, the nurse threw a tantrum which caught the interest of none in the room. Finally, when Barrow calmed down and the transfiguration abated, Bailey uttered, "…Odd."

"Wha odd now?"

"This man is in perfect health. No injuries or ailments of any kind." Barrow had stopped inspecting his gut and focused on the mummy before him, and after some prodding Collins eventually stirred.

"D' you think someone got to him first?"

"That is a possibility…" *But who else knew about this incident?* The more pressing question on Bailey's mind. Whoever it was, also had the ability to conceal themselves. Then there was the matter of this person's allegiance. Was it friend or foe? A pair of hazel eyes popped out from beneath the heavy dressings, shifting from one side to the next.

"Where…?" Collins remembered a black-and-white world. The stinging rain on his skin. The rapid staccato of his heart. The snake's silhouette and— "Nadia! Where's Nadia?!"

Bailey didn't flinch when the Rasta sprang upright. "She went out for coffee."

"So … She's all right?" When Bailey nodded, Collins released a fit of giggles before lying back down again. "H-Holy Shit… What about Cutup? What happened to him?"

"Mr. Collins, we were only informed about your condition

at the hospital. Anything outside that is beyond our knowledge. Sorry." Bailey said. It dawned on Collins that he had no idea who they were.

"Who are you?"

"My name is Athelston Bailey, and my associate..." The boy lingered on the word as the middle-aged man seemed engrossed in fondling himself, scrupulous in making sure no parts were missing. "My associate here is Voghn Barrow. We are both members of White Soursop. Pleasure to make your acquaintance."

Collins was incredulous as he watched the two bow their heads; their greeting far from the standard in Caribbean society. "White ... Soursop?"

"Yes. I believe you already met our superior, Mother Sally." Upon hearing the name, Collins saw Father Hoe's grave, the elderly woman with the wide-brimmed hat and her three veiled bodyguards. All in his mind's eye. He shivered.

"Yeah, I remember her... *Shit!* Kyle! I gotta warn him—" Collins bounded off the bed, tearing off the bandages and groping around for his cutlass. "Gulfsyde. Dem men worse than we thought! I—"

"I'm afraid we cannot allow that, Mr. Collins." Bailey gave a stern reproach, and Collins wondered how this little school boy could possibly stop him. "Our job is to guard you from any attempt on your life, and to prevent another tragedy like Seifert Brathwaite."

Collins swallowed hard at the name. He was still coming to terms with his master's identity. "Look. I ain too sure who you guys are or what your angle is, but there's no way I gine abandon my friend."

Collins's face became a portrait of resolution, and Barrow examined it with high esteem. "Nice look. I think me and this guy would 'gree. His heart is in the right place."

"That's because you are gullible, Barrow."

"Stupse." Barrow sucked his teeth. "Look, it ain nuh harm in letting the man contact his friend. You got a phone?"

Collins looked around, but he figured his clothes were in a laundry room somewhere in the building. "It in my pants pocket…"

Bailey felt a vibration from one of his marbles. The ladies were returning, and he imagined their reaction to Collins's sudden recovery would draw attention to the ward. A scenario he wanted to avoid at all costs. "It appears your friends have finished their coffee and are on their way back. Of course, we can't be here when they arrive, especially with you in this state. Too many questions will be raised."

Collins recognized the dilemma. After the battle with Cutup, he imagined being pretty close to death minutes ago. There was no plausible explanation for his bill of health, at least none that Nadia would believe. Bailey continued, "So I present to you two choices: either you stay here in the comfort of this room with your loved ones until this matter settles, or you venture into hell once again to save your friend."

"Bailey…?" The boy was on a train of thought that Barrow could not catch, and as a passenger Bailey saw an opportunity to combine both tasks effectively: guarding Damian Collins and monitoring Damien Harding.

"Whatever you choose, we will be there to escort you."

Collins considered these options, but he couldn't pick one. The last thing he wanted was to hurt Nadia with his disappearance, but he couldn't abandon his comrade at the eleventh hour. Especially since he, himself, couldn't describe how he survived. "Okay. I'm going to see Kyle."

"Are you sure?"

"Yeah." The doorknob twisted while a marble appeared just above his forehead, and as Nadia and Charlene entered, they vanished; at least that was how it looked, for another spell of concealment had been cast. Collins instantly regretted his decision when he saw the horror on Nadia's face. While she combed the room in a panic, Collins stifled the urge to reach out and embrace her.

"As much as I would like to observe this spectacle, I'm afraid we don't have the luxury of time."

"Don't be so cold, Bailey. Let de boy say his goodbyes." The two strangers vacated the room first, leaving Collins to stare awkwardly at Nadia, who darted into the corridor to find someone in charge.

She probably thinks something went wrong … or worse. Judging from the fresh set of tears on her face, the latter notion was more accurate. It was painful to watch, more painful than any slash from Cutup's palm leaf. "I'm sorry."

Collins's farewell before following his escorts outside; whether it was his last remained to be seen.

Butterflies were in Rasheda's stomach as she pressed in her front door. The living-room walls still had scars from the first Over de Wall attack. Bullet holes. Scrapes on the pitch-pine lumber. A few gaping cavities that she could see the next room through; all clumsily decorated with pictures and ornaments. It wasn't a total mess, as her Aunty Yvette cleaned up most of the blood smears around the room. It was halfway into this housekeeping that Rasheda entered, and the woman—who was well into her seventies—turned around to greet her.

"Oh, child… How you holding up?" Aunty Yvette pulled the handkerchief from her nose, revealing a mournful expression. By then, news of Glenn's demise had reached all over the village, and being well aware of her great-niece's affections for the boy, she expressed her sympathies with every conversation they had.

"I'm okay." And Rasheda, who was not in the mood to discuss those events, brushed off her condolences like usual. "Look, Aunty … I'm leaving."

"You leaving? Part you gine, child?" Yvette resumed her chores, taking a paintbrush to the floor and applying some varnish over the wood.

"I gine and look for work. Should be leaving by the end of the night."

"What type of work you gine be doing?" Rasheda, who

hated interrogations, endured this line of questioning from her aunt, knowing that this may be the final conversation they had together.

"I getting sort out with that. Don't worry."

"It got to do with your meeting with Betty this morning?" By now Aunty Yvette had turned in her direction. Her face was weathered with years of struggle and perseverance, but still her eyes burned with a youthful vigor that her great-niece always admired. It was under this gaze that Rasheda swallowed hard. "Child… I know after everything that happen down here you feeling a little antsy, and I don't blame you for wanting to get out. But I been down that road already. I seen how hard it is; not just for me, but for your Mum and Daddy, too. It ain nuh sweet bread— even next to dem bad johns that come through here guns blazing. So, unless you sure—"

"I sure." Rasheda glared at her aunt with the ferocity of a cub eager to abandon the pride and conquer the wild on her own. Yvette recognized this look; she used to wear it herself long ago. "It's something I have to do. Sorry."

"You don't have to apologize, child. I just want you to be careful is all. That world gine chew you up and spit you back out. Tek care."

Aunty Yvette's words stayed with Rasheda as she lay motionless on the floor; the warmth of her blood enveloping her, drowning her. And when she craned her sights to the yellow chattel house she grew up in, Rasheda regretted not ever visiting her home even after Aunty Yvette died. She should've listened, Rasheda thought. Then she looked at the reason for her departure, the reason she started this career of carnage. *Glenn…*

But it wasn't exactly him. Yes, he wore the clothes they buried him in: a pair of jeans, a black T- shirt, and a hat that made his afro puff out at the sides like Mickey Mouse, but it wasn't Glenn. Glenn would never hurt her. But *this* Glenn did. He gutted her like a member of Over de Wall, with cold efficiency. Rasheda's body was still in shock as she glanced at the thing who resembled her lover.

It was clear to Kyle Harding that this was not a man. Despite the likeness of a human being, there was something ominous about this person. His eyes had an absence of life, with grey pupils much like the skin over his thin frame. Swathed by death, this Glenn was an emissary from the underworld, and Kyle thought very hard about making the first strike against him.

Dangerous. This person is more dangerous than Headgone. Kyle looked at Rasheda who was catspraddled in a pool of red. *Anjèd San* was nowhere to be seen, but he was still stifled by this noxious atmosphere. In the distance, the Amplifier rang with more intensity and Kyle felt the electrified air press harder against his skin. The barrier of cane cuttings still orbited his body, but he was hesitant to direct them at his new target.

Glenn made the first move, shifting forward with the slightest of motions, but before his heel left the earth, a stone shot towards him with clinical accuracy. Disregarding the laws of human movement, Glenn twisted his neck just enough to avoid it.

"What I tell you 'bout fighting these men by youself?" Sniper asked upon landing, his eyes never off the doppelganger of his comrade. "I ain tell you to stand home?"

"Collins is in the hospital." Kyle replied.

"So wha? You wanna join him now? Shit, how de hell you manage to last this long?" Sniper's answer came when he saw the cuttings floating around the canewielder. *Guess that cane of his finally evolve, nuh?*

Aside from the sugarcane's protection, Kyle felt relieved by Sniper's presence. Sniper was a pillar of nonchalance, with one hand in his pants pocket and the other tossing a rock up and down. Compared to Kyle, who was firmly rooted, Sniper ambled towards Glenn with suicidal poise. It was only when he moved his bandana from his forehead to his face that Kyle recognized how serious Sniper was. "Never thought I would see you again."

Glenn said nothing.

"Wait, not even a greeting? That ain like you atall. Looks like you lost you manners along with you life." Upon reaching a certain range something activated inside Glenn, similar to a trigger for an alarm, and with a whip-like motion he flung an object at Sniper. Fast and sharp, the item ripped through the air so that Sniper barely had enough time to evade.

"Heh. You ain forget yuh techniques, though."

Sniper stepped forth again and was met with the same reaction. This time the shot was more precise as it nearly took out his eye. Sniper wasn't afraid. If anything, Kyle swore he was smiling under that bandana. *You ain even bothering to hide it no more, nuh?*

Glenn engaged his prey, zigzagging across the graves with screwdrivers in his grasp. Sniper kept his distance though, placing projectiles in between hops. The bottle case on his back gave Kyle the impression of a Ninja Turtle.

I... I can hardly follow what's happening. Kyle thought as the shadows danced about the graveyard. It was a mixture of speed and power that made intervention impossible for him—even if his cane got a new ability. Kyle stole a glimpse to his side and the radiant white of his mother's dress caught his eye. She was still there, even in this hellish scene.

"I surprise you ain catch rigor mortis yet." Sniper jeered after flinging more stones. His attempts were becoming less effective. *This bastard swatting away my attacks so easy...*

But Sniper wasn't surprised by Glenn's skill. It was exactly as he remembered. Glenn's small stature and nimble steps would keep any man at bay. However, Glenn possessed something even more troublesome for the Pel-Ting: knowledge. Distance, velocity, slant range, projectile weight, and atmospheric conditions were just some of the things to consider with each throw. And like any seasoned Pel-Ting, Sniper randomized his attacks to hide any pattern from the enemy. And yet Glenn parried them all, closing the gap in just a few steps.

Shit! The motion startled Sniper, if only for a moment, but when that ice pick came near, a Bomber Bottle dropped from its case.

BOOM!

Kyle shielded his eyes from the explosion, only spotting two streams flying from the ball of smoke. They were still mobile though, Sniper breaking his stride first with another Bomber Bottle leaving his fingertips. The placement was perfect. Escape was impossible and yet... it didn't detonate.

"Huh?" Kyle and Sniper were equally confused, with the

latter inspecting his payload for any faults.

I thought these supposed to be better quality. Truthfully, they were expertly crafted, without a blemish to be seen. Putting faith in his purchase, Sniper pitched another bottle at Glenn, whose next move revealed the true nature of the malfunction. *Rangate… The bastard's disarming them?!*

Sniper cursed as he landed on a nearby tombstone. Bomber Bottles can detonate upon moments of impact or after a set period of time. They are triggered in a two-step process: where the stopper sends a signal through the glass and to the intricate runes inscribed on the label of each bottle. If, for any reason, these steps are interrupted, the contents of the bottle will not ignite and be rendered useless. This was essential knowledge for any Pel-Ting. However, neutralizing a live Bottle in mid-air required unprecedented levels of skill. "Friggin bastard. I always knew you were hiding something."

Glenn was a statue; his face an illustration of demise. And the more Sniper beheld him the more infuriated he became.

"You knew too much; de Bomber Bottles, our attack formations, projectile theory—everything people outside de family had no idea about, *you knew.*"

Kyle was clueless but he listened in earnest, gathering as much as he could in case the worst scenario occurred.

"It was at the back uh my head but I really ain study it. Not until that day we fight Mix Drink."

What little life that remained inside Rasheda, she clung to it, gorging herself on the answers she spent years trying to obtain. Even if they came from the mouth she despised. Sniper continued, "It was you who took him out, wasn't it? Not the girl. By the time she land that chop, he was already dead. You thought no one noticed, nuh? That speed. That accuracy. You don't see a shot like that unless it from a Pel-Ting."

"Pel…Ting…" Rasheda never guessed that Glenn came from such an illustrious background. It was the lead she needed, and suddenly her aimless vocation of slaughter had direction. But the world was slipping away…

Unseen from those on the battlefield, two spectators observed the events in Layer's Gap. They were not residents, as one clad in a tattered lab coat fiddled with the elaborate glasses on his face, and the other wore an amused simper while brushing aside his long onyx hair.

"Is everything to your liking, sir?" The researcher trembled as he spoke to Sulemann.

"Yeah, man. The project looking very stable from what I could see."

His words exhilarated the scientist who, after many days of labour, struggled to complete the task given to him. Nevertheless, this praise validated his efforts.

"Thankfully, I had a proper specimen to work with. Unlike the Two-Blank, I don't have any method to bring someone back from the dead. However, the reanimation process was very successful, due to the corpse being relatively preserved."

"Yeah, storing him for ten years was a bit inhumane for me. Best if he got to stretch his legs, yuh know?" Sulemann said with an air of sympathy. "You ever heard of the Two Prodigies, big man?"

The researcher, who was by no means a "big man", shook his head.

"In our circle, you know you don't hear the term *genius* thrown around too much, right? Especially when it come to the Pel-Ting family, 'cause when you on that level of skill, it's kinda hard to stand out. Yet, there were two who managed this in the midst of all that talent. One was a once-in-a-generation prodigy, who grasped all the techniques and abilities from young, and by the time he could set Common Entrance, he reach the point of mastery. The other one was the opposite. Without any noticeable ability he was an outcast in their ranks, but through hard work and some innovation, he mastered their martial arts, too. And the craziest thing: those two were only a few years apart. They even became friends."

"I see…" It dawned on the researcher just how significant that specimen was, and justified the tedium he endured all those years. If he did get to experiment on one of these prodigies, he was eternally grateful.

"And even if the Pel-Ting family refuses to admit it, those two advanced their martial arts in unorthodox ways. Pay attention, 'cause this is a duel not many people get to witness."

The researcher followed Sulemann's instructions, but it was Sulemann whose interest lay elsewhere. Regarding Kyle Harding with rapacious eyes, *Especially you, Inheritor. Show me how much further you gine grow today.*

Kyle understood nothing that occurred before him. While he watched the standoff from the sidelines, and heard names like Pel-Ting and Mix Drink being called, all that filtered through his mind was: *It's not safe here. This is beyond my level.*

The reality shattered any confidence Kyle had when he entered Layer's Gap. He wanted to escape; to return home with Damien, where he could pray for refuge away from this violence. An impossible dream, he knew, so he tried his hardest to swallow as much information as he could. Sniper was the first to break the stalemate, creating a cloud of smoke from an ill-placed Bomber Bottle, and attacking in roundabout ways with stray rocks. This proved futile, as Glenn's mastery simply surpassed any strategy Sniper conceived.

"How long, nuh? How long were you hiding these crazy skills?" There was a resentment in Sniper's voice that Kyle didn't recognize. Sniper knew that the corpse before him didn't have Glenn's soul. He could tell from its eyes and lack of charisma—which Glenn had in surplus. However, this was still Glenn's body, and within it was nineteen years of experience, practice, and technique etched into its very bones. Thus, even without cognition, Glenn was able to match his abilities; a fact that mortified Sniper.

"Do you understand yet, the fundamental ways in which these two are prodigies?"

The researcher shook his head. Despite his intellect, he never paid much interest to anything beyond the magical.

"The Pel-Ting Arts usually revolve around the concept of placement, angles and direction. Much like archery, there are many factors to consider before one takes that shot, which often forces the average Pel-Ting to secure himself from a distance. However, Sniper elevated his style to include movement and acrobatics. Using momentum in tandem with marksmanship, it made him all the more dangerous, not to mention that he circumvents the glaring weakness that most Pel-Tings have."

Kyle understood this point fully. As Sniper zipped around the graveyard, it was clear that he had the advantage when it came to a standard long-ranged battle. Yet with Glenn there was a certain exception. *He's getting closer. Between the intervals when each projectile is thrown, Glenn is slowly closing the distance.*

Kyle's learned eye was not wrong, and Sulemann corroborated this fact to his companion. "The other prodigy advanced the Pel-Ting Arts in a different way, you see. Due to their focus on long-ranged combat, a marksman is often helpless if someone traps them in a closed-quarters situation. However, this doesn't apply to Glenn."

"Why is that?" The researcher asked in earnest; this was his first time speaking with the Conductor on such intimate terms.

"…Because when it comes to close-quarters combat, Glenn excels just as brilliantly."

At that moment none comprehended this as much as Sniper, who, in a panic, swung his bottle case at Glenn when he was within arm's reach. The attack was slow and clumsy compared to Glenn's grace. Not only did he slide around it, but he managed to tack a couple screwdrivers into Sniper's arm—immobilizing it.

"*Frig!*" Jolts of pain shot along his joints, while Sniper scrambled in the dirt, trying to create space. Glenn wouldn't allow it, though. With the directive to slay everything in its path, that cadaver followed Sniper with deadly efficiency. Scissors on high and death imminent, the sharpened edge teemed with bloodlust until…

Fwip!

Glenn turned his attention to Kyle, who had sent a cutting straight at his temple. After a pause and altered directive, Glenn dashed towards Kyle with homicidal intent. Excitement bubbled in Sulemann's chest. *How will you handle this, Mr. Harding?*

Kyle also wondered as the distance between him and death lessened. Making a bastion with his cane cuttings he braced for impact, and hoped that some miracle would present itself. But it was only a slithering serpent that Kyle saw last…

Dario was home. After dedicating many years to its upkeep, he was sickened by the state it was in now. The scars from past raids remained, with moss and lianas dressing each wound after ten years of neglect. Dario was lost in the scene, gaping at the perforated door and shattered windows for minutes before venturing inside. The floor cracked beneath his step, with harvested debris littering the boards he swept every day. His home was alien to him, aside from the dingy scent of menthol in the air.

"I'm home." Dario greeted the mildew and traversed past the living room, through the dark corridor, and into the chamber he came to visit.

...

Dario was taken aback when he entered his master's room. The roar of gunfire and motorcycle engines clamored in his mind. He could smell the rotten sulphur; taste the dry, wooden dust. And moments later he would find it, preserved under some boards and rocks.

"Did you miss me?" The portrait of an old man patting a younger Dario's head was still intact, save for a few singes around the edges. He recalled the gentle grip of sallow fingers through his hair; how misleading it was. "Probably not..."

Dario held the last vestige of his master's shrine, resentment eroding any reverence in his heart. His devotion crumbled like the house he stood in.

"I know you never cared for my well-being." he told the frame. "Not truly. You may have had your reasons for giving me instruction, but it was never out of the goodness of your heart. Nor was it pity ... I at least learned that much." Dario squeezed the photo, digging his nails into the image. "I do thank you for your instruction, however inadvertent it may have been. Without it, I couldn't have risen to the point I am today."

Dario slipped through the maw in the wall and into the front yard. His old palm leaf was resting on the step; he picked it up and began sweeping. It was instinct to make those swirls in the dirt. Both defined and undefined. A result of the endless routine he was subjected to. Dario paused, the afternoon sun was pressing on his back, rekindling the wounds from a generous whip. Dario did not wince, but caressed the pain, claimed it. "You meant to awaken something in me. Something that revealed itself when you first saw me. I figured it out."

The palm leaf halted its sway while memories of that day came rushing back. It was a violent initiation for that dreadlocked boy who watched his family's slaughter, the resultant void bottomless. There was no fear or anguish in Dario's blood-soaked face; the part that bore such emotions was struck down, too. "I wanted to kill you. Of course, you knew that, after how many times I tried and failed. But I suppose that's what made you curious. Or at least made you spare my life." Dario nodded. "I was curious too, after a time. I learned. However, your techniques have not sated me … I want more. I *need* more."

Dario resumed his task, the motions of the bristles soothed him, and then placed the photograph on a mound of dirt sheltered by an adjacent shed. Bowing to the new shrine, he said, "I'm leaving. Not for selfish reasons, mind you, quelling my hunger is icing on the cake. But there is someone that I have to protect."

Kamilah's desperation was aflame in his mind. "I suppose it is my obligation, given everything I have done. I owe him that much."

Dario imagined his master's reply. How peeved he would be upon hearing the words of his captured ward. *"You only dulling yourself with such fickle notions,"* he would've said. But Dario would've ignored it then just as he did now.

"I suppose you wouldn't know much about that either. Duty. Obligation. It really is odd that I spent most of my life wanting to surpass you, when your knowledge wasn't sufficient to begin with."

The house, much like its inhabitants, was always governed by order and routine. They would manage the chores, practice their drills, nourish their bodies and rest their minds, and on the next morning they repeated it again. There was no interruption, aside from odd jobs, errands or the occasional murder attempt. This process was perpetual. Yet, as Dario left the yard, he found that stability ruined. He didn't mind. Now he had a reason for his violence. An excuse. A duty.

…Until now.

Order was shattered when Dario reached the graveyard. Rasheda, his partner, his responsibility, was lying in a pool of her own blood—lifeless and broken. Glenn, his fallen comrade, his creditor, was hovering over her like a wraith to reap the dead. Dario didn't register these events at first. Why was Glenn alive? Why was Rasheda hurt? Was Glenn the one who hurt her? A questionnaire unfurled in his mind before the malice infiltrated and manifested itself in his palm leaf.

From Kyle's point of view another monster had entered the pit. Cutup was a different beast from what he witnessed at Sheraton. For one, the bloodlust was sharper and there wasn't a hint of civility to barricade it. Also, his palm leaf was not bandaged; glistening with bristles as black as his hair. Kyle thought if Collins was brave enough to face this fiend head on, then a superior warrior he would be. The bus stop screamed and Kyle felt that electric reaction in the air.

…*Another Amplification?*

Dario's weapon fanned out, so that one palm became four. Through the blades and the dreadlocks, Kyle saw a glimpse of Dario's eyes which burned with pure hatred. If Glenn still had a soul it would've quivered under this gaze, but the corpse didn't flinch. Not even as the serpent split into two and devoured both of his arms in a single bite.

"Cha. There goes the moment." Sulemman sucked his teeth. But the scientist was ecstatic, beaming as his test subject was torn to bits. This was the opportunity he had waited years for.

"I do not know who you are, but you are not Glenn." Dario didn't face him yet, his gape transfixed on Rasheda's bloody form. "It's just as well. I can carry on my work without remorse."

Dario vanished once more, and the serpent reemerged on Glenn's side—where he would have difficulty defending if he still had limbs. With the two-pronged palm leaf ready to carve dead flesh, Glenn appeared powerless to prevent it. But

Sulemann saw the scientist's simper... *Shink!* There was a roar of steel against sheath, heralding the protrusion of countless blades from the gashes where Glenn's arms should've been. In an instant the snake was caught, and through the silhouette Kyle saw Dario's body crumple from the collision.

"*Gahaha!* Do you see that? It's even more brilliant than I imagined." The researcher bathed in his triumph though he sensed Sulemann's displeasure. "I hope you didn't mind, Conductor, sir, but I took the liberty of making a few modifications of my own. At first, I was overjoyed to be working on such a fine specimen as this, but I thought: 'what if we went further than just reanimating a dead form? What if we modified the form itself, creating a fusion of human and weapon unlike anything seen before?' I know I disregarded my boundaries but..." Upon this point he thrust his arm to the battlefield. "...you cannot deny these results, can you?"

Sulemann was silent, observing how the subjects reacted to this anomaly. Dario was on his feet immediately, his left arm was broken from the impact of those blades, and the left cheek and abdomen were dripping blood. Most likely he twisted at the very last second to reduce the damage. In spite of this, Dario showed no pain. With stable breaths he stood before the monster.

"You desecrate his body by turning him into this." Dario spoke to Glenn the Puppet but it was the master who heard his words, and he was not pleased. "By not letting him use the skills he perfected in life, you disgrace him even more with this transformation in death."

Sulemann agreed, nodding his head solemnly much to the researcher's chagrin. His Practitioner's pride was on the line and he refused to surrender it. "Hmph! What would a *consumer* like you know about the intricacies of Dark Arcs? Your kind only cares about using our products, but you know nothing of the effort required to perfect them!"

Dario heard none of this and continued his discourse with the cadaver. "From the moment I saw your abilities, I've coveted a duel with you, Glenn. But not under these circumstances. Not with this husk of your former self. Don't worry; I will free your body from this torment soon."

Kyle couldn't figure out how. Aside from a broken arm, Dario stepped with a limp, his divine speed should be cut in half but there wasn't any lethargy in the serpent at all. Small puffs of dirt and gravel erupted after every zigzag in a clash that Kyle couldn't see. He heard the bangs of crashing metal though, as palm leaf met scissors, screwdriver, or whatever random blade the researcher forged into Glenn's body. Kyle imagined that every ring was a successful parry or an ill-timed counterattack, but then it was foolish to fathom a battle of this level.

Sniper wriggled forward, unnoticed by anyone else in the graveyard. Dario's interruption spared him from severe injury, but he was still unable to stand or partake in the battle. Sniper found the scenario perfect. While the two monsters killed each other he would make his escape; though no longer a Pel-Ting, he still upheld their notions of self-preservation.

Kyle held a similar idea, but rejected it upon recalling his goal and his mother—or her soul, rather—which seemed to support him as her warmth touched his arm. She calmed him, much like she had all along. "Any moment now…"

The countdown was on. Dario and Glenn approached their limit, and since one was undead the odds were not in Dario's favor. Sweeping his black fan like a performer at the Chinese opera, he controlled the space and rhythm of his opponent with ease. If Kyle could track the battle, it would seem like Dario had the upper hand. But it was Glenn who adapted, parrying the cautious swipes of that palm leaf so that he was upon Dario in moments. The timing was flawless, like it was calculation rather than instinct. And as Dario was in mid-thrust with one hand broken, there was simply no means of defending himself. Thus, he was forced to let go.

The air ripped.

From Glenn's stomach came several sharp objects aimed at skewering Dario, but only one would succeed.

"*Gahah!* All that chat, and he still fell before my design." the researched jeered.

Sulemann wasn't as joyous though, paying silent respects to the warrior who didn't utter a croak in his defeat. He was reminded of that day when Over de Wall fell, and now in a quirk of fate, Gulfsyde should do the same. The researcher asked,

"Well? How do you like it, Conductor, sir? Are you pleased with the results?"

"It's aight." Sulemann focused on Kyle Harding— the true objective of this excercise. "But the true test ain really start yet."

Kyle stopped. Not just his movements, but his heart, his breath, his very synapses had come to a screeching halt. Glenn was the neighborhood Rottweiler that was known for mangling any trespassers that came across its path. And Kyle was now in the yard, facing the beast as he caught its attention. Fear froze him on the spot, for the Rottweiler hadn't barked or growled upon noticing him. It just stared with dead eyes, waiting to see what Kyle would do next.

It was in this lull that Kyle experienced the purest horror. Unlike previous opponents who were puppets, or mere beings with agendas behind their violence, Glenn killed purely on instinct. Like a rabid dog trained to maul the nearest piece of meat. He was unpredictable, dangerous, and Kyle had no idea how to proceed.

"I don't know how to handle this…" Kyle told his cane, but his mother didn't respond. Maybe she was never there to begin with? A simple mirage to console himself. Truth is, Kyle knew exactly what he had to do, his agenda hadn't changed, and as he adopted his stance only one command resonated in his core. *Survive.*

Sulemann smiled. The researcher sneered. And Glenn marched forth, sighting the target his body had been fashioned to kill.

Kyle was the first to strike, guiding two cuttings at the cadaver while he darted forward. A rudimentary attack when compared to Sniper's, so Glenn handled it with a Pel-Ting's proficiency.

That won't work… Kyle thought. Even with this new ability, Glenn clearly had the advantage in long-ranged battles. If there was any hope of victory, it could only be grasped up close. But those blades: the Rottweiler's fangs were oh so menacing, indeed.

Time slowed. The air burned. The buzzing in his ear made his head swim. Still Kyle ignored all of it and focused on Glenn's abdomen, where a myriad of jagged objects protruded. *Clink! Clink!* Cane upon metal serenaded the graves while Kyle struggled against the barrage. In a familiar pattern of leg, torso, neck, arm, repeat, Glenn knew the fundamental spots at which to target, albeit simultaneously. And if it weren't for the segmented cane cuttings, Kyle would've been perforated long ago. Kyle was on borrowed time with every guarded thrust and slash, but thankfully he settled into the flow of battle which he'd grown accustomed.

Leg … Torso… Neck … Arm … The cogs were in motion, and the waves of fear ebbed so he could find some fault to exploit. But…

"There is no weak point, fool." The researcher asserted, eager to impress Sulemann with his achievement. "My design is flawless. You could as well curl up and die now, so we could get on with other business."

But there ain no other business… Sulemann thought. So much depended on the outcome of this battle; things far beyond the scope of innovation or pride. But despite how much Sulemann supported Kyle Harding, it was manifest that he would not survive.

Keep attacking … Just keep attacking … Kyle recited between shallow breaths. He never fully recovered from his duel with Rasheda, and his body was fettered by exhaustion and blood loss. Whereas Glenn's body was immune to such effects, or so he assumed.

"Be careful, Kyle." Veronica Harding cooed in his ears; Kyle instantly felt a pang of relief.

"I know, Mom. I know." Kyle whispered, concentrating on the enemy ahead. Glenn resembled a nightmarish porcupine with shears, needles, picks, and all forms of gruesome quills coming from his body. A terrifying sight that made Kyle tense, but it wasn't Glenn's weaponry he focused on. Glenn's flesh looked even more pallid than before, hanging from his bones like an oversized coat on a mannequin. Also with this transformation Glenn hardly seemed as agile anymore. Therein lied his solution. *So far he's excelled at any distance, but he never attacks unless a target has reached within a certain range… let's say five metres.*

Kyle skipped away, gauging his distance with one or two cuttings to keep Glenn occupied. "Skill aside, he's got the upper hand when it comes to momentum—hell, he even out maneuvered Cutup in a swordfight. Which means…? I need to attack him all at once."

Without any command, his cane disassembled and attacked Glenn like machine-gun fire. As expected, the quills shot out to intercept the bullets, rendering Kyle's salvo meaningless. But Kyle was satisfied with the discovery he made. "Those blades are limited. Glenn could only make a certain number at a time."

Sulemann recognized the flaw, too. "Our subject like it slowdown since it change into this new form. How comes?"

"I don't understand how you mean."

"I dunno. He isn't as efficient as before." The researcher wouldn't dare admit it, and Sulemann didn't ask again.

But everything was clear in Kyle's eyes. He noted the interval at which the quills returned to Glenn's body—about five seconds at most—and knew what he had to do. "Mom… Is it possible to extend this cane's length?"

There was no reply but the segments returned to their complete form, which stretched the cane to bo-staff length. *I need to pierce him during that moment. But I can't reach across there in that space of time.*

Kyle coveted Cutup's speed. Upon looking at Dario's battered frame, which was flimsy compared to the mighty serpent in battle, Kyle began to pity Glenn. These were his friends whom he massacred. People he cared for. People he loved. At this point Rasheda's body came into view, and for a moment Kyle remembered the people he endangered himself. *I'll stop you, Glenn. I'll stop you and go home to my family. No matter what it takes.*

In response to this thought Glenn rushed forth, but Kyle didn't panic—there was no room for it. All the pain and exhaustion was plastered by pure resolve, and Kyle adopted his stance— perhaps for the last time. Glenn's movements were stricter than Dario's, swaying from side to side while he ran, but Kyle managed to follow the blur and the cane divided again in kind. There wasn't any energy to match Glenn's sprint, so he sent cuttings by the pair to compensate. *Fwap! Fwap!* The cadaver swatted them away like flies, but for Kyle that was enough to distract Glenn from his true intent.

Now! Kyle focused his will on the single cutting he had left. He wanted it to get longer, to form a long and powerful lance that would reach through Glenn's bladed rampart. And in answer to his call, the cutting stretched and stretched and stretched… with such force that Glenn flailed away to escape.

"Elongation." Veronica Harding said. "Along with the ability to divide, the sugarcane can extend itself several metres away from your person."

Kyle was elated. He didn't expect his plan to work, nor for the cane to have that ability. Yet, as Glenn stood with an arm flopping at his side by the bare tendons, Kyle reveled in the small victory he obtained.

"Yooow… that one pretty tight, though!" Sulemann whistled, while the researcher held his balding head in disbelief.

Bolstered by this new skill Kyle resumed his formation, directing a few cuttings at his enemy before harpooning him. On this occasion, Glenn lost his left shin which he quickly replaced with a pair of shears. The battle hardly resembled a contest of martial arts anymore and entered the realm of nightmare. Yet Kyle found himself quite comfortable in this world of screaming bus stops and purple hues.

Th-Thunk! The tearing of Glenn's flesh made a sickening sound. If he wasn't dead already that wound would've done the trick.

"My work!" The researcher cried as Glenn slumped to the ground, just a few feet away from Kyle. His decrepit frame collapsing under the onslaught, and his final attempt on Kyle's life squelched much like his own. There was no agony in Glenn's face, no emotion at all, but Kyle believed that if the corpse still had life, it would thank him from the bottom of its heart.

Sweet relief anointed Kyle as he flopped in the dirt. The world had fallen silent. The bus stop ceased its song, the air stopped ringing, and his mother's voice had disappeared. Was this death? Kyle wondered for the second time that day, but again the drumming of his heart provided a suitable answer.

"I survived… haha… I survived…." Kyle thought of Damien. Was he at home reading comics in his room, safe and secure? Would he be able to join him soon? These notions settled in his mind as the world turned to black and the grip around his sugarcane waned…,

"Well, I guess that is that." Sulemann clapped his hands together before stretching them in the air. The experiment took longer than expected, but he was satisfied with the results. The researcher, on the other hand, buried his head in his palms, refusing to acknowledge what just transpired.

"I… I don't understand what just happened. I really don't. Everything was going so well and then…"

"It's fine, really. I think the whole thing come off good, when you study it." The researcher wouldn't hear it, shaking his head without facing Sulemann. "If anything, we could count our losses and look forward to the future."

"I'm so sorry, Conductor… I promise—you have my word that I will do my utmost best next time to bring you positive results!"

Sulemann observed him for a while, and likened the researcher to another person he commissioned in the past. Like him, she had a wealth of talent and knowledge of the Dark Arcs—truly a joy to work with. But she also had something that was toxic to Sulemann's ambitions. Pride. An ego that spent decades fermenting under past trials and feats, so that when faced with any instance of failure she rejected it. Like a minor smear on a pristine white shirt, she obsessed over it, troubling the smear until the entire shirt was ruined. Rachel Pringle and the researcher were the same. Cut from the same cloth. And as Sulemann regarded the groveling Practitioner, his high spirits soured with each passing second.

"Uh yeah… I have another appointment, so I think this is where I'll make my exit." Sulemann maintained his smile. "But I truly appreciate all of your hard work over the years. It was a pleasure doing business with you."

The researcher couldn't place a finger on it, but he knew this was the end for him. He blinked at the Conductor, who still had an appeased grin, and felt the chill of death on his back. Then he sensed it on his forehead, the domino which hovered just above his skin. Then he felt the heat, the flames crackling beneath his vision and the void that swallowed him whole.

Betty had a hard time on the job today. After setting up shop at her usual spot on Wednesdays—an indoor vendors market located in Palmetto Street in town—she found her business particularly slow. Amidst the other hawkers trading their wares, fruits, vegetables and clothes, Betty was the only one selling roast corn and magic. No one wanted roast corn for lunch and few wanted to purchase any magic. Thus, as the old hawker inspected her pot full of crackling coals and blackening cobs, she lamented on busier times. This wasn't the only source of her sorrow, however.

"I guess that was the end of the road for you, nuh, child?" Betty sighed while caressing the hilt of *Anjèd San*. The sword had returned to its maker upon the death of the person wielding it—an incantation Betty placed to prevent it from falling into malicious hands. "I'm sorry, Yvette. I shoulda never give she it."

Betty poked the cobs to even out the roasting, replaying the sales she made ten years ago in Layer's Gap. Dario came to mind; the quiet young boy with the veil of dreadlocks draping his face. Back then she wasn't surprised to have him as a customer—he was a member of Gulfsyde, after all. What did surprise her was the boy's reason for patronizing her lowly stall.

"Normally I would trust my own abilities, but I need something sturdier than this." Young Dario said, while bestowing a weathered palm leaf. Betty didn't offer any of her Lickerish Arms because that palm leaf had seen enough death to warrant a place in their collection.

"Gine into Debt Collection too, child?"

"Yes, I am." Dario had to say no more. Betty knew he was following Rasheda's footsteps. His intentions might not be noble, but protecting her was one of them. With that in mind, she agreed to augment the boy's weapon and the service cushioned her decision to sell *Anjèd San*. But Betty was naïve. She realized that now, and only guilt flooded her heart as she regarded her creation.

"I'm sorry."

"Having a hard day, Coalpot?" Startled, Betty turned and found an old acquaintance.

"Oh hello, Mother Sally, I wasn't expecting you in this part of town." Mother Sally read her discomfort, and replied,

It's okay, Betty. We're not breaking any regulations by having an afternoon chat."

"You sure? After everything that happen wid Seifert, I really ain want nuh more trouble." Betty looked at the three bodyguards standing nearby. They failed to blend in with the hustle and bustle of the market, wearing brimmed hats and veils to conceal their faces—like the overseas insurgents seen on TV. They were dangerous though, Betty was certain of that, and Mother Sally was also capable of taking care of herself.

"Positive. I was given a bit more room to breathe by the Admins. Hell, I could even buy some wares from you if I wanted—provided they were minor, of course." Mother Sally chuckled, mostly at the notion of needing items from Betty—a Practitioner of lesser ability.

"You right to mek mock sport at me, Mother Sally."

"Just breaking the ice, dear." She said, while conjuring a snow cone out of thin air. None in the market seemed to notice. "So, I guess another Greedy Weapon has returned to your possession."

Betty caught a knot in her throat. It was clear what Mother

Sally insinuated, and any incorrect response would cost her life. "Yes, *Anjèd San* has returned. Look. I didn't know that it was involved in Seifert's—"

"Please, dear. Do you really think that Father Hoe: *The Last Canecutter* would succumb to one of your weapons? No disrespect. It is excellent craftsmanship, I'm sure, but... come now."

Betty swallowed the defiant retort burning her tongue, and thought of her conversation with Linseed. "I suppose you right..."

"We suspect other forces at work here and are forming our own investigations. I just thought I'd pass by. Yuh know, see how you doing for the time being. It's been so long."

"It has."

Betty and Mother Sally weren't close. In fact, they didn't even run in the same circles most of the time, which served Betty well as she wanted no association with the rogue group known as White Soursop. She suspected Mother Sally wasn't interested in "catching up", though.

"What have you been up to?" Mother Sally cloaked the question with a smile and twinkling eyes.

"Nothing much, yuh know. Just trying to survive in this slow period." Betty took out another cob while Sally sipped from her snow cone. They were a portrait of traditional city life in the Caribbean.

"Times rough, fuh truth. I been having problems with my own business myself." In the aftermath of the Parish War, it was a wonder Sally survived at all, let alone continued her own practice, Betty thought. Sally gestured towards the cone in her hand. "Not much people into snow cones these days either. Diabetes stirring, they say."

They both chuckled. A random nut seller riding a bicycle was stopped and coerced by the three bodyguards to take a different route. His colorful use of the Bajan language flooded the market, and everyone's eyes veered in their direction. Betty cringed beneath their glowers and regretted the conversation with this woman even more. Sally continued,

"When Seifert Brathwaite came to your stall, what exactly did he purchase?"

"Um…" This time the question was naked, exposed in its candor. Betty's mind went blank for a moment before she answered. "He wanted some Rejuvenating Tamarind Balls and some Noni-Juice."

"Perfectly ordinary items for an old man who needed some extra energy…" Mother Sally chomped on the chipped ice. "…Or a veteran warrior eager to get back in action. That must be the pretext they used for his arrest. The slippery bastards…"

"Oh no, I… I didn't mean to…"

"It's all right, Betty. No one is blaming you. As far as you're concerned, you were just selling your wares to a client as per usual. No obligation to reject a sale, even if it is against the law—technically."

"Even so, I'm sorry. If I knew this would happen—" Sally held up her hand and disposed of the empty plastic cup. She'd had enough excuses and sweets for the day.

"Nothing you can do about it now. Worrying isn't going to bring Seifert back, so we might as well move on." Mother Sally then rubbed her hands in her thick skirts, wrenching the fabric in between her fingers. Her voice was low and sharp. "But lemme tell yuh, tighten yuh belt, hear? Because things gine change in Bimshire. There gine be a reckoning, you best believe that."

From her declaration Betty imagined another Parish War, engulfing the island again like the embers in her own pot. It was just as Linseed said: things will get worse now that they kicked White Soursop's nest. Mother Sally came close to a bitter hornet queen as she examined Betty's stall. "One more thing, Betty… would you mind showing me *Anjèd San* for a moment?"

Betty swallowed hard. "I thought you say my Lickerish Arms couldn't take down Seifert."

"Just to be certain, dear. My misguided confidence has no place in this investigation." Betty mulled it over first, then reached into her pot—oblivious to the searing coals—and pulled out the handle of the Greedy Weapon. Chains bounded *Anjèd San* once more, and as Mother Sally inspected the accursed blade, particularly the red digits which flashed in its eye, all doubt disappeared.

"...*Anjèd San* not only records the amount of Blood Money it collects, but the depositors, too. So if Seifert's blood was in there it would show up."

"I assume this was the first thing you checked upon its return?"

Betty nodded. A lie; the first thing she checked for was Kyle Harding's blood.

"This confirms it, then. Please forgive my trespass, Betty."

"I understand. If anything, it raises more questions 'bout what happened, nuh? You think it's an accomplice? Or…"

"Someone else." The Conductor came to mind but Betty said nothing, lest she fuel Mother Sally's interrogation even more. "Anyway, my girl, I best be off. Again, thank you for your excellent service, as usual."

"It is my pleasure, Mother Sally." Betty bowed, while the three bodyguards swooped around Mother Sally and escorted her out of the market. It would be several steps later that they vanished into thin air, unseen by the other people within the square.

With a sigh Betty stowed her creation, hoping that *Anjèd San* would never see the light of day again. As fate would have it, that one transaction between her and Rasheda set into motion a different kind of chaos. And as she dolefully packed up her stall for the afternoon, Betty could only think of Veronica Harding's boys and her friend Linseed.

Damien turned the front doorknob as carefully as he could manage. Sneaking into the house was an impossible task with Mr. Beckles around, but he just wasn't in the mood to talk to his master right now. *Creak!* Damien winced with each moan of the hinge, but after several steps he soon realized that,

"No one's home, nuh?"

A rare occasion where the Harding household was left completely unattended. Just to be certain, Damien swept the house the way Mr. Beckles taught him, and his brother before that. Bedrooms, bathrooms, closets, windows, yard—all clear and secure, and with that confirmation the boy allowed himself to relax. Usually this would entail kicking off his shoes, diving into his divan, and either reading some comic book or playing a video game. But not today. Damien's mind was occupied with magic and witches and a business that involved them both.

"It's finally starting to make sense." He muttered in the face of overwhelming evidence. The Heart Man encounter replayed in his head, along with Sulemann's elaborate magic displays. All the pieces were there, he just had to put them together.

Damien turned over to face his dressing table, on the mirror his own reflection stared back at him with an unruly head of hair and pensive frown. How naïve had he been, thinking he had a normal life? There was no ignoring his master's constant drills or his brother's obsession with safety. Obviously, danger was afoot. Damien kicked a comic book from the foot of his bed, wondering just how much Kyle knew about this new world of magic.

"*I will clear my debt!*" Damien focused on the Heart Man's plea when he attempted to kill his brother. What debt could he possibly mean? And how was Kyle going to help him clear it?

"Maybe I should ask Kyle when he gets home…" Perish the thought. He remembered Kyle's face at the hospital and how fiendish it looked. Vengeance etched that expression, and the likelihood of his brother not returning home had dawned in Damien's mind. "…Or should I call him now?"

Damien imagined the cell phone ringing in the middle of a gruesome battle, breaking Kyle's honed concentration at a critical moment. The result could be disastrous. "Better not…"

Yes, better to trust in his brother's abilities, trust that he'd return safely—battered, bruised, but safe. Kyle was no slouch in combat, Damien knew that much, though the last encounter in his backyard left him with some doubt. Especially since Collins had to rescue him last time, and at present that support was wrapped up in an ICU at the Queen Elizabeth Hospital. Oh, how times have changed, when Damien is the one who worried about his brother.

"Screw it. I need some air." To his alarm, Damien's room became more like a prison than the haven he'd enjoyed over the years. A fake world covered with fictional characters, closed drapes and stacks of mindless entertainment. He needed a change of space, somewhere to let his mind process all the pieces.

His search had finally led him to the sparring post in his backyard. Stick-licking didn't stimulate Damien. Yes, he excelled in it, almost to a virtuoso degree, but he wasn't driven to practice it like Kyle did. There was no reason to, or so he believed. It was the backyard which reminded him of the Heart Man attack. Damien wasn't afraid to be there anymore, but those flashes of blue and yellow were potent in his mind's eye, even in the afternoon. He lashed the wooden figure for ten minutes before tossing his stick aside. This was useless.

Damien then toured the house. It never occurred in his twelve years under its roof to look around his home. *Really look around.* He had visited every room but never paid attention to the details. Like the way the white-and-peach concrete blocks caught the sunlight, even in the hours before dusk. The slight flicker where the galvanized paling met the connecting beams. The rooftop shingles that flaked violet and caused the birds to veer away from above. Inside, Damien felt the cozy familiarity that he had taken for granted. It calmed him, just barely, but it was enough to hush his thoughts and alert him to the creaking in the verandah.

"Kyle?" He cracked open the door and saw, not his brother, but the stunning young lady Kyle was friends with.

"Hello." Lianne waved. She seemed more formal than Damien remembered, with her dark, curly hair tied into one and dark blue pencil dress. He still blushed as he met her emerald eyes.

"Kyle's not here yet."

"I know. Actually, it's you I came here to see."

"...Why?"

"I'm an associate of Sulemann—The Conductor—and he requests your presence." Damien entered the verandah. It was the way she said Sulemann's name, as if it had authority. Then an epiphany bloomed.

"Wait a minute ... are you a witch, too? I mean, Practitioner?"

Lianne winced at the term; she never liked being compared to the common street vendor. "Sort of—we run in the same circles."

"So that means you can do magic, then?" Damien asked, eagerness polished his face.

Lianne blinked, and then she replied, "Yes. I can."

"What can you do? Cloaking? Illusions? Or do you have different powers than the conductor fella." Damien's heart raced. He drank from the well of knowledge that Lianne had offered at his front door. Parched. Delirious. Damien swallowed it all in big gulps.

"Wow. You really aren't like Kyle at all." Lianne giggled, but Damien's interest was ablaze. "Tell you what. If you come with me, I guarantee you'll see my powers in no time."

"Sounds like something a kidnapper would say." Damien was enthralled but not at the sacrifice of his judgment. Lianne's grin hadn't faded.

"Once we understand each other, then."

At this point, many ideas came to Damien like the world after a night's slumber. Sulemann wasn't a friend, despite the acts of support he offered in the past. In fact, Sulemann had been following him all along, or if not him, his allies. Those like Lianne or the Heart Man; they were in some way connected to Sulemann. And Sulemann targeted his brother as well. *Stupid.* He should've known better. But curiosity had gripped him back then and it gripped him even now.

"What does he want with me?"

"I don't know." Lianne answered truthfully. Damien tallied his options; he still had a stick in his hand. But what could Stick-licking do against magic?

"Fine. Lemme get some things before I go."

"Okay." Lianne recognized the discernment in her hostage. *He's a smart kid. I could see how you two are related, Kyle.*

Lianne didn't like this situation. Contact with Sulemann had been sporadic lately, which wasn't very strange given his position, but at least she was an accomplice in his schemes before. Now Sulemann was off the grid, and only corresponded when he needed a task done that couldn't be handled himself. Collecting

Damien Harding was one of those tasks.

Then there was the Harding household, which was obviously a structure of magical integrity. Lianne noted a force field of sorts around the house, with concentrated currents of energy embedded within each board and brick. A bomb, perhaps? No. From the way Kyle regarded his mother, it was clear she intended to protect her children at all costs. Truly a model parent, Lianne was a bit envious. The building was probably a shelter of some kind, providing asylum for all those who entered. The question was: on what condition? Based on Lianne's knowledge, structures like these required a key or invitation, and from the intricacies of the enchantment it was probably the latter. Lianne should've coerced Damien into inviting her inside the house as a guest. But the boy was no fool.

Damien mulled over escape routes as he packed his haversack, but there were none. Not when magic was involved. He glanced at his cell phone, "I gotta tell Kyle…" but there was no response. The Amplifier in Layer's Gap had disrupted the signal. Damien tried four more times before swallowing the fact that his brother wouldn't pick up.

"He's not dead." He convinced himself and resumed his packing.

Lianne believed the same, brushing aside the rousing guilt as she surveyed her surroundings. Molasses Drive was remote for a countryside village. There were no neighboring houses for several kilometers with bushes, gullies and ackee trees forming natural partitions. Perfect for a Practitioner's abode. Lianne also regarded the hillside locale, scoping its summit for any unwanted passersby. At least if Kyle made it back home, he would be in no condition to face her.

"Oh? I wasn't aware that Kyle expected visitors this evening."

Lianne whipped around. The voice came out of nowhere, and upon setting her sights on its source, she found an elderly man gazing at her. Despite her age, Lianne was well aware of the legends in the Dark Arcs trade. Linseed *Bruggadown* Beckles was among the greats due to his exploits in the Parish War of 1976. The records weren't wrong either; Bruggadown was a strapping man; with an athletic frame that survived the ages, but Lianne knew from the solemn glare that there was more to his strength.

"And who might you be, Miss?"

"Lianne..." She paused. "Lianne DeSilva."

Mr. Beckles didn't balk at the name, instead marching towards her. "And what business do you have here, Miss DeSilva? Kyle isn't home right now. I believe he had some matters to attend to."

This was Kyle's master; she was sure of it. Who else could've bestowed him the skills to survive a Shaggy Bear? Lianne chose her reply carefully while watching his arms. "I came to visit Damien."

"Oh? And what would a lovely young lady like you have to discuss with my apprentice?" By now Mr. Beckles had drawn two batons from out of thin air. There they were: the fabled twin truncheons which caused unspeakable carnage in the past. Lianne saw they were mere bamboo pieces, bandaged in black and silver tape, but by no means did she relax as he approached. In the hands of Bruggadown, bamboo was as dangerous as any Lickerish Arm.

"Should I interpret this as an act of aggression, Mr. Beckles?" Lianne asked coolly.

"Perhaps."

Mr. Beckles shared similar concerns. He had recognized the name DeSilva quite well. The DeSilvas were one of the more prominent families in Bimshire and the wider Caribbean. Blessed with substantial wealth and influence, they often had their hand in many corporate and state affairs, which naturally extended to the arena of Dark Arcs. Furthermore, what made the DeSilvas a force to be reckoned with was their sanctioned possession of a Baku. However, this was in the years before the Parish War, and since then the family had fallen from grace. Mr. Beckles once heard the DeSilvas had to relinquish their Baku, over debts most likely, but he wouldn't allow such hearsay to dull his senses. Not with Veronica Harding's children on the line.

"I would like to avoid a needless confrontation. Last thing we both want is to level this community based on a misunderstanding."

"Misunderstanding? Odd... I most certain this is a kidnapping in progress, correct?"

Lianne didn't respond.

"If so, I'm afraid I cannot let you take my ward away. After all, he is my responsibility."

Of course, an enchanted house alone wouldn't have protected the Hardings. The main reason for the children's survival had been this monster. No wonder Sulemann wanted her hand in this abduction. Lianne was a sacrificial lamb. *You stinking bastard…*

Lianne didn't intend to die here. Her ambitions were yet to ripen. Thus, with a flick of her wrist her bracelet flashed cerulean, the beacon for her ethereal servant to come to her aid. Mr. Beckles was now twenty paces away, marching with the resolve of an executioner.

Two abominable forces were about to converge, and inside the house Damien remained unaware of their impact.

Collins followed his two escorts in amazement. His first option was to visit Kyle's house after he failed to get through to the phone. However, the boy called Bailey suggested triangulating Kyle's position using the very same signal from the call. It took five failed attempts—longer than usual, Bailey asserted—but soon they had found Kyle's location and were well on their way to Layer's Gap.

That was a little too easy… Collins thought while glancing at the members of White Soursop. He recalled how easily Cutup tracked him up to Farley Hill, and the mysterious text messages he received last year. If the enemy had these methods at their disposal, it was no wonder they couldn't hide. This begged many questions but one was more pressing at the moment. "How comes we gine by car? I thought wunna used the bus stops to get around de island."

Bailey raised his eyebrows, mildly impressed that he knew about the Transit. "With ordinary transport it's easier to track

Kyle's unstable signal" —*and I cannot track someone and teleport at the same time. But you don't need to know that.*

Collins was ready to object, but Barrow grunted before the words left his mouth. "I don't like um. Those bus stops, I mean. I don't like um at all. Feels like dem watching our every move."

"Dem?"

"De Admin. 'The Powers that Be.' *Kard 28.*" Barrow explained, though Collins noticed how his stubby fingers tightened around the steering wheel. Collins was tempted to ask more but Bailey announced their arrival.

"We're here."

At first, Collins couldn't understand what he meant. As far as he could tell, they had pulled up next to a rusty paling with an array of bay-leaf trees and bush hanging over the galvanized sheets. However, Bailey was certain this was the place, hopping out of the passenger seat to inspect closer. Collins followed suit, glancing at the old Suzuki which the White Soursop operatives commandeered from some unsuspecting delivery man. He felt a momentary pang of guilt which was quickly replaced by his concern for Kyle and Nadia.

"…You sure we in Layer's Gap?"

"This is where the signal ends." Bailey said impatiently. Two marbles floated alongside him in a ninety-degree formation, pausing at particular intervals where the rust tore holes into the metal. "There's a shroud of some kind here—possibly illusionary—and a dense one at that."

"Fuh truth? Why would a thing like that be all the way out here?" Barrow tramped behind after parking the Suzuki and chucking the keys one side. He had no intention of returning the vehicle.

"Someone's hiding something." Bailey mused.

"That's how Layer's Gap is, from what I hear." Collins chimed in, relishing that he had to inform the two for once. "The entire village was held hostage by a gang call Over de Wall ten years ago. Was pretty nasty. Almost like it was in de Middle East or something—men used to call it De Gulf."

Collins elaborated on Sniper's tale, and after hearing the details Bailey scoffed in disgust. "And to leave this shroud activated for all this time? Sloppy. Very, very sloppy. Then again, I shouldn't expect any more from this current administration."

"What about the people inside?" Barrow asked, urgency written all over his face. Collins couldn't answer, and he imagined how horrific these circumstances were for the Layer's Gap community.

"Best to find out for ourselves, then." Suddenly Bailey's marbles stopped their scouring and revolved on the spot before them.

A flare of white and grey blinded Collins, and the crash of breaking glass tickled his ears. When he gathered his senses, the paling had unraveled to reveal an empty street flanked with dilapidated houses. The smell was the second thing to hit Collins when he entered—a putrid waft from ten years' worth of uncollected garbage had settled into the village. The scent of smoke was also prevalent, though whether it was from adaptive residents who burnt their own waste or from more battle-ridden times Collins wasn't sure. It was just as Sniper described; a model community which had once been featured on the CBC Evening News for outstanding innovative design, making homemade attractions out of recycled tires, cans and wood, but now ravaged by constant skirmishes, bombardments and war. Surreal: the word that popped up as Collins regarded the destruction around him. And wasteful. How many lives were lost back then? And how many were stunted after ten years of exile? Too many.

"Is anyone still alive here?" For some reason, Barrow had his belt off and coiled around his wrist.

"I'm detecting signs of life in the buildings." Bailey said, glancing scornfully at a decrepit chattel house.

Collins focused on the windows, which were boarded up haphazardly with mismatching pieces of plywood or galvanize—shelter from gunfire. But the few panes that remained intact showed curtains shuffling under his gaze. If anyone still resided here, they were too afraid to step outside. Wasteful.

"So why don't they leave, then? It ain like Over de Wall still 'bout the place."

"The shroud was only a mirage type—one which projected outwards— so there was nothing physically stopping anyone from leaving here. Psychologically, however…" Of course, it was fear that imprisoned the villagers of Layer's Gap. Fear of being gunned down in the streets or blown to bits. Mix Drink had left an entire neighborhood shell-shocked—*that* was his legacy.

"But why nobody ain come from the outside? They don't have any family members? No friends?" Barrow asked, but deep down he knew the answer to that question, and Bailey recited it for him.

"Protocol would call for containment when it came to large-scaled incidents like this. Mental Erasures. Environmental Mending. Even Shrouds of this ilk…" Bailey said "ilk" as if the word was rotten. "In our field, it is quite possible to wipe your existence from the face of the earth. Though Lord knows it's cheaper just to kill you and get it over with."

Bailey paused. It was miraculous White Soursop still existed at all. He thought after such overt aggression that Kard 28 would've issued the harshest penalty. But they didn't, and that worried him. Barrow, on the other hand, seemed more concerned with the bottled-up residents, bellowing at the prisoners in hopes of freeing them from their cages. He failed miserably.

"There's nothing to be done about them now, Barrow. They're too attached."

"Nonsense." Barrow ignored him and persisted in his efforts.

Collins sauntered onward with meticulous steps, peeking through every opening and pathway for any signs of Kyle. Instinctively, his hand went to his waist but it was empty. He was defenseless. In this ravaged land without any weapon, he suddenly felt the mark of vulnerability stamp upon his back.

…

Time was running short for Sulemann and he found himself veering away from schedule. Though he was known among peers for his tardiness, timing became of utmost importance to his goals.

"That took a lot longer than expected, but I can't really complain about how it worked out." Sulemann grinned, flicking his wrist so that a domino appeared within his fingers. "Cleaning up took away some time, too."

A smoldering lab coat was all that was left of his subordinate. Honestly, the whole affair had left a bitter aftertaste, and Sulemann was relieved to have settled it. Well, almost. Kyle Harding lay unconscious several meters away. His injuries weren't severe, with scrapes and cuts sprinkled all over his body. It was a blessing he survived with this much. But Kyle Harding was exhausted, and naturally so, after facing *Anjèd San* and Glenn in his Duppy form. Sulemann was impressed that he didn't suffer a similar fate as Damian Collins.

"You really are interesting, Inheritor. I look forward to seeing your growth so we can't have you dying just yet." Another domino was conjured; this time landing on Kyle's back and sinking into his flesh just like with Collins. "Till we meet again, Mr. Harding. Oh?"

A black feline slinked around the lab coat and stopped at Sulemann's feet. Elegant and dangerous, the cat peered up at him with piercing green eyes and slit pupils. "I suppose our business is done here?"

Its baritone voice didn't alarm Sulemann in the slightest. "Yeah, we sort out for now. You could send the Two-Three my apologies for what happen to his guys."

"My master has no use for broken staff." The feline peered at Rasheda, who appeared to have passed moments ago from the wound inflicted on her. Dario was nowhere to be found, though the trail of blood leading out of the graveyard made it clear that he had escaped.

"Ouch. Wunna men ain easy atall."

"I shall take my leave now that this is over. Farewell, human." Respect was in short supply when it came to anyone besides its master, and Sulemann was quite aware. The feline paid no attention to his exaggerated waves as it climbed atop the bus stop and vanished with a pop. Prim and pompous, just like its owner.

"Looks like we got some company, yuh."

Collins had found the graveyard, glancing around cautiously at the broken tombstones and eviscerated crypts. Sulemann was most pleased to see the Rasta in full recovery; rubbing his fingertips together so that the domino nestled within Collins returned to his hand in an instant. Everything was falling into place.

Collins wished he had his namesake with him. As he stepped over several fissures in the dirt and noted the plumes of smoke and debris spilling into the sky, he knew this had been a bitter battlefield, and without any weapon, he was merely a civilian waiting to be killed. "Where the hell are you…?"

Collins recognized the faint tingle in the air, the way his hair stood on end from the charged atmosphere. He shuddered. It was just like Farley Hill; just before the twin snakes bit him. "Kyle!"

Kyle's nose was in the dirt, his limbs bent askew and sugarcane firm in his grip. Even in death Kyle Harding wouldn't release it, Collins thought, but then the canewielder hacked back to life. His first words were, "…Damien."

"Yo, B. You all right?"

"Damien… Where's Damien?" Kyle burbled. Collins helped him to sit up. "My brother… Where's my brother?"

"Looks like we missed quite the skirmish?" Bailey ambled from behind before Collins could answer. His marbles took on a more defensive formation around his body, except for one which glided past Kyle and towards the bus stop seventy meters away. "Some intricate magic—of the more brutish nature, mind you—but still intricate all the same. Several amplifications were involved, too."

"The enemy still 'bout the place?" Barrow's belt was fully stretched with its leather licking the ground.

"No. It seems we are the only ones in the vicinity." Bailey lingered on the stirring Kyle. *So, this is Damien Harding's brother.* Another marble danced around the sugarcane, causing Kyle to shift away in alarm. "Odd. Nothing."

"Wait… What are you doing here? Who are these guys?" Memories of a dying Collins clicked in his mind, overwriting the canefield and his mother's nurturing gaze. Kyle hacked again. There was no blood, thank goodness; in fact, his body felt lighter than it had in months.

Collins explained, to his best ability, what happened between his hospital bed and this graveyard, failing to answer questions regarding his own recuperation and locating Kyle's whereabouts.

Collins also couldn't explain the two strangers that accompanied him, only that they were friends as far as he knew. Bailey had a query of his own,

"How exactly did you find Layer's Gap, Kyle Harding?"

The way this boy said his name made Kyle tighten his grip around the sugarcane. "I … heard the story from Sniper and I figured they—Gulfsyde—would be here. That is, if they cared for their friend." Kyle's stomach tightened at Glenn's image, his features distorted by experiments unknown and the forces of obeah magic. Comrades in arms forced to be enemies; all according to *their* will.

"Yes, but *how* did you manage to enter?"

Collins understood the intent behind the question. If the shroud was untouched for the past ten years, Kyle shouldn't have been able to find it—not unless he was a wizard like them. Kyle mirrored their bemusement, simply glancing at his sugarcane again.

"More important than dah, what really happen here, big man?" Collins asked. And Kyle recited the battle for them, though the details married between dream and reality so much that he doubted the experience himself. Ridiculous. It was all too ridiculous. They swallowed his testimony quite easily though, but Bailey resumed his interrogation.

"You say this sword had numbers on its blade, can you remember if they changed during the fight?"

"I think so … and it made a *ka-ching* noise … like a cash register."

"A Lickerish Arm—that explains the amplification." Bailey's brow furrowed. *To think you encountered one and lived…*

The events at Layer's Gap fascinated Bailey as the details were exhumed from Kyle's mind. Especially the bit about the entity—much like the fabled Duppies of *Cockspur*—who engaged Gulfsyde before attacking the canewielder. Bailey wondered how Kyle managed to survive on pure martial arts alone, but then he resolved the feat as impossible. It had to be the sugarcane.

"Look, can we talk about this later? I gotta get home."

"Yeah, man, you right." The shadow of Gulfsyde hovered over Collins, even with their demise. And his mind numbed with the prospect of an even more malicious force lurking around the corner. "You think you could mek it to where we park out front? Or you ain able?"

"No need to use such archaic methods." Bailey said while looking at the bus stop. Kyle and Collins guessed what he meant and they both asked in unison.

"Do you have a ticket?"

Bailey stifled his surprise, and revealed one of the coveted paper strips that allowed this ethereal transit. Barrow glared at them; those tickets would mark their location like a spotlight would a fugitive. Worst-case scenario: the agents of Kard 28 descend on them the moment they reached their destination, and they'll be dragged into a conflict just like the one that scarred this cemetery.

You sure you wanna do that? Barrow's eyes spoke.

I am willing to take the risk. His partner's wordless reply.

Thus, the four of them approached the bus stop, minding their steps from falling into the craters and cracks along the way. Kyle glanced at Headgone and noticed *Anjèd San* was nowhere to be seen. In fact, Sniper and Cutup were absent as well, not even the remnants of Glenn remained. Just like in his backyard. Just like the Heart Man. Whoever their clean-up crew was, they were working overtime.

Bailey was the first to reach the post, inspecting the red-and-white circle of wood and noticing the faint glint over the letters. A violet tinge still lingered from the reaction. "Stay close to me. Otherwise, you'll be left behind."

The rest complied; each joining hands as firmly as they could. Kyle cast his eyes upon the cemetery once more, grateful to have escaped death's eager touch as the world dissolved.

The bus stop serenaded the demons in the cemetery; its refrain pouring power into their jaws as they tore through one another. This was the nature of a high-level battle. The kind with magic that shreds the land asunder. The kind that Sniper stayed clear from.

"Fuck…" He hissed, while ice picks and shears and cane shoots zipped overhead, clashing at intervals with deadly precision. Sniper was comfortable, though. Conflicts like these were common for employed Pel-Tings, and he managed to avoid any grave injury other than his arm, which still had screwdrivers along the elbow and shoulder joints. The limb sprained horribly, with blood trickling down at a steady pace. Of course, he felt nothing. The blow was surgical and his attention solely on escape.

"Nice work, Justin. I coulda really stand home, fuh truth." Sniper spotted his bottle case fifty meters into the throng; it would have to be abandoned. "Only end up spending more money."

He sucked his teeth and broke into a stride the moment he was out of sight. The canewielder awakened a monstrous magic on par with the worst Sniper had witnessed in his career. Who was he to think Kyle Harding needed help? The question on the edge of his lips; covered by the sounds and flashes of explosions. "Not fuh rangate, though. I got no plans to die here today."

At the corner of his eye Sniper caught Dario, who was in far worse shape than he. His dashiki blended with his scarf, with great splotches of carmine spread throughout. He walked with a limp, most likely a ligament was torn in his leg, and one of his arms was mangled in a nastier fashion than Sniper's. But Dario did not wince as he edged towards the mayhem. His palm leaf barely balanced within three fingers.

"Crazy friggin bastard." Sniper spared no sympathy for him.

The last time he was so generous he ended up on the wrong people's radar. Just keep on walking. Count your losses and live another day—that was the plan. "Shit…"

Rasheda's body lay on the outskirts of the battle: lifeless. In one last act of charity, Sniper flung a pebble at Dario to catch his attention. His target didn't dodge. "Yuh Johnny! She's already gone! Wha de hell you doing?"

"I won't abandon her." His eyes whispered; a maniacal brown peaking over red cloth. Bloodlust overrode nobility.

"Suit youself, boss…" He watched as the wraith-like Dario hobbled to Rasheda, violet light caressing his disheveled locks. Good riddance, Sniper believed, but another pang of guilt shook his core worse than any blow. *What would Glenn do?*

Boom!

Sniper had abandoned honor long ago, long before his last days in the Pel-Ting family. But as he regarded his comrade's cadaver, dancing around the clouds of debris like a marionette from a haunting play, Sniper believed that he owed Glenn his honor. Or perhaps even more than that.

Combat was out of the question. He had no ammo aside from stones, and those weren't enough to enter the fray. Not one of *that* kind. So, Sniper cleared his conscience with less violent means, sprinting to an unsuspecting Dario and yanking him by the collar. The bastard still had enough strength to struggle, exacerbating his injuries even more. But Dario didn't care, he wanted to press forward. To get back to Rasheda. To get back to the duel.

"Unhand me!"

"Stop struggling, you bastard!" Sniper believed that Dario could've killed him, even in this battered state. So he dragged him away, careful to avoid any flailing strikes, lest he lost his head.

It was here that an elongated cane stalk punctured the land a few feet away, the resulting gust blowing both Sniper and his hostage closer to the bus stop. Dario landed horribly on his head, rendering him unconscious, much to Sniper's gratitude. He was taking out his ticket, when the notion of using Dario's bloomed at the last second. *Lucky.*

Now it was just the wait. An Amplifier, once activated, cannot be used for transport. This is due to the energy needed for translocation being already allocated to the magical device in the area. Knowing this, Sniper waited for the battle to conclude, since one of them had to be maintaining the amplification. Kyle or Glenn? It didn't matter, once one of them hurried up and kicked the bucket. Sniper chided himself for the thought.

Then there was silence. Five minutes had passed since Kyle Harding began his duel with Glenn, and now the climax was signaled by the waning rings from the bus stop's surface. It was time. With great effort Sniper dragged Dario's body closer to the post, his arms searing as the increased pressure sent blood spilling from his wound. Any further and he would've collapsed himself. The font on the wooden face still glinted violet as he activated the ticket, the paper responding in kind upon hearing his destination.

"Pico Teneriffe, St. Peter."

Sniper gave a hollow grunt, and soon felt that familiar sensation of his arm being sucked through a powerful vacuum cleaner. The graveyard, Glenn, and Kyle Harding evaporated from his view, perhaps never to be seen again. It was for the better.

Fear. It had been a while since Lianne last felt that emotion. The first time was when her family imposed a Baku upon her; the creature ogled her with such unbridled interest that it seemed like she was under the gaze of God. The second time she had tried to assassinate Sulemann, and failed. Up to this day Lianne couldn't explain why her attempt had flopped, but she was secretly grateful for avoiding his wrath. Now she found herself gripped with terror for a third time as Linseed *Bruggadown* Beckles advanced.

Mr. Beckles held a piece of bamboo in each hand, their blunt ends reaching his knees as he marched. The black bandages around them glinted in the afternoon sun, and after five paces they triggered a reaction in the air. Lianne saw sparks on the tips like some manner of wand, and the leaves and rocks beneath his heel rose as if pulled by a great magnet. The gesture was as effortless as flexing a muscle for Mr. Beckles, and upon seeing this refined aura Lianne ordered her Baku to brace for combat.

Hmmm … Interesting. Despite not having engaged a Baku in over twenty years, Mr. Beckles still had expectations from the encounter. He was shocked to see the creature retain its doll-like form which stood at a mere three feet in height. He anticipated a transformation of some kind; most tamed Bakus often augmented their bodies to access the full brunt of their abilities. But from this one's normal appearance, Mr. Beckles was left to assume that Lianne was either inexperienced or extremely proficient. He placed his bets on the latter.

"Again, sir, we don't have to do this. Think of your neighbors. Think of Damien." Lianne said, her voice had little empathy.

"Please don't take me for an idiot, girl. I been around far too long fuh dem false propositions to work on me." Mr. Beckles caught a flicker of cerulean at the corner of his eye and saw it; a gigantic slab of wood hovering overhead. A cou-cou stick—a massive cou-cou stick—had been conjured during the exchange; ready to smash Mr. Beckles under its weight. Evasion was out of the question. Although he had ample time, avoiding the attack would only leave the Harding household vulnerable, and he couldn't guarantee that Veronica's defenses would withstand the impact. Thus, with a great thrust upwards to parry…

BOOM!

The mass of wood shattered into a blaze of blue, with the embers raining down upon Mr. Beckles like fireworks. A distraction. Mr. Beckles guessed as much, and sure enough the ground rose around his feet, eager to surround him in a giant cooking pot. The black metal walls limited his movement, but a flick of the wrist was sufficient. Pang! Pang! *Pang!* The steel crumpled under the force of his strikes, and Mr. Beckles easily tore himself free, much to Lianne's chagrin.

"You really live up to your title, Mr. Beckles."

"Thank you, young lady, but I ain show you why dem does call me so yet."

Then a domino skipped along the gravel; its sound piercing through the crackling flames. Sulemann appeared between them wearing the most mischievous grin. It made Linseed's skin crawl. "Cha boy, I was really running late fuh truth, nuh?"

Lianne restrained her Baku, the flames in its eyes dwindling into cerulean dots. She thought it unwise to show any hostility to this man, even if she had no way of harming him. Linseed kept his stance, though he wore a deeper grimace as he observed Sulemann.

"I see you have graced us with your presence, *Conductor*."

"The pleasure is all mine, *Bruggadown*. It isn't every day that I'm in the company of such legends like yourself."

Mock praise from both monsters and Lianne backed away from them, fearing what was on the horizon. Like watching a fuse creep toward dynamite.

"Odd. I figure you mussy visit ole Seifert the other day. Unless you disrespect his name along with his body." The air around his batons rippled again, Linseed flexed.

"Nah. You got me wrong there, Mr. Beckles, though I am deeply sorry about Father Hoe's passing." Sulemann bowed, and Linseed resisted the urge to crack his skull.

"Lemme tell yuh, I real surprised at how popular Kyle is. First a DeSilva comes knocking, and now you? It begs the question: what do you intend to do?"

The question wiped the smirk from Sulemann's face, and he regarded Kyle's guardian as the beast that he was. "I believe my associate explained our intent; we've come for the boy."

"I cannot allow that." Linseed said, this time adopting his proper dueling stance; his posture akin to the ying-yang formation that Collins had when he wielded two blades. Linseed understood what this implied; it was an open attack on a member of Kard 28—on the administration of Dark Arcs itself. This act of treason could only result in immediate execution, but he was not afraid. Linseed intended to keep the debt he owed to Veronica Harding. The problem lay in what happened after his death; would Kyle be able to handle their wrath?

Lianne watched in silence, relieved that Sulemann intervened on her behalf. No. On *his* behalf. Only five minutes had passed since Damien disappeared behind the door to secure his things. Any longer and she would have to breach the Harding household herself. Lianne wasn't looking forward to that.

...

Damien's haversack was lightly packed with what he considered the essentials: underwear, some T-Shirts, an extra pair of jeans and his favorite *Potter* novel. Lying on the rumpled covers of his bed was the stick he often trained with, Damien didn't see any need for it. Martial arts were meaningless against magic—his solemn belief.

A cocktail of panic and excitement blended in his stomach. There was danger involved; a vicious, violent, deadly danger that twelve-year-olds should stay far away from. And yet, there was also a wonder that he couldn't deny. It had beckoned him from even before he witnessed the Heart Man in his backyard. Damien exited his room for the final time, engraving every wall, shingle and floor board into his mind. He did the same with the corridor, the bathroom, the kitchen and the front house. On the cabinet, next to some ceramic ornaments of doves and turtles and people dressed in old-fashioned clothes, he saw a photo of his mother with her two sons. He was still a babe in her arms. His brother wore a scowl that gave the appearance of a hardears child—a contrast to the polite recluse he knew. Damien mused, longer than he did in his room, and then took the thin frame and stuffed it into his bag. This was his goodbye.

The door knob was cold in his grip, and as he turned it he silently wished that Kyle was on the other side, staring down at him with disapproval. "I'm disappointed in you, Damien," is what his eyes would say.

When he returned to the verandah, Lianne was still there, though her features hardened with trepidation and a flaming wooden doll stood at her side. "I'm ready."

Lianne didn't see him immediately, craning around to peer at the boy with a jolt of horror. Damien had emerged at the most inopportune moment. "Oh. Right."

"Ah! The guest of honor." Milky white teeth decorated Sulemann's impish grin.

Linseed felt his stomach sink, "Damien, go back inside." Damien didn't respond. "Damien. Go. Back. Inside."

"I'm afraid he can't hear a thing you say." Sulemann confirmed. *An illusion…*

"What's wrong?" Damien asked, oblivious to the standoff but intrigued by the Baku. "And what is *that*?"

"Nothing. Hurry up, we're running kind of late." Lianne beckoned to the boy, eager to leave this den before the lions tear themselves apart. Damien hesitated before coming over; though the Baku didn't notice him, it exuded an aura that made his heart jackhammer his chest. Flames that signaled massacre, dancing brilliantly around its head.

Linseed had to act fast, like a cat-o-nine he whipped his baton at Sulemann. The entire motion took less than a breath. Then—*Brax!* Linseed felt a satisfactory crunch under his weapon, but he soon realized that it wasn't flesh he met. A wall of air intercepted the baton and Sulemann's body, taking the shape of a giant domino card—one with a dot at the top and five dots at the bottom. Linseed frowned at the shield and with another flex the bastion unraveled, shoving Sulemann away with the impact.

Damien still noticed nothing.

Lianne diverted her eyes to Sulemann, fully capturing the moment where the Conductor was actually harmed. A sliver of red trickled from Sulemann's right nostril; he swiped his thumb over the blood and curled his lips in amusement. He wasn't actually struck by the blow, the shield did its job, however an unseen wave of pressure had pierced through like a diamond drill.

"Bruggadown is right. You really do pack a punch."

Linseed scoffed at the damage inflicted; he intended to shatter Sulemann's bones with that last strike. Maintaining momentum, he darted forth, the batons resonating in his grip. There was another rattle—Sulemann skipped another domino on the ground—and before Linseed could shove the two sticks at his target, he realized that he was right in front of a tombstone.

"…Translocation. The little bastard." Linseed muttered while scouring the cemetery, great fissures were carved into the ground and graves had been tainted with debris. A bus stop rang in the distance and the entire area was cast in a violet hue. To his right, the corpse of Rasheda lay in eternal slumber.

The sound of sucking teeth filled Layer's gap, as Linseed sourly mused over what he could've done different. Then after counting five alternative scenarios, he decided it was all spilt milk and proceeded towards the exit. He inspected the bus stop; he didn't have a ticket so it wasn't a viable option. Thus Linseed had no choice but to take the long way home, swallowing the fact that Damien would be long gone by the time he returned.

"Hmm?" Rasheda gaped at him with dead eyes, blood caked on her nose and mouth, and her tongue wagged in a manner Linseed found distressing. He hadn't known her, but he decided that Rasheda deserved at least a proper burial. So out of mercy and personal atonement, Linseed interred the strange girl in one of the openings in the ground, breaking the soil with subtle taps and scattering clumps of dirt until her face disappeared. When his task was done, he entered the village, following equally battered streets to find an exit.

…

Damien jumped when Sulemann suddenly materialized out of thin air. Lianne understood this as the deactivation of his enchantment, most likely due to transporting Bruggadown to some undisclosed location. Part of her worried about his fate, but the rest knew that Mr. Beckles wouldn't need her sympathy.

"All packed and ready to go, nuh?" Sulemann asked Damien.

"Yeah…" Damien noticed the flash of light that came with the Baku's dismissal. "What do you plan to do with me?"

"Didn't you say you wanted to learn? I remember you hollering hard up at the QEH." Sulemann was nonchalant as he spoke; Lianne almost believed he wasn't assaulted minutes prior.

"Yeah, but that's only because you disappear so fast. And there are better ways to collect me than kidnapping." Damien's voice indignant, which only amused Sulemann even more. "By the way … did something happen when I went inside?"

"How you mean?"

Damien caught Lianne's question and focused on her while

he spoke. "Well, that thing … whatever it is that was here just now came out of nowhere and—" He paused to examine the cracks on the pavement, and the smoldering black on the crotons that lined the front steps.

"That was just her method of transport, don't mind that," said Sulemann, his hand swatting away the question. "Anyhow, I running kinda late so we better get a move on."

Damien had no second thoughts, but he did question the methods of his escorts. This wasn't the smooth, impressive display of magic he'd witnessed as of late, but instead shoddy, slapdash parlor tricks greeted him. It was enough to make him go back in the house, and forget the silly fantasies of being an adventurous mage. Not that he had a choice in the matter.

"Fine … you lead the way." Damien said.

"Would you do the honors, miss?" Sulemann turned to Lianne, who grumbled a few words and stretched her fingers before Molasses Drive was illuminated in blue again. This time a donkey—one made up entirely of rusted steel—trotted in their wake. Damien gasped in alarm as the mythical beast blew a jet of steam from its nostrils and gazed at them with blue dots—much like the eyes of the Baku. "Our ride awaits."

"….A Steel Donkey?"

"The one and the same." Sulemann followed Lianne as she mounted the rickety, wooden carriage that was harnessed to the Steel Donkey. Damien questioned the integrity of the vehicle, but as he sat on the rotting wooden seats, his worries went away. It was magic after all; ancient, intricate, stable magic. Sulemann was also content with this fact, lounging like a passenger in a limousine. Lianne would've evaporated him with her stare, if that was within her ability.

There was a rumble from the Steel Donkey as it trotted off, nothing majestic, but Damien felt a rush of grandeur wash over him upon hearing it. The Harding household was moving away from view, and the knowledge of never seeing home again clutched his heart tighter with every step.

Then Kyle appeared.

His brother was stunned at first, the horror embroidering his face along with the pure fury of the enemy invading his home again. Then, in that instant, several structures pierced the air and twisted toward the carriage— thin but powerful. *Sugarcane?* The notion brought images of the quirky item Kyle always carried around; a memento from Mom. However, Damien knew that this too was obeah magic—an artifact of the Dark Arcs. The Steel Donkey brayed and cerulean mist surrounded the carriage, so that Damien not only held his ears from the pain but his breath as well. *Thunk-Thunk Thunk!* Precise, concentrated attacks failing on the nimbus shield and Damien, through squinted eyes, caught his brother's desperation. While the veil of smoke shrouded Kyle and Molasses Drive, Damien had the impression of a boy his own age running towards him, afraid that something dear was being stolen forever. And the clutch on his heart grew tighter.

"Goodbye, Kyle."

The whisper heralding the end, and Kyle knew then that his world was gone.

Thank you for reading *Offset: Children of the Gulf* I hope you enjoyed the journey so far. I tried to make the book as authentic to Barbadian (Bajan) and Caribbean culture as possible without alienating international readers. However, to make things easier for those unfamiliar with the dialect of Bimshire, I decided to include this short glossary of terms and phrases in the story.

As Bimshire is a fictional version of the real-world Caribbean island, Barbados, the characters in the story speak Bajan dialect or Barbadian Creole. Bajan is primarily a spoken language, while standard English is used in print, media and formal situations. As such, Bajan is an English-based form of creole with some terms that are shortened or broken forms of their English counterparts.

Please note, since Bajan dialect has no standardized spelling, the spelling of a number of the words are rough approximations.

•**A de**—means *Of the.*

•**Aight**—short for *All right, Okay.*

•**Ain/ D'ain**—can be used in the following contexts: *Isn't/ Is not/ Am not/ Did not/ Do not/ Does not/ Will not/ Won't.*

•**Ain easy**—to be formidable.

•**Aincha**—truncated form of *Aren't you.*

•**Ainno**— truncated form of *I don't know.*

•**Alla**—truncated form of *All of, Entire.*

•**Alotta**—truncated form of *A lot of.*

•**Amplifier**—these are devices that increase the effects of obeah magic within a specified area. See *Bus-stops.*

•**Atall/ At-all**—means *No-how* or *No-Way.*

•**B**— this is a noun, short for *Big man* or *Boss.*

•**Babylon**—corrupt establishment, status quo or system of control. Refers to the Government and Powers that Be. Perhaps Mix Drink was aware of the Dark Arcs without knowing.

•**Bad**—to be dangerous, to be a threat. For eg. *You feel you bad?*

•**Bad John**—badass, gangster, someone you should not mess with.

•**Baku**—a wooden doll that grants wishes in exchange for a fee. Be careful not to skimp on payments.

•**Bare**—this means raw/ pure, often use as an over exaggeration, too.

•**Big man**—this is a term of endearment/ salutation which usually refers to a person of good standing/ good status. This can also refer to a large male.

•**Big-up**—a person of high status, wealth and popularity.

•**Bimshire**—a Caribbean Island located in the most eastern part of the Caribbean Sea. It is two-hundred-and-sixty-six square miles and is touted as being the Gem of the Caribbean. This is where *Offset* takes place.

•**Blood Money**—a form of currency which uses human blood and converts it into crimson dollar bills. Some transactions are only paid in this currency to this day. See *Anjed San.*

•**Boah/ bo**— this can be used as an adverb, similar to *Nuh* or *Doah.*

•**Bore**—to attack, to push aggressively.

•**Bredren**—*Brethren/ Brother,* generally a salutation.

•**Brek-up**—to fall, to feel exhausted, ill or injured.

•**Bruddah**— truncated form of *Brother*.

•**Bruggadown**—the sound of something falling, or hitting something very hard. Linseed Beckles is called 'Bruggadown' because of the sound his sticks make when he hits an opponent.

•**Bus-stop**—a place where public transport buses stop to pick up or release passengers. The bus-stops in Bimshire are a bit special though. See *Amplifier*.

•**Butt**—to meet or run into someone, to bounce off or knock into something.

•**Cakey**—easy, required little effort.

•**Canecutter**—a bladesman who specializes in using machetes or cutlasses as weapons. They existed since the days of slavery. Damian Collins, Seifert Brathwaite, Rasheda and Aunty Yvette are such Canecutters.

•**Cawblen/Caw Blen**—means *Wow!* This is an exclamation, usually vulgar.

•**Cawblemma!**—means *Oh my goodness! / God blind me if it isn't true!*

•**Cawdee**—*Wow!* This is an exclamation.

•**Cess**—to take, steal or appropriate.

•**Cha/ Cha!**—*Wow!* This is an exclamation. It can also be used to express sympathy.

•**Cheese on Bread!**—an expression or an exclamation. Usually used when frustrated or surprised.

•**Chillax**—to chill and/or relax.

•**Cockspur**—A mythical being that is said to be able to raise the dead. More on this later.

•**Collins**—see *Cutlass*. (Fun fact: Damian Collins was named after his weapon when *Offset* was first created. It was supposed to be a joke.)

•**Come 'long**— means *Come along/ Come with me.*

•**Coulda**—truncated form of *Could have / Could've.*

•**Crop Over**— this is a traditional harvest festival which began in Bimshire, having its beginnings on sugarcane plantations during slavery. Nowadays, it is a great party which tourists should try to attend at least once.

•**Cuh Dear**—to express sympathy or pity, *What a shame.*

•**Cunny**—this is a noun. A vulgar one.

•**Cutlass**—a machete or similar blade. See *Collins*.

•**Dah/ Dah's**—shortened/ truncated form of *That* or *That is*.

•**Dark Continent**—the original motherland where most Caribbean natives originated prior to slavery. More on this later.

•**Dat**—truncated form of *That*.

•**De**—means *The*, but Bajan accent usually makes it sound like De.

•**Dem**—truncated form of *Them*, can also be used in the context of *There*.

•**Den**—truncated form of *Then*.

•**Dey**—truncated form of *There*.

•**Diablesse/ La Diablesse**—this is a devil woman from Caribbean folklore. She typically hides cloven feet under her dress and seduces men to their demise. To beat a Diablesse, one must turn their clothes inside out and walk home backwards. Of course, there has been no proven accounts of La Diablesse in Bimshire.

•**Dis**—truncated form of *This*.

•**Do**—used as a superlative like, *Will you*. For example; *Come, Do!* means *Come, Do!*

•**Doah, nuh**—this is often used as an adverb similar to *Though*. For example, *Look at this fool, though!* would be *Look at this fool, doah!* Sometimes, we add *nuh* for emphasis, like *Look at this fool, doah nuh!*

•**Doan**—truncated form of *Don't*.

•**Don't watch nuttin**—this means *It's okay.* or *Don't worry about it*.

•**Does do/ Does (insert verb)**—some Bajans uses this participle in front of some verbs.

•**Don'cha**—truncated form of *Don't you*.

•**Done know**—this is an affirmation; usually means *I agree with you* or *I/You already know*.

•**Dread**—to be crazy or insane. See *Tear-Head*. Can also be used as an adverb.

•**Dress-up**—wearing your best clothes.

•**Drop**—this means a ride, as in a car ride.

•**Dunno**—truncated form of *Don't know*.

•**Dunce**—a type of sour fruit, goes great with salt.

•**Duncy**—to be stupid, slow learner.

•**Duppy**— a ghost, spirit or zombie.

•**Ease off!**—this means *Back off!/ Give me some space!/Relax!*

•**Fagged Out**— *tired, exhausted.*

•**Feel**—this means to believe or assume.

•**Fella**—truncated form of *Fellow.*

•**Fete**—a party.

•**Fits**—this refers to epilepsy, can also refer to mental illness.

•**Fix he/she goat**—this means to get revenge or to make sure someone gets their comeuppance.

•**Flam**—a girl/ boy that one flirts with; to flirt.

•**Fowl-cock**—a chicken.

•**Friggin**—adverb (vulgar).

•**Fuh**—truncated form of *For.*

•**Fuh Sport**—this means for joke or for fun.

•**Fuh True? / Fuh Truth?**—this means *For truth / For real.* Can be used in the context of a question where someone is incredulous eg. *Are you serious?*

•**Fuh truth/ Fuh real/ Fah real**—It can also be used as an affirmation, to agree with something said, *Indeed.*

•**Fussy**—very particular, proud, boastful.

•**Gallist**—this means a ladies' man or a womanizer in Caribbean slang.

•**Gap**—a street or road.

•**Get de belly**—to have an upset stomach, nausea, diarrhea.

•**Get through/ sort out**—this means to succeed or accomplish your goal or task.

•**Get 'Way/ Get Way**—to escape, run away.

•**Gine**—short for *going/ to be going / going to.*

•**Gimme/ Giwwe**—this means *Give me/ Give us.*

•**Gotta**—short for *Got to, Have to.*

•**'Gree**—to speak on friendly terms.

•**Guh 'long**—Go along, leave.

•**Gypsy / Malicious**—to be overly inquisitive, mischievous. The need to know other person's affairs usually for ill-intent or gossip.

•**Hard-ears**—to be stubborn.

•**Hear?**—this can be used as an adverb. Similar to how people use *See?* as an adverb at times.

•**Heart Man**—a serial killer that steals the hearts of his victims. Dorian Nelson was the latest Heart Man in Bimshire.

•**Heself/ Sheself**—this means *himself/ herself*.

•**Hey**—truncated form of *Here*.

•**Horn**—to cheat on a lover or be unfaithful.

•**How you keeping?**—this means *How are you doing? Are you well?*

•**Hungh!**—means *Here! / Take this!*

•**Is cool/ is time**—this means *It is cool/ It is time.*

•**Island Yute**—this means an Island Youth, the archetypical adolescent from the Caribbean.

•**Jah**—means God, can also be a shortened form of Jahweh.

•**Johnny**—this is what Bajans call an idiot or a fool.

•**Juck**—to poke, stab or push.

•**Just so**—this means *Just like that.*

•**Kixxing**—to joke/kid around/ to take a situation lightly.

•**Lag/ Laggin**—to waste time or hesitate.

•**Lawd**—truncated form of *Lord*.

•**Leff**—truncated form of *Leave*.

•**Leggo**—truncated form of *Let go*.

•**Leh**—truncated form of *Let*.

•**Lemme**—truncated form of *Let Me*.

•**Lemme tell yuh**—truncated form of *Let me tell you*.

•**Less Noise**—to *Keep quiet/ Shut up/Be Silent*.

•**Lewwe**—truncated form of *Let us*.

•**Lick Down**—to get hit by a car, ran over.

•**Lickerish Arms**—legendary weapons that trade powerful magic in exchange for a human offering. For example: *Anjed San* and its blood money (human blood).

•**Lil**—short for *little*.

•**Lime / liming**—to hang-out, chill, or relax somewhere with others.

•**Locks**—this refers to dreadlocks.

•**Looka**—truncated form of *Look at*.

•**Manna Tamarinds**—similar to normal tamarinds, except the fruit grows from a special kind of tree in a special kind of soil.

It has a sweet-sour taste and has medicinal properties. Great source of energy for treating exhaustion.

•**Mashup**— means to destroy.

•**Mek**—truncated form of *Make*.

•**Mek Haste**—truncated form of *Make Haste*, means to hurry up.

•**Mekkin Sport/ Mek Sport**—to joke/kid around/ to take a situation lightly. Example *(you) mekin' sport*.

•**Mighta**—truncated form of Might have.

•**Muddah/ Faddah**—truncated form of *Mother/ Father*.

•**Muh**—means *My*. Bajan accent truncates the pronunciation.

•**Mussy/Mussie**—means *Must be*, *Maybe*, *Perhaps* or *Probably*.

•**Nah**—means *No*.

•**Nain**—means *Nothing*.

•**Never-see, come-see**—this is an over-exaggeration.

•**New Guiana**—a country on the northern region of South Ameris which is considered part of the Caribbean diaspora.

•**Noni Apple**—this is a fruit that has multiple health benefits and medicinal properties. The juice combined with that little extra can heal wounds and ailments.

•**Nuff /Nough**—usually means *A lot of*, but is the shortened form of *Enough*.

•**Nuh**—can be used for *No* or a negative. However, Bajans often use *Nuh* in the context of *Huh* as well. For example, *The sun is pretty hot today, nuh?* It can even be used as a superlative like, *Will you?* For example; *Move, Nuh?!* means *Move, will you?!*

•**Nuhbody**—means *Nobody*.

•**Nuhmore**—means *No more/ Anymore*.

•**Nuttin**—means *Nothing*.

•**Obeah**—Witchcraft/Black Magic/sorcery of West Afreecan origin similar to Voodoo. The primary service which the Dark Arcs was built upon.

•**Offa**—truncated form of *Off of*. For eg. *Get offa me* means *Get off of me.*

•**Offisuh**—truncated form of *Officer.*

•**Ole**—means *Old*.

•**Ol man**—means *Old man*, can also be a term of endearment to mean wise person or respected person.

•**Onna**—truncated form of *One of.*

•**One-Two-Three**—this is a traditional dish of pasta, mixed vegetables and corned beef/ minced meat. Known for how easy and quick it is to prepare while being tasty.

•**Opposition**—the term used to describe members of the obeah trade who were against the ruling administration during the Parish War. More on this later. Also see *White Soursop*.

•**Papa Bois**—translates to *Father of the Wood*, legend tells of a being that abducted travelers unfortunate enough to wander into the forest. However, that being is Papa Bois and that forest is Bewitched Gully.

•**Parro/ Parrow**—a crack-head, someone so addicted to drugs, a homeless person.

•**Part**—means *Where*, used to indicate location. For eg. *Part you gine?* means *Where are you going?*

•**Parish War**—a series of conflicts spanning the obeah trade across the Caribbean region during the 1970s. More on this later.

•**Pel-Ting Family of the East**—a mercenary group that specializes in assassination, reconnaissance and debt collection using using the art of throwing objects with superhuman precision.

•**Pelt**—to throw.

•**Peltin-waist**—to dance, to gyrate.

•**Pickout**—to hit a target from a great distance.

•**Play de fool**—to joke, fool around or to take a situation lightly. See *Mek Sport*.

•**Pon /'pon**—short for *Upon* or *On*.

•**Poppit**—this is what Bajans call an idiot or a fool. See *Johnny*.

•**Prickle**—this means to be unkempt or untidy. Can also be used as a noun to describe a homeless person.

•**Propuh**—truncated form of *Proper*.

•**Rally Girl**—refers to women who tend to frequent the motor-sport rally circuits socially. The more attractive women are often used in marketing for the event.

•**Rangate/Rassgate/Rasshole**—vulgar; a cuss word.

•**Rass**—short for *Rasta* (see definition), can also be an exclamation; vulgar.

•**Rasta**—a Rastafarian. Relating to the Rastafarian movement. However, people with dreadlocks are often referred to as Rastas like Damian Collins.

•**Real**—this means *Very*.

•**Real Ting**—this means *Real Thing* which is used as an affirmation or to agree with someone much like *Indeed* or *Fuh Real*.

•**Red-skin**—someone of light-brown or caramel complexion, usually perceived to be attractive in the Caribbean.

•**Rolling**—to travel with, to associate with.

•**Sain**—truncated form of *Something*.

•**Scrunt**—to scrape by financially, to struggle.

•**Shadow Darts**—an assassination unit that specializes in killing people using blow darts.

•**Shaggy Bear**—a costumed acrobatic dancer usually dressed in rags. In Bimshire, these are threatening inhuman spectres associated with the Dark Arcs.

•**Shite/ Shit**—this means excrement or defecation.

•**Shoulda**—truncated form of *Should have*.

•**Shotta Boss** —a gunslinger who has superhuman prowess with firearms. These are even rarer than guns are in the Caribbean. Most notable Shotta Bosses are Kamilah and Odane.

•**Shun'**—truncated form of *Should not/ Shouldn't*.

•**Sighted/Seen/Safe**—this is usually an affirmation to agree with something said. Like *Okay*.

•**Sinse**—a plant that has various physical and mental effects such as euphoria, altered states of mind, paranoia, nausea and even nerve damage. It is often consumed by burning and inhaling the smoke, however it can also be brewed into teas and eaten as well. Due to its toxic and addictive nature, the drug has been outlawed in the Caribbean. However, it has been rumored to unlock abilities in select individuals.

•**Skylark/Skylarking**—this means to play the fool, or to mess around.

•**Somma**—truncated form of *Some of*.

•**Sorta**—truncated form of *Sort of*.

•**Spot me**—means *Lend me*.

•**Steel Donkey**—this is a fabled creature which appears as a donkey made of steel wrapped in chains, and wreaks havoc upon Bimshire villages. Collins often heard of them in bedtime stories.

•**Stick-licking**—a lost martial art involving the use of sticks in a pseudo-form of fencing. It was preserved during the slavery days by being taught in secret to a handful of people. Current Stick-lickers are Linseed Beckles, Kyle Harding and Damian Harding.

•**Stupse**—the sound of sucking teeth.

•**Sugar Daddy**—this is a snack made from fried dough and sugar frosting. Often looks like a stick.

•**Suh**—truncated form of *So*.

•**Tear-head**—insane, crazy, mental, one who takes risks.

•**Tek off**—*Tek* is a truncated pronunciation of *Take* , so to *Tek Off* means to *Take Off* much like a plane or to move away very quickly.

•**Testy**—means dangerous, difficult, uncertain.

•**Tie-up**—means to entangle, confuse or engross.

•**Ting**—truncated form of *Thing*. Can also be used in a list to indicate further items much like *Et Cetera*.

•**Top Man**—term of endearment, see *Big Man*.

•**Trouble**—to interfere, bother, harass, pickup, take, disturb.

•**Trouble tree**—one who causes trouble, usually refers to bad-behaved children.

•**Tuh**—truncated form of *To*.

•**Uh**—truncated form of *Of*.

•**Um**—means *It*.

•**Unstaan**—truncated form of *Understand*.

•**Used to**—means accustomed, or to do something in the past.

•**Village Ram**—this refers to a playboy or promiscuous man in the village or neighborhood. Often times, they will have several children from different mothers or, at the very least, be charismatic and popular.

•**Wash off**—this means to beat someone badly. Much like beating clothes so the dirt or dust comes off during laundry.

•**Wha gine on**—this translates to *What's going on with you?/ What's new?*

•**Whe-hey!**—an exclamation, similar to *Well, would you look at that!*

•**White Soursop**—an organization dedicated to taking down the current administration of the obeah trade. Mostly consists of Practitioners. More on them later. Also see *Opposition*.

•**Wid**—truncated form of *With.*

•**Woi**—an exclamation like *Wow!* Or *Woo!*

•**Wotless/Wutless**—worthless, misbehaved, can also be used to describe someone who is partying too much.

•**Wuh/ Wha**—truncated form of *What.*

•**Wuhloss**—an exclamation, often used to express disappointment or surprise.

•**Wun**—truncated form of *Wouldn't,* also can be used as a bad pronunciation of *One.*

•**Wunna/Wunnuh**—means *You all* or *You people.*

•**Yeaz**—truncated form of *Yes.*

•**Youngsta**—truncated form of *Youngster.*

•**Yuh**—truncated form of *You.* It can also be used as an adverb, similar to *Nuh.*

•**Yuh Know**—truncated form of *You know.*

•**Yute**—a youth/ child/ offspring.

•**ZR**—pronounced *Zed-R,* a private-owned route taxi (So named because of the license plates beginning with ZR).

I hope this short glossary helps to navigate the nuances of Bajan dialect expressed in *Offset: Children of the Gulf.* However, if you are eager to learn more about the Bajan creole feel free to do your own research online. I highly recommend *#Bajanisms: A Culture. A Language by Mahalia Cummins.*

Thanks to my editor, Thomas, for being such a pain and being so patient with me. Thanks to my mother, Deborah, for continuing to inspire me to move forward. Thanks to all the artists who helped breathe life into Bimshire via artwork and commissions. Especially Matthew for the first *Offset* one-shot comic in his anthology series *MASS Anthology,* and Tristan who has stuck by this story and translated it so well in visual form in the *Offset* comic series. Thanks to Hans, who placed his fullest efforts to illustrate *Children of the Gulf,* and has made this book series a dream come true.

Thanks to my best friend, Jaryd, who planted the idea of a young sticklicker whose mother was an Obeah woman into my mind. Without him, *Offset* would not exist.

Thanks to the members of Beyond Publishing Caribbean for their support. Thanks to all my proofreaders who took the time to see my many manuscript drafts. Thanks to every reader and fan of the *Offset* series, your feedback kept me going.

Thanks to Barbados and the Caribbean region for being such a badass place to live.

Offset is for you.

Delvin Howell was born in Bridgetown, Barbados, in 1987. He attended Queen's College and the University of the West Indies, where the idea for *Offset* brewed in his mind. Shortly after, he completed the manuscript for *Mask of Bimshire* and won the John Wickham Award for the Frank Collymore Literary Endowment in 2010. *Offset* is an official series under Beyond Publishing Caribbean where it won several awards for publishing and design from the Caribbean Advertising Federation.

Offset: Children of the Gulf is his second novel and he hopes to capture the Caribbean spirit with it.

Hans Steinbach is a freelance illustrator & character designer, having worked for game studios such as Capcom (*Street Fighter 4* — costume designs), Platinum Games (*Nier Automata* and *Scalebound* — concept art) and Emerald City Games. He's had manga published by Tokyo Pop and is currently working with Udon Entertainment. With over ten years in the game industry, and experiences travelling the world (including Barbados), he was the perfect fit for the *Offset* series.

OFFSET
BOOK 1
AVAILABLE AT
OFFSETSERIES.COM
THE MASK OF BIMSHIRE

BUS
OUT
OF
CITY
STOP
OFFSET: THE COMIC
AVAILABLE AT OFFSETSERIES.COM